THE INFLATABLE BUDDHA

"Funny, intimate, tragic… a saga of realism and magic… a breathtaking adventure." *Steven Kovacs*

"…sharp, clear and entertaining… powerful and deeply engaging… how ordinary people cope with extraordinary historical circumstances" *Joseph P. Forgas*

THE INFLATABLE BUDDHA

ANDRÁS KEPES

Translated from the Hungarian
by Bernard Adams

ARMADILLO
CENTRAL

The Inflatable Buddha

This is a translation of Tövispuszta © András Kepes 2011
Published in Hungarian by Ulpius-ház

First published in translation September 2013
by Armadillo Central, Great Britain

This POD edition first published October 2013

Translated from the Hungarian by Bernard Adams

© Armadillo Central 2013

Cover image, photographer unknown: © Sándor Kardos

Cover & book design: Caroline Reeves

© Armadillo Central 2013

POD ISBN: 978-1-908539-14-4

Armadillo Central Limited
PO Box 897, Richmond, Surrey, TW9 9EH, UK

www.armadillocentral.com

For my family

Acknowledgments

For The Inflatable Buddha, the English edition
of Tövispuszta, I owe special thanks to
Emma Boden-Cummins for believing in the international
success of my novel and for her enthusiastic and highly
professional approach; to Bernard Adams for his sensitive
and inspired translation and to Suzie Morson for her
unfailing sisterly and spiritual support.

I would also like to thank Sándor Kardos for kind
permission to use the archival photograph on the cover
and Armadillo Central's team of manuscript readers:
David, Stephanie, Angelica, Jennifer and Chris.

CONTENTS

I've endeavoured to compile this account from coffee-stained letters, yellowing, tattered documents, battered diaries and the smell of long-redundant objects. I have a collection of everything from call-up papers to relocation orders and contradictory autobiographies; from a silver spoon embossed with a crown to a chest painted with tulips; from a Hanukkah candlestick to a market-stall picture of Christ and an inflatable Buddha. As I see it, it's going to be a messy kind of story, full of snarling and laughter ending in tears; love and murder; friendships and betrayals; plots and platitudes. Something akin to a soap opera. Or the history of Hungary. I thought, what if events as narrated rather than truth, and people's feelings and experiences rather than fact, were to be assembled and thus shaped reality?

The Tulip-painted Chest

All his life, István Veres had been the cantankerous sort. He'd even quarrel with the good Lord, said the women, but they'd never thought that one day this would actually happen. In 1918 however, when he came home after two years away in the Great War, it was a long time before he went back to church. "Along comes the priest and blesses my fucking gun for me to go and kill people who'd done nothing to me. I said to myself, from now on I'm talking things over with God in person." That's how he put it. Later, of course, he did become a churchgoer again, because it was only right and proper.

One winter dawn in 1932 there was such a wind that it took the crown of thorns off Christ's head. István had placed it there, on the statue at the end of the village, when he was a boy. The parish priest had been telling the Sunday school children how Jesus had suffered. The cruel way in which the Jews had treated the son of God had so upset the little boy that he'd made a wreath of thorny sticks, picked up in the ditch on his way home. He'd then climbed up the stone crucifix in his bare feet and, with his hands scratched and bleeding from the thorns, pressed it down onto the white head. At first the village people were horrified at this sacrilegious act,

11

but the priest sensed a childish piety in what István had done and calmed them. Eventually the stone Christ with its crown of thorns became the symbol of Tövispuszta[1]. The crown dried out to grey and adorned the doleful godhead for years, but now it was gone with the wind, rustling as it rolled among the tumbleweed on the ice-bound meadow.

"Oh dear, oh dear, that means something terrible's going to happen," said the woman next door spreading word of the evil omen. At first István made a dismissive gesture: the old women of Tövispuszta were always seeing signs of disaster, but when old Mariska began to harp on about what he'd done the previous evening, he felt less certain.

The economic crisis had laid everyone low. Hail had damaged the crops, then winter had come. In the farm servants' houses they'd scraped the bottom of the flour barrels and dug the tiniest potatoes and onions, previously overlooked, out of the ground. There'd been nothing to give the starving children.

In the longhouse, among the crowded servants' quarters, nothing stayed secret for long. Thus on the previous evening, as István took the picture of Christ off the wall, hurled it to the floor, then bit the shards of glass and howled, his mouth bleeding, Mariska had clearly heard:

"What sort of god are you, that you can bear to go on watching this? Am I to feed them to you?" He wiped his tears and pointed to his children. The two boys and three small girls clung to their mother as they watched their frenzied father. The same sea-blue eyes shone in their pallid, sunken faces. Sea-blue eyes fringed by dark lashes – such was the legacy of centuries of Veres ancestors.

Word of what István had done quickly spread round Tövispuszta. It also reached Szentágoston, where the Baron lived. Two days later a cart arrived outside the longhouse.

The Tulip-painted Chest

"The Baron's sent this," said the driver, jumping down from the box. "Potatoes, flour, onions, maize and fat. So, share it out!" he continued, as the men unloaded the cart. "The Baron's people heard István as well," was old Mariska's comment as everyone received their share from the sack of flour.

István unloaded the sacks and as he did so he thought of 1919 when, inspired by the Commune, the men of Tövispuszta had set off to strip the Baron of house and land. News of land seizures and the burning of mansions had come from all sides, and those who'd returned from the Russian front, such as István Lázár, Imre Kodelka and Márton Veszelka, had spoken of worker- and peasant-power. The war had left people hungry, defeat had left them bitter, and the disintegration of Hungary[2] had humiliated them. István too had joined the rest in the noisy mob outside the inn and had eagerly approved Veszelka's agitation: don't let yourselves be robbed, follow the example of the Soviet Russian proletariat! But as they approached the mansion and he could see tempers rising and the coarse faces of the stocky Pertli and the powerful Jóska Hetési, he was less and less confident. 'Thou shalt not covet thy neighbour's house,' roared in his brain. By then he no longer wished to be there, but didn't know how to melt away inconspicuously. Besides, curiosity drove him on. He howled along with the others, while a sour taste rose from his stomach to his mouth.

When they reached the mansion grounds and saw the old Baron on the French balcony with a double-barrelled shotgun in his hands, looking determined yet helpless, the two Istváns – Veres and Lázár – could scarcely manage to quieten everyone. Veres referred to the Bible, while Lázár said that it was wrong to take another's property by force, it was tantamount to stealing. The Baron would surely agree

13

to distribute his land among the peasantry as Count Károlyi had done, explained Lázár at the top of his voice, so that the old Baron could hear him from the balcony too. The Baron, however, wasn't as ideologically advanced as Lázár, and so he merely looked at them determinedly, glowering, gun in hand. From behind the curtains the Baroness peered fearfully at the enraged men as her two little boys clung to her skirts in alarm. The men shouted for a while, then dispersed.

István tossed the last sack down from the cart, the Baron's driver climbed back onto the box and cracked his whip over the horses.

"There are times when you've got to shout," said Gáspár Nagy quietly as the cart drove away.

They all nodded, and watched with feeling as it vanished into the distance, as if it hadn't been bringing food at all, but taking it away.

István Veres of the beautiful eyes might have had a dubious reputation in the community, but he was a man of some prestige. When he married Gizella Jónás, his father remarked on the way home from the church, "Lucky girl, our Gizi!" "Why might she be so lucky?" asked the bystanders, thinking of István's temperament. "Because my son's got the biggest prick in the village!" exclaimed the old man. What he based that opinion on was never made clear; a couple of lads nodded sagely though, and from then on Gizella was always known as 'lucky Gizi' in Tövispuszta, even to the children. And István's deserved prestige for manliness grew.

This prestige was further enhanced when his eldest son joined the senior team. He had distinguished himself at an early age for skill on the football field, and the bigger teenage

The Tulip-painted Chest

boys had welcomed him on their side when he was only seven or eight; by the time he was fifteen he was picked as left-half for the Szentágoston senior team, Ágoston Lions. After the very first match the county paper's sports reporter wrote enthusiastically of his speed and fearsome left foot. Later, when Ferencváros came to the area on a national training tour and thrashed the Lions 14:1 by way of a warm-up, the Budapest sports paper also carried a photograph of the boy, taken just as, his head slightly bowed and leaning a little to the right, he scored the consolation goal.

For weeks beforehand the people of Szentágoston and Tövispuszta, and supporters from the surrounding villages, had talked of nothing but the match. They could scarcely wait for the day. The champions changed into their green-and-white shirts and tracksuits in the town's hotel and travelled out to Tövispuszta by coach. When the 'chara', as the elderly called the coach, drew up beside the worn pitch, the villagers swarmed round it, the children jumping up at the windows trying to see inside. Even the sick and the invalids were ferried from all around to the side of the pitch. There they sat, excited to see the miracle, never before witnessed and perhaps never again to be seen – Fradi playing at Tövispuszta. The villagers watched open-mouthed, as if seeing a vision, while the coach disgorged the smiling and waving team: the two Takácses, Cseh, Turay, Kohut, Toldi and the rest.

In the first minutes of the match István, like his team-mates, drifted between the two penalty areas, paralysed by embarrassment, as if refusing to believe that he was on the same pitch as the players who had beaten Uruguay. In the second half he pulled himself together, though, and in the seventy-eighth minute he raced up the left wing and slammed the ball between one of the Takácses and Rázsó and into the top right corner of the net, in a way that had the Fradi players

15

shaking their heads in appreciation. Háda, the goalkeeper, threw his cap at the ground, but then burst out laughing and waved to István. The Tövispusta supporters cheered, hugged one another with tears in their eyes and shook old Veres by the hand and, as the teams left the field, Géza Toldi himself slapped István on the back with a laugh: "My boy, another fourteen goals like that and you'd have won the match!"

István Veres' left foot had, in a moment, raised Tövispuszta from the obscurity of centuries. Lucky Gizi carefully cut her son's picture out of the sporting paper and put it in her prayerbook, right next to the pressed cornflower which her husband had given her on their first date. She also selected a fitting space on the inside of the lid of her tulip-painted dowry chest, where she had recorded the most important events since their marriage.

At the top it said, in curlicued letters:

Gizella Jónás, born 1 November 1897.

István Veres, born 7 April 1889.

Married 12 August 1918.

There followed István's date of birth and the other children's. Here Gizi found a space and carefully wrote:

Isti was in the newspaper 3 May 1936.

From then on István senior took a pride in István junior at every match. At least until the first quarrel. Because the first quarrel in the stand always broke out near István senior. And not without cause. The point is he would pour scorn on the opposition, not from the Ágoston supporters' part of the ground, as might have been acceptable, but from the midst of the other fans, and from there he would shout insults at their players. At first the visiting supporters couldn't make out what the fool was up to, then there was always one that would pass comment, and the argument usually ended with him getting a good hiding.

"Couldn't you get your father to sit with our supporters?" asked Dávid Goldstein in the changing room after one of the matches – he was, in a way, the team manager. His father, the shopkeeper Samu Goldstein, sold team kit for the benefit of the club. In return Dávid, who was no athlete, had been allowed to sit, immaculately turned out, on the reserves' bench, but after a few months had decided to look for something less lowly and more useful to do. So the reserve who never went on the pitch became the spirit of the side. It was he that organised the matches and obtained the shirts, shorts and boots. He was a great fan of Isti, and his unreserved enthusiasm rubbed off on him. This particularly because even in elementary school Dávid had done Isti's homework for him. It didn't bother Dávid at all if the teacher gave him a worse mark than Isti. "Comes of being Jewish," Isti would say, patting Dávid's face, and they would laugh together.

"You see if you can persuade him," replied Isti, because Dávid made up for his lack of mobility by the power of his tongue. To the very great surprise of the village, at the next match István senior was shouting among the Tövispuszta supporters, but this time he was criticising the Tövispuszta and Szentágoston players, berating them for all being flat-footed, just loafing around on the pitch, while only his son knew how to play football.

Sometimes István senior would rebel, but only in Hungarian fashion: to show that he had it in him. Everybody understood. They knew that everything would go back to normal. "There's a proper way for things to be," he would say, and bang on the table with his mighty hand as if to beat it into the table's thick skull as well. "I built my house with my own hands same as my ancestors before me, the stove's in the same place, the kitchen, the parlour, the table, the oven. I wear the same clothes as my old man, the same boots and hat, and I respect work like he taught me to. That's how things must be, otherwise the world'll turn upside-down," he would insist, because at the time he hadn't yet realised that the world was already upside-down.

Szentágoston and Tövispuszta were in effect a single village, both the property of Baron Szentágosztony. The mansion stood on a gentle slope in Szentágoston, surrounded by the richer houses; the vineyards and press-houses were higher up, and lower down in the valley, in Tövispuszta, was the home farm with the farm buildings, the machine depot and the farm servants' quarters. The hills of Szentágoston yielded good wine, but the pride of the village was the cherry orchard. At cherry-blossom time people from the town would visit the area to admire the hillside. They spread blankets on the grass, unpacked picnic baskets and bottles of good Szentágoston wine, and ate and drank all day long.

On the other side of the hill Szentágoston had grown into a smart, red-roofed village, from where the mine and lake at Kesz could be seen, and extended all the way into the valley, past the Catholic and Calvinist churches, to the store-houses and the railway station on the outskirts. After the war and the treaty of Trianon, there stood on a few sidings railway carriages in which refugees had lived for years, having left all they possessed in the lost territories and migrated to 'mutilated' Hungary.[3] There were two inns in the area, one in Szentágoston and one in Tövis, because, as the old saying goes, there must be at least two inns in every village: the one you go to and the one you don't set foot in. The carriage-dwellers and the men who'd returned from the war and were subsisting on the dole spent day after day there, out of work, discussing what Hungary was coming to. The football field, laid out at the Baron's instigation, was located between the two village areas, on the grassland beside the road. Not a blade of grass remained around the penalty areas, and on either side of the pitch the rickety benches had been bleached and cracked by the sun. When the fair came, stalls were set up on the pitch as were the merry-go-rounds, and if there was a wedding in the village so were the stage and marquee. On such occasions, as evening drew on, Zsiga Balogh's band would perform on stage, while underneath, in the maze of scaffolding that supported it, the village lads would cuddle up to the squealing girls in their print dresses and big bows. 'I'll tell your father', the girls would say coquettishly to Csoki if he became too daring, and would point up at the boards in the direction of the *prímás* (first violin).

At one wedding Isti asked Csoki to persuade his father to teach him the violin. "You're not a Gypsy!" said the *prímás* with a laugh.

"You're not a Gypsy!" István senior also exclaimed when his son came out with the idea.

"That's what old Zsiga said too," remarked the boy.

"What?! I'll give him Gypsy," he burst out, "doesn't he want to give my son lessons?!"

And so it was decided; Isti would play the violin. Gypsies weren't to be the only ones in future!

Isti got on so well with the violin that one day Zsiga laughed and said: "I was mistaken, you are a Gypsy after all!" For some reason the *prímás* was more patient with Isti than with his own son. True, Isti turned out to have more talent than Csoki. If his son made a mistake, Zsiga was angry at once. After a while the lessons began with Zsiga excusing himself in advance: "Look out, my boy, I'm really on edge today! I'm likely to knock your block off!" And Zsiga was pretty much on edge every day. One might observe, more and more so. Needless to say the promised box on the ear increased neither Csoki's talent nor his inclination for the violin, and so Zsiga, who apart from Csoki only had daughters, poured all his teaching ambition into Isti. He taught the youngster as his father had taught him. Isti became the star pupil. "Isti gets it right first time!" "Isti practices!" Zsiga taught him fingerings that were cherished as a family secret. They practised in lessons, their heads close together, and the *prímás* even invited him to join his band as an apprentice. Zsiga's wife Zsuzsi shook her head; no good would come of this – Gypsy was Gypsy, Magyar was Magyar. It hurt her that her husband paid less attention to his own son than to the peasant boy. But Csoki didn't care. He reassured his mother and Isti that the violin didn't mean instrument and tunes to him, just thick ears.

From this time on Isti led a golden life. In the family his father gave the order that any domestic work was to be done by his siblings in his stead. "Isti's got to take care of his hands, he's a violinist! Isti's got to take care of his feet, he's a footballer," were his brothers' and sisters' scathing comments as they swept the yard, did the hoeing or fetched water from the well, doing their brother's chores.

"Gizi's not the lucky one, it's István for finding such an easy-going wife," muttered the women of the village. But all the same, as on stifling summer nights they lay beside their snoring, wheezing, halitotic husbands, they often dreamed of Gizi's good fortune. The delicate, almond-eyed Gizi did indeed humbly endure her husband's temperament. "That's why a woman wears a big apron, so she can hide her grief in it," she would say with a demure look if they asked her how she put up with him. Gizi played her part without complaint. At Christmas she made neighbourhood rounds with her basket and took little cakes to four or five children with sea-blue eyes fringed with dark lashes whom her husband had scattered around the area in the course of his debaucheries. Gizi loved István. She loved the way he would steal a look at her of an evening as she took off her headscarf, slipped modestly out of her dress behind the cupboard and put on her nightdress. She'd then sit on the edge of the bed, loose her chignon and with long, careful strokes brush her waist-length auburn hair, in which autumnal streaks were now appearing. At such times she was, in his eyes, once again the seventeen-year old girl that he had courted. The wounded Christ that ascended into the shining heavens in the picture on the wall – bought at the fair – watched her every movement and could testify that at those times, Gizi truly did feel herself to be lucky.

After the economic crisis, life in the village had begun to return to normal. The harvest was good, the summer was warm, the sun shone in autumn and the price of wine was good too. Thanks to Klebersberg and Hóman, the incumbent Ministers of Education, the cultural level of the Hungarian people was rising, national morale was higher and His Serene Highness the Regent was distributing financial assistance. But what saved the Goldsteins from having to sell up was Samu's brother, who had emigrated to America. Once more there were goods in the shop and credit in the inn.

It was stiflingly hot at the end of summer. At that time of year, after the harvest was in, the inn would be full in the afternoons. The sun still blazed on the windows, particles of dust floated in the shafts of light which filtered between the closed shutters, and the golden yellow fly-papers that hung from the ceiling glittered, mottled with struggling flies.

21

The men sat at the tables while the youngsters stood at the tin-covered bar drinking their *libafröccs* – sweetened soda-water cut with vinegar. The smell of paraffin from the ancient floorboards blended with the scents of wine and vinegar. By the window Pertli was reading a newspaper in the half-light; he raised his head and said in an undertone:

"Goldstein and Steiner had better pack up and go."

"So what's your problem with them, Pertli?" asked old Lázár from the next table.

"They're Jews," replied the little man brusquely.

Pertli was the village shoemaker, and he was so short that he'd stood on tip-toe when he was called up for the army so as not to be labelled unsuitable and shamed – the village girls would have laughed at him. When he was being kitted out in the army he was issued underpants that were too big, and he complained that there wasn't a drawstring in them, so his comrades in arms nicknamed him '*Pertli*' – drawstring.

"Have you been reading again?!" enquired old Lázár scornfully, nodding his head at the copy of *Pesti Újság* rustling in the shoemaker's hand. "Other people get cleverer if they read, but the more you read the dafter you are."

The rest roared with laughter.

"Is a Jew only any good when you need credit? And when he cures your old mother? Or fills in a form for you?" asked old Lázár.

"What's the matter, you old socialist, you a Béla Kun[4] supporter? Defending the Jews?" the hefty Jóska Hetési at the next table slapped the old man on the back.

"What's that got to do with it?" the old man shrugged his shoulders crossly. "The Reds shot Steiner's father 'cause they said he was a bourgeois, and the Whites beat him half to death for being a Jew."

An awkward silence fell. There were two Jewish families

in Tövispuszta, the Goldsteins, who kept the shop, and the Steiners, who owned the mill. The village accepted them. In the past anti-Semitic remarks had merely been throwaway lines. If anyone had come out with a proverb, for instance 'You only beat a Jew with both hands', neither the Goldsteins nor the Steiners had taken it amiss, any more than Béla Kaszás, who limped, would have thought of being offended if 'It's easier to catch up with a liar than a lame dog' were quoted in his presence. Samu Goldstein, however, was particularly respected, and people went to the shop for advice as well as to buy things, and since he knew about herbal remedies they were also happy to consult him on medical problems.

"The problem's not with individuals, it's the Jews as a whole," said István. "A Jew's a human being, like Samu Goldstein, Ábel Steiner, or old Braun who saved my life at the front, looked after me when I got typhoid. There's nothing wrong with them, it's the Jews! Those that get rich by fleecing us."

"So a banker, a factory-owner or a politician who isn't Jewish is all right?" asked Lázár.

"They're all Jewish," Veres made a sweeping gesture. "Just take their pants down and you'd see."

At that even Lázár grinned.

"They're selling the country out!" Pertli offered a correction. "That's what I say."

"That's not what I say!" answered Veres. He wasn't going to agree with Pertli. "I've never seen Goldstein selling the country out, and I've been going to his shop for sixty years. What I see him selling is flour, sugar and bread."

"Look here, Pertli!" old Lázár raised his voice. "Samu Goldstein's great-grandfather fought against the Austrians in 1848, same as yours, who was a Swabian, and mine, a Székely. You read rubbishy papers."

23

"At least I don't read that leftist rag *Népszava*!" Pertli hissed at him, though only those sitting close heard.

Previously such matters had scarcely been mentioned in the inn. The subject only came up at the time of the economic crisis, when Pertli or someone else from the village occasionally sounded off with stories they'd read in some racist newspaper.

As he glanced from the gloom towards the inn door István Veres saw three figures outlined against the blinding light. He immediately recognised the stocky shape of Isti and Dávid Goldstein's shorter, slighter build, but the tall, slender young man seemed unfamiliar. How long had they been standing there, how much of the argument had they heard? He squinted to get a better look at the stranger, then in astonishment he said quietly to himself, "It's Szent Pál!"

THE SILVER SPOON
EMBOSSED WITH A CROWN

The hair on Baron Pál Szentágostony's head and temples had become markedly grey, but the eyes beneath his bushy, black eyebrows still sparkled with life. He was smoking a cigar under the pergola on the terrace overlooking the valley. He had adjusted the position of his basket-work armchair until he could eventually see, above the vineyard that climbed the gentle slope of the hill, the sun beginning to set behind the distant mountains. A footman brought him a cut-glass goblet of chilled vermouth which the Baron sipped, focusing his attention on blowing the blue cigar smoke so as to filter the red disk of the setting sun.

In every family there is someone who has the time and persistence to research the family history. In the Szentágostony's this had been the younger brother of the previous Baron's father, uncle Gerzson. In the early 1800s he had travelled all the way to Siena to compile the family mythology. His research showed that in or around 1560 Paolo Saltucci had fled Tuscany because, according to the story, he had saved the life of the Princess Medici. When out hunting the Princess had fallen from her horse, her foot was trapped in the stirrup, and the horse was dragging her to an almost certain death when the gallant nobleman spurred after it and caught Her Highness up in his arms. Philip II of Spain had taken Siena not long before and handed over power to Cosimo Medici. The Archduke was fatally jealous of Don Paolo and resolved that he would extend the rules of Spanish etiquette in Siena to include merciless vengeance for trivial offences. This meant that death awaited Don Paolo because he had taken the Princess in his arms, even though for the purpose of saving her life. It is an entirely different matter that, according to some sources, it was not the first time that Don Paolo had taken her in his arms, though indeed less publicly and not expressly for the purpose of saving her life. After a last prayer under cover of darkness in the church of Sant'Agostino, where in his time he had been immersed in the water of baptism, the Ghibelline nobles of Siena, inveterate opponents of the papist Guelf Medicis of Florence, spirited Don Paolo away disguised in the habit of a Capuchin. Stealing through the dark alleyways he had left Siena by the nearby Tufi gate, never to return.

Don Paolo, assuming the title of Barone di Sant'Agostino, offered his services to King Ferdinánd of Hungary, took part in warfare against the Turks, and so gained the estate that reminded him of Tuscany; thence came the name of the village. The Barons Szentágostony revelled in their Hungarianness, but their links with Italy remained. In the opinion of old Gerzson they had, for example, acted as liaison officers between Kossuth and Garibaldi. The Mediterranean influence was apparent in the mansion: above the walls of red brick and ashlar the building was clad with mossy brown roof-tiles, and Venetian shutters protected the windows and French balconies.

"Where's Pál?" the Baron asked his wife as she joined him on the terrace to watch the sunset, dressed for dinner in an elegant, long summer gown and glass in hand.

"Down in the village," she replied as she sank into a basket-work armchair.

"Came home two days ago, and he's knocking about with that peasant and that Jewish boy already?"

"You mean Isti and Dávid," replied the Baroness firmly. "You know they're nice boys."

"I'm glad you too accommodate yourself so easily to the spirit of the age," Pál Szentágostony grimaced. "When would we have thought of keeping company with a Goldstein or an estate servant? Decent people though they might be."

The Baron knew both boys very well. He knew that Pál sneaked off to the village, played football with the peasant lads, and was close friends with Isti, some years his junior; and where Isti was, Dávid Goldstein was likely to be.

A couple of years earlier, when Pál had told his parents that Isti was learning to play the violin with Zsiga Balogh, his mother had summoned Isti to the mansion and listened to him play. Then, with her husband's agreement, she'd engaged a violin teacher for him. For two years Isti went into town three times a week for lessons with a professor at the Conservatoire, at the Baron's expense. He then expressed his gratitude with a little recital in the mansion. He played some Tchaikovsky, and when the Baroness, impressed, looked at her husband and said "Well, what do you say to that?" the reply came "Not bad, just a touch of a Gypsy accent," and the Baron smiled. It was obvious that he too was satisfied and pleased at having helped in Isti's education, but he was uncertain as to whether they were doing the right thing by it; he could see trouble coming in the world as the old order gave way to new; and in the awakening of the common man to upper-class self-awareness. The Baron divided society into the masses and excellent minorities, and although he meant by this types of people rather than social classes, excellence was rather the preserve of the upper classes. He feared that the world was becoming vulgar and common.

"It's a different world!" replied the Baroness.

"A different world," he repeated, without taking his eyes off the disk of the sun as it slipped behind the mountains. The Baroness, as was always her custom, applauded the sun's performance.

"Will it rise tomorrow?" muttered the Baron. He thought that in a topsy-turvy world it was gradually becoming less likely to surprise him if one day the sun were to rebel and decide not to rise at all.

At seven that evening the Baron, the Baroness and their younger son János were seated, dressed for dinner, at the long table which was laid with porcelain, silver and cut glass. Beneath the huge crystal chandelier only Pál's chair was vacant. A footman waited by the wall for the nod that meant that he might serve the first course, but he knew that the family had never yet begun dinner until everyone was at the table. They'd been waiting for some minutes and in the ever more painful and tense silence, no one spoke.

János stared at a huge oil-painting of the gallant ancestor, commissioned by old Gerzson from an artist with an illegible signature. The deservedly obscure painter hadn't worked wonders with his picture of Don Paolo in armour. As children, Pál and János had admired with a shiver the handsome, grim ancestor who, according to Mother at least, watched from the wall above the fireplace to see whether they ate their greens. As teenagers, however, they'd often secretly sniggered at the intrepid knight's expression, which now seemed silly, and between themselves they merely referred to the rescuer of the Tuscan Princess as 'our womanising ancestor'.

Since the time of Paolo, Barone di Sant'Agostino, the first-born son in the Szentágostony family had always been named Pál. In the area around Szentágoston however people abbreviated the surname and among themselves called the young gentlemen Szent Pál and Szent János, as an allusion to the pride with which the Baron spoke of his sons.

At last a dishevelled Pál junior appeared, having washed and dressed quickly, his hair still wet, and muttered a sheepish apology of sorts as he pulled his chair in. The Baron said grace, nodded to the footman to bring the trout, and only after that spoke.

"It seems that in Oxford the young gentleman has learnt to be unpunctual, contrary to the custom in this family," he said archly.

He liked to provoke Pál in order to teach him a lesson. Formerly Pál had argued back, but a year previously the Baron had become so over-excited that he fell off his chair, clutching his chest. The Baroness then pleaded with her son to respect his father's obdurate principles and to consider his high blood-pressure and his weak heart. Pál had promised never again to quarrel with him. That particular argument had erupted over the mine at Kesző, which belonged to the estate; it had stuck in the Baron's craw to have to sell it to a Jewish speculator because the family couldn't afford to develop it, while for years its maintenance had cost more than it earned. "They're plundering the country," the Baron had raged.

"If the Hungarian gentry are snooty and look down on the world of commerce, why are they surprised when the money gets into the hands of people who understand economics?" had been Pál's swift retort. He was in his third year at Oxford, reading History. János was in his first year at medical school and both had come home to the estate for the summer vacation.

But it was no use Pál's quoting the books that he'd read in the course of his studies, the Baron turned red and choked, and it was feared that he was suffering a heart-attack or a stroke. Since then the Baroness, if she felt – as now – that a quarrel was brewing, immediately made frantic signs from behind her husband's back for Pál not to increase the tension.

"Yes, father, you're quite right," replied Pál imperturbably.

The Baron exploded.

"Do you mind not telling me that I'm right when I know that you don't agree with me?"

He felt that he was regarded as no longer worth arguing with. Pál realised that, and although he too easily lost his temper, it annoyed his father considerably that he kept a respectful silence. Now he merely flushed but didn't say a single word.

"Family dinner and punctuality may seem to be a trifling quirk of the upper class," the Baron went on, "but these days, when the masses are not only aware of their vulgarity but actually demand the right to act impolitely, we have to cling to tradition as sailors cling to the mast in times of tempest. Make a note of that, gentlemen!"

In Pál Szentágostony's eyes vulgarity meant the big city, the Russian revolution, and the Hungarian Soviet regime of 1919, together with the corporal with the big voice and small moustache who persisted in shouting in German, having come to power two years before. The Baron had commanded a regiment of the Austro-Hungarian army during the World War and was certain that the educated Germans wouldn't suffer this buffoon, as he called the Führer, for very long.

Since he'd been studying in England, Pál junior's thinking had changed a great deal. In Oxford he'd attended the lectures of Arnold J. Toynbee, who had worked with General Smuts at the Paris Peace Conference in 1919, and although

Pál regarded the dismembering of historic Hungary under the Treaty of Trianon as infuriatingly unjust, the professor's views against nationalism and imperialism had influenced him strongly. In London, however, he'd got into leftist intellectual company in which there were Hungarian writers and artists who'd sympathised with the Soviet Republic, and there he heard of the parts played by Babits, Móricz, Bartók and Kodály in 1919. In the Baron's circle the Commune[5] was referred to only as a 'Jewish-Communist bloody proletarian dictatorship'. In his childhood Pál had heard of looting, the cruelty of the Leninist commandos, of murder and the burning of churches, and he himself remembered clearly how he and his brother had clung to their mother's skirts in terror as the peasants surrounded the mansion, shouting and armed with pitchforks. Then, when the Regent had re-established order, he'd seen the two *agents provocateurs* Imre Kodelka and Márton Veszelka swinging from a tree on the edge of the village. Before hanging them Iván Héjjas, the leader of the White detachment, had castrated Veszelka with his butcher's knife and stuffed his bloody genitals into Kodelka's mouth. For a long time Pál hadn't known what to make of the new concepts, or of the fact that many of the brilliant minds in Hungarian culture had sided with the Red authorities; he couldn't see where they belonged in the world that he'd been brought up to envisage.

Baron Pál had passed the age of forty when he married Emília, a cultured upper-middle-class girl almost twenty years his junior, but he'd taken good care of himself and they were spoken of as a handsome couple. The Baroness was a strong-minded girl, tall, angular and clever, more socially conscious than average and, what wasn't a matter of indifference, had a better than average dowry. She was well ahead of her contemporaries in spiritual maturity too, and the educated, cosmopolitan, mature Baron made an impression on her, while her family were pleased that their daughter was to be a baroness. Emília's mother believed in the upper-middle-class upbringing: French and German governesses, piano lessons, and although her daughter was a good head taller than her contemporaries, ballet lessons weren't omitted from the curriculum. At the performances staged each year-end, her father almost died of laughter when his daughter, resembling a baby dinosaur in a pink tutu, tried to rise gracefully to her points in her enormous ballet shoes. Emília never forgave him for that. By the age of sixteen she was 180 centimetres tall, and the shoemaker in fashionable Váci utca couldn't believe his ears when her parents ordered size forty-two slippers for her first ball. All her life Emília dieted, to be at least a 'slender whale', as she ironically nicknamed herself. In her thirties, after the boys had been born, she blossomed amazingly, and was surprised to find that men could hardly take their eyes off her. Perhaps to strengthen her self-confidence she didn't reject innocent flirtations, and evil tongues said they weren't all innocent. But are evil tongues to be believed? And is it possible to disbelieve them? The Baron, for the most part, tolerated her blossoming without a word, instead relegating his memories to the little drawer where he kept offensive and painful thoughts.

After dinner Pál asked his mother for use of the open-top Fiat Balilla to drive into town. Isti and Dávid were by then waiting for him by the main road in Tövispuszta. They scrambled into the car, Isti in front beside Pál, and Dávid obligingly in the uncomfortable rear seat.

The Green Ox was packed with men, drinking and talking. The smoke was so thick that a suffocating fog seemed to have settled in the alcoves of the smart hotel's underground rooms. As they followed the waiter between the tables, people patted Isti affectionately on the back, complimented him on the spectacular goal that he'd scored from an impossible angle in the last match, then politely acknowledged Pál.

"If you aren't with us we can't get a table," said Pál to Isti with a smile, as they settled down at the little corner table which the waiter liberated for them, asking a number of guests to sit elsewhere.

There they continued the conversation which they'd broken off that afternoon. Pál talked about Germany, the Nazis, the risk of war, big capital, socialism and anti-Semitism, and painted a gloomy picture of the outlook for Hungary. Isti and Dávid listened to him sceptically; Isti laughed all the time, and Dávid chuckled with him.

Pál's account was more and more hopeless.

"Isti's only a stupid footballer, but didn't you hear enough in the inn? And don't you read a paper?" he asked Dávid.

"I don't really understand this," said Dávid with false naivety. "What am I, when all's said and done? An extortionate Jewish capitalist or an anti-capitalist Judaeo-Bolshevist?"

"A bit of both," Isti laughed loudly. "Like I'm a stupid footballer and a peasant at the same time. Oh, and a Gypsy musician!"

THE HANUKKAH CANDLESTICK

Ignác Goldstein, Samu's father, had been a man who was widely respected. In his middle age he would sit on the bench outside the shop, puffing at his churchwarden pipe and chatting with customers, and even in his seventies he paid careful attention to his beard and the way he dressed. When he finally passed away, the town newspaper carried an obituary: 'The golden-hearted Ignác Goldstein, who never failed to help any that turned to him.'

In his own fashion, he'd been a rational man. When he drew up his will he decided not to divide his estate among his children, because a sixth of the house and the little shop wouldn't have been enough to provide for any one of them. He left everything to one so that in time of need, unfortunate siblings could be assisted. He thought long and hard about his children, deciding who to choose and who could best combine material advantage with kindness of heart. The girls would get married, he pondered, and if their husbands weren't sufficiently generous of spirit, he could hardly expect them to worry about their brothers-in-law. The simple solution would be to pick the eldest son, because Vince was the sort who'd always land on his feet but, although he was Jewish, he was fond of cards and might possibly gamble the business away. Henrik, on the other hand, was interested in machinery and cars, and was serving an apprenticeship in a car-repair workshop in town; he would be unhappy in the little shop, and in any case wanted to be off to America. So Ignác thought, and finally he decided on his youngest son, Samu: he always had his nose in a book, but was very helpful in the shop, and was such a kindly soul that he never went to bed before helping his father off with his boots. Ignác felt that the others would always be able to count on Samu. Once he'd taken the decision he informed his wife Bella of it. They agreed that next Friday evening, when the family was assembled for the usual Sabbath-eve ceremony, Ignác would make his decision known to his children.

The table was spread with a white cloth and Bella, smiling ceremoniously, lit the candles and, eyes closed, stretched out her hands in blessing towards her children. As her husband spoke the words of the prayer, she and her daughters covered their faces with their hands and prayed in the candlelight. Ignác broke the two plaited loaves and distributed the pieces to the family. Everyone took a sip of the wine then walked round the table, looked deep into one another's eyes, embraced and kissed.

"I learnt from my dear parents that you have to give while you're still in this life," he began. "I wouldn't like it if, after I'm gone, you had any ill feeling towards each other, because in this world there's nobody else that you can count on, my dear children, but one another and your family."

This he explained in thoughtful terms, and dealt with the matter of the estate.

"Yes, Daddy," the girls nodded in agreement. Vince and Henrik thought that their father's decision was sensible. Samu was the only one to suffer lifelong pangs of conscience at having unintentionally robbed his brothers.

✳

Especially now that he was relieved of responsibility for
the shop and, as he thought, could leave the care of his
aged parents to Samu in return for the inheritance, Henrik
emigrated to America without a qualm and was at last able
to be in Detroit, among his adored cars in the Ford factory.
He'd scarcely been away a year when he cheerfully informed
the family in one of his letters that he was settled in his new
country and was about to marry. He enclosed a photograph of
Peggy, his blonde, blue-eyed fiancée. The day of the wedding
had been named when he received a telegram from Vince:
father dying stop come immediately stop. By the time that Henrik
had arranged for leave from the factory, bought a boat ticket,
gone to New York, from there by ship to Naples and by train
via Budapest with numerous changes to Tövispuszta, seven
weeks had gone by, and Ignác Goldstein had actually died. At
the funeral the family looked tearfully at Henrik, goodness,
what a real Jewish boy: he'd foreseen his father's death even
though there had been no warning. This expression didn't
worry Henrik. He was so delighted at the family's reception
that he began to believe in his own prescience – it didn't occur
to him to ask Vince how he'd known a month beforehand
that their father was going to pass away when everyone said
that Ignác had died suddenly and peacefully. Nor did it give
him cause for thought when, three weeks later, he received a
letter from Peggy informing him regretfully that all was over
between them; he wasn't to look for her as she was moving
to California. He continued to write to her for a long time,
but when no replies ever came he decided not to go back to
America, but to use the experience he'd gained at Fords and
open a little car repair shop a couple of blocks from Nyugati
station in Budapest. Many years later it emerged that when

The Hanukkah Candlestick

Vince saw the photograph of the blonde, blue-eyed Peggy in Henrik's letter he was horrified at the idea of his brother marrying a Christian girl, and declared: "We're not having a *shiksa* in our family, even if she is an American!" And so he'd ordered Henrik home by telegram. Then he'd written to Peggy in Henrik's name, saying that he was going to stay in Hungary and was about to marry a Jewish girl. When he found all this out, years later, all that Henrik said was: "My dear brother meant well! You see, otherwise I could never have married my dear Ancika!"

By that time Vince Goldstein was living in New York. Clearly, things were going well for him: he had a lovely penthouse in Fifth Avenue overlooking Central Park. According to his story he made his money from textiles and the Stock Exchange, while rumours circulated that after losing a lot of his money at cards he'd insured his hair for a huge amount, then obtained a substance which made him bald. It was only after a lengthy argument that the insurance company had paid him a significant sum. Whether or not this tale was true no one could be sure, but it was a fact that Vince's head was as bald as a billiard ball. It was also a fact that Samu never had to help his siblings and that they all stood on their own two feet, even without inheriting from their parents. This was in contrast to Samu, who was excessively honest in business and whom Vince rescued from having to sell up. When, after the economic disaster, the people of Tövispuszta became so poor that they couldn't pay their bills at the shop, Samu simply allowed them credit. He was ruined.

"If a Jew is clever, then he's very clever, but if he's stupid, then he's very stupid! You're the latter, dear brother!" wrote

37

Vince after sending over the dollars to prevent the bailiffs auctioning his brother's house. "What could I have done?" replied Samu. "Should I have watched those poor people being evicted? The shop would have gone out of business anyway, because they still wouldn't have had any money to buy things." "If you imagine they're going to love you for this, you're very much mistaken," Vince's reply arrived in his next letter. "People don't like being grateful. Especially not to a Jew, with whom they've got little in common. They'll be angry with you because you've disturbed them in their prejudice. So they'll find it harder to account for why they hate you."

Samu Goldstein and his wife Ilus were content with their lot. They made a living in the little shop, and their two sons Dávid and Andor filled them with pleasure. Their only disappointment was that they had no daughter. After the two boys, try though they might, Ilus didn't become pregnant again.

One day, when they'd all been visiting Henrik, they were going home via the Keleti station when they noticed a little girl of about six with a placard round her neck sitting quietly on a bench. On the placard was written: 'I am Elza Kiss. I am travelling to my godparents' house in Dombóvár. If I become lost please notify László Fábián, Dombóvár, Bezerédj utca 19.' The little girl didn't seem to be lost, but was sitting there, quietly munching an apple. Since the Goldsteins had arrived an hour early for the train, as was their usual practice, they were taking a stroll and were somewhat amazed at seeing this honey blonde, dark-complexioned child with green eyes. Half an hour later they found her still alone on the bench, swinging her legs and looking around, and this time they went and sat down beside her.

"Who are you travelling with, Elza?" asked Ilus.

"I'm not travelling," answered the girl quite naturally. "I'm sitting on a bench."

Dávid and Andor grinned in amusement, but Ilus was becoming anxious.

"It says on this card that you're travelling to see your godparents in Dombóvár," said Ilus.

"Mummy put me on the train, but I got off when she'd gone away."

"Where do you live?" asked Dávid.

"I don't know. But Mummy doesn't want me at home. She says she's frightened of me."

The Goldsteins exchanged glances.

"Then we'll go to Dombóvár together and see your godparents, all right?" proposed Samu.

"I'm not going there," replied the girl, looking alarmed, "because a boy died there."

"Who died?" Ilus was horrified.

"A boy. A rock fell on him."

"You can't stay here all alone. It's a dangerous place for a little girl like you," Samu tried again.

"I'm not afraid," said the girl self-assuredly. "I'll beat everybody that's wicked. Mummy doesn't trust me either."

Long minutes went by before the Goldsteins succeeded, with the help of Dávid and Andor, in persuading Elza to go with them to Dombóvár.

The girl's godparents lived on the outskirts of Dombóvár, in a one-storey house in a cobbled street. The wooden gate that opened onto the street led to a paved inner yard, where the way to the dwellings lay between wretched flower-beds and vegetable patches edged with barbed wire. At the end of the yard stood sheds and lavatories. A woman was beating a threadbare rug on the fence, and pointed out where the Fábiáns lived. Mrs. Fábián was the only one at home. On hearing the knock she pulled aside the crocheted curtain at the window then opened the door and, wiping wet hands on her apron, enquired suspiciously:

"Who are you?"

"We found Elza at the station in Budapest. She had a notice round her neck, saying that if she got lost she should be brought to you here," said Samu.

The woman looked down at the girl but didn't so much as say hello to her.

"Isn't she your goddaughter?" asked Samu uncertainly. He looked first at the woman, then at the girl, but Elza's face showed even less interest than her godmother's.

"She's my husband's sister's daughter. But why should you bring her here? Where's her no-good mother?"

"Dávid and Andor, go and play with Elza for a bit, will you, while we have a talk," said Ilus, so that harsh words might not be exchanged within the girl's hearing.

"What am I supposed to do with this brat?" Mrs. Fábián burst out. "There's six of us here, and only one room and the kitchen. Her mother should've thought who she was dropping her knickers for. It's all very well having a child, you've got to bring it up as well."

Samu gave a little cough.

"If I understand you correctly, you wouldn't like the girl to stay here?"

"Right first time!" replied the woman scornfully. "She'll just be like her mother, or my good-for-nothing husband. I don't know what I was thinking when I married him."

"Same thing as Elza's mother, when she...er... as you so nicely put it just now," replied Samu. "Well, let's be going!" he turned to his wife.

At that moment a tremendous crash was heard, followed by sounds of weeping and wailing from the farther end of the house, where the children had gone to play. People ran out of their homes, and Mrs. Fábián and the Goldsteins, white of face, rushed to the children. Everyone looked for their own in case something had happened to them. The Goldsteins breathed sighs of relief when they caught sight of Dávid, Andor and Elza. Mrs. Fábián, like someone expecting the worst, elbowed her way into the crowd. In the middle lay a small boy, his head split open, and beside him on the ground some bricks and other fragments that had fallen from the roof. When she caught sight of the boy lying there bleeding, her eyes started out, and she couldn't speak, merely croaked, and flung herself upon the child as he lay there motionless.

"Oh, oh, my boy," she moaned.

Samu Goldstein bent, trembling, over the child and felt for his pulse. Then he sorrowfully shook his head.

Ilus clasped Elza to her and covered her eyes, while with her other hand she shepherded Dávid and Andor away from the disaster.

Someone hurried off to find a doctor. Mrs. Fábián was sitting on the ground, quivering with shock and holding her dead son's hand. The neighbours stood around her, not knowing what to do, and could find no words but just looked at the sobbing, trembling woman.

Samu asked for a glass of water and took a little phial from his pocket, poured a couple of drops from it, then went up to Mrs. Fábián, put an arm round her and gave her the water.

"Drink this, you'll feel better."

He took out a business card and slipped it into her apron pocket.

"We'll take Elza off your hands. Here's our address, and if we can help at all, please let us know," he said.

Mrs. Fábián made no answer, merely stared in front of her, her eyes glazed.

When they were in the street Elza burst into sobs.

"I knew we shouldn't come here because a boy had died. I told you, a stone fell on him!"

Samu and Ilus looked at one another, then at the girl.

"Good Lord!" said Ilus, horrified. "This child can see the future, only she doesn't realise!" she whispered to Samu.

That night, when they'd come home with Elza, Ilus dreamt that she'd brought the little girl into the world. While giving birth, however, she strangely felt no pain but a sort of other-worldly happiness, and Elza didn't cry, as newly-born babies do, but smiled.

"Just fancy, we've got a sister, and she can walk and talk already," Dávid boasted to Isti when he introduced Elza to his friend.

"Can't have been an easy birth," Isti had his doubts as he looked her over.

Indeed it wasn't. The Goldsteins spent months calling on officials and holding discussions with Elza's parents, until it was finally settled that she could stay with them. Elza's mother didn't hold onto the child but was afraid of being accused of neglecting her responsibilities. She was much relieved when the Goldsteins offered to adopt the girl and give her their name. She ceased to be Elza Kiss and became a Jewish girl, Elza Goldstein.

This happened, broadly speaking, when Satan appeared to Dávid Goldstein in the form of paprika-flavoured sausage in the Vereses' kitchen. A well-to-do friend had given them some tasty morsels from the pig that he'd killed, and Gizi carefully sliced the sausage into paper-thin rings so that all the children should have some without too much being used up. They went up to mother piously, one after the other as if receiving communion in church, and she solemnly, as befitted the rare occasion, placed the slices of sausage in their mouths. Dávid looked on enviously.

"Isn't Dávid getting any?" Isti tried to include his friend.

"Jews aren't allowed to eat pork," replied his mother sadly, "isn't that so, Dávid?"

Dávid looked, as if bewitched, at the spicy, reddish-brown sausage, and after watching the blissful expressions with which the Veres children chewed what was to him forbidden fruit, he felt that he was quite sure to die if he were left out. But God is good, so He couldn't want that to happen, he considered. But finally he shook his head sadly and said thank you but he wasn't allowed to eat it.

"Good thing we aren't Jewish!" sighed Isti.

"Dávid, why are you Jewish?" asked one of Isti's sisters. "Nobody likes the Jews, and they can't even eat sausage. We like you, though," she added on reflection.

Dávid didn't know what to say. He had never seen much advantage in being Jewish, and now, to top it all, he couldn't have any sausage.

"Well, don't be Jewish!" Isti suggested to him later in their den up in the plum tree.

"How could I not be Jewish since I was born that way?" asked Dávid.

"Eat some sausage! If Jews aren't allowed to, and you do eat some, then you won't be Jewish. I've pinched a bit for you," he added, and produced it from his pocket.

Isti's reasoning seemed sound. Dávid examined the sausage nervously, carefully picked off the fluff from Isti's pocket that had stuck to it and sniffed at it.

"If Jews aren't allowed to eat things like this, I might die," he said fearfully.

At that Isti felt uncertain too. He found sausage to be an extreme example of what it would be worth dying for. At the scent of paprika Dávid's mouth watered. He felt dizzy, as if he'd faint if he couldn't eat it. That was what Eve must have felt at that well-known, fateful moment in Paradise. 'Have some sausage!' the serpent now hissed to Dávid. And with a sudden movement Dávid took the bait. At first he was alarmed, thought of spitting it out, but felt that he couldn't do that with such a treasure, and then his mouth seemed to begin to move of its own accord, to chew and gnaw the bit of sausage with ever growing enjoyment.

Afterwards they waited for a while to see whether Dávid was going to die. But he didn't.

"Well, are you still Jewish?" asked Isti.

"I don't know," replied Dávid, not knowing what to make of it all.

Since she'd been a girl Mrs. Goldstein had dreamt that should the Eternal One ever present her with a daughter they would play with dolls together, do handiwork and cook, and what nice little dresses she would make for her. When she caught sight of Elza on the bench in the station in Budapest she felt that her dreams had come true. Even the girl's colouring, her voice and the way she moved seemed familiar from some remote ancestral past, only experienced in her dreams. Her eyes in particular were that indefinable grey-green colour which could reflect every nuance of spiritual state from a gentle dove-grey to an angry green when her mood was aroused. Naturally, she was satisfied with her two sons too.

"Of course, how would I not be?" she'd say if asked. "Dávid and Andor, thanks be to the Eternal One, are sensitive, warm-hearted boys, but a chatty, lively little girl, who'll always cling to her mother, secretly try on her clothes in front of a mirror, slop about in her mother's shoes – that's something else."

One day Henrik's wife Anci had told her the joke about Mary Magdalene, her face radiant, asking the Virgin how it had felt to give birth to Jesus, to which Mary modestly and embarrassedly replied 'You know, my dear, I'd really have liked a girl'. The women smiled with affectionate understanding, while the men failed to understand and just stared stupidly. Ilus had been ashamed at those dreams of hers, because she felt that her desire for a daughter was letting her sons down. Now, with the arrival of Elza, her conscience was clear. "Her eyes are just like my father's," she enthused to the neighbours when they brought Elza home to the village like a wonderful prize. "Her mouth's the same shape as my mother's, the boys have got that as well. She's so much like the brothers! I can't believe she's not my own." Ilus felt as if something had simply gone wrong earlier with the machinery of fate, which the good Lord had then put right. She was a little uneasy about the curious incident in Dombóvár, when it had seemed that Elza could in some strange way foresee the future, but as she herself couldn't explain what had actually happened, Ilus preferred to dismiss her fears and attribute it to chance and the fantasy of a six-year-old girl.

Little by little, however, Ilus had to accept that Elza was only superficially the sort of daughter that she'd dreamt of. Her first shock came when, in great excitement, she bought her two frilly velvet dresses in town, and instead of being pleased Elza pleaded with her not to make her wear them. All that she wanted to wear was the printed dress in which she'd arrived. In a chest in the loft she came across trousers and shirts that the boys had grown out of, and she would have liked to go about in those.

"What will people say? It'll look as if we grudge spending money on you and make you go round in Dávid and Andor's old clothes. Don't do this to me, my dear," Ilus begged.

Then eventually she managed to persuade Elza to put on an infinitely simple pastel-coloured dress. It soon became clear that not only did clothes not interest her, but neither did dolls; she didn't like being cuddled, and being caressed upset her. To Ilus, physical closeness was a natural way of expressing emotion, and it almost made her ill that Elza deprived her of that. She felt that she was incapable of being close to the child and didn't understand her reactions. Elza didn't seem to love her, and she was worried that sooner or later she wouldn't love her either. Sometimes when she was alone she took the frilly dresses out of the wardrobe, laid them on the bed, looked at them, and asked herself where she'd gone wrong. Then she'd give the dresses a stroke and hang them back up in the wardrobe.

One day, when Ilus bent down to comb Elza's hair, the girl took her face in both hands and looked deep into her eyes.

"Are you frightened of me too, like my other mother? Don't you want me to live here, either?"

Ilus burst into tears.

"How can you say such a thing, Elza? You're our little girl, you'll always stay with us!" and she hugged the child to her.

That evening, after Elza had gone to sleep on her couch at the end of the double bed, Ilus told Samu in a troubled whisper about the conversation that she'd had with her.

"Are you in fact afraid of her?" he asked.

Ilus considered.

"I think I am. Elza's very perceptive."

"That's a pity," said Samu quietly. "Fear's a terrible thing, because it leads to hate."

"Everything's gone so smoothly with Dávid and Andor," whispered Ilus. "Perhaps it's harder with Elza because she's not one of our race? Not an *unzere*?"

"I don't believe that the difference between people is in their blood, it's more in their souls," said Samu. "Only this little girl didn't sit on a cloud to pick her parents like other souls do, she was waiting on a dirty bench in a smoky railway station. But it doesn't matter whose body she came out of, she's one of us."

He reached over to the other side of the bed and gave his wife's hand a gentle squeeze.

"You can give me a cuddle, I shan't object," he said.

Even in the darkness he thought he could see Ilus' smile as he felt her warm body snuggle up against him.

From the very first moment Samu and the boys understood Elza better than Ilus did, possibly because they accepted her more readily. True, they didn't have to contend with their earlier dreams. Dávid liked to teach her things, but Elza was happy to go about with Andor, six years her senior, and his friends, whom the strange little girl clearly amused.

"And she can tell the future!" boasted Andor to his friends in a mysterious tone. And he told them how his sister had foretold the death of the boy in Dombóvár. The boys shuddered as they listened.

"Let's try her!" said little Lázár.

"Get her to tell us the lottery numbers!" Jóska Galambos suggested. "We'll get rich, at least."

"That's silly!" Andor brushed the idea aside. "She doesn't

know her numbers yet. One day, when she goes to school."
Then will she say whether Csillag's foaled a mare or a
stallion?" Sanyi Hetési had another idea.

"If Csillag's already foaled, that's already happened, so it
wouldn't be telling the future," objected little Lázár.

"Well, we don't know yet what she's foaled, but maybe
we'll find out. That's future then!" Sanyi protested.

Everybody said that he was right. And so they asked Elza
whether she thought Csillag's foal was a mare or a stallion,
but she didn't understand the words.

"Elza! Do you think their mother's mare's little pony is
a boy or a girl?" said Andor, helpfully.

"She's had a little pony?" Elza opened her eyes wide in
delight. "Can I go and see it?"

"Yes, if you'll say whether you think it's a boy or a girl,"
Andor changed to a stricter tone.

"A girl," said Elza after a little thought. "But she'd like to
be a boy."

The boys were taken aback at the answer, but they set off
with Elza for the farm, laughing and pushing one another.
Outside the stable the old coachman, András Asztalos, was
piling up hay.

"Uncle András, is Csillag's foal a mare or a stallion?"
asked the boys, all talking at once.

"Why all the fuss?" the old man laughed. "She's had
a little stallion."

Andor was disappointed. The boys laughed scornfully.

"Well, there's your future-teller for you!"

"You don't understand!" little Lázár laughed loudly,
clutching his sides. "The girl pony wanted to be a boy, and
now she is!"

✳

The Hanukkah Candlestick

One day Ilus and Samu overheard Elza, in her favourite hidey-hole in the store behind the shop, telling Andor something.

"I'd like to be terrifying," she said seriously.

Andor was astounded.

Ilus gave her husband a startled look as if to say 'You see, there's something really wrong with this child, I told you so,' and was about to intervene, but Samu gently took her arm and raised a finger to his lips for silence, and they waited to see what would follow.

"And why do you want to be terrifying?" asked Andor in astonishment.

"So that wicked people will be afraid of me! Because I'm afraid of them!"

"But if you were terrifying, good people would be afraid of you, not just wicked! Would you like Mummy and Daddy, Dávid and me to be afraid of you?"

Elza pondered this for a moment. Then she said "I'd like to be terrifying but good on the inside, only the wicked people won't know that, so I'll beat them."

"Aha," Andor nodded. "But do you know that wicked people aren't afraid of wicked people?"

"Really?" Elza was surprised. "Who are they afraid of then?"

"Well, good people!" answered Andor seriously. "Because they don't understand what goodness is, so they're afraid of them."

"They're afraid of good people?" asked the little girl, puzzled. "Wicked people are afraid of good people?" and her face lit up. "Then I'm going to be a good girl!"

"There, you see," whispered Samu in his wife's ear behind the door. "They've talked it through!"

✳

The family was preparing secret surprises for Ilus' birthday, competing with one another to see who could give Mummy the greatest pleasure. Samu made *sólet*,[6] which was always a special treat. "There's no tastier dish in all Greater Hungary than *sólet* made to the old Goldstein recipe, provided my brother makes it," said Henrik every time that he tasted Samu's cooking. Dávid spent weeks modelling their house in matchsticks and intended to present that, and Andor had been drawing and painting for days. Elza was the only one who hadn't done anything. When her brothers asked what her present was going to be, all she said was that she already had the surprise and she knew it would please Mummy most of all. On Ilus' birthday the boys presented their gifts after dinner, then when it came to Elza's turn she raised a finger significantly to say that she was coming straight back and ran out of the room. Minutes went by in expectation and then the door opened and in came Elza wearing one of the frilly velvet dresses. She'd grown quite a bit in the meantime and couldn't fasten the zip, and she looked rather like a decorated Easter ham, but there she stood triumphantly, as if to say that she had no doubt which present Mummy would like best, because she'd so wanted to see her in a frilly dress. The Goldsteins' eyes popped out incredulously, as they looked, stupefied, at the little girl who was holding her breath in case she split the tight-fitting dress and was waiting for a reaction. Strange sounds burst from Ilus and Samu, as if they couldn't make up their minds whether to laugh or cry. The sight gave Dávid and Andor no such choice: they burst into raucous laughter. Elza, upset, ran out of the room, but Ilus and Samu quickly ran after her and hugged her, and immediately told her what a splendid surprise she'd given them.

Samu enjoyed being with Elza and liked her to keep him company in the shop, to ladle flour and sugar into bags under the till with her little measure, and to help arrange the croissants in the bread-baskets. He took her shopping and she sometimes went with him if he was called to heal someone. At first in the village Samu had been met with a smile when customers complained of their ailments in the shop and he asked them questions such as whether they preferred sweet things or sour, whether they were perspiring or feeling cold. Sometimes he would question people for an hour or two, and then produce tiny little pills from a drawer, which they were to take. The word soon spread in the village that the shopkeeper could, with his pills, cure diseases that the doctor couldn't. The Baroness asked for his help several times, as did the Baron himself now and then, although on such occasions he always added that he didn't believe in hocus-pocus. Lucky Gizi followed his advice with an almost religious devotion; his little pills often restored the Veres family. "He's a holy man!" Gizi declared at such times. Samu's talent was recognised even by Dr. Kenéz in the town. "That Goldstein has homeopathy in his blood, if I may say such a thing," he told the Baroness. It even happened that, in his capacity as a doctor, he asked Samu's advice, showing what an enlightened mind he had.

Elza was now seven. Dr. Kenéz was just leaving the Goldsteins' after one of his professional calls when she took his hand and looked at him with her big eyes.

"Doctor, could you show me what there is inside people?"

"Are you interested in that kind of thing?" asked Kenéz, pushing his glasses higher on his nose. "Well, there are all sorts of organs inside people, the heart, the liver, the lungs and so on," he answered.

"But could you show me?" Elza asked, now a little impatiently. "I'd very much like to see!"

"Could you take her to an operation at the clinic?" asked Samu, supporting the girl's request.

"Take a seven-year-old child into theatre?" the doctor scratched his head. "Are you sure you won't faint?"

Elza was surprised.

"I know what people are like inside, but I'd like to see if it really is like that."

Dressed in white gowns and masked, Samu and Elza followed Dr. Kenéz into the operating theatre. They stood by the wall, peered through a gap between the doctors and assistants and waited for the surgeon to open up the patient with his scalpel from the rib-cage downwards, and take out the inner organs. The intestines made such an enormous pile on the operating table that if Samu hadn't seen it with his own eyes he wouldn't have believed all that had been removed from one person.

"Good Lord!" he muttered, "How are they going to get it all back in?"

Elza held her father's hand, fascinated, and looked at the patient as he lay there. Afterwards all she said was "That's how I thought it was!"

The Poster

In 1938 Isti Veres was playing for the town team and earning money as a violinist. Zsiga Balogh had more and more requests to bring the 'blue-eyed Gypsy' to weddings. Thanks to Isti, his band had become one of the most popular in the district. Wedding receptions were still held on the badly trampled football field. As Isti played with the band on the stage, set beside the pitch, he watched the half-drunk wedding guests enjoying themselves at the tables. He looked on as the girls, dressed in their Sunday best, squealed happily when the lads chased them and pawed them under the stage, just as he'd done at their age. "What a special place this pitch is," thought Isti, "whether it's football or music, where you come from doesn't matter, it's what you can do that counts." As he was given ever more engagements with the band, however, he found it harder and harder to reconcile the demands of music and football. It was lucky that weddings mainly took place towards the end of summer, in the weeks following harvest or at vintage-time.

Isti enjoyed the popularity that football and music brought him equally: as the fans shouted his name for minutes on end after each goal and as girls stared at him, their faces flushed, at festivities, or revellers asked him to play their favourite tunes.

Isti and Dávid were eighteen. In school their ways had parted eight years earlier; Dávid had gone to commercial school, while Isti, following four years at primary school, had gone to higher elementary school and then left school altogether. István Veres had said at the time "Musicians and footballers don't need doctorates," and indeed he was right. Dávid, according to plan, would go into higher education since his younger brother was happier than he was to remain in the shop. Their father had agreed with them that Andor would keep the business going. It was planned that eventually Elza too would lend a hand. Dávid's studies were going really well, especially considering that in recent years another school – the dancing school – had interested him much more than the commercial.

At the time, the most fashionable dancing school in town was the one known as Auntie Manci's, and the principal instructor was none other than old Jenő Berger, the former competition dancer whose reputation was nation-wide. Auntie Manci had had two enormous flats knocked into one on the first floor of an elegant art nouveau apartment block. There was plenty of space, in what had been six rooms overlooking the street, for forty couples and there were seats by the wall for mothers and aunts. Heavy, dark red velvet curtains covered the windows so that the music shouldn't be heard outside, and similar curtains hung at the entrance too. Music was provided by a four-piece band: a clarinetist, trumpeter, drummer and a pianist with a funny face who, to Manci's annoyance, liked most of all to play fashionable swing or boogie-woogie. She was irritated most of all when László, who called himself Leslie, said "If the girls don't shake their backsides in time to my music and get the boys excited, then I'm playing badly!" The girls shook nothing at all, stepping instead with stiff legs and anxious looks, right-two-three-four, but fortunately this didn't undermine Leslie's confidence in his musical ability. At that age, needless to say, a boy is aroused by the mere touch of a girl and of course the blood in the girls' veins ran no thinner than the boys'; but what girl would get to her feet and dance watched by the staring, inquisitive eyes of the mothers lined up by the wall? Middle-class girls were in fact brought along on Saturdays to learn deportment. Originally middle-class boys were sent there too by their parents, with much the same aim, but for some reason Aunt Manci's admonitions and sharp words of command, as she beat time with a closed fan against the palm of her hand, had less effect on them. Old Jenő, slender and refined in his tight-fitting dance-competition trousers, didn't have the forceful personality required to call teenagers to order when they roared with ribald laughter. On Sundays he went to watch the town team and had great respect for Isti, so thanks to his intervention the boys were admitted to the dancing free of charge. Isti wore a suit, shirt and shoes borrowed from Pál, 'hand-me-downs from the gentry,' while Dávid wore the suit that he'd been given when he left school.

Just as plain girls usually go to parties with pretty girls, Dávid too felt that his chances were improved by appearing among the girls with Isti.

"You've just got to be careful," he said pedantically, "that the balance of the sexes is right, because when the party's at its height people split up. That is, pair off," and he raised a finger in emphasis.

But all that was mere speculation, because things didn't go beyond clumsy kisses and the occasional grope snatched on the dark stairs of the dance school.

"I understand why plain girls go about with pretty ones," said Isti once, as they stood to the side of the dance-floor, trying to raise the courage to ask someone up, "it's because if they came by themselves nobody would so much as look at them. But what's in it for the pretty girls?"

"Being with the plain ones makes them look even prettier," replied Dávid.

"There ought to be nothing but pretty girls!"

"And they shouldn't be too demanding," mumbled Dávid.

Isti had by that time had his first physical experiences. To be more exact, two. Dávid still only imagined such things and questioned his friend in minute detail on numerous occasions so that he could go on imagining with greater insight. On seeing Dávid's wide eyes, Isti's bent for fantasy always came into play and he spiced up his accounts with more and more detail each time until eventually a woman-eating hero took shape in the stories and their telling usually ended in raucous laughter. The boys would roll about on the ground clutching their sides and further embroider the lewd exploits, exaggerating Isti's manly prowess more and more. In fact they both knew that Isti had neither his sea-blue eyes with their dark lashes nor yet his fame as footballer or musician to thank for his triumphs, only the girls' curiosity. The girls of Szentágoston and Tövispuszta soon worked out what the Veres boys had inherited of their father's manhood, such was its fame throughout the region.

The most inquisitive of the girls was Panni Ördögh – curvaceous, chatty, and with a slight squint. When it happened, one warm summer evening, in the hayloft above the stable, she could hardly wait till morning to boast to the girls about it.

"Well, well, what has Isti inherited from his father?" they squealed excitedly.

"His lovely blue eyes!" Panni laughed.

Panni's opinion cannot have seemed convincing, because the blonde, angular Zsuzsi Kántor decided to assess the facts of the matter in person. Afterwards all that she would say, pursing her lips, was "I've seen better tools in the village," which, coming from Zsuzsi Kántor, was to be believed, because she truly had a sound basis for comparison.

"Nothing wrong with that tool!" retorted Panni, her eyes flashing.

"Steady now, Panni!" said the girls.

His father's reputation was always on Isti's mind. Even as a small boy he'd furtively compared his own organ with his father's when washing in the evening, but since his teens, when he'd become conscious of the ultimate difference in dimension, he was full of complexes. Zsuzsi Kántor's opinion, which went round the village in a matter of days, was another blow to his morale. He tried to laugh it off with Dávid, and pretended to be quite the tough guy: he tossed a long scarf round his neck and started to smoke cigarettes.

As they made little headway with the town girls, Isti increasingly asked his friend to go to the inn instead and he would occasionally let himself be tempted away from his footballing friends to the town brothel, which Dávid avoided with religious horror. What worried him even more was that Isti was definitely taking to drink, and after playing into the small hours with the Gypsy band regularly failed to appear for training. Dávid himself turned to the manager of the town team for help and old Gyula, the trainer, told him to tell his friend that, outstanding talent or not, if he carried on in the same way he would sooner or later throw him off the team. At such times Gyula would add: "To my very great regret!" All that Dávid would need to say to Isti after a while was: "Again, it was to my very great regret!"

"My boy, you're like Halley's comet, only seen every seventy-six years," Gyula said to Isti when he finally turned up for training. Bearing in mind Gyula's grasp of scientific concepts, the witticism didn't come from him, but he thought it very amusing, because afterwards he always paused for effect, just as great comedians do. "Mark my words, my boy, two talents are often less than one!" he said, and slapped Isti on the backside with fatherly affection. Isti hated Gyula's familiarity, and it always reminded him that a year before, when he'd joined the squad, the trainer has said to him in front of the others:

"Isti, my boy, don't go wanking too often, it'll ruin your fitness."

The other lads burst into raucous laughter not just at the trainer's line, but also because of the way Isti turned beetroot red, as if caught in the act.

"Don't get worked up, you fathead, the old devil says that to everybody when they join the squad. And we all blushed because because we thought he thought we were the only one doing it," Bandi Czigány, the goalkeeper, reassured him.

Isti was at a difficult age: he was trying to find his bearings – in his dreams, in the adult world and in his natural inclinations. The situation was further complicated because the Baroness decided to persuade Isti to give up Gypsy music and concentrate on classical instead. She called him to the mansion, put one Bakelite record after another on the gramophone, lowered the needle ceremoniously onto Tchaikovsky and Mendelsohn, placed a pile of illustrated newspapers in front of him on the Biedermeier table and leafed through them with theatrical gestures. The pictures were of artists in evening dress playing in the Vigadó in Budapest, London's Royal Albert Hall or Carnegie Hall in New York. Isti had never been to a concert in his life and the illustrated papers showed him a world so remote as to be inconceivable and, what was more, rather funny. He couldn't imagine what there might be for him in that alien place. The thought of all those hours of practice every day also dismayed him, but for weeks he allowed himself to be persuaded because he loved those cinnamon-fragrant afternoon teas in the mansion's drawing-room, and especially the way the Baroness bent quite close as she turned the pages of the papers. At such times Isti didn't look at the photographs, the monotonously dressed gentlemen and the evening-gowned ladies, but inhaled the Baroness' perfume and did his best to peer into her décolletage. Presumably she noticed all this, but it didn't upset her; it even seemed to flatter her vanity a little. Sometimes she would ask Isti to bring his violin and play something. She accompanied him on the piano and listened to him with dreamy eyes.

"If you become a Gypsy musician it'll be as if you've just pushed your head out of the mud," she once said, "but if you became a concert violinist you'd even be forgiven for being born a farm servant."

The musical afternoon teas were brought to an abrupt end by a sarcastic remark from the Baron. One day he came into the drawing-room and saw Isti and the Baroness tête à tête, and said to her "Are you playing Anna Karenina or Madame Bovary?"

Isti didn't know the name of either lady, but it was evident from the blood that suffused the Baroness' face and from her blazing eyes that they didn't enjoy too much popularity in the Szentágostony family. They must surely have been importunate relations, he thought. After the incident Isti excused himself for being a nuisance and didn't set foot in the mansion for years.

At the time Pál hadn't been home for the second summer, nor had he written to Isti or Dávid.

THE INFLATABLE BUDDHA

∗

In the summer of 1939 it emerged that Dávid hadn't been admitted to the university. The new law[7] only permitted a limited number of Jewish students, and he was excluded. As he did on every important occasion that concerned the family, Samu Goldstein consulted Vince and Henrik about the boy's future. They then decided that Dávid should move to Budapest and become an apprentice in Henrik's motor repair workshop.

Ilus arranged a farewell dinner in honour of her son for the last Friday. On Samu's advice Isti was also invited as the lads were going to be a long way apart. It was the first time that Isti had been to a Sabbath-eve dinner, and Samu loaned him a *yarmulka* for the occasion. He was familiar with the little Jewish skull-cap, as Samu always wore it, even under his hat. He also knew that even as boys Dávid and Andor had persuaded their father that they need not wear a *sábezdekli*, as they called it, every day, so as not to be teased by the village lads. Only now, however, did Isti realise that Jews wore it not only in the synagogue but on all religious occasions, and therefore it was worn on a Sabbath eve and at the ceremonial dinner. He felt strongly disposed to laugh when he saw himself in the mirror with the tiny head-gear perched on top of his head like Dávid and Andor, but he stood with bowed head, doing his best to control the spasms that wanted to rise from his stomach, and meanwhile he watched Ilus and Elza as, heads covered with delicate lace kerchiefs, they buried their faces in their hands in prayer. Isti didn't really understand what he found amusing about it all but went on trying to choke back the convulsions. Sounds that came from under Elza's hands, however, indicated that she too was struggling with infectious laughter, and that only stimulated Isti further.

The Poster

When, after the blessing was ended, Samu broke the plaited loaves and tossed the pieces lightly around to members of the family, who were ready and caught them neatly, Isti could stand it no longer and burst out laughing. For a moment the others were dumbfounded, but then Samu too laughed and Elza, Dávid and Andor joined in the merriment without restraint. Only Ilus shook her head and looked at her husband in disapproval.

"Have you ever tried to look from the outside, to see how comical this must be to anyone who's never seen it all before?" asked Samu, wiping his eyes.

Isti gave Samu a grateful look.

After Dávid had gone Isti was left to himself. He felt lost without his friend; this pleased old Gyula most of all – at last, his favourite appeared regularly for training. One afternoon, as Isti and some of the team were going home after the session, they caught sight of a poster at the door of one building. 'COURAGE' it proclaimed in big letters, and invited any that were interested to a meeting of the Hungarian National Socialist Party. It was a well-designed poster, with an eye-catching symbol at the top: on a red background a white equilateral lozenge, containing a green cross with each arm ending in a barbed arrow-head and a capital H in the middle[8]. As they had plenty of time before going for a drink they decided to look in on the meeting since they'd never been to such a thing. They could hardly get in – the big room was packed. At the far end a balding, rather tubby man was saying that the time was ripe for Parliament to pass the new Jewish law, the one limiting the presence of Jews in public life and the economy, because while only six per cent of the population was Jewish that included a third of all lawyers, journalists, business executives and doctors. And the peasantry at last deserved the land reform which the communists had manipulated in 1919 and which Prime Minister Gömbös was now promising. And that if Germany hadn't been helping Hungary for four years with a trade agreement, Hungary wouldn't have known where to sell its agricultural produce and would be starving. People should look at the economic advances being achieved in Germany. A similar future awaited Hungary too if it would only follow the German example, and not in the hesitant manner of the government. Only through the Germans could there be any hope, he said, of Hungarians one day living within their historical frontiers once again. People applauded and nodded enthusiastically in agreement, and Isti found himself nodding too. When the speaker presented the case for the Jewish law he felt less confident, because he recalled Dávid's ill-suppressed tears when it emerged that he wouldn't be able to go on studying, but in the end he let himself be convinced. "It's fair if you consider the ratios, and Dávid too must see that," he reconciled his conflicting feelings. "It's a pity some other Jewish boy wasn't excluded, though," he thought to himself. Then he thought of his father, who, ever since he could remember, had yearned for land of his own. "How marvellous it would be if the old man got his own land at last," he dreamed.

At the door, on the way out, he bumped into Pertli, Jóska Hetési and another man from the village, Balázs Székely. "Well, what d'you say, young Veres, come to your senses?" asked Jóska on seeing him.

"We were just passing on the way from training and looked in," stammered Isti. "Very interesting."

"Mind you tell your Jewish friend Goldstein that as well!"

Pertli called after him in the street, and the rest laughed.

Isti was disturbed. The speech had indeed had a profound effect on him, and in the inn too he and his team-mates went on discussing how lucid and convincing the speaker had been. Only Lapát, the habitually cantankerous outside right, didn't understand.

"Look here, there aren't any Jews in our team, so let's get Goldstein in!"

"Are you stupid, Lapát? Dávid can't play football!" Isti was astonished.

"Well, that's the point!" said Lapát with a laugh. "He can play football, but not as well as we can. If somebody's just got into university instead of him that can actually study, but not as well as Dávid, then we could take him into the side in return so as to correct the percentage here as well. That'd be fair!"

Only a few of them grinned. The rest exchanged puzzled looks.

"This Lapát really is as thick as a plank!"

THE POSTCARD FROM PARIS

As it was the Baron's custom to rectify the unseemly vagaries of reality by way of his pipe-dreams, he told everyone in the village that his elder son had taken his degree at Oxford and then gone to America. In fact, after finishing at the university, Baron Pál junior had gone to Paris to perfect his French. He'd decided to accept no more money from his parents but to subsist by giving English lessons to French students. In the first weeks he lived in a small hotel in the Latin Quarter but found it expensive; he therefore eventually rented a garret that looked out over the rooftops in rue Cujas, near the Sorbonne. A creaking, narrow staircase led up to the fifth floor, and at first Pál couldn't believe that so tall a house had been built without a lift. Only later did he find out that this was the norm in old Parisian houses. "There'll be stranger surprises for me in the future," he told himself with a smile. "What's this compared to discovering that there's a twenty-four piece silver dinner-service, when I've only seen a forty-eight piece one?"

There was no bathroom with the little room, just a battered tub by the fireplace to wash in. The WC was in a cubicle off the corridor, and consisted of a hole in the floor with shoe-shaped concrete blocks on either side so that one could keep one's feet dry. That was all. Previously Pál had only seen, both at home and in Oxford, lavatory pedestals of white glazed earthenware. He particularly liked the one at home, which was a real masterpiece: green-leaved fronds ran round it in high relief with tiny red and pink flowers between the leaves, as if on a vase. The first time he'd encountered the old-fashioned type of lavatory in a Paris café he calculated with great anxiety how to squat on it in order to hit the hole. As he couldn't find the light switch he left the door a fraction ajar and held onto the handle. He was just working out how to accomplish his mission when someone pulled at the door, thinking, as it was open, that there was no one inside. Pál, trousers down, fell forward. Blushing furiously, on all fours, he tried to pull up his trousers, while the other customer was so amused by the scene that he collapsed in laughter against the wall opposite, scraping the wallpaper with his nails as he did so. "My father would really look down on me and my mother would very likely have a fit if they saw where I'm living," thought Pál as he eyed his little home. This gave him strength.

His breakfast consisted of coffee and a croissant in a bistro, where he quietly enjoyed observing the Parisian public. He skimmed through the newspaper, then went out to read and study on the Seine embankment or in the Jardin du Luxembourg. In the afternoons, however, he went down rue Bonaparte all the way to St-Germain; there he sat in Les Deux Magots, where he arranged to meet his pupils. On one occasion he was sitting under the wooden statues which give the coffee-house its name, waiting for his pupils, when he caught the sound of Hungarian being spoken at the next table. At first he eavesdropped a little, then felt ashamed of himself, got up and went over.

"Gentlemen, let me introduce myself, I'm Pál Szentágostony.

I felt I ought to speak, as I'm a Hungarian, so as not unintentionally to overhear your conversation," he said.

"There are few things better than eavesdropping," a slender, red-haired young man reassured him with a laugh. "Perhaps only being a Peeping Tom! That's real entertainment!" His companions laughed with him.

"I saw you hesitate slightly before coming over," the red-haired man joked.

Pál was embarrassed.

"I see, you're an aristocrat!" a stout, bearded man reassured him with a tinge of regret. "Never mind, you'll get over it!"

And so Pál made the acquaintance of the company who became his closest friends while he lived in Paris; the slender, red-haired man was Sanyi Réder, a painter, and the bearded, hefty one was Géza Szegedi, a sculptor. Both of them had graduated at the Academy of Art in Budapest before coming to Paris. Also in the group were Sanyi's brother Tamás, a laconic biologist, their sister, the gorgeous, red-haired Sári Réder, who had been a dancer with an avant-garde company in Hungary, and Imre Bence, a sunken-chested, fiery eyed poet. Emma, the Réders' mother, had brought the three up single-handed, and one evening in 1934 she'd flung the newspaper down on the table and informed them:

"We're leaving! The Nazis keep blowing up coffee-houses in Vienna, and sooner or later it'll be Budapest's turn. I don't want you living in a country like that!"

They decided to take with them the few family jewels, clothes and a handful of cherished books and personal belongings. Emma sold everything else – flat, furniture, pictures, carpets, silverware. Géza, Sanyi's best friend since childhood, immediately declared that he was going with them. When they climbed into the carriage at the Nyugati station they also found a smiling Imre Bence, already seated. They arrived in Paris and lived together on the top floor of a run-down apartment house behind the Odéon, in a big, antiquated flat with five high, north-facing rooms. The flat was always chilly, never caught the sun, but therefore had the advantage of a cheaper rent, and as one room was Sanyi and Géza's studio – in which a constant light all day was desirable – the northerly aspect was absolutely ideal. Sanyi painted and designed graphics for publications, Tamás worked in a research laboratory, Imre worked as an English and German proofreader for a publisher, Sári taught modern dance in a little studio and even Géza had found a keen collector who bought his work now and then.

They liked Pál the moment they saw him. His formal, serious ways bothered them a little, and they found his refined manners funny, but they respected his sharp mind, his broad cultural knowledge and his unrelenting sincerity. In the evenings they sat in bistros and cheap coffee-houses, drinking and talking. After a few weeks they invited Pál back to their place behind the Odéon, and after one of Emma's well-cooked meals they talked until the small hours about politics and art. Emma sat with them until precisely ten o'clock when she said "Well, I'm off to bed!" raised her hand to smother a little yawn and went to her room. Seemingly she had an internal alarm clock, because every time that Pál was at the Réders', the scenario was repeated at exactly the same time.

From their first meeting Pál secretly admired Sári – her deep-set, roguish, chocolate-brown eyes, her slender ballerina's neck and the graceful way she held herself. Although her hair was red Sári's skin wasn't snowy white, and her small, shapely breasts rose pertly beneath her blouse. Pál invariably found himself talking to her, even if he was explaining something to the others, and she listened to him, her head inclined to one side, eyes sparkling. If their gazes met, her smile indicated that she'd noted his interest, but she always stayed close to Imre as if they belonged to one another.

"Watch out with her!" Géza said to him one day. "I can see you like Sári. But she's a dangerous wild-cat. Enticement is what she lives for. Her hair isn't just fiery red, lots of people have burned themselves in it. Even I could scarcely get over her, and now Imre's stewing, and it looks to me as if you'll be next."

Pál dismissed the suggestion in embarrassment, but Géza merely waved a hand:

"I've noticed you."

After that Sári suddenly invited Pál to the dance studio for the dress rehearsal of their next production, and he accepted with pleasure. As he climbed towards the Panthéon in the late afternoon sunlight he couldn't tell whether his blood was pulsing more warmly because of the slope or the excitement. The entrance to the dance studio was via the courtyard of an apartment house. Outside the open door slim, muscular youths and slender girls stood about in tight-fitting trousers and shirts, with thick, coloured, woolly leg-warmers. Big, soft bags hung from their shoulders, or had been thrown on the ground beside them. They were laughing and talking loudly and stared at Pál as he passed through their midst. In the hall Sári and the pianist were talking. She'd tied up her red hair with a coloured scarf, which made her finely arched forehead seem higher still, her neck looked longer than ever and the tight black shirt showed off her delicate figure. Pál stopped in the doorway and looked at her, enchanted. She caught sight of him, ran to him, stood on tip-toe to reach, kissed him on both cheeks, and led him to a bench by the wall where others were already sitting.

Pál had been to the ballet several times at the Budapest

Opera House and at Covent Garden in London, but this was something else. In a stylised set representing an Eastern town the dancers moved, turned and spun to music shot through with oriental motifs. The combinations of movements followed regular rules, like the planets circling the Sun. The love story was brought out by Dervish dance, sacred dances and elements of Asian folk-dance, and resembled a strange, spectacular, mystical revue. During the dancing Pál frequently caught Sári's eye as she glanced at him, looking at once transfigured and roguish. At the end of the rehearsal the people sitting on the bench clapped enthusiastically and shouted 'Bravo'. Sári and her male partner, arms around one another, came over to Pál and she, leaning against his shoulder, introduced them. Looking deep into Pál's eyes, she whispered in Hungarian:

"I was dancing for you!"

As they strolled home down the Boul'Mich' Sári talked about the composer, Gurdjieff, who had been born in the Caucasus and had travelled in search of mystical secrets in Central Asia, India, Tibet and Egypt to find an answer to the question: what is the purpose of human life?

"Do you wonder about such things?" she asked.

"All the time," said Pál with a smile, but what he was in fact thinking about was how charmingly the tiny pearls of perspiration glittered at the roots of her hair after the performance, and how her nipples showed through her soaking shirt. 'What else can the purpose of human life be?' he thought. He stopped, and with sudden daring seized her by the waist, pulled her to him and meant to kiss her passionately on the lips, but Sári turned her face away with a laugh, pushed him with one hand and placed the other on his mouth, laughing into his eyes as she did so.

That evening in the bistro the ballet was discussed again.

The boys had seen a previous rehearsal, had read Gurdjieff's writings, and Imre in particular was familiar with philosophy and mystic learning. He explained to Pál that according to the 'Master' people spent their existence in a kind of waking dream, and that it was only by developing one's consciously lived moments and memories and by the constant practice of self-confrontation that one could attain a higher level of consciousness. Pál found all this interesting, even if he could only hazily follow the line of thought.

"The ballet is about the struggle between the Black Magi and the White," said Sanyi, with a scarcely perceptible cynical smile at the corners of his mouth.

"That's certainly what the world is about these days," said Pál thoughtfully, "but as a historian I can see that in the background there are not esoteric ideas but remorseless economic and political conflicts."

"Nothing of the sort!" Géza laughed. "Economics and politics! The world is run by emotions and myths. That's what has an effect on people. Take Germany, for example!"

Pál wasn't sure whether Géza was being serious.

"My dear Pál, in this company you won't get far on rational principles," said Tamás Réder. "These are artists!" with scornful stress on the *art*. "Be careful, it's catching! Even I'm gradually starting to research biology on an emotional basis."

The young people went to their friends Sanyi and Géza's private views, knowledgeably discussed and analysed the often striking paintings and sculptures, knew about all the latest important novels and good films, saw the more interesting exhibitions, and hung about nightclubs if they heard that American jazz musicians were in town. A few days after the ballet rehearsal they went to the Trocadéro and to the *Exposition Universelle*. At the foot of the Eiffel Tower they looked in amazement at the gigantic German and Soviet pavilions, with the imperial eagle on one and Vera Mukhina's huge peasant girl and working man on the other. The pathos of Mukhina's sturdy figures fascinated them as they brandished hammer and sickle, straining upwards side by side. The two massive buildings stood face to face as if each were daring the other to blink first.

"The struggle between the Black Magi and the White," said Géza, referring to the conversation of a few days previously.

In the German pavilion they looked at the proud achievements of German industry and technology, the photographs of the new roads, newly built municipal areas, and happy citizens of the Third Reich; in the Soviet pavilion the photographs were of gaily harvesting peasants surrounded by fields of golden wheat, the radiant faces of workers in heavy industry, and the new, extravagant metro stations. As they left the Soviet pavilion, passing the embossed panels, reminiscent of the reliefs of the *ancien régime*, in which industrial workers, peasants and engineers worked together in great harmony, they found themselves once again facing the German pavilion. The swastika banners on both sides and the gigantic nude male and female statues on the steps surged towards them.

Géza stopped.

"Don't you see how closely related the two styles are?" he asked.

"Now, how can the ideology of National Socialism, based on racial superiority, and the Soviet Russian system, founded on the righteous power of the proletariat, have anything in common?" expostulated Imre.

"I don't know about ideologies," said Géza, "but I do know about sculpture. Look at the rigid poses, the expressionless faces. They're the spitting image of one another in both pavilions! Those aren't free peoples!"

In the evening they sat on little cushions on the floor in Sanyi and Géza's studio surrounded by clay models on plinths covered in damp cloths and canvases propped against the walls; amidst the mingled odours of clay and oil-paint they drank cheap Burgundy and discussed the way the middle-class world was sinking into moral and economic decay. Pál was in his element: he could display his Oxford knowledge. He compared the prospects for socialism and National Socialism, the free market and the planned economy, and as he did so he watched Sári as she listened, wine-glass in hand.

"My friends in Budapest have written about what a marvellous lecture Thomas Mann gave in the Magyar Színház," said Imre. "So you see, even a philistine like him can't see any way out these days, except socialism."

"If I could choose between Nazism and the Soviet system, I'd opt for socialism as well," said Pál. "But rather than the label 'socialist' I prefer Thomas Mann's term, 'militant humanist'."

Sári went into the kitchen for another bottle of Burgundy and some cheese and Pál, watched suspiciously by Imre, followed her. She was standing at the work-surface, back to the door, struggling with the bottle. She heard steps, looked round, and laughed coquettishly at Pál.

"My militant humanist, would you mind opening this bottle?"

Pál's inhibitions were by then lessened by the wine, and he put his arms round Sári's waist from behind and kissed her on the neck. He felt her thrill with ecstasy. Faces flushed, they took in the wine and cheese.

In Oxford Pál had had girlfriends in the university who, released from the strict and hypocritical environment of noble or upper-middle-class families, were intent on abandoning good manners, abstinence and virginity all at the same time. In London too he'd had a number of fleeting relationships with pleasant, frivolous young things with smudgy lipstick who wore frayed bras, washed-out briefs and darned stockings under their provocative clothes. But he'd never before felt what he did when Sári was there. He worshipped her husky voice, her wavy red hair, warm brown eyes, her neck, the way she moved. Night after night he tossed in bed, unable to sleep, imagining her naked body against his. If they went to the cinema together she allowed him to sneak a crafty hand under her arm, as if he were only putting an arm round her, so as to hold her breast, but she very soon removed it. On the Seine embankment they exchanged lingering kisses, but it was no use Pál making suggestions that couldn't be misunderstood, that she should come up to his garret: Sári always refused the invitation.

One evening they were discussing beauty in Sanyi and Géza's studio. The conversation had started on the subject of art, and had moved from Aristotle's *Poetics* through Chinese philosophy to Kant. Sári was bored and gave a big yawn. Then when Imre quoted the Königsberg philosopher to the effect that a beautiful thing was one that gave pleasure disinterestedly, Sári jumped up. "I'm going to my room, putting on some provocative clothes and going down the boulevard, and you can see how much I get offered. Because everybody can be beautiful when it costs nothing!"

With that she left them. The boys laughed, thinking that she was joking. Half an hour later, however, when they'd passed beyond Plato and even Bergson, Sári came back into the studio. She'd rouged her mouth heavily, put on a lot of make-up and a skirt that was slit to the thigh, her blouse was deeply unbuttoned and she'd tossed a feather boa round her neck. In one hand she dangled a tiny handbag, the other was on her hip as she leant erotically against the door-post. The boys burst into applause. She insisted that they should go with her into the street and witness her success.

Laughing loudly, the group filed down the echoing staircase after Sári, and only Pál held back, ill at ease. On the Place de l'Odéon Sári made for the bus stop, tugging at her skirt, and leant on the side of the green shelter. Passers-by stared, several smiled at her, and others pulled a face. The boys watched what happened from a respectful distance. First a middle-aged man spoke to her, then a couple of young lads. Sári talked to them, and the men strolled on.

"I don't find this very funny!" said Pál crossly. Imre agreed.

"Come on, let her have some fun. She's a dancer! She can't help it! But she'd be the one to take fright if anyone really did come on to her," said Sanyi.

Another two or three men spoke to Sári, and after a brief discussion they all moved on. Finally a young man with slicked-down hair and wearing an apache shirt went up to her. After a few words he began to shake her and was about to hit her. The boys rushed up – with his long legs, Pál reached her first and gave the man a push. He fell down, and as he lay on the ground drew a knife, but when he saw how outnumbered he was and how fierce Géza looked he swore and made off. Sári was shaking from head to foot. She tried to laugh, but crumbled into tears.

"I was getting some quite good offers," she said, "and then along came that pimp and spoilt it all! He asked who I was working for."

"It could easily have turned out badly," Tamás shook his head.

"Sári, this is not like you!" said Pál crossly.

That evening he left his friends early and for weeks

didn't go near either the Odéon or the bistro. Sanyi and Géza dropped notes into his letter-box on rue Cujas asking what was the matter, and he replied in a note left in the bistro, saying that he'd been too busy because he was working on a longish essay. He had in fact been shaking off his melancholy by going to the library and writing the doctoral thesis which he'd left incomplete. He found it hard to explain even to himself why the scene at the bus-stop had so repelled him. He'd known that Sári was only fooling about, playing a role like a silly girl, but he couldn't bear the thought that she would even pretend to sell what he didn't get from her for love.

Autumn descended suddenly, as it does in Paris. Almost from one day to the next the trees became bare, their branches a tangled tracery against the grey sky. Pál decided to go and see Josephine Baker's new show. He knew that Sári too was a great fan of the black *danseuse* and was secretly hoping that they might run into one another at the Moulin Rouge. 'La Baker' was already on stage singing when he looked around the crowded auditorium for his friends. Finally he spotted Géza by a pillar in the gods. Sári was standing with him, her face turned and looking at Pál. She'd obviously seen him first and had been waiting for their eyes to meet. When she had his attention she raised a hand like a shy child in school and beckoned to him with her fingers. From that moment there were just the three of them: Sári, Pál and Josephine. Then there were only two, because they paid no attention to the singer's exaggerated dance moves on stage and only had eyes for each other.

After the show Pál waited for his friends outside the theatre. The three weeks since their last meeting seemingly evaporated with not so much as a reference to the fact that Pál hadn't been seen, except that Sanyi embraced him perhaps a little more warmly than usual. It started to drizzle, and they set out across place Pigalle for the metro. Sári walked with Pál, but, finding it hard to keep up with his long strides, caught his hand as if to slow him down. They carried on hand in hand. They got out at the Odéon with Sanyi and the rest, but said goodbye so they could go on walking together.

"In the rain! That makes sense!" Sanyi laughed.

The wind swept leaves along the pavement, the gas lamps flickered and hissed, and the bistro lights shone dully through the drops of water on their steamed-up windows. The wind blew a burst of rain into Sári's face and an unruly curl was plastered to her forehead. Her face wet and shining, she looked up at Pál and asked in a whisper:

"Are you going to ask me for tea?"

"To a bistro?"

"I'd prefer your place, rue Cujas."

In amazement, Pál looked into her eyes. She blushed and bowed her head.

"It's a bit of a pigsty," said Pál in embarrassment as he opened the door.

"Pity you didn't say so sooner – I wouldn't have come up!" laughed Sári, looking around the flat. "But now I've climbed five flights of stairs I might as well stay."

"I haven't changed the bedclothes for a month," Pál apologised as he tugged the grubby sheet and duvet cover off the unmade bed. "And I simply haven't got any tea."

"Are you trying to get rid of me?" asked Sári, a trifle uncertainly.

Pál went to her, took her in his arms and kissed her. It was a long, lingering kiss, and she clung to him as if she was afraid he would run away.

"Don't be cross, it's just that I've waited so long for this moment... I don't even know what to say," said Pál. "And then, we've not seen each other for the past three weeks... it's as if we've got to start over."

"What about a nice bit of housework?" asked Sári.

"At two in the morning?"

"Well, it is a pigsty if ever there was one. And doing it might help us relax."

They found a tiny spoonful of tea in the bottom of the caddy, put the kettle on, and started cleaning. By the time they'd finished tidying everything up, sweeping, letting in some air, changing the bedclothes and then demurely taking it in turns to wash at the battered tub in the kitchen, Sári now wearing one of Pál's shirts, the tension was indeed broken.

"A man's shirt is very fetching on a woman, don't you think?" Sári struck a pose.

Pál looked her up and down with a smile. The long shirt reached her ankles. She'd fastened collar and cuffs in a feminine way, but even so she looked more like an orphan escaped from a nineteenth-century English institution.

"Oh yes, very fetching!"

He put his arm round her and led her to the bed.

"That tea will be stewed!" she hissed, breaking free as she made for the kitchen.

"Why are you doing this, Sári? Why are you playing with me?"

Sári turned in the doorway and burst into tears.

"I'm not playing. I'm afraid."

"Of what?" asked Pál, shaking his head.

Sári went back to the bed, huddled up like a child, and snuggled into his arms.

"Two years ago I had a lover. It was very painful when we tried to make love. We simply couldn't. I'm afraid of losing you like I did him. And you're very important to me," she gulped, "That's why I wouldn't even come up. But you see, even so I've nearly lost you."

Pál caressed her long and slowly, in silence, and when he sensed that she'd relaxed he gently, lovingly, slipped off her shirt and briefs.

"It only hurt a little," said Sári half an hour later with a chuckle. "But it was very good."

"This evening at the theatre you fascinated me so much I could scarcely keep my eyes on Baker's breasts."

"But you did manage to! I was watching you!" Sári teased him.

"Yours are nicer!" said Pál triumphantly, trailing a fingertip over them.

Sári didn't move officially to rue Cujas because Emma was against couples living together if they weren't married, but she turned a blind eye to the girl's sleeping at Pál's more than at Odéon. Sári learnt to cook and enjoyed shopping. The shopkeepers in the area worshipped her, and whenever she went in, or rushed past with her red hair flying, both the ruddy-cheeked baker, smelling of fresh baguettes, and the fat butcher next door would wave cheerfully from behind their counters. The greengrocer, with his blue apron and big moustache, would wink his tiny eyes and secrete some *primeur* or a little bouquet into her basket along with the carrots, salad leaves and spring onions. They didn't talk about their future together, but Pál considered asking his parents what they thought about him marrying Sári. He didn't speak to her about this, but only said that he was going home for a short visit because he hadn't seen his family for a long time.

The Postcard from Paris

*

Pál drew in a deep breath of the familiar sweet and sour smell of the stable, redolent of straw and manure, which the wind carried as far as the mansion when it was northerly. He'd loved this smell in his childhood. When he took up cigar-smoking in Oxford he realised that this scent, this blend of earth and animal, was what he had tried to find when choosing a cigar: cigar-smoking cured his homesickness. He sniffed the air as he followed his father and brother towards the stables behind the house.

Talján, the Hesse mare, recognised him; she began to stamp in her box as he approached with an apple.

"Now then, what's up, old girl, you haven't got rheumatism in your back yet, have you?" Pál patted the mare's neck and proffered the apple, which she crunched up happily.

"Haven't you gone grey!" he went on, as the stable lad led the horses out and fetched the saddles. While the lad saddled their father's thoroughbred Pál and János attended to their own.

Pál hadn't ridden Talján for years. When he'd been given her as a boy she'd been black, later dapple-grey, and now she was completely grey. She still moved well though, and even enjoyed a gallop despite her eighteen years.

Baron Szentágostony and his two sons rode towards Tövispuszta as they had many years before when the Baron himself taught them to ride. Plum trees and mulberries lined the dusty earth road along which they trotted from the plough-land towards the farmstead; Pál thought how much had happened to him during the past years, while there in Tövispuszta time seemed to have stood still.

János spurred up to his side.

"What news of Isti Veres and Dávid Goldstein?" Pál asked.

"Dávid didn't get into university and is now working in his uncle's car workshop in Budapest. Isti's still playing football and playing the violin with Zsiga Balogh," replied János.

In Tövispuszta, where they were heading, people greeted the Baron and his sons in surprise. He seldom rode that way, and if he went round the estate he usually went somewhere near the lake at Kesző. The sight of the Baron and his two sons in those parts seemed to indicate some special purpose. As the three reached Samu Goldstein's shop a girl came out of the door. She looked quite young, but her youthful figure already had feminine charm. She was at the age when a girl is still a child but the subconscious, flirtatious curiosity to wonder what she must look like to men begins to shade the charm of innocence and purity. As she caught sight of the three riders she stopped and waited for them.

"Good morning, Your Honours!" she said.

She pushed back her honey-blonde hair a little and looked up with inquisitive green eyes at the Baron and his sons.

The Baron nodded, his sons returned the greeting.

"Who are you, then, my dear?" asked János pleasantly.

"Who am I? I'm Dávid and Andor's sister," said the girl with a laugh. "I'm Elza Goldstein."

"You haven't only grown, Elza, but you've found your tongue as well!" replied János.

He clearly liked the girl.

"Say hello to Andor for me, and to Dávid, if you speak to him," Pál called as he turned his horse.

Elza flashed her green eyes at Pál, then, as if she'd suddenly thought of something, blushed, nodded and dashed back into the shop.

"She was a little girl last time I saw her, and she'll soon be grown up," said Pál admiringly.

"Well, poor girl, she's chosen the right time to become Jewish," commented János ironically.

They trotted home saying no more, each lost in his own thoughts.

Pál had intended to make known his plan over dinner, but János forestalled him, and talk turned again to the meeting with Elza.

"Will the Jewish laws[9] apply to her?" he asked. "She's Jewish, but none of her grandparents are."

It seemed that János' question had opened the floodgates, the way that Baron Pál burst out.

"The people who thought up this disgraceful law aren't merely vile, they're stupid as well," he thundered. "No one can accuse me of loving the Jews," he said, "but this law isn't only unworthy of the Kingdom of Hungary, but it's also preposterous from a legal point of view. It's outrageous for citizens of a thousand-year-old country to have to find their ancestors' documents and prove that there've been no Jews in the family! And as for those who come from the lost territories, where records have very likely been destroyed by now, how the devil are they to produce documents? It turns out in the case of several friends of mine, who previously regarded themselves as Hungarians to the core, that one's got a Serbian grandmother and an Austrian grandfather, and another's grandparents were Romanian or Slovak, and even our ancestors were Italian. Does that mean we're not Hungarians? Or does that only apply to Jews? And if someone's grandparents converted to Christianity, the family's been faithful Christians for a hundred years, and now they discover what blood runs in their veins, are they suddenly Jewish? No one's ever destroyed patriotic sentiment in people's hearts the way these fake Hungarians have!"

The Baron began to choke with rage, and Pál and János jumped up, helped their father out of the dining room to a sofa in the drawing room, and got him to lie down. Pál slipped a cushion under his father's head and looked anxiously at his mother.

"We weren't having an argument," he whispered.

"Your father's been at loggerheads with the world for a long time," said Emília quietly.

While the Baron rested in the drawing room, Emília and her sons took their coffee on the terrace beneath the pergola and talked in whispers. Pál took a deep breath.

"I'm thinking of getting married."

"Oh really, dear brother," János enthused.

"Do you mean the girl you mentioned in your letters, Sári?" asked Emília.

"That's right," answered Pál.

"And you've really thought about it?"

"We love each other very much. We've been living together for months."

"How old is she?" asked Emília.

"Twenty-one."

"You're twenty-four. So what's the hurry? Why not finish your doctorate at Oxford first? Of course, when all's said and done you're of age now, you make your own decisions," she added, in a voice that showed that she thought the opposite.

"There's one slight snag," Pál went on, and paused briefly. "She's Jewish. I don't know what Father'll say to that."

Emília turned pale.

"Your father would never accept a Jew in the family.

Nowadays, with the Jewish laws, it'd surely be the death of him."

"But Mother, you heard how strongly he opposes the Jewish laws," Pál tried to persuade her.

"Principle's one thing, practice is another," said János scornfully. "In principle we condemn the laws that exclude the Jews, but we don't want them as daughters-in-law and grandchildren."

"János, stop that sort of talk! This is no joke!" said Emília, her mouth quivering, and turned back to Pál. "You'd bring trouble on the whole family," she said in an almost pleading tone then, getting a grip on herself. "Not to mention the fact that good marriages always come about in similar social circles, where people have similar scales of values, culture and property. I can understand that a pretty little dancer can easily turn the head of an inexperienced young man, and becoming a baroness isn't the worst you can do, but love's one thing and marriage is something else."

"You don't understand a thing, Mother!" retorted Pál.

With that he stood up and stormed off to his room to pack his bags.

THE BOOK OF VERSE

Henrik Goldstein, his wife Anci and their daughter Blanka lived in Kresz Géza utca, in Újlipótváros, and his car workshop was on the ground floor of the same block of flats. Dávid was very familiar with the flat and the workshop, since once or twice a year Samu and the family went up to the capital and stayed at Henrik's. "There's always room for my dear brothers," said Henrik with great pathos, and "There's room for many good men even in a little place! Haha." Dávid didn't really understand the latter remark, because to him Uncle Henrik's four-room flat didn't seem in the least small, especially in comparison with the two-room house in Tövispuszta where the five of them lived.

As a boy Dávid spent a lot of time standing with Henrik at one of the apartment windows, which was on a corner with a clear view of Nyugati station. Henrik would kindly get the binoculars from the bureau, and Dávid could watch the cars speeding up Váci út or the railwaymen working between the platforms on the station, patiently bending and tapping the wheels. He liked going with his brother into the workshop with its smell of oil, and the biggest treat for him was to be taken by a worker into the inspection pit and shown the cars from underneath. The only thing that bored him were

Henrik's stories, because the old man insisted on telling the same tales of America and the Ford works in Detroit. Dávid and Andor only liked two of these stories. One was about Henrik as a young man arriving by ship and hearing stall-holders in the harbour shouting *pina, pina!* [10]
"Well, is that all there is to it here?" Uncle Henrik appeared just as amazed retelling the tale as he'd been at the time. "I was happy, I thought I was in Paradise!" he said every time, with the same laugh.

The punch-line was that it later turned out that the stall-holders were selling *peanuts*, but Dávid and Andor no longer found this amusing in the least. Nevertheless, just to hear the beginning of the *pina* story they often asked Uncle Henrik to tell it again.

Only Ilus was offended at the words the boys used.

"Ilus, my dear," said Anci, "in school these children say even nicer things."

"Is there anything nicer than a *pina*?" Uncle Henrik would carry on talking dirty, to the boys' delight.

"Oh, you men!" Anci would threaten them, blushing and laughing. "Your mouths are filthy! And you eat with them?"

Henrik told the boys' other favourite story as the most tragic item in the family mythology, but Dávid and Andor found it terribly amusing. It concerned 'poor Sándor', Henrik's cousin, who had also emigrated to America; once he'd leant out of a train window and a track-side pole had taken his head off. Dávid and Andor particularly liked the bit in this story where poor Sándor's severed head flew through the open window in the next compartment and landed in a sleeping passenger's lap.

"Hear that, Andor?" said Dávid when they were little. "And what if your head flew in through the window?"

And they both imagined Indians chasing the train,

as they'd once seen in a Western at the cinema in Budapest, and Andor's head looping a little loop between the compartments, flying for a moment above the prairie, watching the wild mustangs galloping beneath it, and then spinning neatly through the window into a sleeping passenger's lap. The head would then, with an inquisitive wink, look up from its worm's eye view to see what the passenger had to say when he woke up.

Dávid rather liked his uncle; it was of course only right to be fond of family members, but the old man had one fault which, in Dávid's eyes, was irredeemable. There was in Henrik's display-cabinet, amongst the porcelain figurines and the snowstorm paperweight that was kept as a souvenir from Semmering, a little ball bearing which he'd brought back from America. Ever since he was little Dávid had been fascinated by the sight of the gleaming steel rings and the sparkling steel balls that rotated so freely between them. When the family arrived at Henrik's on a visit the first thing Dávid did was to run to the cabinet and ask for the bearing. He often tried to wheedle it out of his uncle, but the old man was adamant.

"Know what? When I die I'll leave it to you," he said one day with a laugh. "It'll be your inheritance!"

Dávid felt reassured. Uncle Henrik looked old, and Dávid knew that sooner or later old people die. Perhaps he wouldn't have too long to wait for the bearing to be his. Meanwhile he was tormented by pangs of conscience, and he tried to suppress his wicked thoughts; he knew that he ought not to wish for Uncle Henrik to die, but what else could he do if he liked the bearing so much and if that was the price to be paid?

Then one day, when they came to visit and Dávid, as usual, ran to the display cabinet to ask for the bearing to play with, Uncle Henrik shrugged his shoulders.

"Oh, the bearing? I've given it to the little boy next door, because he was very fond of playing with it as well."
At first Dávid didn't understand what his uncle had said. He didn't want to understand. He simply stood there, wide-eyed, as if he were having a fit. His inheritance...given to another little boy?

For some time afterwards he did wish that Henrik would die – without any remorse now, unselfishly in a sense, because he wouldn't have inherited the bearing.

Dávid's life in Henrik's workshop was by no means as happy as the visits to Budapest that he remembered from his childhood – leaving aside the matter of the bearing, of course. Henrik's daughter Blanka was no longer living at home but had married a baker in Miskolc, with whom she had seven children. Henrik took a serious view of apprenticeship years; that had been his own experience. Dávid was up at five in the morning, and at half past was tidying up the workshop. At six o'clock Keller and Tóth, the two assistants, would arrive, followed by Henrik at half past then at seven the first customers would call in and leave their cars on their way to work. Henrik had bought the garage in the block and the neighbouring storage space and demolished the party wall, so that three cars could be worked on at the same time. On the walls, surrounded by tools and tyres, there hung prominently displayed pictures – brought by Henrik from America – of the legendary Model T Ford. Everyone knew by heart the story of how Henrik had known József Galamb, the designer, personally because they'd worked in the same factory in Detroit, and that the car was nicknamed Tin Lizzie. In America Henrik had infuriated his colleagues in the factory by saying

87

that without the Hungarians, proud America would never have come to anything. "What do you think of, when people say 'America'?" he asked. "Hollywood and cars, right? Well, we Hungarians invented both of them!"

After returning home Henrik had filled everyone's heads with his American stories. "The things I saw over there!" he would say and throw up his hands in resignation, as if still amazed. "When's it going to be like that here?" he would add with a disparaging gesture and wry face. These exclamations were regularly followed by incoherent, intricate stories with little, unfinished digressions, incomplete lines of thought.

Keller swore that several customers, although perfectly satisfied with Henrik's professional competence, preferred to go to other repairers because they couldn't spare the time to listen to his complicated, rambling stories. This problem was solved by the new Jewish law, when in 1939 Jews were expelled not only from public offices, newspapers, educational establishments and the theatre but were also refused licences for trade and industry, and those that had previously been granted began to be withdrawn. One day Henrik called his assistant aside in the shop.

"Keller, would you, for a consideration, put the business in your name? I needn't explain why I ask, need I?" he said drily, because he'd decided in advance not to let himself down by weeping.

"I don't need money for that, boss, that little raise that you promised me some time ago will do nicely," said Keller with a smile, and embraced Henrik, who, decision or not, burst into tears just the same.

Keller shifted from one foot to the other in embarrassment. Their relationship wasn't the kind that would enable him to console his boss, the embrace had just been an instinctive outburst of emotion on his part. He felt sorry for Henrik as he stood there, humiliated and wretched.

"My name's Aladár," said Keller, with a lump in his throat. "I'm sure you know that these days people in Budapest call a front man a 'turkey'. I'll be Aladár the turkey."[11]

"Aladár the turkey! That's a good one!" said Henrik, wiping the tears from his eyes. "I never even thought of that." From then on Henrik was a mechanic in the workshop, but somehow his stories dried up and after that it was Keller who dealt with the customers.

Dávid didn't know what to say if he was asked whether he felt at home in Budapest. The big city excited him, but its impenetrable size and its bustle strained his nerves. Even in his free time he only wandered about in the vicinity of the workshop: down Csanády utca or up Váci út, past Nyugati station to the Nagykörút. He went to the cinema or looked at the shop windows on the ring-road, the rumbling trams, the people. Sometimes he would stop in front of an elaborately decorated house or two, close one eye and detach it in his imagination from the adjacent houses in order to examine it better. Then his gaze would minutely, as it were inch by inch, review the details of the building as an inquisitive lizard might examine the pages of a huge picture-book. People sometimes stopped beside him as they hurried along, or simply looked in the same direction as they passed, to see what he was looking at, whether someone was about to fall from a window. But when they saw nothing of interest they pulled a face to show they couldn't understand why he was gazing into the void. Dávid would look at pillared doorways, timpana above windows and caryatids that supported balconies, and gaze at length at the breasts of a hefty female nude statue. At the age of eighteen he could see that the world was wallpapered with female breasts; they flirted with him provocatively from beneath the blouses of the girls that loitered on the ring-road, from advertising columns, cinema posters, even, indeed, from the walls of houses. As he walked on the ring-road he sometimes wondered what would happen if he simply went up to a woman as she came towards him and said: "Excuse me, I really don't want anything from you, just let me hold your breasts. It's nothing to you, you can do it to yourself any time, but it would mean a very great deal to me."

Dávid felt lonely in Budapest. He made no friends, Uncle Henrik and Aunt Anci weren't entertaining company, and in the workshop it was mostly Tóth, the younger assistant, who spoke to him. Although Keller was friendly too and since he'd been promoted took it as his duty to train Henrik's nephew, he spoke to him exclusively about professional matters. Dávid did the work that he was given properly, but wasn't overly enthusiastic about cars, and as Henrik said 'Anyone that isn't in love with machines won't make a real car mechanic'. Dávid would have preferred to be in love with girls.

Dávid knelt on the oily floor and, stretching between the wheels of an ageing Ford, handed the tools down to Tóth in the inspection pit. As he worked, Tóth sang a strange song to himself – it sounded even stranger because of the dead acoustic quality of the pit:

> *What's the prospect for a man*
> *who can have no plot to hoe,*
> *scrapes along as best he can,*
> *and lies idle, full of woe;*

who tills others' for a share
as he's no land of his own,
and in handfuls falls his hair
though he doesn't seem to know?[12]

The final two lines in particular caught Dávid's attention – he'd previously heard mostly folk songs and cinema hits.

"What is that?" he asked Tóth.

"Do you like it, my boy?"

"Very much," said Dávid, nodding thoughtfully. "It could be about Tövispuszta."

Next day Tóth brought in a slim volume of Attila József's verse for Dávid.

"I hope you like it! Poor Attila died last year, committed suicide under a train at Szárszó," he said. "We were helping him to sell his books, and we've got a heap left. We've scarcely managed to sell a few dozen. People don't want this sort of thing nowadays."

Dávid liked poetry. When they were little Samu used to read to his sons, and later to Elza, the works of Arany, Petőfi, Ady, Babits and József Kiss.[13] Petőfi's *János vitéz* and Arany's *Toldi* had been among the children's favourite tales, but lines and images like those that he met in the unfamiliar poet's work were something new to Dávid.

When beloved crossed the road
Doves flew down to call on sparrows.
When she reached the side, so dim
Gleamed her ankle, neat and trim.
And her shoulder's tiny motion
Drew a small boy's admiration.[14]

As he read the poem Dávid felt that he was falling ever more in love with the girl who existed only in his dreams,

91

and the lack of her was even more painful. He read the book through more than once, and the lines stuck in his head. Sometimes he would mutter a fragment or two at work as if it were a prayer. "How can anyone invent such lovely images?" he asked Tóth enthusiastically. "It's almost painful to read them, and at the same time they're so profound, like a bottomless well. And people don't want them?"

Tóth suggested to Dávid that if he would like to meet the sort of people that did like such poems he would take him on a hike at the week-end.

He and Tóth met on Széll Kálmán tér. The mechanic was wearing plus-fours and hiking boots with thick socks turned down over the tops, and was carrying a big green canvas rucksack. Dávid had come in his ordinary trousers, well worn at the knees and the seat, a sweater and shoes. He looked at Tóth's hiking gear with envy.

"Now don't call me 'Mr. Tóth'," he said, "call me Jani, like my friends do. And call me *te*.[15] As of now we're friends outside working hours."

Dávid was beside himself with pleasure. He could even call Tóth, that is Jani, his friend?

They met Jani's friends at Hüvösvölgy and all set off. They sang folk-songs and joked together as they walked the paths through the woods and eventually settled down in a clearing. Rugs were spread on the ground and containers of food, flasks, balls and books were produced from rucksacks. Jani could see from Dávid's face that he was embarrassed at seeing everyone unpacking rucksacks, because he was the only one who hadn't brought anything.

"Don't worry, I've got something for you," he reassured him. "As we say: if you come you'll be there, if you bring something, you'll eat. But we've got a few factory workers in the group who aren't well off, and in fact a number who are out of work and can scarcely afford anything to eat. So everyone brings what they can and everyone eats what there is. This is communism, my boy! Everybody contributes to the common good according to their ability, and everybody receives according to their needs," he said, laughing out loud.

At first Dávid was only politely interested in the delicious looking cheese, goose-fat, bacon, paprika, onions and fresh bread that were set out on little plates in the middle of the blanket, but then the others generously offered it all around: don't be shy, everybody's at home here, so in the end he overcame his nerves and shared everything. Except the bacon. Because since that time at the Vereses' when, as he put it, he'd had a taste of Christian life as a boy, he wouldn't miss out on sausage for the sake of God – bacon, however, seemed to be going too far.

"How did you get here?" asked a girl with short hair and a boyish figure at the very moment that Dávid had decided to take a large mouthful of bread and dripping. The question caught him off guard and he tried to chew and swallow as fast as he could in order to answer. "Oh, sorry," the girl apologised with a laugh, "I asked at the wrong moment."

Dávid blushed with a final swallow.

"I'm a friend of Jani Tóth," he replied proudly, with emphasis on the word 'friend'.

"There's going to be some very good entertainment, I expect Jani's told you about it," the girl chattered, as she took a bite out of a hard-boiled egg.

"There's going to be entertainment?" Dávid was puzzled, but dared not ask, because as Jani Tóth's friend he obviously ought to have known.

After the empty plates and kitchen utensils had been packed away a young man in glasses unrolled a large piece of

cardboard and the short-haired girl helped him to prop it up
against a tree. Then the man in glasses sat on a three-legged
hunting-stool in front of the cardboard and asked the rest to
join in with the singing when prompted. He started to sing,
drawing on the cardboard at the same time.

> *Here's the straight and here's the curved,*
> *and here's the head of Hitler...*

The girl then picked up a long stick and urged the others
to sing along as she pointed to the drawings.

> *Straight, curved, Hitler's head,*
> *straight, curved, wooden wheel,*
> *oh, how pretty, oh, how pretty,*
> *this three-legged stool is!* [16]

The young man in glasses triumphantly held up the
three-legged stool at the end. Everybody laughed, and Dávid
was also amused to see that while they were singing the
young man in glasses had drawn the straight, the curved,
the wooden wheel and Hitler's head, with his hair brushed
characteristically sideways and his cropped moustache.

There followed another song, performed by a little choir.
Dávid was shocked to hear it satirise the Regent.

> *Horthy, great warrior,*
> *the mounted mariner,*
> *as much brain as we've got sea*
> *Oh, oh, such a brain, Horthy the great warrior!*

Everyone clapped and laughed. Dávid joined in with some
misgivings. He didn't really dare to laugh, but dared even

less not to. He found the song amusing, with its pun on
tengerész ('mariner') and *tenger ész* ('sea mind'), but was also
perturbed: how could the Regent be satirised in that way?
"Anyway, what's wrong with the Regent?" he hesitantly
asked the short-haired girl, whose name he'd found out was
Erzsi Török.
Erzsi looked at him as if he'd come from outer space.
"Do you live under a tub?"
"I came up two months ago from Tövispuszta, where my
parents live, and I've been living at my uncle's in Budapest
since then," answered Dávid seriously.
"And are people in Tövispuszta happy with the way things
are?" asked Erzsi scornfully. "Because here in Budapest the
workers are exploited, and it's not good. In Csepel, Kőbánya
and Angyalföld, where I was brought up, people work for a
pittance, they're crowded with four children into one-room
rented flats – it's not right. And I dare say the peasants are no
better off in your village either. Do you think this is right?"
"There've always been rich and poor, haven't there?"
Dávid replied, unsure of his question.
"So it's got to be tolerated?" was the immediate retort.
"Wouldn't a fair society be better, one in which the means of
production were in the hands of the workers, and in which
the bourgeois didn't get rich on high profits without lifting
a finger; one in which the people who did all the work could
have a better life?"
Erzsi spoke with such conviction and passion that her
face flushed and Dávid couldn't take his eyes off her. But he
didn't really understand what she was talking about, because
although he'd been taught in commercial school what means
of production and profit meant, he couldn't envisage a world
in which there were no rich or poor.
"You've got a lot to learn," said Erzsi, like a little

schoolmistress. "Come out with us next week to the Danube, to the centre at Göd. There'll be comrades there from whom you'll be able to learn a lot. Do you like reading?"

"Yes," Dávid nodded.

"Just a moment, then, I'll get some books you can borrow." With that she jumped up, went round the little groups sprawled on the grass talking and debating, and came back with three books.

"Géza Féja: *Viharsarok*," Dávid read out in an undertone.

"Don't let people see that, it's been banned," said Erzsi.

"Gyula Illyés: *Puszták népe*," Dávid read the second title.

"And Lenin's *Állam és forradalom*," added Erzsi. "Keep that out of sight as well! Now, if you read these three books you'll understand what's wrong at home in Tövispuszta – and what's wrong with the Regent."[17]

THE NEWSREEL

Isti Veres' trainer Old Gyula had found his favourite striker a job so that he could concentrate exclusively on football and no longer claim that he had to play with the Gypsy band at the weekend because he needed the money.

"Now, no more nonsense and stopping out all night, right, my boy?" said Gyula as Isti just managed to jump aside and avoid the slap on his backside.

Dr. Béla Sárády needed little persuasion to employ Isti in his law office as a sort of office-boy. "At last a healthy Hungarian peasant lad after all those sickly intelligentsia and crafty Jews," he said to Gyula. Dr. Sárády was in fact a keen football fan and looked after the team's legal affairs. He knew Isti very well on the pitch, and so was quite happily forthcoming in addressing the future employee's salary. As he saw it, doors would open quite easily to this young man, even in the town hall – with the gentlemen because of football, with the ladies because of his good looks – and he would be able to deal with things much better than the blockhead whom he'd had to dismiss the week before because he didn't dare to knock and disturb anyone, but preferred waiting for hours in the corridors of power on the off chance that someone would eventually come that way. The lawyer wasn't mistaken,

Isti carried documents confidently to the town hall, the court and to other officials, waited his turn and dealt with things, and Dr. Sárády was satisfied with his work. After working hours, or even during, if he'd nothing else to do, he enjoyed talking to him – at first only about football or politics, and then gradually he introduced him to family affairs. This began when one day the lawyer came into the office looking depressed, with dark rings under his eyes, and although he was otherwise as immaculate as ever there was no freshly cut flower in his buttonhole; he wore a black silk arm-band, a black tie, and a black silk handkerchief protruded from his breast pocket.

"My mother's died," he said brokenly, and the thin, clipped moustache on his lip quivered. Isti was touched by the effort which the lawyer was making, even in deep mourning, to preserve his usual strict dignity.

"You know, my boy, it's hard to know when a person's going to choose to die," said Dr. Sárády. "My father, for example, left a void when he went. He was alone in the house, even the servant had a day off, when he fell off the WC. He didn't give himself or the family the consolation of our being with him when he set off on the great journey. My mother, poor woman, has died at a good age, if one can say such a thing," his voice failed, and he paused for a moment and swallowed a few times to choke back his tears. "She'd have been eighty-four this summer," he went on. "Mentally she was totally alert, and even these last few days she would say if there was something in the paper that I'd missed, but physically she'd lost control. The result was what she'd been afraid of all her life, she'd lost her independence. Her body made her ashamed, she had to be washed by somebody else, wear incontinence pads. She waited just long enough, three months, for us to see that she couldn't stand it any longer, so she asked us to let her go. Her presence hadn't become a burden, and the loss of her will be painful. You see, my boy, that's how it is if someone has an exceptional sense of values. Arrange things so that you're there when your parents go!" said Dr. Sárády, and sighed deeply.

On 15 March[18] 1939 Isti ran into Dr. Sárády and his showy wife and two, shall we say, less than showy twin daughters in Fő utca on the way to Kossuth tér, where the civic ceremony was being held. The spring sun was shining, and in honour of the occasion the lawyer was wearing a cockade in national colours in his buttonhole, while the ladies were elegantly dressed, with ribbons in national colours in their hair.

Isti knew Mrs. Sárády by sight; she was considered notable in the town as a pianist, but outside the county her name seemed unknown in musical circles. Naturally, this caused Dr. Sárády pain, but he realised that this was part of the usual conspiracy of the Jews and the world of art, which, to his regret, even the Jewish law had failed to alter. The Sárádys' relations with music critics hadn't been trouble-free. The opinion generally expressed in the cultural columns of the local papers was that Böske Sárády was very nice to look at as she played the piano, it was just unfortunate that one had to listen to her. But the height of discourtesy was truly reached when a dastardly culture-scribbler had the impudence to write in the county paper that 'during the concert the performer's face was as if she were enjoying the delights of love-making, but her playing selfishly left the audience out of the fun'. According to rumour in the town Sárády had challenged the insolent columnist to a duel, and as he'd served as an officer of hussars would obviously have cut the cowardly critic to pieces. The latter, however, hadn't even dared to stand up to the offended husband in a mere pistol duel, making the ridiculous excuse that duelling had long been prohibited. It hadn't been the hostile criticism that really upset Sárády, since over the years he'd been obliged to get used to it – otherwise he would have had to fight a duel after every concert – but the idea that the writer had had the effrontery to fantasise about his wife. His face flushed as he imagined some lousy little journalist watching with his mind's eye Böske at the pinnacle of delight in bed. Since then, every time that his wife appeared on the concert platform, Sárády scanned the faces of the audience jealously, wondering if they too had their minds on her erotically transformed face instead of listening to the music. The most annoying thing about it all, of course, was – a fact known to Sárády alone – that while she was playing Mrs. Sárády's expression was indeed precisely the same as when her husband pleasured her. The audience in return watched the lawyer husband maliciously as if they wanted nothing more than to annoy him: now then, what's up, Sárády, you're down here while your wife's making love to the piano on the platform…?

Sárády obviously liked Isti. "Well, my dear boy, what do you say to the way things have turned out? Marvellous, isn't it?" he enthused. Seeing that Isti was mystified he went on, his face radiant: "Haven't you heard the news? We're getting the Kárpátalja back!"[19]

The Sárády girls seemed excited too, though a distant observer, unable to hear what they were saying, could easily have believed from their movements and glances that what had roused the young ladies was actually the sight of the blue-eyed young man. The twins, Csenge and Enese (Enese, not Emese, as was often emphasised when someone mistook the name), to their father's regret, didn't take after their mother but rather his sister, who had remained unmarried; the family took this as a bad omen for the girls' prospects. Anxiety was further fuelled by the fact that they were now twenty-eight, and on one occasion a friend of Mrs. Sárády had flung at her in an argument that people in the town called the twins 'the two when one would have been plenty'. After that Böske had sobbed for a week, and the lawyer had come close to striking the former friend.

The next few days were full of the excitement of military activity, and three days later, after twenty years, the thousand-year-old Hungarian-Polish frontier had been restored. People talked about it in the streets, in offices and shops.

"One of our horse-drawn armour-piercing cannon has destroyed a Czech tank," Isti overheard in the shop, as if an incident in a football match were being described, "and the Czechs were so terrified that they ran away full pelt," one of the customers gushed. "We've got the Pass of Verecke back again, where Árpád crossed the Carpathians at the time of the Honfoglalás!"[20] said the newsagent emotionally. Isti was affected by the enthusiasm too, especially once Sárády explained the political background.

"These symbols are particularly important to a nation that has been humiliated and annihilated!" he said. "The western countries have their wealth, we have our past. One more ancient and glorious than theirs! Just as the Germans are proud of their Teutonic past, we must take pride in our Scythian[21] ancestors, because that gives us strength. If that is taken from us, there goes our self-respect too."

The lawyer gave Isti books on the Hungarian forebears, the mighty Nimrod, grandson of Noah, and his sons by Enéh, Hunor and Magyar. Then Isti realised that Enese's name was actually a version of that of her ancestor. He had, of course, learnt the old myths in school, but at the time they'd made little impression on him, they just seemed like good stories.

The books that he got from Dr. Sárády, on the other hand, dealt quite differently with the Hungarian heroic past, with Scythians and Ancient Hungarians, and from them it was clear how superior the Hungarians were to stupid Slovaks, hairy-footed Romanians, blood-thirsty Serbs and materialistic, exiled Jews. They really gave him resolve and faith. From one of Sárády's books, for example, he even learnt that Jesus hadn't been a Jew, as the Jews told everyone, but a Scythian, therefore in fact a Hungarian, because as it said in the Bible, Jesus came from Galilee, where the Scythians had lived for a time. Isti listened with pleasure to his employer, from whom he learnt a lot, and Sárády instructed him in history, politics and decent Christian standards.

Then one day the lawyer invited Isti round for tea. By then Isti was living in a tiny rented room in the town, where by special permission of the old lady owner, Panni Ördögh was a frequent visitor. The other Veres children were still living at home in Tövispuszta and going out from the house to work. Isti's brother and the two older girls had jobs at the farmstead, while their little sister helped in the shop at Szentágoston. Isti was glad that he'd at last escaped from the cramped peasant house and could live independently. It was the first time in his life that he'd had a bedroom to himself, and after the many snatched lovemakings in haylofts and ricks, under bushes and in the shed, he and Panni could finally lie completely naked in a bed. Now he walked over to the Sárádys' like a gentleman, dropping in at the florist's on the way. He was in such a good mood that he even tossed a few coins into the beggar's hat on the corner, although the flowers were so expensive that he drew his breath in sharply on hearing the prices.

The Sárádys lived in Fő utca, on the first floor of an ornate neo-baroque house. Isti walked up the curving marble staircase, awe-struck. His sweating hands held three bunches of flowers, one for each of the ladies; anyone that has tried will know that this wasn't an easy task. The double mahogany front door was so big that a giant could have walked through it. Since his right hand was full, Isti rang the bell with his forehead as if heading in a simple goal, then looked round quickly and nervously in case someone had seen him. In the wide hall a maid in white apron and cap offered to take his coat, but with both his hands full, he looked around uncertainly for somewhere to put the flowers while taking it off. He thought at first of giving them to the maid, but then how was she to take his coat with her hands full? Fortunately the glass door in the hall opened and a smiling Enese stepped out. She immediately appreciated Isti's difficulty.

"It would be good if people had as many hands as they bring bunches of flowers, don't you think?" she asked with a laugh, and to solve his problem helpfully took the flowers. They went over the soft rugs in the hall, which was hung with numerous pictures, to the drawing-room; the family were sitting on a sofa and armchairs in a bay window, talking and drinking tea. As he sniffed the air Isti caught that same scent of wealth that he'd known in the Szentágostony mansion. The lawyer's son Csaba was home on a visit; he was a subaltern working with the staff in the Army Ministry, and so was able to give his father up-to-date inside information. He knew that there was no greater gift for his father than news that he was the first to hear – he prided himself on being well informed. Like his father, Lieutenant Sárády was a keen believer in Hitler and Germany.

"Hungary's a small country, we haven't much choice here in the middle of Europe. We obviously wouldn't choose Bolshevism, it's not fit for a white man! We know what that's like from 1919," he explained to Isti over tea. "And there's no one but Germany that could defend us from the Russian bear. The British are vain and the French conceited, and have let us down twice, at Trianon and during the economic crisis. Germany has helped get the economy on its feet, and only in Hitler can we place any hope of regaining the stolen territories. Fortunately General Rátz knows this as well. The General's an outstanding man, he was my tutor at officer cadet school, my commanding officer in the staff and now he's my minister.[22] It's a disgrace that the excellent staff officer Major Szálasi has been so vilified.[23] It's a pity that the Regent, the Prime Minister and a number of other politicians can't see what would be best for the country."

Lieutenant Sárády explained things to Isti, but the boy wasn't concentrating; his thoughts were on the kindness of the lawyer and his family. What an honour it was for the son of a farm servant, even if he was now working in a law office, to be received as if he were a real gentleman. As they talked Isti looked now at the Lieutenant, now at the lawyer, now at the still elegant, blonde Mrs. Sárády, and from time to time he stole a glance at the girls – but not so furtively that Eni, as she was known in the family, failed to notice. And if their eyes met, in some strange way she didn't look away but returned his gaze kindly, naturally, interestedly, almost encouragingly. "She's not so bad looking," Isti thought to himself. "Why does everyone say she is? Her eyes are quite beautiful. Or rather, she's not ugly. And she's got a pleasant smile," he thought. In his imagination he undressed her. "Hmm, no bust, no backside, but good proportions." And what could absolutely not be denied was that Eni too had that same alluring, refined scent of purity just like the other middle-class girls at Aunt Manci's dancing school.

After Isti had taken his leave of the Sárádys, Eni saw him to the door, and, furthermore, leaned over the bannister and waved to him, which wouldn't have gone down well with Auntie Manci. What disgraceful manners! A young lady saying goodbye like that to a young man that she hardly knew! But Isti liked this immediacy and naturalness, so unusual in girls. It was what he liked best about Panni Ördögh.

The conspicuously marked attention which Eni paid to Isti stirred up a storm in the Sárády family, almost as great as it did in Isti. Lieutenant Sárády in particular was puzzled when he realised that his sister liked the peasant lad.

"How old is he, then, dear sister, if I might ask? Eighteen?"

"Twenty," Eni corrected him. "He'll be twenty..."

"Fine, twenty," he checked her. "And can you see yourself with an ignorant peasant, when you could just about be his mother?"

"That's quite an exaggeration," Csenge chipped in – she was the more sensitive of the two about age and marital status. The twins were only similar externally. Csenge was quieter, more withdrawn and prickly, while Eni was more an extrovert, lively and clever. They'd always got on very well together; they understood each other without a word being said, played only with each other and even excluded their parents from their private world. As is usual with twins, they divided their tasks: the assiduous Csenge dealt with things in the background, while the more assertive Eni maintained contact with their parents and the outside world, arranged their joint affairs and acted as their spokeswoman.

"Dear Csaba," said Eni with a smile, rather off-handedly, and put a hand on her brother's knee, "you're used to giving orders in the army, but I'm sure you know that the emotions can't be ordered about. Before you get too hot and bothered, may I ask why you're so concerned? What's happened? A pleasant colleague of Father's has been to tea, a good-looking, intelligent peasant lad. That's all."

Csaba had been on the right track but was still too young, and so what his sister said reassured him. He hadn't yet had enough experience of life to know that when men are still unsure whether to bother to court a woman, women are mentally already putting photographs of their future children in an imaginary album. The Sárády parents, on the other hand, had worried extensively about their daughters' future marital status and had lain awake discussing it; at the end of the day, as may be read in advertisements, any solution was of interest to them. The young men whom the girls had liked hadn't even noticed them, and the girls considered the suitors who had occasionally appeared old, ugly, boring or plain repulsive. Csenge wouldn't so much as speak to them, while Eni treated them to such stinging irony that they fled headlong. Things had continued in this way for some eight years now. Isti was the first young man in a long time to have obviously made an impression on Eni, so the parents weren't willing to discourage it, even though they thought it nonsense for a well-to-do, educated, clever Sárády girl, even if no beauty, to marry a penniless, unlettered son of a farm servant eight years her junior.

"Let's see what we can change and what we can't," said Dr. Sárády to his wife that evening when they were alone. The lawyer approached all questions as if preparing a court case.

"We can't change Isti's family background, but that barbarian peasant world has the kind of ancestral strength that would bring fresh blood into the family, which is something that the country could do with as well. The main thing is that he comes from a patriotic, decent, Christian family, and his parents are hard-working people. We can't change his age, but youth doesn't last forever, and time will take care of that. True, Eni will always be eight years his senior, but we've seen marriages that have been extremely successful even with such a difference in age. He's got no money, but how many rich men do we know who started out with holes in their pockets and now own factories? The easiest thing to change is his education, he'll have to enroll as a private pupil at the grammar school. He's got such a good brain that with a little help he'll pass the entrance exam, and he's sure to matriculate."

"What sort of little help are you thinking of?" asked Mrs. Sárády.

"We've done the headmaster enough favours, he's sure to welcome the chance to do one back," the lawyer smiled mysteriously beneath his moustache, "and Eni will be happy to help him study."

Mrs. Sárády gave a knowing laugh and got up to fetch a glass of water. As she passed her husband she bent to place a kiss on his lips, and he took advantage of the movement to stroke his adored wife's breast.

"Goodness, if only our girls could have the life that you and I have," he said with a sigh.

Next day, to Isti's great surprise, his employer promised him an increase in salary if he passed the entrance exam and enrolled at the grammar school. He also said that Eni would happily study with him. At first Isti was alarmed and tried to evade the offer, giving football and work as his excuse, but Dr. Sárády would have none of it.

"How many years do you mean to kick the leather, my boy? And if you ever have a family, how are you going to support them? Think of the future! When are you going to get another offer like this, with your employer paying for you to study instead of working? Who do you think I am, Kunó Klegelsberg? [24] If you refuse I'll have you out of here so fast your feet won't touch the ground!"

This seemed like a rational argument. Isti decided to accept the generous offer.

*

Eni turned out to be an excellent teacher. She was able to explain even mathematics succinctly and enjoyably, and gave entertaining accounts of literature, history, and the history of art. Isti swore that at such times she became prettier, and it suddenly came to him that he looked forward excitedly to her company, loved being with her. The first kiss took place over a successfully solved mathematical problem which Eni unexpectedly rewarded with a kiss on the cheek. Isti found the courage to kiss her, after which things took their course, and the old lady shook her head when she saw both Eni and Panni regularly visit the little rented room.

The Sárády girl also managed to astonish Isti in bed. Panni had been unselfish and inventive, but Eni, good, thorough teacher that she was, had collected theoretical sexual knowledge since her girlhood and now, with complete lack of inhibition, released the entire collection on Isti, overwhelming him with pleasure. The girls in the brothel with their tired routines, whom Isti and his friends had previously visited every so often, were mere beginners compared with the many ideas that Eni came up with at every opportunity. It was as if she did nothing between their meetings but devise ever newer means of mutual delight. And her fantasies seemed inexhaustible.

Because Isti was being cowardly about breaking up with Panni, saying that he felt sorry for her, his fitness began to deteriorate rapidly and this was becoming evident on the pitch. Fortunately one day the old lady, who disapproved of the two girls taking it in turns with Isti, gave him an ultimatum.

"You're an absolute rotter!" she said. "No good will come of this! Hurry up and decide which girl's staying, because I can't stand seeing dishonesty."

After that she was always standing in the hall, leaning on the tiled stove, as if to say 'You'll see!' when Isti tried to slip in with either girl.

Poor Panni squinted even more than usual when Isti confessed to her that he loved another. Then when she found out who it was, she sobbed out some home-spun wisdom: "You're running after a carriage, when a cart would gladly give you a ride!"

At lunch-time Sárády usually resorted to a little restaurant named Paprikás, a couple of blocks from his office. Since Isti was doing well at the grammar school he often went with him. He not only paid for lunch but, while he had his wallet out, would also occasionally slip him some cash so that he could take Eni to the cinema or out for dinner. This embarrassed Isti at first, but seeing that Sárády did it as naturally as if he were his son, he soon stopped demurring, and only expressed appropriate gratitude for the assistance.

They were sitting in the garden, and Sárády was delivering his usual little lecture. It had become customary for Isti to drink in his employer's words and for adjacent tables to fall silent as people began to eavesdrop on the lawyer's train of thought; once he noticed this he raised his voice out of vanity – though it might have been as a matter of pure courtesy.

"If I were British or French, perhaps I'd believe in democracy," he declared aloud to Isti. "But I feel about it the way I do about sea-fish, lobsters and shellfish. On the Riviera or in Abbazia I'm happy to eat them, but not here in Hungary, because the sea's a long way away and by the time they arrive here they've gone bad. Well, that's how I feel about democracy. It may be all right for the British, the French and the Dutch, but by the time it gets here from the West…" at this point he broke off, held his nose, and pulled a face as if aware of a very nasty smell. "Let's just stick to good Hungarian stew and tripe! So, enjoy your meal!" and he turned his attention to his plate.

People at neighbouring tables smiled and turned towards him, and a ripple of applause was heard.

Eighteen months had slowly gone by since Isti had first had tea at the Sárádys. He'd finally left Zsiga Balogh's band, and now only played the violin to please Eni or himself, but still took football seriously. There was a rumour that he was talked about even at Ferencváros. Officially he and Eni were only friends, but there wasn't a single person in town who didn't suspect more, so often were they seen together in cafés and the cinema or walking in the park. Eni taught Isti to drive, and they went for trips in the country in the Sárády car. At first they were frequently gossiped about in the town and everyone considered Isti a gigolo, interested in the plain but well-to-do girl for her money, but after a while it became obvious even to the distant observer that their relationship was completely harmonious, and just as every wonder lasts three days, soon people accepted the unusual couple.

"The Sárády girl's become quite nice-looking," said some.

"Isti Veres has made her look younger," said others.

"It's good enough for a film script, like the one about the managing director and the secretary," added a middle-aged lady dreamily.

Eni had been asking Isti for ages to take her to Tövispuszta to meet his parents, but he'd always evaded the issue, saying that the time would come. He couldn't imagine what the upper-middle-class girl, accustomed to a six-room flat, would say of the farm servants' quarters where he'd grown up. He felt ashamed of the yard, foul with chicken manure, the decrepit mud-brick walls, the tattered roof, his father's uncouth manners and his mother's servile ways – and he was ashamed of being ashamed.

They'd been to the cinema when Eni finally extracted the promise that Isti would take her to see his parents. The newsreel had shown the celebratory review in Kolozsvár, and applause and cheering had broken out. Isti saw for the first time what it meant for the citizens of mutilated Hungary and of the part that had been cut off to join once more in celebration after twenty years – some on the screen, some in the cinema. "The capital city of Transylvania welcomes, to the enthusiastic acclaim of the population, the Regent, Miklós Horthy of Nagybánya, and his lady on their arrival in Kolozsvár," said the commentator, but his voice was drowned out by the uproar in the auditorium. In the cinema the sound of the band leading the procession on screen and the noise of the crowds lining the streets, cheering wildly and waving Hungarian flags, blended with the shouts of the audience as they shook one another by the hand. "*Csonka Magyarország nem ország! Egész Magyarország mennyország!*" [25] someone cried out, "everything back, everything back," people started to chant, then someone else began to sing the National Anthem and Isti and Eni rose and joined in with the rest of the audience.

Eni insisted that they shouldn't go to Tövispuszta by car because she didn't want to make a show. To Isti's surprise, when they met that morning she wore only a simple printed dress so she would merge easily with the village girls. She brought with her a little basket containing two bottles of wine for Isti's father and some sweets for his mother and the children. They took the train to Szentágoston and from there walked to Tövispuszta – a good half-hour along the main road. Isti's shirt was blotchy with perspiration by the time they arrived – the effect of excitement, rather than the heat. He was surprised to see that Eni was quite at home in Tövispuszta. In her light sandals, she was more careful than local people in avoiding the chicken manure, but she spoke to those that they met and looked cheerfully and inquisitively at the surroundings, the houses and the people.

"I'm interested in everything to do with you!" she told Isti, and planted a kiss on his cheek.

Maybe Lucky Gizi was in a state of greater excitement than Isti. She'd been cooking and cleaning all day. When Isti and Eni reached the house she was standing by the wall, nervously fiddling with the edge of her freshly ironed apron, and when they met she couldn't bring herself to look Eni in the eye. Finally Isti felt sorry for her, picked her up, swung her around and kissed her on the cheek.

"This is my mother!" he said.

"Oh, you mad thing, what are you doing," she laughed shyly, "you'll break every bone in my body!"

While the visitors and the men ate chicken soup in the kitchen Gizi and the two girls busied themselves at the stove and served. Eni asked them to sit at table, but in vain. They were even more reluctant.

"We can't do that, miss!" replied Gizi.

"Oh, please don't call me 'miss'," Eni was horrified. "My name's Eni."

"Yes, Miss Eni," said Gizi.

"Let my mother please herself," Isti whispered to her,

"it'll be easier for her." And he started a lively account of what had happened in the cinema.

Old Veres's eyes sparkled. "There, mother, that's something you can write in your chest!" he called to Gizi.

"That's only for family events," said Lucky Gizi severely. "I've been waiting for this twenty years!" István was excited. "We fought through the war, then we lost two-thirds of the country. And in 1919 even the reds fought over the country but now at last we've got the Kárpátalja back, and the Felvidék and the Székelyföld.[26] Only trouble is, there's going to be another bloody great war as a result."

"If there is, so be it!" retorted Isti proudly.

"The only people who talk like that are those that haven't ever been to war. Those that haven't seen guts spilled out, mutilated corpses, dead children. Or, of course, they're fools," Veres growled. "In a war it's always the poor that get it in the neck while the rich get richer. I don't see much good coming of that Jewish Hitler!"

The Cigar-band

On 26 June 1941 retired colonel Báron Pál Szentágostony became old. There had been signs of it in the preceding weeks, but this Thursday was memorable. Although the Baron wore his age lightly – he was sixty-four – and if we disregard stomach trouble, backache and a slight prostate problem which, if not obligatory, is common enough at his age, he was in fact healthy. As a vain man, however, he was increasingly troubled by the twenty-something year gap between himself and his wife. He seemed to take the passage of time as a personal affront. Since he couldn't avenge himself on time, he made his wife the target instead. To justify his jealousy he looked for signs of betrayal in Emília's behaviour. He now found her basically cheerful disposition, which twenty years earlier had enchanted him, frivolous and irresponsible. If the Baroness appeared too relaxed in the company of others he called it 'tastelessly provocative', and if perchance his wife expressed a desire to travel or have some fun he told himself that she intended to break away from their relationship. He beset his lively wife with scornful remarks in an attempt to crush her spirit. He had, however, no cause for worry. In his wife's eyes he still appeared an outwardly attractive man, and he did all that he could to achieve this. He was careful about his diet, took regular walks, rode, played tennis, did press-ups and abdominal exercises, and by means of an ancient Indian yoga practice, kept his double chin in check. With regard to his appearance the Baron had since his youth been concerned about two matters: layers of fat under his chin and around his waist.

"I just hope I never develop a flabby dangling double chin or the hips of a neglected woman," he once said as a young officer to a newly qualified psychiatrist friend; they were strolling on the Danube embankment in Pest and caught sight of a middle-aged man, his midriff rippling with fat, his arm round a young girl on a bench.

"Aren't you afraid of the Great Evil Notary hearing that?" asked his friend.

"What Great Evil Notary?" asked the Baron, laughing in disbelief.

"Oh, don't you know?" replied his friend, keeping a straight face. "Up in heaven on a cloud sits the Great Evil Notary, and if he hears anyone say the sort of thing that you just have he says: "Aha, now I know what that Pál wouldn't like: a double chin and a spare tyre! Well, he'll get them!'"

Baron Pál laughed, but ever since then, for a good thirty years, he'd regularly and suspiciously examined the front and side views of his chin, and the rear and side views of his midriff, with the aid of two mirrors.

On that early May morning he was standing in front of the bathroom mirror, carrying out an, also routine, examination of his ears. As he began to age hairs sprouted from them, and as a disciplined ex-soldier, he indignantly regarded this as intolerable untidiness.

"It's understandable that some parts of our bodies are covered in hair, that's how we deal with nature," he said, recalling what he'd been taught in years long past.

"Our eyebrows prevent perspiration running into our eyes, our hair protects us from the sun and from cold, the eyelashes and nostril hairs keep out foreign bodies, but what do we need hairs in our ears for?"

Baron Pál had a radical method of expressing dissatisfaction: he simply pulled the offending hairs out of his ears.

"Oh, if only things were that simple in politics!" he said to his sons Pál and János, as they smoked cigars on the mansion terrace. "We'd simply cut out the communists and the Nazis like the hairs that stick out of our nostrils; pull them out, like the superfluous hairs in our ears."

Pál and János weren't acutely aware of their father's inner struggles and found it difficult to follow the old Baron's biological and political allusions. To understand that line of thought called for a few extra years and some extraneous hair.

In recent weeks the Baron had been paying even closer attention than usual to political events. His former fellow officers had visited him more frequently of late, and they had spent hours discussing the way in which Hungary was being swept unstoppably into the clutches of the Reich.

"The peace conditions imposed at Trianon meant a slippery slope for Hungary with a precipice at the bottom," said the old Baron one day. "No decent Hungarian can pursue any policy other than the recovery of the lost territories. That, however, necessarily pushes the country in the direction of a war, while the army is not equipped for another." Bitterly, he said to his friends, "The Regent is a ditherer. What's become of the hero of Otranto? Yes, even in 1919 he couldn't restrain Prónay and the mindless, murderous terror squads, it was no use Count Apponyi pointing out that those excesses would be used against us in the peace negotiations.[27] And you see, he was right. Is he now going to offer an amnesty to

The Cigar-band

Major Szálasi, the national socialist? There's only one way to deal with the extreme right and the communist rabble: with a heavy hand!" The Baron quivered from head to foot. His older son's visit was the only thing that had lifted him out of the increasing despondency of the past weeks.

Pál had arrived from England the day before and had brought his father and brother a big box of Havana cigars each. The three of them were smoking contentedly on the terrace, sipping a fine single-malt Scotch as they did so – this was also a gift from Pál.

"Anyone who isn't pro-British must be mad!" said the Baron, happily savouring his drink.

"Hats off to Cuba as well," János made a sweeping gesture towards his father with an imaginary hat, and drew at his Havana.

"A gentleman drinks either wine, like the Italians and French, or whisky, like the British. Beer is for peasants. No wonder the Germans drink it!" the old Baron laughed.

"Actually, the English drink beer too," János attempted to correct him. "Although it's English beer."

"And that is something completely different!" said Pál with a smile.

"And not to mention Goethe, Bach, Beethoven, Thomas Mann and a few more not-so-peasant Germans," János winked at his brother.

"And let's not forget Marlene Dietrich's legs!" laughed the old Baron with a waggish good humour that he hadn't shown for quite some time.

Emília looked happily at her husband and her two grown-up sons; she was trying to work out when had been the last time that they'd all four sat together enjoying themselves on the terrace.

When, almost two years previously, Pál had rushed home

from Paris to announce that he wished to marry Sári Réder, the visit hadn't even lasted three days. He'd taken his parents' disapproval so badly that for a year afterwards they hadn't even exchanged letters. On his return from Szentágoston to Paris he'd struggled inwardly for weeks over whether to risk opposing his parents' wishes before finally persuading himself to wait a little before proposing marriage. He was ashamed to tell Sári what had happened at home, and couldn't explain why family traditions were so important to him, enlightened man that he was, and why he wasn't capable of standing up for their love. Sári sensed the unspoken secret in Pál's behaviour and didn't know what to think. She believed that his problem was with her, and it only made things worse when she asked him what was wrong and he assured her in an increasingly heated manner that it was nothing. Pál's constantly uneasy conscience ate like acid into their relationship. Eventually, in order to explain his behaviour, Pál said that the unfinished work for his doctorate was on his mind, and he proposed that they move to England; he was certain that in the end his parents would accept Sári. She, however, was unwilling to leave either the ballet company, with which she was having greater and greater success, or her mother and brothers. Finally they agreed that Pál should go to England, finish his studies, and come over to Paris now and then for a few days. At first their letters were emotional and tender, but later, as the sustaining vital fluid of personal meetings dried up, they became drier and drier, until they merely gave one another an account of their daily lives. Sári wrote about the performances that she was rehearsing for, what she'd seen at the cinema, what exhibition Sanyi and Géza had had, and Pál told her about his studies.

At the time Professor Toynbee was mainly living in London and working in Chatham House, the Royal Institute of International Affairs. He invited Pál to work with him and at the same time complete his thesis. In addition to scientific research the Institute regularly made analyses for the British government and the secret service, but Pál found it hard to come to terms with the idea of entering politics as an academic researcher.

They were sitting in the Professor's study, Toynbee in front of the bookcase which was stacked to capacity and behind a huge desk littered with books and files, and Pál facing him in an armchair on the other side. The blind was half lowered because strong light troubled the Professor's weak eyes, so that even in the daytime he worked by artificial light.

"Professor, how is it possible to honestly reconcile objective science and the practice of day-to-day politics, which is necessarily biased?" Pál asked anxiously.

"You're familiar with my work," replied Toynbee. "If we compare civilisations it emerges that they're destroyed not by external forces but by themselves. Those cultures that receive serious challenges and find good responses to them survive, but others collapse before their time. At present Western civilisation is facing such a challenge. National socialism offers one response, communism another, and democracy a third. Anyone who maintains an intellectual distance, hides in silence in the cool depths of a library and leaves the decision-making to others, will likewise be responsible for their own destruction."

"The thing is, I'm incapable of simplifying the world and seeing it in two dimensions, dividing it into left and right, when we know that it extends in both space and time," Pál objected.

The sound of the London streets filtered through the open window. Toynbee ran a palm over his lofty forehead and pushed a book away across his desk as something to do while he considered. "History is the science of facts, politics is the realm of the instincts. It isn't surprising that politicians build on people's instincts. Which, incidentally, is practical thinking, because everyone has instinct while few have brains," was the Professor's reply.

Working for the Institute provided Pál with the assurance that, despite the increasingly tense political situation, he would be given permission to re-enter Great Britain. Now that he was home, visiting the family, he brought with him a commission to obtain the latest information on Hungary's war plans.

The Szentágostony boys decided to spring a surprise on Isti: they would go to the match on Sunday and look him up in the changing-room. It was a good game, Isti was in brilliant form, but Pál often caught himself sneaking glances at the faces of the spectators in the stand rather than keeping his eyes on the pitch. Had these people, as they shouted so enthusiastically, any inkling of where the world was heading? Did they know what was in store for them in the years to come?

As early as March a letter had passed through Pál's hands which had been sent by the Prime Minister of Hungary, Pál Teleki, to the ambassador in London. This had been delivered, almost without precedent in international diplomacy, by special British courier because Teleki, fearing Gestapo influence, didn't trust his own Foreign Service. From this it emerged that he was anxious that Germany was about to attack Yugoslavia, because a military coup by anti-German forces had taken place there. As an expert on Hungary,

Pál had been invited to the conference at which the British government resolved to inform the Kingdom of Hungary that if German troops were permitted to cross its territory Great Britain would sever diplomatic ties, and that if Hungary took part in an attack on Yugoslavia, in breach of the treaty between the two countries, a state of war would exist. By the time that Pál reached Szentágoston in early May Hungarian forces had already entered Yugoslavia in support of the Germans, despite the British warning, and Prime Minister Teleki had shot himself in shame. "We have taken the side of the evil-doers... We have become body-snatchers. The most despicable of nations. I failed to restrain you. I am to blame." So wrote Teleki to the Regent in his letter of farewell.[28]

A few months earlier the mention of Oxford University would have provided Pál with the entrée even to people who weren't especially well disposed towards the British. He could, however, see that although London, perhaps less heated as a result of Teleki's action, had not yet declared war on Hungary, he would do better in his information-gathering to make use of his father's old military contacts, elderly officers who had sworn allegiance to the Emperor Franz Josef and who were keen supporters of the erstwhile imperial admiral, the Regent Horthy.

"I don't believe it!" Isti gave a great shout when, after the match, Pál and János walked into the crowded, sweaty changing-room. He and János had met now and again in the town, but he hadn't seen Pál for years. They looked each other over: they had both changed, matured. Pál congratulated Isti on his marriage, and he in turn happily introduced the Szentágostonys to members of the team and other friends who'd come to the changing-room to offer congratulations.

"My brother-in-law," he pointed to a young officer who was enthusiastically analysing the match with a number of perspiring, half-naked team members, "Lieutenant Csaba Sárády." The young man gave a soldierly nod.

"Csaba's on the staff," said Isti proudly. "Baron Szentágostony, on the other hand," indicating Pál, "has himself read more books than the rest of us in the changing-room put together. If we don't include János," he corrected himself with an apologetic grin to the younger Szentágostony.

Isti was so glad to see Pál – it was like getting an unexpected gift. Pál too was pleased at the chance of seeing his old friend, but for him the real stroke of luck was that fate had brought him into contact with a staff officer, through whom he would be able to make important connections. The appraisals of anti-German senior officers and generals became known in Chatham House through British intelligence channels; such officers had watched indignantly the tragic lack of military expertise in the entry into Transylvania, the bad decisions by commanders, the failures of transportation and the inadequate victualling of the troops, who sometimes didn't eat for days. The old Baron too had confirmed to Pál that he'd heard from his former senior comrades that after the entry to Northern Transylvania, the Regent himself had indignantly placed the responsibility on the Chief of Staff. The British diplomatic service and secret service, however, had difficulty in establishing contact with pro-German Hungarian staff officers. Pál felt that Lieutenant Sárády could open this channel for him.

The lieutenant was proud of his new acquaintance, the cultivated, landowning aristocrat, whose father he knew to be a retired colonel, and invited him to several gatherings at which his fellow officers talked freely about the political and military situation. The fracture-lines in the army could be measured precisely in the Officers' Club: the pro- and anti-German officers sat at separate tables beneath the gilded pargetry of the ballroom with its mirrored walls. As he walked through the room under the crystal chandeliers with Sárády, Pál could feel enquiring eyes from other tables and from the balcony overhead: who was this tall young man being escorted to their table by a well-known supporter of the Hitler party? After the introductions Pál politely apologised for obviously interrupting an interesting conversation. He was curious to know what Csaba's friends had been discussing so heatedly before their arrival.

"Have you been to the International Fair?" asked a stocky, moustachioed captain.

"I only came up to Budapest from the country a few days ago," Pál excused himself.

"Well, we were saying how astonishing it is that thousands go to the Soviet pavilion to admire the Bolshevik propaganda films. And you needn't think that they're only communists, Jews and Social Democrats, they're decent, sane Hungarians as well."

"That's quite astonishing," Pál agreed. He found it surprising that people's curiosity should overcome their prejudice. "Perhaps they enjoy being frightened. Like people who go to horror films in the cinema," he added with a smile.

"That's possible, we didn't think of that," answered the captain.

The officers laughed knowingly.

A steward in a dinner jacket offered Sárády and Pál tall glasses of champagne from a silver salver. "They'll get the chance to feel frightened if we march on Moscow," said a slim, blonde major in glasses, first waiting for the steward to move to a discreet distance.

The others nodded.

"We're going to attack the Russians?" enquired Pál innocently.

"Sooner or later Germany will attack the Soviet Union. Only by allying ourselves to them shall we recover the lost historical territories," said the major. "The only question now is whether General Werth[29] will manage to persuade the Regent and his surrounding doves."

"Has he persuaded the Prime Minister?" asked Pál, feigning indifference.

"Fortunately Prime Minister Bárdossy[30] is more of a rationalist than Teleki was," remarked the captain.

"And if he can't persuade the Regent?"

"He will," the captain assured him. "General Werth will take care of it."

"With a little German assistance," added another captain, with a smile.

"And what's the guarantee that Germany will defeat the Russians? Even Napoleon couldn't," Pál objected. He was trying to stir a balanced mixture of agreement and doubt into the conversation so as to extract as much information as possible from the staff officers, but at the same time not to lose their sympathy.

"If Napoleon had had air power and tanks, like the Führer has now, he'd have stood a better chance," Sárády laughed.

"Let's hope that the Russian mechanised army gets bogged down on the Kutuzov line,"[31] said Pál.

"I can see that the Baron has no confidence in Germany," said a young, girlish-looking lieutenant in a somewhat offended tone.

"There's no doubting that the Führer's men have had some impressive success," Pál nodded. "I'm just worried about Hungary. And it made me stop and think when the Führer's deputy defected to the British."

"We don't know why Hess went there," the major interposed. "It may be that he flew to London for talks on

The Cigar-band

Hitler's instructions to safeguard the Reich's rear for the attack on the Soviet Union."

This explanation surprised Pál too. He had as yet received no information from London about Hess' desertion.

"The Baron says that he's worried about Hungary," said the girlish-looking lieutenant. "All he need do now is decide whether to worry about mutilated Hungary or historical Hungary."

"Hungary is one. Isn't it?" Pál answered with a question. Everyone took that the way they pleased, and so all agreed.

From the conversation in the Officers' Club and notes that he made of a later meeting Pál had enough information to be able to report to London: the pro-German staff officers of the Hungarian army weren't going to acquiesce in not joining in the attack on the Soviet Union, and in this Prime Minister Bárdossy would support them.

Then on 22 June the radio announced the news: Germany had attacked the Soviet Union. Italy and Romania had allied themselves at once. Pál was somewhat reassured to hear that the Kingdom of Hungary had only broken off diplomatic relations with the Soviet Union. He was further relieved when, a few days later, he learned that the Soviet foreign minister had informed Bárdossy that if Hungary remained neutral, the Soviet Union would recognise her territorial claims. At last the Regent held a trump card: he didn't have to abandon the revisionist policy, but neither was he going to be forced to take the country into a devastating war. So thought Pál, and on hearing the good news, he went back home to Szentágoston at once. He couldn't speak to his father

125

and brother about what he'd learnt. They, however, couldn't understand why Pál was so optimistic; he, on the other hand, wasn't to know that Bárdossy hadn't revealed Molotov's message to the Regent or to the council of ministers.

Next morning he was woken by János, deathly pale, rattling the door of his room.

"The Soviets have bombed Kassa!" he said.

"That's impossible!" replied Pál sleepily. "They've no interest in dragging Hungary into the war," and he shook his head. "This can only be provocation."

"It was on the radio," Janos confirmed.

Pál grabbed his clothes and went out onto the terrace. The radio was on in the drawing-room, and he could hear the news out there, where the old Baron was sitting, wrapped in his silk dressing-gown and deep in thought. That afternoon the Parliament, to shouts of acclaim, voted for mobilisation. The bill was signed on 26 June 1941.

The Summons to Forced Labour[32]

It was dawn. A bluish vapour wafted above the hillside. In the dawn breeze the only sound was the panting and groans of people trudging along, exhausted, and the curses of their Arrow-Cross escort. The squad containing Samu and Andor made its way along the muddy road, 'to the accompaniment of shots in the back of the head' as they said among themselves. The front was approaching from the east and the forced labour squad was being marched westwards. The guards took care to avoid places of habitation so that the workers would have difficulty knowing where they were going, but from the general direction and the countryside that spread before his eyes Samu worked out, to his surprise, that they were heading for Tövispuszta. They were passing the cemetery in the neighbouring village when bombers appeared overhead. Machine-gun fire from one of the escorting fighters raked the column. Then bombs began to fall. Everyone scattered and tried to take shelter among the graves, but the marble tombstones gave no protection from the ear-splitting explosions. Fragments of marble caused almost as much damage as did splinters of steel.

"Practical, when all's said and done, to kick the bucket in a cemetery," said Andor to his father as they cowered behind a tombstone.

Samu hadn't appreciated Andor's gallows humour for quite some time. "The gallows is no laughing matter, my boy! It's too real," he'd said one day.

"Never mind if you survive this, you stinking Jews, you'll die just the same!" shrieked a hard-faced, sunburnt Arrow-Cross man with a strong local accent.

"He's scared," said Samu.

"Don't go feeling sorry for him, father."

Samu was aware that Andor, in self-defence, did his best to dismiss even the most dire situations with bitter humour, but he found it hard to bear. His father's endless toleration, on the other hand, got on Andor's nerves.

"Look at how his shoulders are raised, his body's contorted, the veins on his face are standing out. He doesn't just want to frighten us, he's trying to overcome his own terror by shouting, poor chap," Samu explained.

"Bugger the filthy murderer!" was Andor's response.

Samu had for a long time been unwilling to admit what was in store for them. When news arrived in August 1941 of the camp at Kőrösmező, into which the Hungarian authorities had herded eighteen thousand Jews, mostly refugees from Galicia, and then sent them out of Hungary to Kamenets-Podolski, where German death squads machine-gunned them, the majority didn't guess that that was a foretaste. Nor that anyone who said "That's the price we have to pay to the Germans, let's hope it satisfies them", would later be unable to escape the shameful bargains. Samu had simply not believed the depths to which people could sink. Or at least he tried to find redeeming features in them. It was as if the Creator had omitted to give him any ill humour, and without it he was incapable of understanding what was happening. After the news from Kamenets-Podolski he shook his head: "That's impossible, because the Regent took the Poles in," he repeated. When Margit Schlachta, head of the Catholic Sisters of Social Service, together with a number of other figures in public life reported with startling force on what they had seen at Körösfő, Samu had immediately come out with "You see, there are honourable people, there's always hope!" All that Andor retained, on the other hand, were the details of the eye-witness accounts that the soil swiftly piled on the old men, women and children who had been shot and thrown into bomb-craters had continued to heave for days.[33]

Since then three years had gone by. Samu had learnt of the harsh Jewish laws, had endured inhuman treatment during two years of forced labour, hadn't rebelled when he experienced the precise thoroughness and readiness with which the gendarmerie and Hungarian officialdom assisted the Germans in driving the provincial Jews into ghettoes and thence into cattle trucks from May 1944 onwards. He learnt through friends how, one after another, Henrik's daughter Blanka and her family had been rounded up and deported from Miskolc, as had his and Henrik's sisters Sára and Margit and their families from Makó and Kecskemét respectively. By the time that the Regent put a stop to the deportations in early June there was no one in the family left. From the account given by two Slovak prisoners who escaped from Auschwitz there was no doubt of the fate that awaited the deportees. "Still, it's lucky that Henrik's family and Dávid are safe in Budapest," even then Samu looked for hope. At this time Samu Goldstein was the only Jew in Eastern Europe that still trusted in human goodness.

"What do you still trust in, father?" Andor asked him.

"I've got a little box," replied Samu. "In it I collect my memories of decent people. And although it's still not full the little that's in it gives me the strength to live!"

"Ah!" Andor made a disparaging gesture. "I don't even

believe in God any more. That must be why he's punishing me," he added sorrowfully, feeling ashamed.

"The Everlasting One isn't angry if you don't believe in him. At the most he pities you. He knows that it does him no harm, only you!" said Samu.

The bombs were falling. Samu was praying aloud.

"Back on the road!" shouted an Arrow-Cross man and cocked his sub-machine gun.

Among the explosions and the dust that covered the cemetery, a number of the forced workers emerged from their hiding places.

"Come on, father," whispered Andor, and began to move towards the field of maize alongside the cemetery. "If we're going to die anyway, at least let's not do it here, like cattle in the slaughterhouse."

Samu slipped after Andor, but shook his head as if indicating that they were doing something wrong. "He's mad! Father's letting correctness come before the survival instinct!" thought Andor in amazement. Crouching low, they crawled between the posts in the damaged fence into the field, and began to run as fast as the maize would let them. Samu was panting loudly. Andor took his father's arm and tried to help him along until they collapsed, breathing heavily, sweating from exertion and fear. Then they heard the shouts of the Arrow-Cross men in the distance and a few short, random bursts of sub-machine gun fire.

"Perhaps some others have run for it as well," said Samu.

They lay among the maize until evening, filled with anxiety but feeling more relieved.

"Well, such is freedom!" said Andor as they set off, looking at the starry sky. They had only just turned onto the road when they found themselves face to face with two soldiers on patrol. There was no chance of running away. The soldiers, rifles with bayonets slung on their shoulders, momentarily looked at them from a distance, then exchanged glances and moved towards them.

"What are you doing here at this time of night?" asked the older, a ruddy-cheeked man whose twirly hussar moustache made him look like a toy soldier.

"We became separated from our unit during the air-raid this morning. Thought we'd take a rest somewhere, then go on tomorrow," said Samu uncertainly.

"They were looking for a few this morning near the cemetery here, who'd got separated from their unit. Suppose we'd better escort you back. Or would you rather spend the night in the gendarmerie?" asked the second.

"One idea appeals more than the other," said Samu bitterly. "but right now we don't know which to choose."

Andor appreciated his father's sarcasm. The soldiers smiled.

"If you don't care for either, we suggest you go in the other direction, you might do better," said the one with the moustache, and to the Goldsteins' surprise the soldiers saluted and turned away.

"Just a moment," Samu called after them. "We've got nothing left, but I'd like to give you this," and he began to pull the wedding-ring off his finger.

"Don't insult us, old chap," said the toy soldier. With that they turned and went on their way. Rooted to the spot, Samu and Andor watched them go.

"Are there such people?" asked Andor, astounded, shaking his head in disbelief.

"You can see for yourself, my boy! Into the box they go!"

Their road led to a distant farmstead, where they might be able to hide for a while. Through the window a flickering light could be seen. After a brief consultation they decided to go in. After all, according to the soldiers it wasn't advisable to go towards Bátakér. In Tövispuszta, on the other hand, they would immediately be recognised, but it couldn't possibly be advisable to stay in the maize for weeks, until the front reached the area. They knocked on the door of the house and went into the kitchen. There were three men there, sitting at a table. Two were younger, about twenty, and one older. As the door opened they were startled, and looked at Samu and Andor in expectant alarm.

"Good evening," Samu said politely, and repeated what he'd said before. "We got separated from our unit in the air-raid this morning and we're trying to catch them up. We'd like to stay the night here, then we'll go on in the morning."

The three men nodded. They looked Samu and Andor up and down. Their faces showed that there was no need to tell them what kind of 'unit' they'd 'been separated' from, but they said nothing.

"There's a bowl of soup left, if you like, you can have it between you," said one, who introduced himself as Ferenc Mayer, Franci, and spoke with a thick Swabian accent. He took the pot off the stove, poured the soup into a bowl and put it in front of them with a couple of spoons.

Samu and Andor bent over the bowl and spooned up the soup without a word. In the flickering light of the paraffin lamp it seemed that their faces were flickering too. They both concentrated on not letting it be seen how hungry they were.

"Where are you from?" asked one of the younger men, also with a Swabian accent.

"Not far from here, Tövispuszta," said Samu, looking up from the bowl. "Chance has brought us this way."

"That's right!" said Mayer. "You're the shopkeeper. Thought I recognised you."

"Yes," Samu nodded. "And this is my son. Now you'll

know everything. Don't suppose you've heard anything about my wife and daughter? We've had no news of them in months."

Ferenc Mayer knew perfectly well how the gendarmes and the Arrow-Cross had cleared the Jews from nearby Tövispuszta. The village people had talked about how the Steiner family from the mill, the old man, his wife, daughter-in-law and grandchildren and the wife and daughter of Goldstein the shopkeeper had been taken to the end of the village. The story had gone round the whole area that when they went for the Goldsteins, Ilus had begged them to leave Elza at least, because she wasn't Jewish. The entire village could confirm they'd adopted her. The gendarme and Jóska Hetési, bulky in his Arrow-Cross uniform, hadn't known what to do. But then Elza turned to Ilus and said with determination:

"Please don't disown me, Mummy! You took me in as your daughter when I was little and I'll still be your daughter now!"

Ilus sobbed. She put her arms round Elza and tried to push her away at the same time as she clung bitterly to her.

The villagers looked on shamefacedly. One or two women dabbed their eyes, but only Lucky Gizi dared confront the men in uniform.

"What kind of men are you?" she shouted with uncharacteristic passion.

"Clear off, old woman, while you're safe," said the gendarme, embarrassed.

Isti and István Veres watched what was happening, looking grim.

"Didn't a mother give birth to you? Shame on you!" Gizi shouted. She ran to Ilus and Elza, put her arms round them and tried to pull them to her, and to protect the Steiners' grandchildren too.

Jóska Hetési sprang at Gizi and pushed her aside. She fell to the ground. Then Isti rushed at the Arrow-Cross man like a raging beast and kicked the big man hard on the thigh with his famous left foot.

"Hit my mother, would you, you animal?" he roared.

Hetési collapsed and his gun fell to the ground. His face contorted in pain, he clutched his thigh with one hand and with the other reached for his weapon. But then István too came up with a long-handled axe in his hand.

"I'll split your skull!" he shouted in fury, and had Isti not grabbed him was on the point of doing so.

"There must be no bloodshed!" said Elza, gesturing for the people to be quiet. "We're going as well."

And she set off up the road, the Steiners and Ilus behind her. Hetési got to his feet and limped after them. He shouted back to Isti "Veres, fuck your mother, you'll regret this."

Ferenc Mayer remembered the event precisely, but in reply to Samu's question only shook his head in embarrassment. No one spoke. In the silence, artillery could be clearly heard to the east.

"The Russians," he said, his face showing that he was thinking of something. He was silent for a while, then thoughtfully, with a weary smile, he went on "You can hide in my stable while you look for your unit."

The stable was dark, but the moon shone through the window and in its silver light a skinny cow could be seen lying on the straw, while a horse was outlined at the manger. When Samu and Andor went in the animals became a little restive; the cow swung its tail a few times and then settled back into its previous gloomy apathy. The Goldsteins climbed the ladder into the hayloft and burrowed into the musty hay. From up there they saw through the grimy window the older man setting off along the road towards the village.

"If he's not gone to report us we really are in God's hands," said Andor.

They tossed and turned until dawn in the straw, cold despite the horse-blanket that covered them, hardly daring to sleep. At every sound they thought that someone had come for them. Then early in the morning they saw through the window the man coming back with a sack over his shoulder. As he reached the stable door he called in "Good morning! Here's your breakfast! Come into the kitchen!"

There he emptied the sack: a smallish loaf, some fat, potatoes, bacon and onions and set them out on the table.

"Tell you what," he said afterwards. "I'll hide you till the Russians get here and you can say a good word for us for having saved you. What do you say?"

"And why would you need anybody to speak for you?" asked Andor.

"The youngsters are deserters from the Waffen SS. They volunteered because they were hoping for an easier time during the war, and they didn't want to be stinking Swabians in the Hungarian army. But they couldn't take any more. If the Arrow-Cross, the gendarmes or the Germans catch them as deserters they can expect a bullet, same as you. If the Russians catch them and you, the bullets will only be for them. That's why they need somebody to put in a good word for them."

"Right," Samu nodded in relief.

"We're under the same roof as filthy SS soldiers?" Andor was indignant later in the stable.

"These lads are only saving their skins like anyone else," said Samu. "It's not surprising that they preferred to join a German elite unit in the rear rather be taken to the front and the Don bend."[34]

They had been hiding in the stable for some days when

Franci brought himself to tell them what had become of Ilus and Elza.

"We've got nobody left," Samu sobbed. "I'd like to at least know how Dávid's getting on in Budapest."

Franci offered that if he heard of anyone from the village going to Budapest in the near future to take food to relatives, he'd send them to Kresz Géza utca and try to find out at the workshop what was known about Dávid.

Henrik, Anci, Dávid and a good twenty others were being herded by three men in black uniforms and Arrow-Cross armbands towards the Pest embankment of the Danube, from where the sound of gunshots indicated that the preceding group was being shot into the river.[35] The Arrow-Cross men had driven the Goldsteins out of a 'starred house'[36] in Pozsonyi út, which served as a ghetto. The column of women, old men and children, all with yellow stars on their coats, were moving towards the embankment in as orderly a fashion as a nursery-school crocodile. As they passed people drew back from windows, passers-by looked away; just a few stared at them in curiosity, pity or Schadenfreude, storing for life the memory of a humiliated elderly face, a terrified pair of dark eyes, or a small child skipping along at its mother's side without the slightest idea of what was going on.

Another two Arrow-Cross men appeared from the direction of the garden. They hurried with quick strides and searching eyes towards the group as it advanced with bowed heads. They stopped in front of Henrik, and one of them struck him a blow in the face laying him flat on the ground. Wiping his bleeding mouth, he looked up at the Arrow-Cross man towering over him. The others, all pale, drew back and watched. The three escorts were brought up short, and looked questioningly at their furious colleague.

"Let me have these swine!" said he. "They've tortured me enough, at least let me have the satisfaction of liquidating them."

Henrik, Anci and Dávid suddenly recognised in the shrieking Arrow-Cross man their former mechanic Jani Tóth.

"You just see to them, brother!" called the commander of the escort cheerfully. "Enjoy yourself!"

At the park Jani and his friend led the Goldsteins not towards the Danube but into a side-road. They took them to a little pick-up truck that stood in the forecourt of a building, told them to get onto the load-bed and lie down. Tóth sat in the cab, while the other Arrow-Cross man climbed into the back of the vehicle and covered the Goldsteins with a tarpaulin.

A few minutes later they felt the truck go cautiously up a ramp and stop with a squeal of brakes. The tarpaulin was pulled off them, and the first thing that they saw was the old poster advertising the Model-T Ford.

"Excuse the rough treatment, Mr. Henrik," said Jani Tóth, as he looked round to see if anyone in the street could see into the workshop. He'd deliberately stopped the vehicle in such a way that the load-bed blocked the rear of the garage. He held a hand out to help the old people climb down.

"I overdid the slap in the face rather," he apologised, "but it had to be convincing, otherwise those evil Arrow-Cross men might have suspected something."

By then the Goldsteins were beginning to realise what had happened. Anci and Dávid clung to the two men's arms in gratitude. Henrik, however, was less pleased.

"Have you lost your marbles, my dear boy?" he asked Jani. "I never hit you like that, even when you were my apprentice! And you deserved it often!"

Jani and his friend pushed aside a tool-cupboard in the corner of the workshop. Behind it the wall had been demolished and it was possible to crawl through on all fours into the cellar, where three mattresses lay on the floor. Henrik, Anci and Dávid hid there and the cupboard was pushed back into place. In the daytime the workshop was busy as Keller and Jani worked on cars, but in the evening the cupboard was pushed aside so that the Goldsteins could have some fresh air, empty the chamber-pots into the WC and have something to eat. Towards evening or in the small hours, when the curfew emptied the streets and not even a glimmer of light showed from the blacked-out windows, Jani and a few companions put on Arrow-Cross uniforms and made the rounds of the 'starred houses' to save people. Erzsi, whom Dávid knew from the hikes, obtained Swedish or Spanish protective passports for them, and later, when genuine papers were no longer available, documents were forged.

Artillery could be heard from the direction of Kispest when one morning a downy-chinned peasant boy arrived at the workshop and enquired for the Goldsteins.

Keller, now in charge, looked at him suspiciously.

"Far as I know, they were taken to some 'starred house'. But whether they're still alive... Why are you looking for them?" he asked

"I've been asked to find out what's become of them," said the boy.

"Who wants to know?" asked Keller with a frown.

"I'm from Bátakér, near Tövispuszta, if that means anything to you" said the boy.

Keller raised his eyebrows as he pondered this, and to gain time searched for a cigarette in the pocket of his overalls. He took his time to light up and inhaled.

"Sorry, I can't help you," he said, "but come back tomorrow, just in case I hear anything."

After the workshop had closed Henrik and the others emerged from their hiding place and Keller told them what had happened that morning. They discussed at length what they should do. The young peasant had seemed genuine and honest, and it made sense that Samu would try to make contact with his son and brother.

"I wonder whether the family just wanted to give a sign of life in the hope of getting one back, or maybe they need help?" asked Dávid anxiously.

"Perhaps they need money. It may be that people won't hide them for nothing," Henrik thought. "If we send some we'll give ourselves away. If we don't, we may be sentencing them to death."

Finally they decided to send some money with the boy, but Keller wasn't to say that it came from Henrik.

The boy called in the next day.

"The Goldsteins are in a 'protected' house," [37] said Keller, "but I don't know which one. They sent word by a go-between."

He carefully took an envelope from his overalls pocket.

"Would you take this to whoever sent you here, my boy?" he asked. "It's from me, in case they're hard up."

The boy nodded and slipped the little package into his trouser pocket.

It was dark, just before dawn. Both the land and the horizon looked dirty when the four SS soldiers and two Arrow-Cross men went to the farmstead for Samu and Andor. They were woken by the sound of the jeep and the motor-cycle combined, and then a German soldier and an Arrow-Cross man kicked in the doors of the house and stable while the other two SS stood guard outside. With weapons trained on them they were forced out into the yard; they had no chance to escape or defend themselves. All the same, the Arrow-Cross men, perhaps out of self-justification, struck the Goldsteins in case they resisted. Samu and Andor could only look with pained expressions at the two from the village: Jóska Hetési and Balázs Székely. The two Swabian lads were the only ones to plead with the soldiers, in German, but to no avail. The SS officer demonstrated with a mighty blow how little their knowledge of the language impressed.

The fugitives were marched towards Tövispuszta with the Germans and the Arrow-Cross escorting them in the jeep and on the motor-cycle. By the time they reached the village it was light. The noise woke everyone and tousled heads peered from behind curtains as the two Goldsteins and the young Swabians trudged by, heads bowed. Samu, his back bent, was just passing the Vereses' house when Gizi looked out of the window.

"Sweet Jesus!" her voice failing as she crossed herself. The low sun shone into her eyes from behind Samu's head and its blinding, golden red light illuminated the bloody, bearded head like a halo.

"Sweet Jesus!" she sighed again.

She was still standing at the window, motionless, praying with lips that scarcely moved, when the sound of the volley came from the cemetery.

THE TELEGRAM

Mass had just ended, and the soothing perfume of incense still hung in the air of the church. Lucky Gizi and the parish priest were standing by the little altar, in front of the confessional box, and she'd spent some minutes, her face passionate, trying to persuade him to ask the Pope to declare Samu Goldstein a saint. The priest didn't know whether to laugh or weep.

"Do you think I have lunch with the Holy Father every Sunday?" he asked.

"No, but you know the bishop, and he certainly knows His Holiness," she assured him.

"That seems very simple," smiled the priest. "And yet, my dear daughter, how do you suppose that the name of St Samu or perhaps St Goldstein would go down in the history of the church?"

"That man was a saint," Gizi insisted.

"On what grounds?" asked the priest.

"He was full of love, helped everybody, healed people, gave them strength."

"Then let's say that he was a good man," the priest agreed. "But look here, every good man can't become a saint! Furthermore, he was Jewish. How could a Jew be made a saint?"

"Jesus was a Jew, and his Holy Mother," said Gizi adamantly.

"But in those days Christianity didn't exist yet, dear lady! And the Jews rejected the Lord! You've read the New Testament, haven't you?"

"These days the Christians reject the Jews," Gizi retorted. "And each other."

A yellow ray of sunlight came through the window above the altar, piercing the cool gloom of the church, and lit up her face as if the good Lord up above, or perhaps Samu Goldstein, was watching to see how she was getting on with the priest. She paused for effect before playing her final card.

"I saw the halo on Samu's head," she blurted out.

"A halo on his head?" asked the priest, astounded.

"Yes," said Gizi. "I saw the halo on his head when he was being taken to his place of execution. Just like on Our Lord."

The priest looked affectionately at the old lady's gentle, excited face. He didn't want to upset Lucky Gizi, who sat in the front pew at every mass and sang the psalms more loudly than anyone else.

"Do you know what, my daughter? I'll dedicate a mass to Samu Goldstein next Sunday."

"And Andor," Gizi added.

"And Andor," the priest assured her.

"And Ilus and Elza."

"Quite so," the priest nodded.

"And the Steiners," Gizi bargained on.

"To them too," said the priest, and by then he was smiling. "But let's agree that it's up to the Jews to make Samu a saint!"

✳

The Telegram

Three Arrow-Cross men were digging on the edge of the Tövispuszta cemetery. Jóska Hetési, Balázs Székely and the short Frédi Müller, known to everyone in the village as Pertli. There was blood on their faces and they dug in silence, resolutely, their eyes mere slits; the only sounds were the clink of spades and the thud of the clods being tossed up. Four armed policemen and a detective in civilian clothes watched them; sometimes they looked at the cold sweat on the Arrow-Cross men's faces, sometimes they peered into the hole. Hetési was the first to utter as they came to the first corpse.

"Who is it?" asked the detective.

Hetési bent to take a closer look, as did Székely, but Pertli turned away with a grimace.

"I think it's one of the Swabian lads," said Hetési.

"That's right," said Székély.

They dug around the body.

"How do we get him out?" asked Hetési.

"How do you get him out? With your hands! If you could shoot him and throw him in you can get him out as well, you mother-fuckers!" said one of the policemen.

With marked repugnance the two Arrow-Cross men took hold of the mud-coloured body and laid it on the side of the hole, then wiped their slimy hands on their trousers. After a little while they dug up the other deserter too. Then there lay the corpse of Samu Goldstein – rigid, muddy, its face unrecognisable; green flies were buzzing above them in the sweetish corpse-smell when an ancient truck arrived in the cemetery. A detective in civilian clothes climbed awkwardly down from the seat next to the driver.

"Isti Veres!" whispered Székely in horror to Hetési.

Isti limped over to the hole. The policemen saluted, and the other detective acknowledged him in silence. His face expressionless, he looked at the corpses, their eye-sockets

143

blackened holes, and then, as if he didn't even recognise Hetési and the others, he ordered:

"Get on with it!"

The Arrow-Cross men dug on, and from beneath the muddy earth there emerged the yellow and black body of Andor Goldstein. The solitary shot had hit him in the right eye: in its place gaped a hole the size of a fist.

"The sons of whores!" said one of the policemen. "They ought to be shot instead."

The three Arrow-Cross men wouldn't have been surprised in the least, especially on seeing Isti. "We didn't kill him, so now he's going to kill us," thought Hetési. When the peasant lad let out in the pub that Franci Mayer was probably hiding Jews on his farmstead, Pertli had immediately rushed round to Hetési's with the news, and together they had gone to the Germans. The SS officer and the Arrow-Cross had first arrested Franci as he worked in his garden in Bátakér. The moment he saw them he realised that he was in trouble. Two blows were enough to make him tell all. He was sitting in the Germans' guardroom, beaten black and blue, when the soldiers and Arrow-Cross surrounded the farmstead in the small hours. He was sent on the final transport to Mauthausen, and could thank his lucky stars that he hadn't been shot on the spot. After that came Isti Veres' turn, but that was just a personal affair with Hetési and Székely. They waited for days for him to visit his parents in Tövispuszta and caught him by the stable behind the house. Székely and Pertli took him from in front, Hetési from behind, and simply knocked him flat.

"Shall we shoot him or beat him to death?" asked Hetési, and gave Isti a great kick as he lay there.

"It'd be enough to break his golden leg, the one he kicked you with, and his musician's fingers," Pertli laughed aloud. Hetési and Székely liked the idea too.

"Just for the sake of our long-standing friendship!" said Hetési with a grin.

They fetched a shoeing-hammer from the stable, and with it systematically smashed Isti's legendary left leg from the tip of his toes through his ankle to his knee, and then one by one broke his fingers. He'd been lying unconscious for hours behind the stable when Márton Jónás found him and carried him to his parents' house. When old Veres saw Isti, frozen and bloody, he let out such a shout that people came running. Lucky Gizi just looked at her son stupefied, without a tear, and couldn't conceive what had happened. Next day she wrote with shaking hand on the lid of her dowry chest: *Isti crippled 12 December 1944.*

Isti limped towards the truck and took out three pieces of cardboard from the cab. These had loops of string attached, and daubed on them in red were the words 'WE ARE ARROW-CROSS MURDERERS!'

"Hang these round your necks!" he said in a voice that brooked no opposition, and threw them to Hetési, Székely and Pertli.

"Now put the two lads on the back of the truck, then pick up Samu and Andor in your arms and start walking in front of the truck to the village."

The Arrow-Cross men dared not object. They picked up the Swabian lads' bodies by their hands and feet and tossed them onto the truck. Hetési picked up Samu's rigid, muddy body while Skékely and Pertli, with evident reluctance, took Andor, whose yellow and black arm resisted stiffly and went on beating against Pertli's side as he walked as if he, in death, were as disgusted at being touched by the murderers as the Arrow-Cross men were at touching him. So they went all the way to the village, the corpses in their arms, like a *pietà* of horror. Behind them came the truck with its load-bed open, so that people could see the bodies of the Swabian lads too. But no one wanted to see them. The people of Tövispuszta peered, horrified, from behind their windows, as they had some months previously when the four men were being driven towards the cemetery.

From the autumn of 1944 Isti had spent more time at his parents' in Tövispuszta than with his wife in town. His relationship with the Sárády family had broken off after the Chief of Staff himself informed the family by telegram that Lieutenant Csaba Sárády had been killed in action on the Russian front. Even though they had been dreading that moment for months, added to which, after the tragic destruction of the Second Army, no one of their acquaintance had been spared a similar telegram, the Sárády parents refused to believe the news. They put the black-edged telegram on the mantelpiece beside the picture of Csaba in uniform, and stood for hours, arms round one another, as if hoping that suddenly the wording would change and it would all turn out to have been a bad dream, or that Csaba would ring the doorbell and say that the documents had been mixed up. Dr. Sárády couldn't forgive himself for failing to dissuade his son from volunteering to serve at the front, indeed, he'd even been proud of him, and now had to find a scapegoat so as to come to terms with his conscience.

"I fixed it for you to stay at home because Eni begged me, my boy," he threw in Isti's face. "Poor Csaba volunteered for active service, and has died for his country."

Böske Sárády clung to her husband's arm and tried to calm him, but she couldn't restrain her sobs either.

"What could I do, Béla?" Isti tried to excuse himself, looking round at Eni and Csenge for support, "I tried to talk him out of it, but he insisted that honour came first."

"What would have happened if everyone had been a coward and backed out?" asked Sárády, his embittered gaze cutting deep into Isti's face.

Isti made no reply, merely lowered his eyes as if ashamed of himself, and as he did so thought that his father-in-law clearly couldn't accept how blind he'd been to have faith in the Führer's glorious victory; he must now be feeling that he'd paid for his enthusiasm with his son's life. Eni too was upset by her brother's death, but wouldn't take sides with either her father or her husband in the undignified argument. Meanwhile hatred, like carbon monoxide seeping through the cracks, imperceptibly permeated the family, poisoning the atmosphere and relationships.

Eni was thirty-one. The hormones were rioting in her nervous system, banging furiously on the door: we want a child! If she needed to pass water more frequently, felt dizzy or sleepy, she immediately began to believe that it was a sign. In the evenings she pulled Isti on top of her so passionately, clung to him so bitterly, that it seemed that she wanted to squeeze a triumphant drop of seminal fluid out of him by force. For months she'd burst into tears when her period came round, then she would start over, persuade herself that she had morning sickness if she was off her food or if her abdomen was painful, and then once more disappointment would come when these symptoms turned out to be simple indigestion or a menstrual cramp. When she was finally certain that she was expecting, it wasn't just her long-held desire which was fulfilled. The excellent refuge offered by motherhood also meant that she would be able to escape the increasingly intolerable atmosphere in the family. As in every situation throughout her life, once again she found a loyal companion in Csenge. From the first moment of the pregnancy the twins, closely closeted together, whispered about the delights, pains and anxieties of motherhood. Csenge wanted to know every single thing about it, down to the last detail, so that she could at least vicariously experience motherhood. Isti took it amiss that his wife confided more in her sister than in him.

"This is women's business, you know," said Eni, with a consoling pat on his cheek.

When the labour pains became more frequent and Isti took Eni to hospital, Csenge came along too, and while Isti, excited and powerless, nervously paced the corridor, Csenge held her sister's hand in the delivery room. The doctors knowingly said that she'd experienced the birth to such a degree that afterwards she needed nursing alongside Eni. Isti was filled with envy as he listened to them, not venturing to say that he too deserved a little recognition: after all, had he not stood his ground in the corridor and not fainted, for instance?

Since his mother had been Enese, or Enéh, in keeping with the mythical family, following Dr. Sárády's wish the little boy was christened Hunor, and also István after his father, and so his nickname became Pityu. Naturally, Hunor István Veres was immersed in the water of baptism by Csenge.

Isti was surprised to hear his wife speak of the child in the first person plural: we do our business, we pee, we suck...

"You too?" he asked scornfully at first.

But when he noticed that Csenge was also using the plural, he began to take offence.

"Are you all sucking, shitting and pissing together here, and I'm left out?"

"Csenge hasn't got a child, probably never will have now, let her feel that he's her own, after all we're almost one," said his wife later, in such a way that Csenge couldn't hear.

"So, I've produced a child for her as well?" Isti grumbled. After the birth Eni gradually took less and less interest in anything but Pityu. All day long she tossed him on her shoulder, cuddled him, kissed him, they did their business, peed and sucked, and in the evening she took him to bed with her and slept with him.

"I've waited for him so long, let me have a bit of pleasure in him!" said she to Isti.

If Isti shyly snuggled up to her in the evening to make love and stroke her breasts, Eni gently pushed his hand away.

"You know, darling, I can't do that now. My breasts belong to Pityu."

Isti felt that it wasn't only Eni's breasts that belonged to Pityu but her body, her head and her very breath. When she was breast-feeding with Csenge and Isti was sitting with them, as he looked on he had the feeling that the baby was slowly swallowing his wife, leaving for Csenge nothing more than a few unconsidered trifles, the way that after a meal people toss bits of chicken skin or a bone under the table to the cat, to stop it meowing. When Pityu was taking his afternoon nap – in Istis's opinion, to gather strength for bawling at night – Isti would sometimes sneak into his son's room, sit on the floor by the cot and look at him, trying to discover something of himself in the child, just in case there was anything. If he was awake, the blue eyes fringed with dark eyelashes were like

149

his, but asleep Isti could see only Sárády features: it was as if
Dr. Sárády himself were lying there – in miniature, of course.
Isti tried in vain to discover in himself any of the paternal
feeling of which he'd heard so much; apart from his father-in-
law, the sleeping child reminded him mostly of the new-born
kittens which he'd often watched in the loft as a boy.

Isti felt ashamed, and so couldn't even tell Eni how much
he missed her attention, her consideration, her body. In the
evening he often felt offended, and spent more and more time
in the bar at the club, meeting his former team-mates, and
once more took to drinking, spending ever longer periods
back home at his parents'. He was hoping that at least his
absence would re-arouse his wife's interest in him, but it
simply had the opposite effect. Eni too complained, naturally
in the plural: "We don't interest you any longer."

Mrs. Sárády accused Isti of taking to the bottle and
neglecting his family.

"It looks like once a peasant, always a peasant!" slipped
out of her mouth one day.

It was then that the warning that Panni Ördögh had once
uttered came to mind – "You're running after the carriage,
when the cart would gladly give you a ride" – he packed
some things and didn't return to town from Tövispuszta
for weeks.

He convalesced there after being crippled by the Arrow-
Cross. That had hurt him physically, but even more so
mentally; he spent hours staring bitterly at his misshapen leg
and crooked fingers, and felt deprived and lonely. He'd been
beaten back into the working class. They had taken from him
what had made him feel equal to the middle-class, what had
lifted him out of the servants' quarters. When Eni heard what
had happened to Isti she rushed to him, but then persuaded
her husband and herself that there would be no room for both

of them and Pityu there; for months, however, Isti wouldn't hear of sleeping in town, depressed and humiliated as he was. At first Eni came to see him every week with the child, but Isti treated her off-handedly and roughly, so after a while she stopped going.

"Why should we go if he isn't even pleased to see us?" she said.

By the time spring had arrived hostilities were over in the Tövispuszta region. The Germans had fled and some of the Arrow-Cross after them. Hungary was licking its war wounds; some travelled around town and country with packs, collecting food for their families or trading in it, others awaited the future with hope or trepidation. There were those who had hailed the Red Army as liberators, and those who dismissed their former fears or, learning from their wartime experiences, looked anxiously at the invading Russians. The Soviets chose the golden mean: they called themselves liberators but behaved like invaders, thus there was nothing to wonder at when the Communist Party suddenly became very popular, at least as far as the number of members was concerned. Before the war the illegal party had had at the most four or five hundred members, but in the autumn of '45 almost half a million had come forward, applauding one another, in the Soviet-type party, and people flocked to join the other opposition parties too, the Smallholders and the Social Democrats. Battle had been joined for the new power, because even then it was apparent that a struggle between the Hungarian parties was going to break out.

In Tövispuszta Isti was sitting on the bench outside the house when a black car stopped on the dirt road. A man in a suit alighted from the rear seat, came forward past the communal baking oven and made his way self-confidently towards the house as if he knew where he was going. The old women sitting on the benches outside their houses, like crows in a field, watched him stop in front of Isti Veres.

After greeting Isti the man asked if they might go into the kitchen as he wished to speak confidentially.

He introduced himself as Lieutenant Markó from county police headquarters, and after expressing in a few words his pleasure at meeting Isti personally – he'd been a fan of his – he quickly came to the point: he asked him if he would like to join the police.

"A disabled policeman?" asked Isti scornfully, pointing at his leg.

"We won't call you a stormtrooper," the officer tried to fend off the awkward situation. "There are a lot of things that can be done perfectly well even with a bad leg."

"Such as?" asked Isti.

"Look here, I'll speak frankly. The country's in total chaos, in the towns people are being robbed in the streets, we're trying to clear away the dead, the carrion and the Arrow-Cross posters, but as we do so the Russians are driving the police out of the barracks and the police stations. There are now three thousand officers and other ranks in a prison camp in Gödöllő. To take their places we're getting droves of Jews who've survived the death-camps or forced labour and are thirsty for revenge. What we need is recruits from the peasantry. Especially people who've completed their schooling, like you. The communists are trying to take over the entire police force. After what the Arrow-Cross did to you, nobody will have any doubt which side you're on and they'll have confidence in you, although you're neither a Jew nor a communist."

Isti made his mind up fast, and after that advanced quickly in the police force. After a few weeks training he was posted to the department charged with tracking down Arrow-Cross and other criminals, and a few weeks later was working in Budapest, at 60 Andrássy út, the Political Security Section of the State Police. One might sat that in basing the communist political police in the former Arrow-Cross headquarters, the instruments of oppression had displayed a rare continuity of taste.

Isti had been to Budapest only twice before the war, and now looked in amazement at the destruction wrought on the city, the houses disembowelled, the spines of their roofs broken, and the bridges which hung, crippled and wrecked, into the Danube; it was as if he saw his own deformed leg everywhere. But life sprouted in the broken body of the city, like wild flowers and weeds on untended graves; determined people were clearing up the rubble, Russian cavalry horses ate hay from a deserted piano in the road, and here and there in gateways and on the pavement, things were on sale that hadn't been seen for a long time: pork and veal, real English tea, Swiss chocolate, perfumes, women's stockings and material for clothes. "The Hungarian can't be crushed!" thought Isti proudly; he was also inspired by the declaration of the Provisional National Assembly, which, alluding to the heroes of the Hungarian struggles for freedom,[38] proclaimed itself the repository of the 'national will' and 'Hungarian self-determination'. In the Provisional National Government, in addition to the anti-Nazi Horthyist general, Prime Minister Miklós Béla Dálnoki,[39] two other generals and Count Géza Teleki held office, and along with the communists, the Smallholders and the Social Democrats were represented too. "That was a considerable exaggeration, what Lieutenant Markó said about the communists seizing power," Isti assured himself.

The first thing that made him stop and think was a remark from his superior, Major Vári, who simply gestured deprecatingly when the declaration of the National Assembly was mentioned: "No need to take that nationalist drivel seriously!"

Seeing Isti's startled expression, he went on "I shouldn't think the Soviet comrades would think much of the jingoist outpourings of a hostile country".

Isti didn't really understand what was supposed to be jingoist about the struggles against the Habsburgs, as the left and right of the country celebrated 15 March as the glorious day of national independence, and he too put on his cockade every year. But he respected Major Vári: he obviously knew what he was saying as he'd lived for years in the Soviet Union and was now a frequent visitor to General Belkin[40] in Vilma Királynő út, from where the Soviet State Security general directed the chiefs of the Hungarian police.

"Just think, Comrade Veres! Who can national independence slogans now be against?"

Vári was a hard and embittered man. He'd fought against the Germans as commander of a partisan unit, and after the war discovered that everyone in his family had been deported to a death-camp.

"Next thing it'll be the Fascists' turn to play the Jews!" he repeated sourly to Isti, but to tell the truth he also deplored the Jews. "Just went to their deaths like cattle," he said of them.

Only a matter of months after making the Arrow-Cross parade their victims in Tövispuszta, Isti ran into Pertli in the corridor at 60 Andrássy út. He looked at him as if he were seeing a ghost. If he hadn't witnessed him being arrested with his own eyes, he'd have believed that the little man had stayed in the building since Arrow-Cross times, hiding in a deserted corner or in a corridor where no one had been since then.

The Telegram

"Hello, Veres!" said Frédi Müller with a grin. "We've become colleagues,"

Isti didn't reply, strode on furiously up the corridor and went to see Major Vári.

"Comrade Major, with your permission. Is it possible, comrade, that a former Arrow-Cross man from my village, Alfred Müller, is working for the political police?" he asked, beside himself with rage.

"Why shouldn't it be possible?" said Vári.

"But the man's a murderer!"

"He didn't murder, he only reported. On that basis we could have half of Hungary arrested. Müller isn't on the staff, he does nothing but what he did before: reports. And don't forget, Müller was also around in 1919, an organiser of peasant demonstrations under the Soviet Republic. He just managed to survive the White Terror, unlike Veszelka and Kodelka. You ought to know much better than this! Yes, later he went wrong. But we need these lesser Arrow-Cross men. Don't worry, we've got them by the balls."

Isti stared uncomprehendingly at Major Vári.

"And what's the score for someone who used to applaud at Arrow-Cross meetings with his fellow football team members, whose father-in-law's an Arrow-Cross man, Comrade Veres? We know all sorts of things, you see, that don't occur to you."

Isti opened his eyes in surprise. And he stayed like that for years.

The Relocation Notice

Baroness Pál Szentágostony, or now more correctly Mrs. Pál Szentágostony, stood beside the meadow and looked at the goods train as it clattered on the horizon. Goodness, she thought, what has been made of the triumphant invention of the nineteenth century? For years it has been made to carry replacements for the dead to the front or the death-camps, and now people stripped of their homes are swapped to and fro on it by victorious powers, across frontiers drawn to suit themselves, as if they weren't even living beings but chattels: Hungarians are carried from Upper Hungary and back go Slovaks to Czechoslovakia, Swabians to Germany and so on. The cattle trucks come and go with weeping, waving people in them who've been torn from their native lands, from the graves of their ancestors, from their friends and neighbours, and on the outside of the trucks big letters announce "Farewell, my beloved country!"

Emília hadn't felt self-pity for a long time now, had tried, if not to take things lightly, at least to accept them and in this her native wisdom and wry sense of humour helped her. The baronial title had gone, with the re-allocation of land so had the estate, the mansion had been taken from them, her parents' factory and apartment houses; 'easy come, easy go', she thought acrimoniously, like a gambler inured to success and failure. 'Never mind; at least we're alive, and these days not everyone can say as much.' Not only had the estate been divided into five-acre holdings, but Szentágoston too had ceased to be. The county authorities had classed the name of the village as a clerical remnant, and first wanted to reduce it to just Ágoston, but although the idea seemed ideologically attractive, in the end, on the recommendation of the Party committee, the two neighbouring villages were rather united under the name of Tövispuszta, which better expressed the taste of the agrarian proletariat and sounded more 'people's democratic'.

"Tomorrow perhaps the whole country will be a Tövispuszta," said Pál Szentágostony, pulling a disdainful face.

The Baron had endured the tribulations far less well than his wife. He'd collapsed spiritually when Hungary entered the war and since then his health had deteriorated steadily. From the first day he'd been sure that the Germans would be defeated, but he also hated the Russians; with his ingrained opposition to both Germans and Soviets he could place no hope in either Hitler or Stalin and, unlike Pál, he hadn't expected the western allies to reach Hungary in the course of operations. When, however, it turned out that the allies had landed in Normandy instead of the Balkans, the Baron lost all hope.

"If the Germans invade, there'll be Nazism here, and if the Russians do, then we'll have communism. One thing's for sure, we can only come off badly," he'd said to Pál, whose view was, on the contrary, that against Hitler they should join forces with the devil himself. After winning the war they would have time to decide what to do about the Generalissimo. The influence of the anti-Nazi alliance would even enable the two social orders to come closer together, he thought, as he believed that the western democracies would have something to learn from the societal struggles of the Soviet Union.

"The allies are playing for time, they want to bleed the Russians to death," the Baron countered. "But they don't know that an empire founded on autocracy can't be bled to death, because there human life has no value; for every army that's destroyed, two more come forward, and if anyone dare open his mouth, he's shot. It doesn't even interest Stalin that half the country's starving because of the war economy. By the time the allies wake up the Russians will be parading in Berlin."

Acting as liaison between the Regent and the Soviets, Pál also secretly went to Moscow in order, with the help of some of his father's former fellow officers who were loyal to Horthy, to pave the way for Hungary to withdraw from hostilities. The old Baron, however, had no faith in a separate peace. "It's too late now," said he bitterly, "that should have been thought of earlier." Pál met Horthy junior on the morning that the Gestapo trapped and kidnapped him in order to put pressure on his father to appoint Szálasi. When he heard on the radio that power had been handed over to the Arrow-Cross, Pál leapt into the car and didn't stop before reaching Switzerland. 'My father was right again,' he thought. Whether it was his military expertise or his pessimism that helped the Baron to assess the situation clearly remains uncertain; indeed, at times tragedy does follow pessimism, as it can also fuel persecution mania, and then after the event earlier, fears of disaster are called wise foresight.

Pál and Sári's correspondence broke off as early as 1941, when the Germans occupied the French capital. Pál went to Paris to look for her, but found the flat behind the Odéon shut up, and the neighbours couldn't tell him anything about the Réders. In the bistros and coffee-houses which he and his friends had previously frequented there were now rowdy German soldiers; he went round the district but found no trace of them. Later on Sanyi wrote and told him that at the time of the occupation he'd been working in the south, in the studio in Nice, and so had escaped, but the others had been trapped in Paris. The Germans had deported Sári, Emma and Tamás, while Imre and Géza had joined the maquis, the French resistance. Later, Pál took part as an interpreter with the British forces in the liberation of the death-camp at Bergen-Belsen, and to the last hoped that he might find Sári among the prisoners, though he didn't even know to which camp she'd been sent. He looked in horror at the mounds of half-decayed corpses and the skeletal, typhus-riddled survivors. He found to his alarm that disgust overcame his sympathy. He struggled against nausea, but his breath came in tiny, broken gasps, he couldn't control himself, retched, bent double and vomited. He looked round in embarrassment in case he'd been seen, but there were only a few young soldiers near him; they were in a state of shock at the sight of the mounds of corpses and the living dead, and had been looking fixedly ahead.

Pál didn't find Sári. At the corner of one building, however, a girl stopped in front of him. She was shrunken to the bone, her head shaven.

"Do you recognise me, sir?" she asked very quietly.

In alarm, Pál searched the familiar grey-green eyes.

"Elza Goldstein?" he asked hesitantly. The girl stood there, her face yellow, motionless as a corpse buried upright. And she didn't move even when Pál shuddered and took her in his arms.

He entrusted Elza to the medics, making a careful note of where survivors were being sent. He gave her his address in

England and promised to come and see her when the chance arose. As he was attending to Elza, Sári came into his mind: where could she have got to, was she in a similar state – if indeed she was still alive? Peasants trooped past him with a military escort. On the orders of the British commander, inhabitants of the nearby villages were being shown round the concentration camp so that they should see what had been going on in their neighbourhood. Men and women with terrified eyes, who could only repeat "We didn't know about this! We aren't to blame!"

Three months later Pál was back living in London, and from there he went to visit Elza in a small Dutch town where a number of former prisoners were being cared for in the hospital. The medical director was well aware that Elza was one of the few lucky ones, because only one in four surviving prisoners recovered. The rest were in such poor physical condition that they died in hospital after being liberated. Elza had been cured of typhus but was thin and weak; she devoured the chocolate that Pál brought her without a word, and allowed him affectionately to stroke her hair, which had grown to stubble during the three months.

"Do you know, even now you're beautiful?" said Pál hesitantly.

"I think so," said Elza with a weary smile. "They say that typhus makes you beautiful."

"What are the doctors saying, when will you be able to go home?"

"I've written to Dávid, I wouldn't like to go straight home. I won't be able to face people there. And I still can't talk about what's happened."

Pál suggested to Elza that once she was out of hospital she should come and stay with him in London to recover her strength. He gave her news from home, how the Smallholders' Party had swept the board in the elections. His pleasure, however, didn't last long. When he returned to England, Professor Toynbee, who was a principal adviser to the western allies, tempered his enthusiasm. He made it clear to him that at the Yalta Conference the Americans, British and French had abandoned Hungary to the Soviets, and it was to be expected that at the peace negotiations in Paris the country would be forced back within the Trianon frontiers. Pál tried in vain to persuade the professor to intercede so that at least Hungarian territory should be extended along ethnic lines. Toynbee merely repeated that the decision would be in Soviet hands and the balance of power could no longer be changed. He advised his pupil to move to London, there would be a guaranteed place with him at the Foreign Institute, but Pál preferred to take the post of First Secretary at the Hungarian Embassy, which he'd been offered by the Foreign Ministry in Budapest. He thought that he could be of much more assistance to Hungary as a diplomat and would become an important link in the chain of relationships binding the country to the western democracies.

Elza had been discharged six months previously from the sanatorium where she'd been sent after her hospital treatment. Pál went to fetch her back to London by train. She was waiting for him in the sanatorium lobby, ready to leave. Pál took both her hands as if they were dancing, and smiled at her.

"I'm getting all mixed up, Elza. Until now I've thought of you as a girl, but now I can see you're a woman."

"If you could see inside me, you'd also know that I'm an old woman."

"An old woman of eighteen?"

"Nobody's as old as their date of birth indicates. Over the last two years I've aged as much as others do in fifty."

"Know what? If you're that old you can call me *te*,"[41] said Pál with a laugh, and kissed her on the cheek.

Physically, Elza was on the road to recovery. She was no longer thin but slender, the short hair suited her, as did the dress that Pál had brought for her to travel in. But she couldn't laugh yet.

Gradually Pál accepted the fact that he'd finally lost Sári, and lived comfortably with Elza in the little flat near Covent Garden. He treated her as a younger sister, they shopped and cooked together, he taught her English, they talked about what they read, went to the cinema, to concerts and restaurants. They themselves hardly noticed their relationship deepening. It wasn't the mutually rending, tempestuous love that he'd had for Sári; everything happened as naturally as if it couldn't be otherwise, as the seasons change or night follows day. Pál hadn't forgiven himself for not daring to oppose his parents when he'd wanted to marry Sári. This time, he decided he would have his own way and not even ask Elza about marriage. There was a little church in the next street, Pál arranged with the priest to join them in matrimony, completed the formalities and asked a couple of his old university friends to act as witnesses. On the day of the wedding he produced a package from behind the cupboard and gave it to Elza.

"Put it on, if you like it," he said.

Elza laughed and undid the package.

"Is this a wedding dress?"

"I'm marrying you," said Pál.

"Right," said Elza, as if nothing could be more natural.

"No surprise, no sobbing, no tearful rage?" asked Pál, a little offended.

Elza flung her arms round his neck and kissed him on the lips, long and passionately, then turned her head to one side and wiped a tear from the corner of her eye.

"Well, here you are then!" said Pál with feigned severity, then took a diamond ring from his pocket and put it on Elza's finger.

There was a special atmosphere in the church, enhanced by its situation in the middle of the city. It was as if a little village chapel with no side-aisles had squeezed in between the houses. It was simple and intimate. Vine tendrils ran up onto the altar and their leaves gleamed in the sunlight that streamed in through the lead-framed windows; the face of Christ that looked down on the quiet ceremony from the crucifix above the altar wasn't agonised but gentle and compassionate. The elderly priest spoke unaffectedly, in a natural voice, as if he were their father: something about people committing so much sin against one another during the war that even Christ buckled under the weight, and yet here were young people such as these two being joined together here in the sight of God. But Elza and Pál had eyes only for one another.

"Remember years ago, when you rode through Tövispuszta with your father and János?" asked Elza after the wedding. "I was still a young girl, and I happened to come out of the shop. You told me to say hello to Dávid and Andor, and I blushed and shot back inside."

"I remember, clearly," said Pál.

"The reason I blushed at the time was that this picture flashed before my eyes. Me standing in front of this altar and becoming your wife."

War criminals were brought before the people's court and hanged, while Arrow-Cross men, gendarmes, and other known extreme right-wing public figures vanished. According to local sources the Russians had removed them to Siberia, among them lawyer Sárády, who had unsparingly placed his professional expertise at the service of the gendarmerie when the Jews were being rounded up and deported.

"The railway trucks came into Hungary with returning prisoners of war, the Russians are thrifty people and wanted to make use of the capacity to send things back," said János maliciously.

In 1947 the Communist Party activists voted so strenuously that not only did they put voting papers in the ballot box like other electors, but by the kindness of the Interior Ministry, directed by the Communist Party, received voting papers or 'blue chits' by the thousand, and so were able to vote in more than one constituency. The Party, prepared to go to any lengths, took them to different parts of the country in well-organised lorry-loads, and the outcome of this unrelenting effort was the communists' huge majority in Parliament. The victorious party wasn't idle for long and tried hard to make wise use of the power that it had gained, and so Pál in the London embassy received a series of communiqués concerning the dismissal from public office in Hungary of politicians and anti-German army officers who, in the preceding political era, had been considered honourable, whom everyone had believed to be resolute and honest supporters of the national army.

When the rustling of the iron curtain that was poised to fall became audible János Szentágostony suggested to his parents that they should slip out under it. "Anyone with any sense is going," he said, but the old Baron replied "You can't transplant an old tree," and he certainly wasn't going, the communists could instead. The communists, however, had no intention of going as they had only just arrived, and János wasn't prepared to leave the country without the old people. "He that is not a believer in socialism is an enemy of the people," was the ideological principle proclaimed by László Rajk [42], and then, scarcely two years later, his own comrades demonstrated that he that did believe in socialism actually was the enemy of the people. First the Foreign Minister and then General Pálffy were arrested, after which, a few months later, Pál was ordered home from London. His friends advised him not to even think of going back. Elza begged him as well, but he replied that it would be cowardly to run away when his parents and brother were still there, and in any case he'd nothing to fear. He was mistaken. On arrival, he was informed in the Ministry that he was suspended from his position, and he was requested not to leave Budapest until a decision had been taken about his future. He and Elza spent four months in uncertainty in Kresz Géza utca, during which time Rajk and Pálffy were both executed. When the radio announced that the death sentences had been carried out János happened to be at Pál and Elza's. Scornfully he exclaimed:

"Our beloved Comrade Rákosi [43] knows that there is need of an opposition. Now that the genuine opposition has been annihilated they're taking on the noble task themselves with legendary communist self-sacrifice, and hanging one another."

"I'm afraid this is only the beginning," said Pál gloomily.

One January dawn men in leather coats came to Kresz Géza utca for Pál and Elza, and arrested them both. Henrik Goldstein, who, having two weeks previously lost the workshop again – this time because it was nationalised – was becoming senile with alarming rapidity and was tottering around in the hall at the time. "Are they here again?" he asked. "Who, darling?" asked Anci, his wife, in tears. " The Arrow-Cross, of course," said Henrik. "Old fool!"

gestured one of the ÁVH men, who had heard him. "János was right, we should have got out, and Pál ought not to have been allowed back," lamented Baron Pál. "He's gone to prison because of my obstinacy," he said, bursting into tears. Emília and János looked at the old man aghast; they had never seen him weep. "Excuse me, it looks as if I'm getting old," and he wiped his eyes, like a child caught in the act.

The ÁVH[44] interrogators didn't know what to make of Pál. Without exception, other arrestees denied having worked for western news-gathering organisations, whereas Pál openly acknowledged that during the war he'd had close links to the Intelligence Service. He explained patiently to his interrogators how the western allies and the Soviets had worked together against Hitler, and what tasks he'd performed personally in revealing the Hungarian war plans, and how he'd tried to help the Regent in his attempt to extricate Hungary from the war.

"Don't tell me, I wasn't born yesterday!" the interrogating officer – a former gentlemen's tailor – screamed, affronted.

Pál answered the questions with an unconcerned expression. He made no attempt to deny that after the war, when working as a diplomat in the London embassy, he'd thought it important for Hungary to continue to maintain good relationships with the parliamentary democracies of the West. "If that's a crime," said Pál, "I admit it."

"You do?" asked the interrogating officer scornfully. "If you're lucky, you'll get off with fifteen years."

Pál found himself sharing a cell with a former army officer.

The Relocation Notice

"Do you recognise me, Baron?" the stocky, moustachioed man asked Pál when he stepped into the cell. He introduced himself as Lieutenant-colonel Lóránt Bánoss.

"Give me a hint, please, where did we meet?"

"Lieutenant Sárády brought you to the club before the war, that was where."

Pál examined the man's face for a moment, then suddenly remembered him: the moustachioed staff-captain of Csaba's acquaintance.

"I remember," said Pál. "You all tried to persuade me of the wonderful prospects for Germany and Hungary in the war. Looks as if you were wrong."

"We wanted to avoid what's happened. The Russian occupation. We hadn't reckoned on the western powers preferring the oriental communist hordes as an ally rather than the Führer," said the colonel, looking at their third cellmate.

This was a former ÁVH major, László Vári, the most stubborn and embittered of the three. Whereas Bánoss openly confessed to being opposed to the Stalinist regime and Pál too understood exactly why the communist leadership felt that his values were dangerous, Vári found it hard to explain why his former colleagues were beating him half to death – him, who considered himself a dyed-in-the-wool communist. He was regularly taken off for interrogation, sometimes for days on end, and returned with marks of beating and torture on his face and body.

Bánoss found consolation in the Bible. If his doubts assailed him, as was often the case, he would open the Bible or St Thomas à Kempis' work *Imitatio Christi,* and find the answers to his problems one after another. Pál looked on with envy.

"Give it a try," said Bánoss, "it'll help you as well."

"I'm afraid the answers to my problems are in other books," said Pál with a smile.

"Try, anyway, I'd like to know where you open it."

Pál picked up the New Testament. He found chapter ten of the Gospel according to St Matthew and began to read. 'Think not that I am come to send peace on earth: I came not to send peace but a sword. For I am come to set a man at variance against his father, and the daughter against her mother, and the daughter-in-law against her mother-in-law. And a man's foes shall be they of his own household. He that loveth father or mother more than me is not worthy of me: and he that loveth son or daughter more than me is not worthy of me.' Pál closed the book.

"The communists could have written that as well, don't you think, Vári?" He turned to the major. "God is important to me, but I can't accept any idea that requires me to love Him more than my parents or children."

"It's not a question of an idea, Pál!" Bánoss retorted, "but of Christ and faith!"

"Anyone that lacks faith and passion won't be able to understand these sentences either," said Vári, lying back on his bed, looking up at the wires under the bunk above. "But what matters is, is life worth living without faith and passion?" he added, still not looking at the others.

"We're looking good, Pál," the colonel laughed. "An ÁVH thug teaching us the Christian faith!"

"Not Christian, just faith," Vári was more specific.

"I'll tell you something," Bánoss turned to Pál. "I was visiting an architect friend of mine, a practising Christian, in Rome. He took us up to the top of several Renaissance buildings and pointed out what was behind their facades. And do you know what's there?"

"What?"

The Relocation Notice

"Nothing, my friend! The Gothic period, the Middle Ages, built the entire building because they believed in God, they knew that God could see everything and behind everything. Since the Renaissance, Man has only believed in himself, the external has been the only aspect to interest him. Man has turned from God, and look at the state we're in!"

"I think the trouble started not when Man turned from God, but when Man turned from Man. Because then God turned from him as well."

Bánoss and Vári shook their heads.

Pál had no liking for Vári, but when, following a torture session, the major was dumped back into the cell like a sack of rubbish, he couldn't help taking care of him, bathing the raw, exposed flesh where nails had been torn off, trying to keep his spirits up with words of encouragement.

Bánoss had no sympathy for Vári.

"He had it coming," he said to Pál.

"Is that a former staff officer speaking, or the Christian love of a man that has found Christ?" asked Pál with undisguised irony.

"I'll decide who I love in Christian fashion and who not," answered Bánoss.

Vári was tortured until he broke and signed everything that he was asked to. He was convicted according to regulations, got eight years for espionage, and seemed to be content with that.

"Now you can tell us what you did," Bánoss turned to him, when the major returned to prison from the hearing.

"Nothing," replied Vári.

"That's impossible," said the colonel with a scornful smile, "for 'nothing' your friends are only given five years."

As the months went by Pál felt that his situation was less and less hopeful. At first his reliance on being right

169

still sustained him. He had confidence in his intellectual superiority, felt that he was capable of finding rational explanations for the political situation and the *status quo* in general. When, however, it dawned on him that there had been no rational ground for a long time he lost confidence. He'd never known what to do about moods and hatred, thought them irrational and couldn't deal with them. "If eventually there were to be a court verdict, at least I'd know where I stood," he thought. But no verdict was forthcoming, because neither the Hungarian nor the Soviet organs of State Security would have liked Pál to refer in court to the British and Soviet collaboration in intelligence-gathering, and in particular to certain less-well-known details of the former Soviet-German agreement. They were reluctant to execute him, because they knew that Stalin had prevented even Horthy from appearing before a court because he'd approved of the attempt to withdraw from the war. But they excluded Pál from the world. He didn't even receive news of his family. He was worried about Elza, what could be happening to her, had she been able to have the child, and if so where? Then he calculated how old the child must be, tried to imagine what it must look like, which of them did it take after? He hoped that the secret police would be satisfied with having arrested him and wouldn't disturb his family. And at the same time he secretly envied Vári and Bánossy: faith sustained their strength.

Early one morning in June 1951 officials in the dark-blue hats of the State Security Authority arrived at the Szentágostony mansion with the order for relocation.

"Does Baron Pál Szentágostony live here?" asked a

fleshy-faced lieutenant of Jani the footman, at the door of the mansion. He was on the point of answering when a sleepy-eyed János did so first.

"The Comrade is indeed very attentive, but we no longer use the title as it has been banned," he said politely.

The officer was nonplussed and for a moment examined János' innocent face without speaking; he was unsure whether he was making fun of him or being serious.

"Who are you?" he then asked, as if in cross-examination.

"I'm his son, Dr. János Szentágostony."

"Doctor?" asked the lieutenant.

"I can still say that, can't I? I'm a doctor of medicine," said János lightly, in an apologetic tone.

"You're going to put your foot in it one day with your scornful remarks," Emília told him after the ÁVH had left. "These people have no sense of humour! Think of Pál!"

Eighteen months has passed since Pál had been arrested. There had been no court case, nor had there been any news of him. Asking Isti to look for him had been futile; he'd replied that it wasn't his department and he dared not show an interest for fear of arousing suspicion. At the time, the family was living in just four rooms in the mansion, and the entire ground floor had been taken over by the collective farm and the district Party office. In the other upstairs rooms Emília had put white covers on the furniture – such as remained and hadn't been commandeered into the offices or simply dispersed, as was the polite term for 'looted'; she'd done the same in the old days, when they went to Tuscany or Abbazia for the summer. The shutters had been pulled to on the windows. The staff had been dismissed long ago, and only Lenke had stayed with them as housekeeper, chambermaid and cleaner, and her husband Jani (the Baron's batman in his army days) as footman, concierge, gardener and driver.

He, like a quick-change artist, changed his clothes three or four times a day as his various roles required, because although Emília never stood on ceremony the Baron insisted on outward appearances. "If we give that up too, what will be left?" he asked.

The Szentágostonys knew what awaited them: one by one, reports had reached them of internments and relocations. Emília's parents had been sent to the Hortobágy.[45] Some of the aristocrats and upper middle-class people who were stripped of their property and homes, especially the more elderly, had no clear idea of what was happening to them. Why were they enemies of the people? Emília struggled with tears and laughter at the same time when she heard that Count Manó Csáky had asked the ÁVH officer to allow him to go to his designated place of relocation by taxi because he had a phobia of crowds on trains, and that as she packed, Countess Andrássy had pondered over which dresses to take to wear to afternoon teas. Baroness Kohner was obviously being sarcastic when she asked the officer with the blue collar-tabs in which category she was being relocated: as an aristocrat or as a Jew? The Szentágostonys, however, could guess the future from more than news coming through friends and relations; some weeks before, Lucky Gizi had been up to the mansion to take Emília a plate of freshly baked cinnamon and apple strudel and had told her that Isti had been home and had charged her in great secrecy to warn the Szentágostonys to get ready, they were going to be relocated. All the help he could give was that if they wanted to, they would be relocated in Tövispuszta.

When the fleshy-faced lieutenant handed them the relocation order and informed them that they had twenty-four hours, repeat: twenty-four hours, for packing, Emília had in effect already packed everything. The old Baron wasn't capable of lending a hand, but said that Emília should do as she thought fit, he wouldn't like to attend his own wake. He shut himself away and while the packing took place lay silent on his bed in the darkened room. Officially they were allowed to take five *mázsa* [46] with them, but what Emília managed to select came to no more than three chests-full and a few favourite pieces of furniture. She spent days packing and sorting old letters and documents so that they shouldn't fall into the wrong hands. The fire blazed on the hearth and she sat in front of it surrounded by huge heaps of paper; the red light danced on her face, and the crackling tongues of flame, like hounds panting in anticipation of their reward, seized eagerly upon each new tit-bit of paper. Only when her diary came to hand did she show uncertainty. She turned the pages, read here and there, and couldn't bring herself to throw it in the fire. "A faithful account of this time must be left for our sons, if the truth is to be written one day," she murmured to herself. As she sorted and packed, long forgotten objects and documents emerged. "Things that have disappeared are always so mysterious," she thought, "they've been lying there somewhere, just not to be found. When we come across them we could swear that we've looked for them there, but it seems that they're temporarily swallowed up... It's as if, when they're being looked for, someone hides them in a great, public lost property office where the shelves are full of forgotten names, dates and stories." Together with the rediscovered letters and documents, the old family stories also emerged; Emília was burning the Szentágostony family's past. Objects had somehow lost their significance. She remembered the tale told in the village of how, when the Arrow-Cross were taking the Steiners from the mill to a ghetto, one of the grandchildren began to gather up the family porcelain and the hanukkah candlestick, but her grandmother told her: "Those are no longer of any interest."

173

"Not of interest?" asked the little girl. "What about the family photograph album, the seder-plate, grandfather's favourite chiming clock on the wall?" "Nor those," said grandmother. If the family's private treasures, the past and everything that had hitherto been important were no longer of interest, then the trouble must be very great, thought the little girl, and began to shed bitter tears. This story came into Emília's mind as she looked at their chests, and the bedclothes wrapped up in a sheet. The Steiners didn't make it back from the death-camp, she said then, into the air in front of her. It seems that there always has to be someone to be hated.

The Szentágostonys found themselves on the outskirts of Tövispuszta in a single-storey, wood-beamed outhouse with a room and a kitchen on the property of a *kulak*[47]. Emília let her husband have the room, although she officially lived in it too, and spent most of her time in the kitchen, which would have been János' place. The Kallós family wasn't officially reckoned kulak as they owned only fifteen *hold*[48], but in the village they were considered to be among the rich and so were saddled with the Baron's family. "Little village, little kulak," commented János. Mrs. Sárády, her two daughters and grandson had by then been living for almost a year in cramped quarters – in the Hetésis' former summer kitchen and their back room overlooking the chicken-run. As Hetési had been hanged for the murders and Dr. Sárády was either in prison or Siberia – no reliable information had been received – there was room for them all in the two-room peasant house. Their relationship was understandably not free of tension, as Eni's former husband Isti was an ÁVH officer and had earlier been crippled by Hetési, who in turn had been made

174

by Isti to carry the murdered Goldsteins through the village, shortly after which the People's Court had sentenced him and Székely to death and they had been executed. Now they were living together there, sharing kitchen and lavatory. Lucky Gizi suggested to Eni that she and Pityu move to their house, but Eni felt that she couldn't let her mother and Csenge down. Therefore Gizi visited her grandson regularly and took them what she could – fruit, vegetables and poultry, though the Vereses had little enough themselves.

A few days after the Szentágostonys, the other dispossessed and relocated persons arrived, and the villagers peered from behind their curtains, just as they had a few years before when the Jews were being deported, at the 'kings, princes, counts, idle rich and bourgeois'[49] moved into Tövispuszta. There were families whose members were brought by train from Budapest or the county town and then transported by peasant cart to their designated places; others arrived, sitting on their furniture in the backs of ÁVH lorries. Most of them had been utterly unable to think what it was worth bringing with them. Countess Zichy arrived with a voluminous cabin-trunk full of silk dresses, lace underwear and high-heeled shoes, cherished mementoes of her youth from which she couldn't bear to be parted. In the stable where she was lodged she slept on the trunk, her feet resting on a stool. Old General Kárpáthy had been dragged out of his sick-bed, couldn't walk, and on the train had had to be given injections to enable him to stand the journey.

In the round-dance, as formerly in Aunt Manci's dancing school, everybody had moved on at the word of command. This time to the left. After the war a number of peasant families quickly moved from their longhouses into the Steiners' mill and the Goldsteins' shop so as to grab the homes of the deported Jews. The enemies of the people were moved into the farm servants' quarters, the deserted longhouses and the outhouses of the Tövispuszta farmsteads: the new functionaries of Party and State settled in the villas of dispossessed counts, factory-owners and generals. Mansions became children's homes and workers' *sanatoria*.[50] The Szentágostony mansion too was given a more equitable, nobler role than the former: the rooms became the offices of the Aranykalász ('Golden Sheaf') collective farm and the regional Party organisation, while the library and dining-room became the collective farm granary.

In Tövispuszta the peasant children vied with one another over what sort of family had gone to whom.

"We've got a count!" boasted Laci Veréb.

"We've got a princess!" replied Mari Bódis.

"Princesses are only in fairy-tales!" retorted Vince Lázár.

"Yes we have, we've got a princess, a Russian princess," insisted Mari.

"Russian? The Russians are communists! A communist princess? Come off it!" and Vince made a dismissive gesture.

Emília found her husband harder and harder to tolerate. Old age is like the importunate caricaturist who, in inferior coffee-houses, tries to persuade his victims to have a cartoon portrait drawn. He won't just exaggerate their features, so that anyone with a big nose or ears will have them even bigger, but also their characteristics. The failing brain-cells devour the upbringing, culture and social inhibitions which, over the years, have been studiously built into a personality, and the old person stands there half naked: if his basic nature is philanthropic, by the time that he's old he becomes tolerant and just, but if, on the contrary, it's resentful and headstrong, he becomes like the ageing Pál Szentágostony. The older he became, the more intolerant he was, or perhaps he was rather less prepared to appear tolerant. He wandered aimlessly round the house and garden, at times striking telling blows with his stick at anyone that crossed his path, and especially at those that tried to help him. Externally it seemed as if he was angry with others, but in reality he was angry with himself because he, colonel and landowner held of old in respectful awe, was now reduced by his body and circumstances to helplessness. He did all that he could to torment his wife. At first Emília tried, if only for the Baron's sake, for them to lead as normal a life as possible under the circumstances. With the few bits of old furniture that had been brought with them she charmed the outhouse into a welcoming place, tidied up the yard at the back, used a tree-stump and a mill-stone to contrive an attractive little table at which they could sit and talk in the shade of the walnut, and with the help of Lucky Gizi, who never forgot that the Baron's family had helped Isti in the past, she even planted a little flower and vegetable garden along the fence. In order to lift her husband out of his grinding thoughts she decided to invite round a relocated couple or two with whom he would have something in common, because he wasn't inclined to leave the house.

It was a sunny afternoon in late September. The guests arrived, having smartened themselves up in memory of former times, as was the done thing when calling on others, even if the menu would be garlic bread toasted on the kitchen fire and tea. Everyone put on the best that they had brought with them, but when Emília looked for her husband and called out to him, he was nowhere to be found. She was annoyed, but decided that he would appear if he chose to. They sat under the walnut at the mill-stone table, on which there were flowers and a pot of raspberry syrup, and talked, crunched

177

the toast, and sipped the Russian tea with blueberry jam.

"The important thing is for one to maintain one's dignity, come what may," said Mrs. Miklós, wife of a wealthy lawyer. The rest nodded in agreement.

"I was in the field this afternoon as the cows were being driven in, and as one got up from where it had been lying I looked at how the grass had been crushed under it," Emília said. "Then, after a while, the flattened stems began slowly to move, came to, and gradually straightened up. And I thought, that's how we shall be. If this new regime tramples on us, certainly for a while we shall be downtrodden, but then we shall come to and straighten up."

The others laughed, they liked the simile.

And then, from behind the lavatory in the garden, appeared retired colonel Baron Pál Szentágostony – stark naked. The women screamed, and clapped their hands to their eyes, while the men gasped audibly in astonishment. With a disdainful smile on his face the Baron raised his arms and, none too steady on his feet, began to dance; his once muscular body was the colour of parchment, the sinews hung limp on his drooping chest, his pubic hair was white and in the weird St Vitus dance he shook his shrunken penis, so further abasing himself in humiliation. Emília jumped up and fled, sobbing, while the guests excused themselves and, pale, helped each other homewards. The Baron, with his accustomed courtesy, waved them goodbye.

Emília was so ashamed that she never again invited guests, nor did she accept invitations. The others reassured her in vain that it wasn't surprising if the Baron had become deranged, in fact the surprising thing was rather that anyone did remain sane in that mad world. János no longer lived in Tövispuszta, as he'd obtained a position as doctor and a flat that went with it in neighbouring Bátakér, and he too did his best to reassure his mother: "When cerebrosclerosis is combined with psychic trauma strange things can happen," he said, and advised her to treat the old man simply as a sick person, affectionately.

That, however, was easier said than done. After the painful incident Emília avoided company, but she didn't stay in the house, preferring to sit on the cracked, leaden tongue of mud by the narrow brook. On the far side spiny tendrils wound around the willows and poplars as if the thorns intended slowly to suppress, to overwhelm everything. The village lads watered their horses in the shallow, muddy stream, and Emília even washed and bathed there wearing a costume which she had made herself for the purpose from thick, black underwear and a short skirt.

Emília took up the rhythm of village life so that she shouldn't become deranged like her husband. She was up at dawn, helped the household and took the fresh milk to the collection-point for the Kallóses.

"Really, how can a baroness do such a thing?" Mrs. Kallós objected at first, but when they saw that Emília was serious they left her to it. When she came back in she would make breakfast for her husband and herself on a little spirit stove – fried bread, lightly done toast and tea – wash herself and the Baron in a basin, then drive out the Kallóses' three cows to the field and tether them, driving sharp stakes into the earth with a heavy hammer and chaining the cattle to them so that they shouldn't stray. After that she would do some hoeing in the garden and pick some vegetables. Most of all she liked to talk to Lucky Gizi: after living with István Veres she'd had many years of experience in the sphere of intolerable husbands, and gave Emília wise and gentle advice.

Under the peasant woman's guidance Emília began to appreciate some quite surprising things. Previously, for instance, although she'd really enjoyed chicken, especially in the form of fried legs, she'd hated the birds themselves: they were noisy, dirty, woke one up with their crowing and cackling and covered the yard with their feathers and excrement. While she lived in the mansion she'd mostly seen animals at a distance, and close to only when they were quiet, tidy and tastily served up on plates. One day Gizi gave her two tiny, fluffy, bright-eyed, day-old chicks.

"Just look at them, they're hardly out of the shell, but you can tell what they'll be like, same as with people. This one," she picked one of them up, "is lively and active, this other one is clumsy, which must be why it's so miserable."

Emília began to take notice of the domestic animals and her surroundings. With Gizi's help she soon learnt to distinguish cock, capon, hen, pullet, drake and guinea-fowl. After a few weeks she realised that she enjoyed cleaning the chicken-coop and saw how the birds matured; how the little trusting, harmless chicks changed into malignant young cockerels with bare, wrinkled necks and angry eyes; the way that they pecked, hit and tormented one another, started futilely to court the evasive, timid pullets, or how the braver tried with the mature, matronly hens, that indignantly squawked and drove away the self-confident, impudent teenagers, or endured their clumsy attempts with motherly good humour so as afterwards to cluck and discuss with their girlfriends under the mulberry what it had been like with the hot-blooded lads.

In church too she sat in the same pew as Lucky Gizi, but the villagers were careful not to be seen in public with the relocated otherwise than in the course of work, for fear of being reported for associating with reactionaries and enemies of the people who might wish to reverse the wheel of history. The parish priest did his best to persuade Gizi to avoid the company of Mrs. Szentágostony and Mrs. Sárády if she didn't wish to cause herself unpleasantness. "Aren't you afraid of the ÁVH, my daughter?" he asked in a warning tone. "No, father, I fear only God," replied Lucky Gizi. "Don't you yourself fear God, father, that you should give me such advice?" "No, my daughter, nowadays I fear only the ÁVH," he answered.

One day Lucky Gizi whispered confidentially to Emília that in addition to Jesus and the Virgin she prayed more and more often to Samu Goldstein, who had once appeared to her in a dream and offered his assistance. Since then Samu had answered her doubts from heaven and performed miracles. Not long ago, for example, the hail had missed them, and another time in almost miraculous fashion their young goat had got stuck on the lip of the well and hadn't fallen in, and most recently he'd calmed the raging István, who'd been threatening to run the bailiffs through with a pitchfork – fortunately, in their absence – because of the compulsory deliveries of produce. Samu had dazzled Gizi with this last miracle in particular, because Isti had warned his father more than once that it wouldn't matter that he was an ÁVH officer – if he were deported he could expect no help from him, and it was even possible that he would be deported too.

That day István had cursed mercilessly.

"Those mother-fuckers, all my life I've been waiting to have some land! Károlyi promised it in 1918, Gömbös in 1935, and even the sodding Arrow-Cross did. Now that the communists have given me a plot at last, do they want to take it off me straight away? What the fucking hell are they after?

Do they think they can pay me sixty forints a *mázsa* for maize when it costs me two hundred and eighty? They want to force me to give my land up voluntarily to the collective. Well, I'm not going to! I won't join the collective farm, I'll sooner stick a pitchfork in 'em and hang myself in the loft."

While István was fulminating, Gizi closed her eyes and prayed to Samu, and behold, a miracle! István was suddenly silent. He clapped his hands to his chest, slapped his left arm, gasped for air, collapsed onto the stool, and said no more. When Dr. János Szentágostony was called to him and heard what had happened, he told István that he'd do better to control himself a little, otherwise he wouldn't need to hang himself in the loft because the matter would be dealt with by a stroke or a heart attack.

Emília was sitting on a bench in front of the house, like the peasant women did. Beside her sat the wizened Szonja Esterházy, whom no one was keen to talk to because she was so deaf that she could only hear what was shouted into her ear. The princess of Russian origin, with her humorous face, seemed to act the part of a benevolent demon after an accidental mix-up of characters in a fairytale. She lived a few houses farther along, in her room in the Bódis family's yard. She came to see Emília from time to time, sat on the bench, and they would sit and stare at each other in silence. If Emília was asked how she managed for hours on end with the deaf princess she always answered "There's no one that I can stay as quiet with as I can with her."

Suddenly a party of Pioneers[51] on an excursion turned into the street and, singing loudly and waving, marched past in front of them.

"The red flag will always triumph, and every vile reactionary will hang! But where? On the post! The lamppost, nice and high! String 'em up!" with a roar of laughter at the end.

Emília listened, stiff with fear, as if the song were meant for them, but the hard-of-hearing devil-princess, on the other hand, although she couldn't make out a word of the song, looked with bright face and loving smile at the children as they sang vigorously.

"What are they singing?" she asked with her Slav accent, holding a hand to her ear.

Emília looked the aged woman in the eye, then after a brief hesitation shouted into her ear:

"They're singing that they're as happy as squirrels up a tree!"

"Well, that's really charming!" replied the deaf woman with a broad smile, and waved cheerfully to the pioneers.

THE PORCELAIN BUST OF STALIN

To Dávid and his family's consternation, the tool cupboard covering the entrance to their hideout was moved away not as usual in the evening, but in the morning. A shaft of light from a torch swung around in the darkness, followed by the muzzle of a sub-machine gun, and then the light of the torch shone on their faces one by one, blinding them. By that time Dávid had been in hiding with his uncle and aunt in the cellar behind the workshop for almost three months. Most of the time they had sat on their mattresses – in the dark, so that the paraffin lamp shouldn't exhaust the oxygen – and talked, immersed in themselves. For Dávid, the nastiest aspect of the concealment wasn't the constant fear or the being shut in, but these so-called conversations; they mainly consisted of Henrik talking unstoppably and disjointedly, as if talking to save his life, like someone that dare go through a dark wood only if he sings aloud all the way. Over the years with Henrik, Anci had developed a number of special abilities; for example, she could completely shut off her hearing even when her husband was muttering directly into her ear, and she'd learnt to sleep with her eyes open, so that she could look into Henrik's face with genuine interest at the same time. She could also suspend her sense of smell; generally she didn't notice Henrik's unbearable bad breath, which, with the restricted opportunities for hygiene in the cellar, was as overwhelming an excess as his compulsion to talk under the influence of fear. It is possible, of course, that Anci didn't develop these abilities herself but that they were all the result of a sort of specialised evolution, like the air-breathing of the climbing perch; just as for these fish brachiate gills were the only chance of survival in the shallow water at monsoon times, so her abilities were *sine qua non* for Anci's survival with Henrik. Dávid, however, wasn't given the amount of time that Anci had had in which to adapt her social behaviour, her senses of perception and, indeed, even the volume of her brain to Henrik; thus after a few weeks he found confinement with his uncle so intolerable that he was planning to ask to be released from the cellar and to surrender to the Gestapo. Then at least his sufferings would have a speedy end whilst Henrik was slowly driving him mad. Every evening, when they were let out for a short while, he implored Jani Tóth to give him something to read to occupy his mind. In the poor light, however, his eyes soon became tired, and he couldn't read for any length of time. And then Jani, with surprising foresight, brought him a Russian grammar book.

"The Russians are getting very close now," he said, "learn the language, it may come in useful."

Dávid applied himself to studying Russian. He spent every available moment while the lamp was burning with his nose in the book so that he would no longer have to talk to Henrik, and memorised grammar and vocabulary so that after three months he could read Russian quite well.

Then the time came for the oral exam which was conducted by a little Tartar soldier, the holder of the sub-machine gun and the torch.

"*Nyemtsy? Fashisty?*" he asked, crouching and peering into the cellar.

"He's looking for Germans and Fascists," Dávid interpreted readily.

"Well, we'd look good if they were here as well," muttered Henrik.

The Soviet soldier ordered them out of the hole, and in the open two other grim-faced soldiers in battledress were waiting for them, one covering Keller and Jani by the wall while the other, ready for anything, covered the aperture.

"*Daragiye tavarishchi, druz'ya!*" Dávid greeted them as he crawled through.

The soldiers looked at him enquiringly. "Dear Comrades, friends?" He wasn't making a political statement?

"*Ty gavarish pa-russki?*" asked the one with Tartar features, with a grin.

"*Da, ya gavaryu pa-russki. Minya zovut* Dávid Goldstein," Dávid introduced himself politely, following the book.

The soldiers liked this, but it seemed that they were in a hurry, because all that they said was '*chasy*', and made signs to Henrik that he should be quick and give them his watch because they didn't have one.

"Tell them that this was actually my late father's watch," said Henrik to Dávid, as if the soldiers had come to trade, not to plunder.

"*Eti chasy u vashi otets,*" said Dávid. "*My lyubyom velikaya krasnaya armiya.*"

"What did you tell them?" asked Henrik anxiously, because the soldiers began to laugh so much that they slapped one another on the back.

"I said it was Henrik's father's watch and that we loved the great Red Army," said Dávid in confusion.

"*Maladyets,*" said one of the soldiers. "*Nu, dayte vashi chasy tozhe.*"

"What did he say?" asked Henrik.

The Porcelain Bust of Stalin

"He said that if we love them so much we should all give them our watches."

When the soldiers had collected the watches and left, still laughing and slapping Dávid on the back as they went, Henrik continued to sulk. "Are you such an idiot, my boy? Was that the best you could do? Was that what I spared no trouble or expense having you taught Russian for?!" Then he burst out laughing. "I loved that watch, damn them, but anyway, it saved us from the Germans and the Arrow-Cross. We owe them that for it."

Dávid might have failed to save the watches, but his knowledge of the language eventually laid the foundation for a flourishing business. With Henrik's encouragement he began to talk to the Soviet soldiers as they passed through. The Soviet army made a mockery of the Stalinists' planned economy of the previous fifteen years. They delivered such excellent proof of both commercial and logistic acumen, that had Stalin recognised it in time and entrusted the Soviet national economy to the private soldiers in the army, the world economy's leading powers would have found a worthy competitor. Dávid learnt the Russian words for car components, Henrik ordered spares from the soldiers as they advanced towards Berlin, and within a couple of weeks the items that they needed would appear: Ford clutches, Opel gearboxes, Volkswagen pistons, whatever the esteemed customers asked for. Trade was so brisk that the workshop flourished, Henrik and his staff bought new premises and in a few months' time there were a dozen mechanics working for Henrik Goldstein and Aladár Keller. Goldstein & Keller's became the leading car servicing workshop in town, and customers came in droves.

Jani Tóth was the only one who didn't remain at the

187

workshop. As a proven illegal communist, the district Party committee considered him a political colleague, and he threw himself heart and soul into the rebuilding of Hungary. He took part in clearing up the rubble and helped to organise the food supply. Where needed, he personally drove the lorry which delivered food, study materials and medicines to schools and hospitals. Workers and peasants with ruddy, shining faces smiled down on passers-by from posters in the streets. Jani smiled back. It gave him a good feeling when he discovered more and more red stars on factories and in public places. He applauded and sang enthusiastically at Communist Party rallies. He agitated, and tried to persuade people to build a more just and finer future in which all would be equal, where the big fish wouldn't swallow up the little fish, and where no one would prey on anyone else. He waved the red flag in the breeze and sang happily that 'by tomorrow we'll turn the whole world'.

"In the course of eighteen months we've rebuilt more than a dozen bridges on the Danube and the Tisza, the trains are running again, and there are as many cars on the road as before the war! We communists are rebuilding Hungary!" he boasted to Dávid, who often attended the meetings.

Jani was living with Erzsi Török at the time. Theirs was a real marriage of true minds, based not only on love but also on political principles: they scrutinised each other and themselves critically – not easily done, as they hardly ever met. While Jani was turning night into day and building a country of iron and steel, Erzsi was hard at work in the Democratic League of Hungarian Women, educating the outlook of women and girls. She gave practical advice to her fellow women on housekeeping and the rearing of children, simultaneously giving lectures on the fundamentals of Marxism, the equal rights of women and the enviable situation of Soviet women. At the week-end they and Dávid went for walks on Margitsziget, went rowing on the Danube, or took hikes in the Buda hills, singing the songs of the workers' movement as there was no longer any need to fear the Horthyist police. Jani was also proud that Hungary's reconstruction wasn't reliant on foreign aid.

"We'll have a few lean years, and perhaps for a while people will only get half of their pre-war incomes and the peasants will probably make a bit of a fuss, but we're independent. We mustn't kill the goose that lays the golden eggs, because that's our future!" he said, quoting Comrade Rákosi's simile.

At the time it didn't occur to Jani that that goose might actually die of hunger.

It was easier to clear the dead from the streets than from people's minds. There wasn't a single family that hadn't mourned someone, or wasn't awaiting the return of someone from a Soviet prison or labour camp, or from a German death-camp. For the rest of their lives Henrik and Dávid's consciences were tormented because they'd survived while the others hadn't. If only they'd gone through hell like Elza, they thought, it would be easier. It was as if they'd suffered a sort of bereavement. Henrik in particular was gnawed by the thought that his well-meaning endeavour had been the precise reason that landed Samu and Andor in the killers' hands; if he hadn't sent money with that lad, his brother and nephew might have survived the war. He never spoke of it, but he dragged the crushing burden around with him. Only once did he sob out his thoughts to Anci, and naturally he never dared mention to Dávid what he thought. In the end, however, the unspoken pain came between them, drove them apart, and even made Dávid reject his faith.

One yellow and red autumn afternoon Dávid was walking at Nagyrét in Hővösvölgy. The trees were shedding their leaves and a red carpet covered the paths. Erzsi was sitting cross-legged on a check blanket; she was expecting and stroked her belly like a self-satisfied buddha, chatting with the others while Dávid and Jani went for a stroll in the forest. Dávid kicked at chestnuts as they walked, talking about his childhood, and about how since the age of twelve he'd been uncertain of his Jewishness. He adored his father, but secretly he would have liked to be like his friend Isti, and through the memorable incident of the sausage he seemed ritually to have sacrificed the religion that he'd inherited from his ancestors. Now, after the war, disgraceful or not, finally he didn't like belonging to the weak, the subjugated, the humiliated, who'd been unable to defend themselves and each other.

"You don't have to feel ashamed about that," Jani reassured him. "It's perfectly understandable. In my view the Jewish question can best be solved if the Jews blend into the Hungarians, and if we stop stirring it up. Then it'll just fizzle out, like the State."

Dávid nodded thoughtfully.

"Are you religious? No!" Jani went on, answering his own question straight away. "So you don't keep the Jewish faith. Is your native language Hebrew? No! It's Hungarian. You don't even know any Hebrew, do you? Is your culture Jewish? No! That's Hungarian as well. So what would make you a Jew? In fifty years' time there'll be no classes, no religions, no nations, and everybody will earn according to the work they do," he said triumphantly.

Dávid listened to Jani, his eyes sparkling, and as a sign of agreement patted his arm.

The Porcelain Bust of Stalin

"There's only one thing about you that's Jewish: your name," Jani continued. "This Goldstein, if you don't mind my saying so, is very Jewish. You ought to change it."

"I think my nose is suspicious as well," said Dávid, "and if I take my pants down the expert observer can see this and that down there too. But if possible, let's leave my nose and my what's-its-name out of it," he said with a laugh.

He and Jani discussed for a long time what name he might assume. Dávid would have liked Rákóczi, Zrínyi, Hunyady or the name of some such historical hero in whose place he'd liked to picture himself when reading books as a boy, but of course there could be no question of that. He thought about whether to keep the existing initial and perhaps become Gonda, Gombos, Gáti or Gács, or whether to have a name with a similar meaning to the original. As a surname Aranykő[52] sounded stupid, and plain Arany alone would sound as if he was imitating the great poet. Aranyos sounded as if he was attaching a mawkish adjective to himself: 'Good morning, I'm a sweetie'. In considering his new name Dávid was struck by what an ancient, magical and poetic charm there is in bestowing a name. We try in one word to refer to personality, character and destiny, a person identifies with his name, and those few letters can mark him for life. He'd thought that by that gesture he'd cast off his past, his disinheritance, his former fate, as if by changing his name he would be seeking to change his future, his whole life. He remembered his mother telling him, when he was a boy, that as a girl she'd had diphtheria and was at death's door when, in accordance with an ancient rite, her parents gave her a new name, so that when Death came and called for Miriam they were able to tell him 'You've come to the wrong house, Death, this little girl's called Ilus', and he had to move on perplexed. Dávid was subconsciously hoping that the same would happen again.

Some time elapsed before, with Jani's help, he'd convinced himself that he wouldn't be rejecting his ancestors if he changed his name, since the family had only assumed the name of Goldstein in 1787, the year when the Emperor Josef II had ordered the Jews in the Empire to take German surnames; nevertheless, he felt as if he was performing a little self-amputation. In the end he remembered his native village, Tövispuszta, and decided on the name Pusztai[53], and so Dávid Goldstein became Dávid Pusztai. With Jani's encouragement he applied for university. At first he resisted because he thought he was too old but in the end he allowed himself to be persuaded.

"Studying isn't an upper-class privilege any more," Jani insisted. "Thousands of workers' and peasants' children go to university, and they'll be the intelligentsia of the future. The Horthy regime turned you down, so now the people's democracy will accept you," he said ceremoniously.

Since the Red Army was no longer on the move but now, as its half-century occupation of Hungary was loosely termed, 'temporarily stationed' in the countries of Eastern Europe, the Soviet supply of parts gradually dried up in the car workshop, although it was possible for years to buy stolen kerosene or sub-machine guns in the vicinity of Soviet barracks. For that, however, knowledge of Russian wasn't required, nor was it needed in the workshop; people understood each other much better in the language of the black market than they did with the aid of professional simultaneous interpreters at Comecon conferences. For quite some time Dávid would have liked to get away from his uncle, who, since he had no one left but his wife, devoted all his energy to trying to run Dávid's life. He'd decided to go to university and chose the School of Economics. Henrik actually took the view that this was quite superfluous, that 'Economics' didn't exist; wealth was a matter of acumen and capability, 'just look at him', and 'who ever saw a rich academic?' But he liked the idea of Dávid going to university; he could boast about it in synagogue. He supported Dávid's studies, and from then on began to refer to him in synagogue as his son. "My son's a university student! He's a Goldstein as well, only he's Magyarised his name! He's going to be a scientific businessman!" he said to the other old men who nodded pensively at him.

One day Dávid ran into Isti outside the Milk-bar. He was wearing a silk raincoat and limping along, his head lowered. At first Dávid wasn't sure that it was him.

"You haven't been to see me!" said Isti reproachfully after they had hugged each other.

"No, because I'd heard you'd become a detective, and I didn't know whether to," answered Dávid. "You haven't been to see me either."

"No, because these days not many people like having the political police call in on them," said Isti, pulling a face.

They went into a dismal coffee-bar on the ring-road. At the back its dark red paper made it so gloomy that the wall lights were left burning even during the day. A couple of middle-aged lovers, their heads together, were at one table and the only ones in the main room. Dávid and Isti glanced at them, then sat at a corner table in the dim light of the low-powered bulbs and tried to recall their shared past in fits and starts. So much had happened to them in the course of a few years that it was difficult to identify the stage at which

193

more things bound them together than had since separated them. Isti told of his marriage to Eni Sárády and how Dávid's mother and sister had been deported, then how the Arrow-Cross had killed his father and brother, how he'd been crippled and how he'd made Hetési and Székely carry Samu and Andor's bodies through the village. Dávid had tears in his eyes as he listened, and then told of how Jani Tóth had saved them from being shot into the Danube, how he, Henrik and Anci had hidden in the cellar at the workshop in Kresz Géza utca. It was agreed that if Dávid could summon up the courage to face his memories they would go to Tövispuszta and visit Isti's parents and his young son. They decided to renew their friendship, and if Isti's work allowed they would go to football matches together. In fact, nothing came of the idea of meeting frequently, but on 20 August Dávid and Isti did go home together.

St István's Day[54] had traditionally been the most important festival in the Veres family. From time immemorial the eldest son had been named István, and when Isti was born four generations of Istváns had sat round the table because great-grandfather Veres had still been alive. Istváns, Istis, Pistas, Pistis and Pityus[55] continued to drink mournfully on their name-days[56] in the circles that celebrated them – mournfully, because it wasn't called that any longer. By central decree and in the struggle against reactionary clericalism the king and founder of the State had been demoted from St István to István I, and just as in honour of the people's democracy Szentágoston had become Tövispuszta, so St István's Day had become the 'Festival of the Constitution'. In 1949, surreptitiously, the socialist constitution had been promulgated on that day in order to distract attention from the first king of Hungary, who had adopted Christianity.

"Your name-day's Constitution Day, you could be called

Constitution Veres," said Dávid to Isti with a laugh as they pulled their chairs close together in the kitchen, downing large spoonfuls of Lucky Gizi's renowned chicken soup.

"Veres is right enough, the Constitution's red, the buggers," István acknowledged.[57]

"Better talk about the village gossip, mother, because if father starts talking politics it'll only lead to trouble," said Isti.

"The ÁVH'll cart me off in the end, you mean? After all, they're sitting at the table."

Isti's brother and sister tittered in embarrassment at the old man's remark. Isti merely shook his head.

"There's no good news, son," said Lucky Gizi. "Life's hard. I kept that chicken for your name-day."

They didn't even go into the Sárádys' house. Dr. Béla Sárády had been released from prison a broken man, and looked at them from a distance over the garden fence, his eyes expressionless and his face stern. Isti didn't want to meet them or the Hetésis' in whose house they lived, so they waited in the street for Eni to bring Pityu out for them to take him to the fair.

The people of Tövispuszta still held the fair on that same day just like in the olden days. Apart from weddings this was the only event in the year, and people rejoiced that the harvest was in and said goodbye to summer.[58] More recently they'd also been saying goodbye to the harvest, a large part of which had to be surrendered. Isti held the blue-eyed boy's hand and limped through the crowd with Dávid. People stared at them nonplussed. At least that's how they felt. Isti could see that the warm affection which was present when he used to play in Zsiga Balogh's band and had been outside right in the football team had vanished from people's faces. Now that it was known that he was an ÁVH officer he was politely greeted but feared. Dávid, on the other hand, the only Jew to return to the village since the war, felt that he could sense guilt in the villagers' eyes. A few shook him by the hand and said some kindly words of regret about the family, but the majority didn't know how to behave towards him, just like when people avoid the eyes of a disabled person.

Dávid's stomach was in knots as he walked round the house where he'd been born, and the shop, and memories welled up inside him. When the new occupants came out to keep an eye on the stranger who was lurking around the house and then suddenly recognised him, they slammed the door in his face, fearing that he meant to exercise his rights of possession. Having not been to the Tövispuszta fair for years, Dávid was surprised to see, next to the roundabout and between the shooting gallery and the decrepit Turkish delight stalls, the new bread displayed on a nicely decorated platform rather like an altar.[59] It was festooned with ribbons in national colours, but above it the new coat of arms with red star, hammer, sickle and wheat-sheaves proclaimed the power of worker and peasant. He'd seen it everywhere, but there, in the village, at the fair, it was an unaccustomed sight.

Somehow the peasants weren't enjoying their power. Maybe this was because three days earlier the inspector and the inspector's inspector (a teacher and a council official respectively) had arrived to supervise the collection of produce. People said they weren't malicious, as they'd been the previous year when they'd searched lofts in a number of houses and dug up storage-pits to see if the peasants were concealing any produce. So strict were the regulations governing the handing in of produce that families were scarcely left with enough to live on, and the pig was left with only just enough maize to keep it to become the next thing to be surrendered.

The Porcelain Bust of Stalin

✳

The building in Szerb utca, which had once been a monastery and later a prison, wasn't really suitable for university teaching. There wasn't even a big lecture theatre, and so the lectures for entire years of the School of Economics were given in the neighbouring Law Faculty. There was an audience of three hundred, which offered a good opportunity for students to become acquainted, but Dávid found it hard to make friends with his fellow students, among whom there were both young workers and peasants of limited educational background and the well-schooled children of cultured intelligentsia. There were other people with families, whose partners were still working in fields or factory. Dávid didn't feel that he belonged to any of these groups, but he was at ease with Laci Bartos, a pleasant, happy-go-lucky young man who secretly wrote verse and published it under a pseudonym in literary journals. Laci had the reputation of being a womaniser, and at first Dávid thought that the hero in the rumours must be their source. Later, however, he was rather envious when he found out that the stories about Laci were true. He started to study his style in the hope of picking up some tips, and realised that his friend didn't chase the girls at all: they were simply wild about him. He dressed carefully, walked with a gingerly, almost mincing gait down the university corridor and the girls flocked to him from all sides like pins to a magnet. All that he had to do was to choose whom to take to the attractive little attic room, overlooking an internal garden, which they shared in the centre of the city.

"No need to push," said Laci impudently to the girls. "Everyone'll get their turn!"

Dávid had never had a serious relationship, and had no practice at courtship. It seemed as if he was afraid of girls, but in fact he wasn't, nor was he afraid of a serious relationship – he'd yearned for one for years – but he was apprehensive of its breakdown. What would happen if he tired of a girl, how would he tell her without causing pain? Samu and Ilus Goldstein had brought their children up to such a stern moral code that it had all but crippled Dávid's later intimate relationships. He'd just reached the age when he was beginning to go with girls when his mother told him "My boy, if you're going to court a girl keep one thing in mind at all times: would you like it if a boy behaved like that towards your sister?" In those days, when he held a girl close at Auntie Manci's dancing school and she could feel his swelling interest in her through his trousers, or if his hand slipped and apparently by accident reached her breast, he thought of what he would say if someone else did that to his sister. He was no longer capable of considering what the girls said about it. Elza in those days was only ten, and Dávid felt that the whole line of thought was perverse. He didn't realise that his anxious aloofness and doleful dark eyes attracted the girls, who would try with him for a while, make eyes at him, urge him on, but when they saw that he was a hopeless case gave up on him. It was futile for Laci to encourage him as well.

"Don't be stupid, Pusztai, the girls adore you, and the way you pretend to be dead meat and wait for them to jump on you unsuspectingly is fantastic. One more step and you've got 'em!"

Dávid had been used to playing second fiddle to Isti and now became Laci's companion. In fact, it was Laci that he had to thank for Anka Deutsch. She was a pretty girl, swarthy, with wavy black hair, and at first Laci had marked her out for himself, but when he realised that his modestly withdrawn friend excited her much more he worked at bringing them together.

The Porcelain Bust of Stalin

"See how well your method's working, old chap?" he applauded Dávid, and in so doing was filled with pride: not everyone is capable of such selfless largesse.

✳

Anka's father was an engineer of some repute and they lived in an old villa on the Rózsadomb.[60] Before the war they'd owned the entire house, but by the time that they'd returned from forced labour, deportation and hiding, two other families had moved in. The Deutsch family retained the former servants' quarters that opened onto the garden. "Let's hope nobody's paying attention any more," said Ferenc Deutsch calmly.

"Actually, we're lucky to have been left with this much," he said over dinner to Dávid and Anka, as he served the *lecsó*. "It's a bit spicy; is it all right?"

Ferenc Deutsch was convinced that despite all the trouble, he was born lucky and nothing interested him other than that he and his family should be left undisturbed.

"I was lucky on the Don Bend as well," he told the story, "Our labour company was sent out with the order that none of us was to return alive, and it has to be admitted that everything possible was done to achieve that. I meant to escape, to swim the Don, but I had the good luck to step on a mine," he said cheerfully.

"Oh, very lucky!" said Dávid in astonishment.

"Quite so," answered Deutsch. "Because if anyone managed to swim the river the Russians shot them, and if they stayed where they were doing forced labour *that* killed them. But I got into hospital. Furthermore, they didn't cut my leg off because I wouldn't let them. And I was right, I survived. So, that's how I was lucky!"

Dávid looked at Anka's father as he mopped up the

199

juice of the *lecsó* with his bread. He regarded him as a clever man and so couldn't decide whether he was being ironic or whether his view of the world was optimistically confident. He thought of his own father, who likewise had been confident until the Germans and the Arrow-Cross shot him into the pit. It is said, he thought, that the only thing that distinguishes the optimist from the pessimist is lack of information. That, however, didn't apply to Samu Goldstein and Ferenc Deutsch. They'd both known precisely what was in store for them, and if they'd been unwilling to believe it they'd been driven by obstinate gentleness rather than fear. Which, indeed, in certain situations can scarcely be distinguished from naivety.

Rózsi, Anka's mother, sat by the tiled stove with her plate on her lap. She was essentially a young woman, possibly forty-five, but even in summer didn't like to move away from the stove; she walked with a stick because, as Dávid learnt from Anka, Dr. Mengele had performed medical experiments on her in Auschwitz.

"Tell me, my boy, why do you call yourself Pusztai?" asked Deutsch.

Dávid didn't answer, merely looked thoughtfully into space; after what Anka's parents had been through, what explanation could he give?

"I understand, of course," said the engineer. "On the off chance of missing the next transport, eh? Believe me, my boy, it's no good trying to pretend you're not Jewish, there'll always be somebody that'll remind you. I thought that after Auschwitz it would no longer be possible for people to be fed all kinds of vileness because everybody would see what inspired hatred and where it led to. But it seems it isn't so. I expect you've read that there were more pogroms in Kunmadaras and Miskolc.[61] But when all's said and done we're fortunate, because it's no longer allowed," he ended in a satisfied tone.

As it turned out it wasn't at all fortunate that Henrik & Co's workshop became so popular, because this meant that it fell among businesses on which the State fixed its eyes. After losing the workshop, the pride of his life, for the second time in a few years, and after what happened to Elza and her family Henrik finally lost contact with the outside world. He suffered a stroke, and could neither hear, speak nor move, but just sat in the big, battered armchair relieving himself where he was. As far as he was concerned, that was his opinion of the machinations of the imperialists and of the reactionaries in Hungary, the developing international situation and the successes of the proletarian dictatorship. The most distinguished lecturers were beginning to disappear from university and scientific life. Some were dismissed, others escaped abroad. Icons of Comrade Stalin and his best Hungarian disciple Comrade Rákosi appeared on lecture-room walls, and the liturgy of the new religion illumined textbooks and lectures. Dávid and Laci were at a lecture on accountancy: Varró, the lecturer, was just beginning to expound Comrade Stalin's revolutionary advances in the field of book-keeping and had no sooner uttered the Generalissimo's name, than a few over-zealous students were already on their feet applauding loudly and chanting 'long-live Sta-lin, long-live Sta-lin'. The rest followed suit in alarm, and after a brief hesitation the lecturer too joined in, and for long moments the hall resounded to the fervent celebration of the savant leader, equally well versed in all branches of science and culture.

The compulsory enthusiasm of the majority, which was

sincerely held by Jani Tóth, would probably have infected Dávid too had the arrest of Elza and Pál, coupled with the nationalisation of Henrik's workshop, not cast a shadow on his outlook. He found it hard to come to terms with what had happened to his family, but as a confirmed follower of rules it was easier for him to accept a situation that obviously couldn't be changed than to question it. He continued to go with his fellow students to Dunapentele on 'shock-work' at the week-end, helping to build Sztálinváros, the pride-to-be of socialist industry[62] but he and Anka were no longer as keen at mass meetings, and kept straight faces as images of the wise leaders were paraded and Stalin or Rákosi were acclaimed, but they waved as they passed the saluting base in the Mayday procession.

It was some months later, at a League of Working Youth meeting, after the League secretary had, as usual, read out the leading article from *Szabad Nép*[63] – on this occasion analysing the triumph of socialist agriculture and saying how in a matter of years the collective farms had become ten times as numerous and their members twenty times – that Dávid timidly observed that he'd been to his native village of Tövispuszta. He thought that this might perhaps have been achieved in a more sensible manner since the majority of the peasants were seriously disenchanted. A shocked silence followed, but after that, heartened by Dávid's daring, a number of young peasants confirmed that in their villages people weren't overjoyed either. The secretary was lost for words. This hadn't been in the script and he became paler still when Laci spoke.

"All that would need to be done is to reinstate the big estates, since they did at least work," he remarked.

At this point the atmosphere became somewhat chilly. Laci realised at once that what had been intended as a witty comment could lead to big trouble. He tried to smooth things over by saying that what he really meant was that some kind of socialist-type big estates ought to be created from the collective and State farms, if that was the right way to put it, and he could see that that wasn't quite correct. But it was too late. A few blinkered listeners hurried to the secretary's assistance, and declared Laci a reactionary hireling of the *kulaks*. Dávid and a number of his fellow students were disciplined, and Laci was expelled from the university.

It so happened that when on 5 March 1953 Josip Vissarionovich Djugashvili, otherwise known as Comrade Stalin, the wise leader, gave back his soul to the Creator – if indeed that's who he got it from, and not the Devil, as Laci Bartos maintained – Dávid could no longer grieve with a clear conscience like the workers in the factories, the peasants in the fields, and the engineers at the drawing-boards did. Or at least, that's how they appeared on the newsreels.

Following the reburial of László Rajk,[64] events speeded up in October 1956. During the afternoon of 23 October Dávid and Anka were walking on the small ring-road with Peti, their little boy, when they heard the noise of a crowd. With a nervousness born of years of such experiences, Dávid's stomach immediately knotted up and he looked anxiously round to see if the police were coming. By then, however, the agitated crowd had reached them, some waving cheerfully at passers-by on the pavement as if in a Mayday procession, others shouting eagerly as they walked arm in arm "Worker and peasant children, come with us!" There were only youthful faces; some people carried children on their shoulders, and Anka recognised a number that she knew, former fellow students from university and younger lecturers, who beckoned them to come with them. As they joined the march someone started to shout 'Russians, go home! Russians, go home!' which was at once taken up by the crowd. At Nyugati station the morning shift was leaving for home and joined the marchers.

"There's Jani!" Anka pointed to the spectators on the side of the road. Dávid ran over and pulled Jani in with them.

"What's all this about?" asked Jani, his face registering both enthusiasm and alarm.

The city was bathed in autumnal sunshine as they crossed the Danube by Margit híd. By the time they reached Bem tér the crowd was so big that all that could be seen was the tops of heads. Dávid and Anka stood to the side of the square with little Peti for fear of being trampled in the mass of people. Someone said that Péter Veres [65] was speaking, but they couldn't hear much of him. Then they were swept back with the rest to Pest, where everyone gathered in the huge square in front of the Parliament building.

"There's at least two hundred thousand of us," said someone good-humouredly.

By then daylight was fading. The rumour spread that the statue of Stalin in the Városliget had been pulled down and cut up with oxy-acetylene torches, and that the head was being dragged by a lorry towards Blaha Lujza tér.

"Stalin's been beheaded!" someone commented

"About time too, the swine," shouted a young man.

People round him laughed and applauded.

"Imre Nagy into the government, Rákosi into the Danube!" people were shouting.

Dávid and Anka wanted to hear Nagy speak, but the speech was postponed repeatedly and Peti was becoming increasingly restive, and so, with him now asleep on Dávid's shoulders, they walked home to Kresz Géza utca. It wasn't until the next morning that Jani phoned and told them that the insurgents of the previous evening had occupied the radio station building following a fire-fight. Dávid and Anka held the receiver between their heads so they could both hear Jani's account.

"This is revolution!" said Anka. "There's no way back, only forward."

"This isn't revolution, it's counter-revolution," replied Jani sourly.

"The public mood is understandable, they've had enough of lies and humiliation. And the ÁVH even fired on the crowd? This regime must go!" shouted Anka down the telephone.

"I wouldn't care to side with the armed insurgents, nor with those that murdered them!" said Jani calmly.

"But Jani, anyone that isn't on the side of the revolution is supporting the murderers!" replied Anka heatedly.

"I've never sided with murderers!" said Jani in a choking voice. "Not in '44, nor since. I've always been on the side of socialism, that's what I believe in. Trust me, killing can only lead to killing by the powers that be."

"And if the powers that be kill, so will the revolution!" was Anka's firm rejoinder.

Events seemed to conspire to justify their exchange of words. The next day ÁVH soldiers on the rooftops opened fire with machine-guns on a crowd of unarmed demonstrators outside Parliament. Hundreds of dead and wounded lay in the square. Fighting had broken out. Anka's parents begged them to seek refuge in their cellar, or at least to stay in Kresz Géza utca, but she was so taken by what was happening that she seemed to be afraid of missing the equivalent of an unrepeatable concert. "It's not as if you can take part in a revolution every day of the week," she said excitedly. They left Peti at home with the grandparents and went out onto the streets. Shooting could be heard in the distance. Lorries loaded with young armed civilians passed by and above the cabs flew flags in national colours with their centres cut out.[66] There were long queues outside the bakers' shops. They walked towards Széna tér because Laci had sent a message: he'd joined the insurgents, they should come too. Near the square the fighting had stopped, a burnt-out Soviet tank stood rammed into a wall and the burnt body of a young soldier hung from the turret. Anka looked away.

Laci was waiting for them. He had a sub-machine gun with a drum magazine slung over his shoulder and wore an armband in national colours.

"A bloke tossed a Molotov cocktail into that tank half an hour ago, the rest got away," he said excitedly. "Do you want guns? We've just had a new delivery."

"Couldn't we help without guns?" asked Anka anxiously. "I don't know how to handle one, and I don't think I could bring myself to shoot anybody."

Dávid approved, with a sense of relief.

"Your place is with the boy," he told her.

"You could help with ferrying the wounded," Laci suggested. "The ÁVH are holding a lot of patriots prisoner in the Party HQ, and hundreds are imprisoned in the cells under the square. We're going to attack tomorrow."

"You're not normal! Peti needs his parents," Rózsi Deutsch wept hysterically when she found out what Dávid and Anka meant to do. "Haven't we suffered enough already?"

"Can't the revolution take place without you?" asked Ferenc sarcastically. "There'll be enough there! You just stay at home and keep out of it."

"I hid in the cellar all through the trouble in '44," said Dávid. "I was cowering while others were saving lives. Since then I've felt ashamed of myself. I couldn't face it if other people settled my future for a second time."

"Dávid's right and I'm going with him," Anka said the final word. "We'll take care of ourselves, we promise."

As they approached Köztársaság tér Dávid and Anka heard shouts: "The ÁVH are killing people!" They quickened their pace, but on the square there was only sporadic firing. Laci had joined the Corvin köz group,[67] the insurgents who were attacking from the direction of the theatre building, and Dávid and Anka remained hidden between the trees, waiting for the medics to arrive so that they could join them. Machine-gun fire was heard from the theatre roof. An attack was launched aimed at the Party HQ, but the defenders beat off the first assault. Dávid and Anka watched Laci anxiously; if he was momentarily out of sight they stiffened, and when he eventually reappeared they gripped one another's hands. The Baross tér group from Kenyérmező utca succeeded in making a breach in one of the windows using hand-grenades, but from the theatre side a T-34 tank with a Kossuth coat-of-arms trained its gun on the building. It only fired once every ten minutes, but even so wrecked almost every upper floor in the Party HQ. Dust and smoke flew in clouds. At about half past one other tanks arrived from the direction of Légszesz utca with a tremendous roar, and a warning shot was fired into the air from the command vehicle. The freedom fighters took to their heels and the square was soon deserted. The command tank then went round the theatre and stopped in the middle of the square, facing the Party HQ. The insurgents began to trickle back into the square and waited tensely to see what was going to happen. The tank swung round uncertainly, as if it didn't know where it was or what it ought to do, and then lined up with the T-34 that had been firing on the Party HQ from beside the theatre. The insurgents cheered. At that the command tank, as if realising that it had made a mistake, moved off again, but only one followed it. The two tanks cleared their way with a sharp burst of fire and left the square, but the one which remained shot the Party HQ to pieces. A good half-hour later the firing stopped, and from the door of the Party HQ a white flag appeared, hastily contrived from a tablecloth and a piece of window-frame, and with it three unarmed men. Shouts went up: "Don't shoot, they're surrendering!" But they'd scarcely gone a few yards when a club-footed insurgent in a cap stepped forward from behind a tree and fired at them. Others joined in, until the three that wanted to negotiate had fallen. Dávid and Anka watched in horror from a distance and then, once the shooting in the square had stopped and the insurgents were storming the now wrecked building with shouts of triumph, the medics and first aiders moved forward as well, picking up the wounded. The latter were taken to ambulances and driven to nearby hospitals. As Dávid and the others approached the building, they could see that inside, in the meantime, the enraged insurgents had immediately begun to settle scores. The defenders were beaten up and the ÁVH shot on the spot, including several soldiers wearing blue collar-tabs. From the second floor a woman hurtled through the window onto the concrete below. Some of the other insurgents did their best to stop the lynchings. "Don't hurt the women, we aren't animals!" shouted someone. Anka saw Laci throw his own coat over a wounded defender and smuggle him out of the building, where a lynching mood had now taken over. Two other insurgents seized two defenders, their heads bleeding, by the clothes and dragged them out through the door into the square. Dávid watched them, unable to move: he recognised one of them as Isti Veres. He tried to go after him to help, and could still see him as people in the square set about him again, but then he vanished in the crowd. Several tried to save the non-ÁVH defenders from the hands of the mob. One first-aider was shielding a wounded man with his body and called to Dávid to help take him to the ambulance. Anka too rushed over, and as they left the building with him they saw one man, beaten to a bloody pulp, hanging head down from a tree while those around kicked his head and spat on him. Flash-bulbs were going off, Hungarian and foreign photo-reporters and cine-camera operators were at work trying to get shots of one seriously injured negotiator being seized by his arms and legs, kicked and cursed. "Down with the ÁVH!" shouted several, intoxicated by the opportunity to take part. "Let's tear his heart out!" howled someone. "Let's do that!" screamed others. A long knife was handed to a young woman, her eyes gleaming with hatred, and with a powerful blow she drove the blade between the writhing man's ribs. As she pulled it out blood spouted over his silk raincoat. Two men grabbed the body and with bloody hands began to open the wound so as to tear out the dead man's heart and show it to the crowd. The woman threw down the knife with a look of uncertainty and turned away. Dávid and Anka, however, stomachs heaving, faces contorted with horror, tried to distance themselves from the square as far as possible.

The train rumbled towards the frontier, its passengers laden with rucksacks and suitcases. 'Let's get out, let's get out!' overwhelmed Dávid and Anka's minds. They stood side by side at the window, Dávid carrying Peti, and wept as they looked at the scenery. It was just about the first time that they'd been out of the house since the battle in Köztársaság tér, and they'd spent days in a state of shock in the Goldsteins' flat in Kresz Géza utca. Jani Tóth and Erzsi had hurried over to them as soon as they heard their anguished voices on the telephone, and tried to cheer them up. Anka sobbed her heart out on Jani's shoulder. "Why did they have to befoul the revolution?" she asked through her tears. "What have those raving murderers to do with freedom? That was our revolution!"

When, a few days later, Soviet forces launched a dawn attack, the flashes of gunfire so lit up the dark sky that Dávid and Anka at first thought that it was a thunderstorm. In the streets freedom fighters were keeping up the bitter struggle against the invading troops, but by that time the couple had decided to leave the country. The Soviets were obviously going to reinstate former conditions, they said, and they could no longer live in the world of the past ten years. They rang Jani and Erzsi, and Laci, to ask them to come with them. Laci replied that there was still work for him to do in Hungary, but Jani said "Off you go, you may do better abroad, but Erzsi and I are staying because somebody has to rebuild this country now and then." Dávid and Anka covered the last few miles to the Austrian frontier on foot with a group of refugees. They lugged suitcases along, helped the elderly and carried the smaller children on their shoulders or in their arms. They were led in small groups over wooded hills to a region where the forest had been cleared. "This is no-man's-land," said one of the guides, a peasant in a cap and storm-coat. "No-man's-land!" repeated the others, passing the word from mouth to mouth. And the refugees sighed with relief as they looked at the bare strip of land which for ten years had separated the two jarring Europes.

The Fashion Magazine

W hen the insurgents who'd forced their way into the Party HQ came across Isti Veres he received the first blow from the butt of a sub-machine gun from behind. His ear was split, blood immediately gushed forth and he fell to the floor stunned. A woman kicked him in the genitals. Isti howled with pain, tears flooded his eyes, and his mind filled with memories; he re-experienced being lamed by Hetési and Székely. Cursed, beaten, he lay curled up on the floor, both hands held up in front trying to protect his head at least from the kicks: between his crooked fingers he glimpsed hate-filled faces and expected to be beaten to death. Surprisingly, however, it wasn't the most important moments in his life that flashed before his eyes, as he had heard said, but the ÁVH tortures. He hadn't in fact taken part in interrogations; special 'enforcement operatives' were used for that work in the political police, and only a few of his keener colleagues had assisted in the exhausting work of beating people up; the majority had at the most taken an occasional part, overcome in the heat of the moment. Isti had, however, often heard the screams through the door, been in the cells, knew the methods, had seen the results of torture and the humiliated victims. At first he had believed that they were all guilty

211

as charged, enemies of the State, but when tried and tested communists were brought to Andrássy út, and his immediate superior, the totally loyal Major László Vári, was arrested and charged with espionage, Isti became less confident; if those were all enemies, who wasn't? Isti was among those forced to make a statement in the Vári case. At first he thought that he'd stand his ground, stick to the truth, but when confronted with the face of his former superior, deformed by torture, he pondered no longer and signed the statement prepared for him, giving evidence that Vári had been spying for the Americans. Over the years he'd seen so much dirty dealing, so much monstrosity, around him that he felt that he had to pay the penalty for everything which he'd been involved in: they had every right to beat him to death.

Then he heard someone shouting: "Leave him, we'll sort out the rubbish!" It was a man with a wrinkled face and a moustache, in a tram-conductor's uniform. He picked Isti up off the floor and dragged him out of the enraged circle, while a young man who looked like a student pulled another bloodied defender after him and they were both hustled through the door. Outside in the street a number of insurgents set about them again, but the conductor and the student shielded them and in a noisy argument persuaded the furious crowd to leave them to it, they were going to deal with these filthy communists in the corner. At the side of the square, however, Isti and the other man were led to an ambulance where the man with the wrinkled face handed them over to first-aiders; he looked hard into Isti's eyes and all he said was: "Tell your murdering mates that the revolutionaries aren't animals like you!" They didn't wait for an answer, turned on their heels and set off back towards the Party HQ.

At the hospital in Péterffy Sándor utca wounded attackers and defenders waited together in the corridor. Standing by the

The Fashion Magazine

wall and lying on the floor as they fingered their injuries, they looked the new arrivals up and down, wondering on which side they'd been. Isti made straight for the lavatory, where he tore up his ÁVH identity card and flushed it away. It took three attempts, and he pulled the chain harder and harder as if to make his past vanish down the glazed pedestal. He checked anxiously to make sure that the incriminating document had been destroyed; if it were found on him, it could cost him his life. Fortunately he hadn't needed to wear uniform, and so there was nothing to betray him as an ÁVH officer. He just hoped that no one that knew him would turn up and recognise him. He agreed with the other rescued man, a lecturer in the Party college who had been hiding in the building at the time of the siege, that if questioned he would confirm Isti's status as a lecturer. They took their places among the other wounded and held the dressings that they'd been given in the ambulance over their wounds. The doctors gave priority to the seriously wounded and the first-aiders and assistants took the unconscious or moaning bodies to the operating theatre at the double; 'French photo-reporter,' was said of one. Then there was something of a commotion among the nurses as the sheeted body of one of the hospital doctors was brought in; he'd been fatally injured by a shot while on duty in the square. For hours, people waited patiently for their turns.

From the hospital Isti went straight to Keleti station. He arrived in Tövispuszta with his head swathed in a white turban. Here and there blood had seeped through the dressing, and the neighbours looked at him in dismay as he doggedly made his way to his parents' house, head firmly bowed, exchanging greetings to right and left.

"Jesus, my boy," said Lucky Gizi when he stepped into the kitchen. "What have they done to you? Hetési and Székely's sons have been here looking for you."

"They said they'd beat you to death if they caught you," added István as he sat by the table, "but I got the axe out. They understand that sort of language."

Isti limped about Tövispuszta. János Szentágostony came over from Bátakér from time to time to dress his wound. He took the stitches out in the guest room with scissors and forceps. István watched, leaning on his elbows at the end of the bed, his head to one side.

"Well, what does the young gentleman have to say about it all, have the Jews and the communists come back?" he said to János.

"Don't go on about the Jews, István, I don't like to hear that."

"But there'd be every reason to! The communists have locked your brother up, taken all your property, and made the Baroness into a peasant woman."

"You can curse the communists for me, if you aren't afraid they'll come and get you, but don't speak ill of the Jews, it's not right."

"The communists were Jews in '19, and it's the same now. Jew or communist is the same thing, isn't it?"

"No it isn't. Because it wasn't only Béla Kun and Rákosi that were Jewish, so were the Goldsteins and the Steiners. What was wrong with them? Just because Hitler and Stalin were Christians you wouldn't think of identifying them with Christianity, would you now?"

"They were Jews, the pair of 'em! Pack of work-shy wasters!" István made a disparaging gesture. He struggled to his feet and left the room.

János shook his head and packed his equipment in his doctor's bag. He then wrapped the stitches in a piece of gauze and put them in a little paper packet. He looked at Isti. "A wise man once said that history's main lesson is that people learn nothing from it. Presumably he knew your father."

As István limped out of the room János watched him go.

"What's wrong with your father?" he asked Isti.

"Goodness knows, he's been dragging his leg for a while. He says it's very painful."

János followed him into the kitchen.

"I'd like to look at your leg, István."

"Leave it alone, young sir. There's nothing to see, it's an old man's leg."

"That's why I'd like to take a look," János insisted, and told the old man to lower his trousers.

He drew in his breath sharply when he saw István's discoloured, dark blue leg.

"This is very bad, István!" he shook his head. "I'm surprised you can even walk. You ought to go straight into hospital."

"Oh, rubbish!" the old man waved the idea away.

"Pack a bag, Gizi, I'm taking your husband into hospital," said János in a tone that brooked no dissent, and István, like a naughty boy, docilely followed the doctor.

After some initial unease, István felt fine in hospital. He was, however, a little put out when the young nurse began to undress him to be washed, but then he waited curiously to see what the girl would say when the famous vision was exposed to her. He raised his backside in anticipation so that she could slip his trousers off first.

"Let me help you, Mr. Veres," said nurse Zsuzsi, and pulled down his pyjama trousers. Then she simply stared at the pride of Tövispuszta, which, in its pleasure at being freed from the trousers, or perhaps simply wishing to show off, was rising steadily between István's legs. She blushed and looked at him, and then, seeing from his amused face that he was enjoying her embarrassment, turned away and bought time by slowly reaching for the basin of water and sponge. Then she felt her bottom being stroked.

"Have you gone mad? What are you doing? You dirty old man!" she burst out angrily. "How dare you?" and put the basin down so hard that the water slopped over, fleeing the ward in tears. The old folk in adjacent beds grinned.

After a brief interval in came Margó, the hefty nurse, in militant fashion; she picked up basin and sponge and performed István's ablutions without batting an eyelid.

"Keep your laddish tricks for after the operation, Mr. Veres!" she said as she gave him a firm sponging down.

"They're treating me like a lord," István boasted to his son when he came to visit. "They won't let me out of bed, I shit and piss into basins, they bathe me like a child," he said with a proud laugh. "It's just the little blonde one who wouldn't let her bum be touched. But to punish her I shat myself so she'd have to clean it up!"

A few days later István was operated on. He was dazed when he came to. In the November half-light he looked cautiously round the ward, the dark, shaded neon light tube on the ceiling, the window frames, the white iron beds, the drip stands, the patients, either staring blankly into space or sleeping, and saw a whining Gizi and their two daughters who, arms around their mother, watched in tears as their father came out of the anaesthetic. István's attention then strayed to his bedclothes. By his right leg, where previously the outline of his leg had always raised the coverlet from the thigh downwards, the white hospital sheet lay flat on the blanket. He looked at it in alarm, then questioningly at his wife as if he couldn't believe his eyes, seeking reassurance from her that it was only a bad dream – but in Lucky Gizi's eyes he could see only profound agony and sympathy. István closed his eyes and was still lying there without having said a word when, hours later, Gizi and the girls gave him a silent caress and took their leave.

Once the night nurse had made her ward rounds the room was plunged into darkness, and only the cold light of the moon cast shadows on the wall. István looked round; apart from him everyone was asleep and the old men snored and hissed. István pulled the drip tube out of his arm, felt for the floor with his remaining leg and tried to crawl off the bed. He could feel two more tubes hanging from under the bedclothes, both ending in heavy-duty plastic bags on the floor. A quick investigation revealed that one of these led from his wound, the other from his sexual organ. He tried to stand on one leg, but didn't have the strength and sank back onto the side of the bed. He rested for a while, then sank to his left knee, clutched the two plastic bags to him with one hand and dragged himself to the window; summoning the remainder of his strength he clung to a radiator, stood on one leg and looked outside. The ward was on the fourth floor, and the window opened onto an internal courtyard. He opened the window, lay across the sill and looked down, calculating where he would land if he jumped. In the dark yard, directly beneath the window, lay an enormous roll of rusty wire surrounded by builder's rubble. "Sod it, if I fall into that rusty shit I'll end up with blood-poisoning," he thought. As he was considering the issue he began to shake convulsively from head to foot. "What kind of suicide candidate am I, to worry about my shitty life?!" He sprawled there on the windowsill until the nurse and the doctor on duty, cursing, helped him back to bed.

"You pig-headed old man!" said the doctor in charge of the ward on his rounds the next morning. "That's all we needed! What do you want? Septicemia as well as arteriosclerosis? You've pulled out your catheter and opened the incision up and we'll have to operate again."

Following the second operation István developed a high temperature and despite heavy doses of antibiotics, fever spots burned on his cheeks. It was no good Lucky Gizi bringing in her husband's favourite foods every day and trying gently to get him to eat. Like a wilful child István turned his face away. He spoke to no one, wouldn't eat, and lay silent on his bed.

"If he gives up, there's nothing we can do," said the surgeon to Isti. "It's not enough for the doctors to want a patient to recover, he has to want to himself."

After a few days István was being artificially fed, three weeks later he was at death's door. He was lying on the bed, his face sunken and deathly white, his eyes closed, when Lucky Gizi bent over him to kiss his forehead. Suddenly he opened his eyes, grabbed her by the throat with both hands and began to strangle her.

"You're coming with me!" he croaked.

Such was the force with which he gripped his wife's throat that had Isti not been there he would surely have throttled the little old woman. Isti pulled at his father's wrists with all his strength, but even so was scarcely able to wrench the bony fingers from his mother's neck. One last time István turned his sea-blue eyes with the fringe of dark lashes to Lucky Gizi, as if he wanted to take her face with him; then he fell back, never to move again. Gizi, however, gasped for air and looked at her husband with the same startled, gentle eyes as she had done for forty years.

By the time that Isti went back to Budapest and reported for duty at the Ministry of the Interior the fighting was over. To

The Fashion Magazine

his surprise he was received in the Ministry by Vári, whom he
hadn't seen since 1949, when the major and others had been
arrested on the basis of his statement. Vári had aged in prison,
his face had grown thin and haggard, but his eyes had their
former fire. He was wearing a Russian army sweater with a
belt and a pistol-holster on one side. When Isti walked into
the office Vári immediately noticed his consternation and the
embarrassment in his eyes. He went up to Isti and shook his
hand.

"I know what you're thinking," he said. "But I bear no
grudge. There was nothing else that you could have done, and
in fact I testified against myself. I believed that by so doing
I would be helping the Party, and then when you've had your
balls beaten with a rubber truncheon and not been allowed to
sleep for a week you'd end up confessing to having stabbed
Julius Caesar."

The events of the following weeks wore Isti out: the
arrests, the savage sentences of the 'hanging judges'. Many
ÁVH personnel who'd gone into hiding during the uprising
quickly joined the authorities after the Soviet counter-attack
and were now boasting of their heroic deeds and listening
with some satisfaction to news of the executions. "If as many
had fought against the counter-revolutionaries as are now
boasting of doing so, the Soviets wouldn't have had anything
to do," said Vári with profound disgust.

In Mérleg utca there was a sour-smelling, smoky, rough
inn where, after dark, in the hissing neon lights sad-faced men
stood drinking alone, or talking quietly with those standing
beside them. "*Che serà, serà,*" someone sang the prohibited
song as he dolefully peered into the bottom of his glass, but
no one informed on him even though men from the Ministry
of the Interior who worked in nearby offices went there after
hours. They would drop in for a beer and a slice of bread and

219

dripping with onion, then go their various ways. Isti and Vári mostly stayed, like the rest, and carried on drinking wine together and talking. A few weeks later, when the two of them had once again lingered on, Vári told Isti how his former ÁVH colleagues had tortured him. When the fighting had broken out in October he and several ÁVH men had gone at once to Tököl,[68] where they reported to Soviet HQ. They had fought on the Soviet side against the insurgents, and fired into the demonstrating crowd without a second thought.

"I thought that after what they'd done to you, you'd have hated the regime," said Isti.

"The regime?" repeated Vári uncomprehendingly, toying idly with his glass of wine on the counter. "That would be like hating myself. And if I didn't belong here, where then? With those who murdered my parents and brothers? Or with those who looked on as accomplices? There's no middle way here, old chap; either we kill them, or they kill us."

The wine-drinking became a ritual. Their colleagues watched enviously as Isti and Vári conferred regularly during the day and met after work. They both felt out of place among the others, and their future also seemed to be without hope. His years in prison had destroyed Vári's relationship with his wife; no family was waiting for Isti at home, only a stuffy rented room and an uncomfortable couch, on better days the occasional woman, who would pull a face and turn her head away the next morning when she caught the smell of stale wine and tobacco on his breath. Isti and Vári didn't become drunk, they just sipped their wine and chatted as if trying to ease their loneliness by being together, although they were both aware that two lonely people never become two social beings; even in company they remain lonely.

As the months passed Isti noticed Vári's disillusionment and deepening depression, but try though he might he

The Fashion Magazine

couldn't help him. Then one day Vári was summoned by
the newly appointed young and well-groomed head of
department (the 'man of the future', as he was called in the
Ministry) and informed that he was being detached from the
Interior and transferred to some new cultural organisation.
Vári rushed out of the office in a rage, slamming the door
behind him. The director leapt up from his desk, tore open
the door and shouted after Vári:
    "Come back at once, Comrade Major! I demand!"
    "Don't you demand anything from me, my son," said
Vári without even looking round, and then he stopped and
turned. "You were still pushing children's toys around the
playground when I was fighting the fascists with real guns,"
he said with a harsh, scornful look on his face.
    The colleagues watched with ill-concealed grins.
    "You're on a charge!" shrieked the young departmental
head, crimson at the public insult. "I'll have you up in front
of the Party!" he added malevolently.
    "While they were shitting themselves that they'd
be strung up on the nearest tree we did all right, we old
Bolshies," said Vári that evening in the pub. "But now, when
they've got nothing to be afraid of, they've even hanged Imre
Nagy, and we're a thorn in their flesh. We're the disgraceful
past, a hindrance to consolidation. Just imagine, a few days
ago some idiot rang me up and asked how I'd like my funeral
to be conducted! Look here, I said, I'm still alive! At which
he started to stammer that he was ringing from the central
Party undertaker's department or some such, and his job was
to ask old comrades what sort of funeral they wanted. Are
these people in their right minds? I told him I'd only got one
request: I wanted to be buried face down. Which startled him
– 'Oh really, Comrade Vári, why?' So that everybody'll be able
to kiss my arse, I replied, and slammed the phone down."

221

When, a few days later, the local Party Secretary announced from his presidential desk with its red covering that Vári had been disciplined, everyone discreetly watched the major. Vári, his face harsh and expressionless listened to the verdict, then left the room without waiting for the meeting to be over. The colleagues were singing the Internationale when the dull sound of an explosion was heard from the lavatory: Vári had shot himself in the head.

Major László Vári's last rites were performed at the workers' movement plot in the Mező Imre cemetery. The Workers' Funeral March[69] played softly from the loudspeakers. His colleagues, their faces unemotional, surrounded the bier and official wreaths were laid by policemen in dress uniform detailed as pall-bearers. His widow and twelve-year-old daughter, dressed in black, sat alone in the row of seats for relatives.

"Laci Vári knew that the weapon that the Party had given him shouldn't be used against the Party, so he turned it on himself," someone said in an undertone. A few people tittered quietly, others snorted.

Then the cortège, consisting of friends and old comrades in arms, formed up by the coffin. With no fuss, their faces impassive, they found their places in the line. And it was then that Mrs. Vári burst out in a sudden, inarticulate shriek.

"That man who grassed on Laci in the Horthy police in '32, you get away from there!" and she pointed a shaking hand at a man standing by the coffin. "And the one who informed on him in '41 in Moscow, you too!"

Confusion grew around the coffin. The men in black suits and police uniforms looked at one another, unsure what to do. A number lowered their heads and slunk away from the coffin, others were righteously indignant. Mrs. Vári, however, continued to shout.

"And you who ruined our lives, you who imprisoned Laci in '49, though he hadn't done anything, how have you got the nerve to stand there? And you," she pointed at the 'man of the future', "you who humiliated him and drove him to suicide, how dare you come here?!"

Two of Vári's colleagues hurried to her, took her arms and whispered something in her ear, but in such a determined and forceful manner that it seemed as if they wanted not so much to calm her as to take her away. She covered her face with her hands and sobbed, and didn't look up again until the funeral was over; meanwhile her little daughter clung weeping to her.

Isti searched the faces of the mourners, and smiled grimly; he was thinking, have they really buried Vári face down in the coffin, as he wanted, because these people really might kiss his arse.

In the interests of stabilisation some of the condemned revolutionaries were pardoned, while most of the former ÁVH men were transferred to so-called 'politically sensitive' enterprises and cultural institutions in which they made up for their lack of know-how by their reliability. Isti remained in the Ministry for the Interior, but moved to the economic section. His task was to observe and, if necessary, catch secret agents whose cover was foreign trade or the domestic economy, and dealers who faltered politically or commercially. He acquired more and more friends: small businessmen who ran gebins, premises rented from State enterprises, and the

223

sort of middle-men who assisted in the acquisition of permits for small businesses. Both parties were happy to meet with Isti's readiness to collaborate and all saw the usefulness of this, not to mention rising socialism. Indeed they also saw the usefulness of Auntie Bözsi, manageress of the Öreghárs, because the intimate little restaurant was an ideal meeting-place for middle-men who weren't devoted to the puritan lifestyle and small businessmen who managed their affairs successfully. The Öreghárs was essentially a family place, with big, leafy lime-trees which gave it its name, tables with checked cloths, expert, good-humoured waiters and hidden private rooms. The *Wienerschnitzel* overhung the plates, the pickles were home-made, the chicken soup and fisherman's stew inspired hit songs, and those in the know could even have tripe, *körömpörkölt*,[70] and indeed cold – cold! – beer, which was definitely in short supply nation-wide. A Gypsy band played outside in the garden in summer, indoors in winter, and in the evening, but in the basement and exclusively for select regular guests, a hoarse-voiced bar pianist performed. Auntie Bözsi was discreet, and saw to it that the mood of regular guests, bowed down with the burden of political or commercial responsibility, was lightened by pretty girls; she provided private rooms for intimate working dinners and evocative corners for romantic rendez-vous in the basement bar. On the upper level of the Öreghárs there were also two little rooms which guaranteed that a number of important comrades were devoted to ensuring the uninterrupted licensing of the Öreghárs and to Auntie Bözsi's personal trustworthiness and discretion. She knew everything about everybody, artists and Party leaders of nationwide repute sobbed out their amorous woes on her shoulder, as did philandering husbands and cheated wives.

The first time that Isti set foot in the Öreghárs, as the

guest of a businessman who enjoyed official concessions, the
prímás struck up his tune. Isti looked at him in astonishment.
For a moment the music stopped. Everyone looked that way.
"Csoki," exclaimed Isti loudly, and hurried over to the *prímás*
to give him a hug. The rest of the band went on playing while
they embraced.

"Are you playing here?"

"I thought you'd come in because you knew," said Csoki
with a laugh. "After all, there's a notice up outside saying that
Zsiga Balogh junior and his folk musicians are performing."

Weeks went by before, one vinous evening when few
guests were left in the restaurant, Csoki finally prevailed on
Isti to take over the violin. He hadn't had the instrument in
his hand for twenty years. He struggled with his crooked
fingers, eventually got out a few bars, then handed it back.
"It's no good," said he, fighting back tears. "Maybe one day."

The Öreghárs became Isti's favourite watering-hole.
Auntie Bözsi introduced him to the life of the bar and to Klári,
a beautiful but terribly inhibited model who'd only recently
left her lover, a well-known council leader.

No sooner had the love of Isti and Klári begun to burgeon,
as the saying goes, than it went into full bloom, and then, when
the Ministry promised him a councillor's flat if he married,
they tied the knot. Klári's tubby, six-year old daughter also
took to Isti, and at first everything in the garden was rosy.
With Isti's help Klári appeared more frequently on the cat-
walk, on the title pages of fashion magazines and in the
newsreels that preceded films in the cinema. They sat in the
auditorium and watched proudly as Klári, in a slightly stiff
manner, walked across the screen in *Elegant* dresses from the
Vörös Október dress factory, made for export to the West. But
Isti assured her to no avail that her movements weren't stiff in
the least, and that it was in fact her very inhibitions that gave

her personality its charm. She found it harder and harder to believe, and felt that she was awkward, clumsy and devoid of talent. The fact that she often heard her colleagues' muttered remarks suggesting that she wouldn't be allowed on the cat-walk if her husband wasn't an officer of the Ministry of the Interior had a lot to do with this.

Klári started to drink. The first tot that she downed before a fashion show did indeed greatly relax her movement, but the second, third and later the fourth led rather to loss of balance, until one day she fell off the cat-walk in front of the audience and broke a leg. By then they were quarrelling daily at home. Isti would regularly come home from work to find Klári dead drunk on the carpet. There was disorder in the flat and nothing in the fridge as Babi, their little daughter, in her desperation had eaten everything in it and then lain weeping on the floor beside her helpless mother. The first few times Isti rummaged in the wardrobe, grabbed some money from beneath the underwear and rushed out to the Öreghárs. There he asked Csoki for the violin and, suffering agonies with his twisted fingers, played his favourite tunes with tears in his eyes, buying several rounds for the guests so that they might endure his performance. They, however, weren't in the least cross with him, and some looked on his unhappy suffering with pity, others amusedly; people are grateful if they can see the representative of a fearsome power being even more unfortunate than themselves. Furthermore Isti was definitely charming when he picked up the violin. It seemed that the instrument evoked his former sensitive personality.

At first Isti was careful never to strike Klári in front of the little girl. Later he found it hard to control his temper and, setting aside his educational beliefs, he slapped her when he found her drunk. He threatened to leave her, but then didn't because he was afraid that divorce would wreck his career.

In the Ministry the domestic circumstances of staff were taken seriously, and while wife-beating was acceptable, divorce was not. And then, to tell the truth, Isti did love Klári. Or rather, he did when she was sober.

Breaking her leg came as a turning-point. Klári couldn't appear on the cat-walk, and therefore no longer felt pressure. She hardly drank at all.

"If you could get me a licence to open a boutique, that would be the answer to everything," she said to Isti one day.

"Licence for a boutique," he pondered dreamily. "A little place by the Balaton, and a place on the list for a Trabant. That's what everybody wants. It won't be easy, but I'll see what I can do."

THE GYPSY GRAMMAR

P ali had heard the story so often that he gradually convinced himself that he remembered that it had happened. He'd been five. He was playing in the garden when a tall, thin man stopped outside the gate. The crumpled balloon-silk coat hung from the man's gaunt body as if the latter were a hat-stand, and in his hand he held a bag. He looked at Pali as he played and didn't speak. "Who are you looking for?" asked Pali. The man carried on standing there and looking at him, holding onto the fence with both hands as if afraid of falling. "Is this where the Szentágostonys live?" he asked hoarsely. Pali was startled, ran to the door, and called inside: "Daddy, a gentleman's asking for you!" János came out and, rooted to the spot, the two men stared at each other intently. Then they put their arms round one another and held each other tight for a long time, swaying, as if wrestling. Mother then came out, and on seeing the man burst into tears. Then they too embraced and wept together. The stranger bent down to Pali, picked him up and asked if he might give him a kiss. His face was unshaven, and his clothes and skin had a sour smell. "You're smelly, I don't know you," exclaimed Pali and pushed him roughly away. Mother was sobbing. The adults asked him to go back into the garden and play, and they talked quietly in the kitchen. Then the stranger came out and played football with him, taught him to head the ball, told him tales. Later he slept with Mother in the big room while Pali and Daddy slept in the little room.

Now in his teens, Pali was making an effort to reconstruct the story of his life, piece by piece. He had to struggle for every detail because he had difficulty in prising things out of his parents. Elza told him that when they returned from London and were arrested she'd been in her fifth month. She'd given birth to the little boy in the prison hospital where she'd been allowed to nurse him for a month, then despite her pleas and wails, the child was taken from her and she wasn't allowed to see him again. When she was released two years later she kept asking for her son to be given back, but after a lengthy search and much pleading the only information she was given was that he'd been taken to an orphanage in Buda. It wasn't known where he went from there, because in the meantime his name and details had been changed.

The woman in charge of the orphanage looked perplexed as she examined the official document empowering Elza to recover her son. The carers were clearly sympathetic but really couldn't offer her any definite information. They told her that at the time, several children had been brought to the orphanage whose parents had been executed or imprisoned, and all of them had had their original details changed. Elza, in despair, did her best to wind her memories back to the day when her son had been separated from her, so that they could leaf through the thick register for details.

Fortunately one of the carers remembered the nurse from the prison hospital bringing in the blanket-wrapped child to the babies department. Since the nurse was forbidden to divulge the child's real name he'd been registered as József Nagy. Eighteen months later little Józsi had been transferred to the home at Berkesz, in Szabolcs county,[71] said the carer, "But keep that to yourself, will you, comrade," she went on anxiously, "because I could find myself in jail for telling you."

At the children's home in Berkesz, Elza had to pick out her small son from half a dozen Józsi Nagys. She tried to recall the month-old infant's features, looked for any family resemblance, worrying about her ability to identify her own child; then, relying on instinct, she went towards a slender, brown-haired little boy. "This is him," she said decisively. When, however, she tried to give him a hug the child screamed, kicked, scratched and even defecated; he didn't want to be separated from his carer. "Are you sure it's him?" asked the carer, looking startled. "Yes, this is my son," said Elza, satisfied.

Pali's brain had so protected him from trauma that, as he far as he could tell, every painful memory had been erased. Although he still looked up on hearing the name Józsi, even at the age of five, he could remember nothing of the time that he'd spent in care. Elza applied to the authorities for information about her husband in vain – her letters went unanswered. No one dared say so openly, but apart from Elza, all the family were convinced that Pál had been executed, sent to Siberia, or simply died of maltreatment in prison.

Following his years in institutions Pali still couldn't recover his name. Officialdom blocked Elza's choice and the boy would have to remain József Nagy, or could take his mother's maiden name of Goldstein. János suggested to Elza that he should adopt Pali so that in a country strong on prejudice she need not appear to be an unmarried mother, nor the boy illegitimate. After much petitioning he finally became a Szentágostony once more; the documents, however, named János as father. In order to avoid official suspicion Elza and Pali joined János in Bátakér, where a flat went with the surgery.

The Gypsy Grammar

✳

"I thought my uncle was my father," said Pali to Tamás Kárász at the counter in the Nárcisz coffee-bar, struggling to find the right words. Tamás was leader of the working-party on Gypsy studies, and well known in student circles as a dissident. "At home in the village the old people sometimes address me as 'young Baron', although I haven't seen any of the family wealth," Pali went on. "At other times they try to insult me, calling me a Jew because of my mother, even though I was born a Christian of Christian parents. And what's more, I'll never know by what right they do it all, because I'm not even sure that my mother didn't bring some other József Nagy back from the institution."

"An identity-challenged boy searching for explanations in an identity-challenged country," replied Kárász with sympathetic irony. He already knew all about Pali's history, because he almost always talked about it when he'd had a drink or two. He patted him on the shoulder. "You go home, old chap, and sleep it off. You look a bit done in."

The girl who was watching them from behind the bar apparently hadn't understood a word of the conversation, but as she polished glasses and served drinks she kept turning her head so as to have her ear towards them.

Pali watched his friend leave. Then, when he was alone, he loitered at the counter for a while longer, shaking his head as if puzzled, holding his glass in his hand and hunched up a little, as if feeling the burden of life on his shoulders, or at least the light weight of a bottle of brandy, even though he'd only drunk three glasses. The girl behind the bar was very pretty. With her chestnut hair, big brown eyes and taut blouse she reminded Pali of the young Lollobrigida. She watched the sad-eyed boy, fascinated.

"Are you a student?" she asked.

"Uhuh."

"What are you studying?"

"Hungarian and French," said Pali.

"You speak French?" asked the girl.

"Uhuh. Sort of."

"It's a beautiful language. I once met a real Frenchman. He spoke French, didn't know any Hungarian," she said brightly.

"Yes, it's beautiful," Pali agreed. "So are you."

The girl blushed. Pali tried to smile pleasantly, but he felt that his facial muscles were stiff from the alcohol and he only managed a forced, lop-sided, inane grin.

"I'd love to go on talking to you, but I'm exhausted," he said. "What's your name?"

"Olga. And yours?"

"Pál. Pál Szentágostony."

"We could meet tomorrow, if you like. It's my day off," said the girl, cocking her head expectantly.

"Half three at the EMKE?"[72]

"Right," said Olga happily, and blew a kiss to Pali as he left.

It had been five years since the National Theatre had been demolished to make way for the Metro, but nevertheless, when Pali was on Blaha Lujza tér he still looked round for the building. The image of the old theatre was so etched into his memory that even now, years later, the square looked improbable without it. "Something like phantom pains," he thought. "If someone has a leg amputated the place where it was can still itch. Then a new generation grows up that can't imagine what the square was like with the old National. I'm becoming like the old idiots that still call Népköztársaság út Andrássy út, November 7 tér the Oktogon, and Moszkva tér

Széll Kálmán tér, as they were before the war.[73] In this country nothing is what it is, nor the opposite."

He looked for Olga in the afternoon crowds, among the people strolling and loitering in the square. Then suddenly he spotted her. She was coming from the direction of the Corvin Warehouse, and people were staring at her. She was wearing a short figure-hugging evening dress sewn with silver spangles, her hair piled high in a beehive style, and her eyelids were so thickly painted purple that Pali could see them clearly fifty yards away. She was hurrying towards him, smiling happily, while he looked around to either side in case anyone that knew him was witnessing this painful scene.

"Are you going to a ball?" asked Pali, instead of a customary greeting.

"I wanted to please you," said Olga, and the happy smile vanished from her face. "I've put my best dress on. I got it last week at the Gólya Warehouse. It's a bit second-hand, but it's foreign!"

Pali felt sorry.

"I beg your pardon, it's just that you're so splendid that on a bright sunny day like this it's rather extraordinary among all these dingy, down-at-heel people."

"Where shall we go?" asked Olga, mollified.

Pali looked round uncertainly. "If we go towards Rákóczi tér," he thought, "the prostitutes will stare at us, and if we go towards Kossuth Lajos utca we might run into my university friends, and that would be terrible."

"There's a nice little strudel shop on the corner just here," he said, "let's go there."

"You like strudel? Oh, that's good! So do I," Olga welcomed the idea.

"This girl's pretty thick, but she's very agreeable," thought Pali as he watched her elegantly slide half her backside onto

THE INFLATABLE BUDDHA

the high, aluminium bar-stool, carefully adjust the spangled evening dress and take a mouthful of morello and poppy-seed strudel. 'The best thing would be to go to a cinema,' thought Pali, 'there at least it's dark. And at this sort of time in the afternoon there'll be nobody that knows me.'

"There's a good film on at the Bányász, it's called *Walls*."[74]

"*Walls*?" Olga savoured the name. "Is it a love-story or a war-film? I prefer love-stories."

"I haven't seen it," Pali answered. "But I believe it's neither. Just a good film."

"And you think I'll understand it?"

"Why not? You're a clever girl," said Pali without conviction.

Olga watched patiently for half an hour as Miklós Gábor[75] discussed the problems of practical socialism at a production conference, a party and in a café, then she whispered into Pali's ear:

"Do you really like this?"

"Well… "

"I can't understand a word of it."

"Then would you rather go to your place?"

"Might as well."

Olga lived in Salétrom utca, in an apartment house with a *gang*.[76] The semi-basement flat consisted of one room and a kitchen and opened onto the courtyard with its broken tiles. It was officially occupied by Olga and her grandmother, but the latter had for some months been in a hospice and Olga didn't expect her to come home, and so she'd painted the walls lemon yellow and daubed the assortment of furniture – chairs, cupboards, beds and tables – with a uniform white gloss. The flat was tidy, a vase on the table contained a carefully arranged bunch of colourful flowers, but a musty smell came from the walls. Pali looked round and discovered a telephone among the framed photographs on the little cupboard.

"Goodness, you've got a telephone!"

"Yes, but it isn't connected," said Olga, blushing. "I'd very much like a telephone, and well, like this it's almost the same."

"Ah, yes," said Pali, "very nearly."[77]

The working-party on Gypsy studies, led by Tamás Kárász, met weekly in the Napoletana restaurant in Váci utca. He had for years been visiting Gypsy settlements, had learnt Lovári, and with his friends collected money, clothes, school material, toys and books for the poor. The middle classes, with their first taste of the thaw that replaced the terror, regarded the Gypsies as shiftless, feckless wasters.

"What do you want?" Pali was asked at the university by a young lecturer, charged by the Party organisation with dissuading students from going to dissident meetings. "Look what's happening in Romania, Czechoslovakia or the GDR! Is that what you're after? You're an intelligent, capable person, you ought to understand that there's a frontier within which the Hungarian Party leadership can operate, and these political frontiers are drawn up in Moscow with the agreement of the West. Haven't you learnt from what happened in Prague? Would you like the Warsaw Pact to march in here? The Czechs, Romanians and East Germans would love to come! Is that what you want?"

The last time they'd met, in the Napoletana garden, Bea Szakács, a busty, final-year medical student angrily related how she'd gone to see a well-known painter to ask him for a picture for an illegal auction, the proceeds of which would be used to help the poor. The painter's wife wouldn't even let her into the hall. She listened to what she had to say through the part-opened door, then asked: "Have you got a fiancé, my dear?" "No," replied Bea in surprise. "Well, my dear," said the famous painter's wife, "get one quick, get married and have some children, then you'll calm down!" and she slammed the door. When the deeply offended Bea told this story in her high-pitched voice Pali could hardly withhold a grin. Bea was one of the medical students attached to the working party, which also included technical students and economists. The majority came from villas in the Buda hills or spacious flats, their parents were former leftists or even influential leaders who, in the young people's view, had betrayed the revolution and stagnated, leading a life of ease. Members of the working-party were only distinguishable by their designer jeans (received as presents from the West), whereas students from less well-off homes mostly went about in Hungarian-made Trapper jeans. Otherwise they wore the same popular footwear from the Alföld Shoe Factory, and carried the same kind of embroidered shoulder-bags or gas-mask cases which had been customised as bags. They carried out assessments in the Gypsy settlements, each in the terms of his specialism, from health, sociological or cultural points of view. Kárász taught them the Romanian Gypsy language, and so when they arrived at the settlement they offered a greeting in Lovári, which the inhabitants found rather odd.

"*Taves bahtalo,*" they said politely.

"*Taves vi tut. Zhanes romanes?*" asked a suntanned, middle-aged man at the door of a shanty, but with that, any conversation in Lovári came to an end since the working-party's knowledge of the language lacked substance. Kárász was the only one to reply in Lovári, saying that the others were still just learning the language.

They stood politely at the entrance to the mud-brick,

earth-floored shack and peered eagerly inside.

"May I ask how many generations there are in this shack?" enquired the bespectacled Feri Bagi importantly.

"How many what?" the man returned the question suspiciously. "We've got nothing like that here, we keep clean! I'll bet I've got more clean shirts than you!"

With that he stepped to the rickety cupboard, pulled open the door, and took out half a dozen neatly ironed snow-white shirts.

"Nobody'd better call me a dirty Gypsy!"

"You misunderstood me," Feri excused himself in alarm. "I wouldn't dream of such a thing!"

"Are you Jewish?" asked the man.

"What's that got to do with anything?" asked Feri, perplexed. He took off his spectacles and began to wipe them.

"Because the only people that come here are Jews," said the man. "And the police," he added. With that he turned his back and went inside.

"Only Jews come here…" grumbled Feri, and began to steal furtive glances at the profiles of the research group. "How can you tell who's Jewish?" he muttered to himself.

Kárász felt sorry for him.

"To be fair, it would make sense for people who've themselves suffered exclusion for centuries to be a bit sensitive about it, don't you think?"

"Somebody who's socially sensitive has to be Jewish?" Feri exclaimed.

"Let's change the subject," said Kárász with a dismissive gesture. "We've come to do some work, right?"

The party split up and talked to the inhabitants of the settlement, collecting what they learnt in little notebooks.

"If you were to get a few chickens I'd make you a nice Gypsy chicken *pörkölt*,[78] and we could have at least a bit of

237

meat as well," said one plump Gypsy woman in a head-scarf. The idea appealed to the party. "We've never tasted Gypsy *pörkölt*, " said a few.

"What's it like?" asked a girl who was studying economics.

"You'll see," said the woman with a laugh.

Kárász stroked his beard and smiled. Bea Szakács immediately went round the group, forints came from pockets, and she and the Gypsy woman went off to the nearby shop. They came back with three dressed chickens, some onions, a huge loaf, some pickled gherkins and three bottles of cheap red wine. A fire was lit in front of the shack, a cooking-pot placed on it, the cut-up chickens and onions went into the fat and the cooking began. The breeze carried the scent of onions and chicken far and wide.

Pali dipped a wooden spoon into the juice of the *pörkölt*.

"Very tasty, but what's Gypsy about it?"

"Well, a Gypsy woman's cooked it," and the woman laughed and wiped her hands on her apron.

The *pörkölt* simmered gently in the pot while the party were hard at work. They asked the inhabitants of the settlement what income they had to live on, what hygiene conditions were like, what illnesses people had; the architecture students prepared drawings showing how waste water might be drained and how the shacks might be made more habitable on a small budget. Pali and a few Gypsy children did some weeding, and provoking plenty of laughter he showed them how the settlement might be made to look nicer. They had just started playing football when some dreadful swearing and shouting was heard.

"They're stealing the food!" shouted the woman angrily. "Damn their eyes, rot their guts!"

Two workmen had sneaked between the shacks, taken the pot off the fire and were making off with it at speed. Pali,

The Gypsy Grammar

Kárász and two more gave chase, and Feri Bagi – holding his glasses on his nose – trotted after them. The workers waddled as they ran carrying the pot, slopping the red liquid onto the ground. Then, as the boys had almost caught up with them, they threw the pot and well-cooked pieces of chicken and paprika-laden juice away, scattering the steaming meal all over the ground. The two workmen ran on a few yards, then stood there laughing, swaying backwards and forwards and slapping their thighs, as the sobbing Gypsy woman cursed them. It was at that moment that Feri Bagi's faith in the equitable nature of the world order was destroyed.

Kárász took Pali into a cellar in a street off Főtér. They made their way cautiously down the steep stairs to where a young man with matted hair and a beard, accompanied by a guitar and drums, was singing Karel Gott's song *Lady Carneval* [79] in Czech.

The group was standing on a heap of doll corpses, wailing rapturously. Around them lay dolls made of plastic, porcelain and rag, their eye-sockets empty or their eyes upturned, on a mound of amputated hands and feet, as if waiting, following a monstrous massacre, to be buried in a mass grave to the sounds of the Czech star's velvety song.

At first Pali looked in astonishment at the scene. "What's this, Prague in 1968?" Then, when he saw the grins lurking behind the audience's apparently serious faces, he felt relieved at being allowed to smile. Several greeted Kárász and he introduced Pali, whispering each time in his ear whom it was that they'd met. "Avant-garde painter, here from Szentendre," [80] he said of a bearded man in a cap, "film director," of a gaunt man with a pony-tail. "Writer," he said of a bald man in black,

239

"but be careful with him, he's probably a police informer."
There followed a contemporary composer, an avant-garde
theatre director, a performance artist and the rest.

The group played, but the long haired singer with
a moustache didn't actually sing all that often, instead
speaking the lyrics in a dull voice, which became increasingly
determined and loud, until eventually he was beside himself
and shouting. By the end of it Pali was grinning uninhibitedly,
and was as happy as the rest; he was having his first taste
of being accepted in such company and was roaring out the
refrain with the others.

Pali never really did get close to his father. He couldn't ever
make up his mind whether it was because of the missing
years, when they should have been together, or whether Pál's
severe, elegant aloofness was the reason; it encircled him like
an impenetrable shell which only Elza could occasionally
pierce. Perhaps it was the fierce contest for the favours and
attention of a mother, which always sets fathers against sons,
that kept them apart. When Pali was told at the age of seven
that Pál really was his father he burst into sobs, insisting that
János was his Daddy and that he would always call him such.
In the end Pál suggested that it would be quite in order for
him to go on calling János Daddy, and he could be called Pa.
This didn't make the situation any simpler if they all four
went anywhere together. People were dismayed to think of
the peculiar family relationship that they must have. Pali
never dared ask his mother whether, during his father's long
years in prison, there'd been more than a familial friendship
between her and János – nor did he enquire what his father
thought or knew about this. He didn't venture to ask his

father or János whether they'd ever spoken of the matter either. In any case, János was separated from them, remaining in Bátakér in his official flat while Pál and the family moved back to Tövispuszta, to a little peasant house, so that at least they could be of help to Emília in caring for the aged Baron. Pál translated technical literature from four different languages and Elza had a position in the town library.

Two years later, following the revolution, Pál was imprisoned once again. In the earliest days of the revolution his sometime cell-mate Bánoss, recently liberated from prison, had sent him a message that ex-officers were preparing to fight and were awaiting him in Budapest. Later he was asked to join the town's revolutionary council, but he refused both invitations. "Everybody from the communists to the former Arrow-Cross believes that this is their revolution, and meanwhile they can't see that the status quo that has arisen since the war won't be altered by an uprising," he said. At home he followed events on the radio, read novels and listened to classical music on records. But although he was the only person in his neighbourhood to have been certain from the outset that the Soviet Union wouldn't tolerate the developments in Hungary, when the Soviet attack started Pál had been the most embittered. Then it turned out that, contrary to all his wisdom, deep down he nevertheless trusted in the impossible: what if Hungary succeeded in winning her neutrality and, together with Austria, became part of the buffer zone between the Soviet Union and the West? A suppressed and frustrated hope burst out of him like an explosion. The town revolutionary council had been disbanded and a lot of people had fled the country when Pál went into town for the first time. The miners and factory workers were holding a mass meeting outside the offices of the Mine Trust. When a number of people in the crowd recognised him he was dragged onto the platform and asked for his advice: ought they to join this national strike or not? Pál thought for no more than a couple of moments, then said in a firm tone: "The strike is probably pointless, the revolution has failed. All the same, I say Strike! For your own sakes! Because if you don't, you'll feel that you're worthless, and you won't be able to look your sons in the face."

For that speech of just a few sentences, Pál was given 5 years in prison, and in articles justifying the retribution after the revolution, illustrated with photographs of the lynchings in Köztársaság tér, his name was often included among those of former Horthyist officers, priests and aristocrats who had sided with the insurgents, because lo and behold! the former ruling class had seen that the time had come to recover its power and property.

First the old Baron was buried, then three years later Emília was carried off by cancer. Elza nursed her in the final months of her illness, moving into the Kallóses' outhouse to be with her, because after being relocated the old people had stayed there since there was nowhere else for them to go. Elza fed her mother-in-law, washed her and changed her incontinence pads. Pál wasn't paroled, even for his parents' funerals. János was once again a frequent visitor to Elza and the others, and so things went on until Pál was released. When János disappeared a second time from Pali's life the boy was angry with his father for separating them in this way. Later too if any problem arose he would consult János or his mother rather than his father. Pál built an ever higher and thicker wall around himself; he would write in the kitchen, working on his translations until the small hours. At night the yellow light of the reading-lamp filtered through the gap under the door and they had to tip-toe round the house in the morning because Pál was asleep in the darkened bedroom. Then he would read or listen to music, or go for solitary walks round the village. Elza occasionally went with him, but she would never accompany him to the embankment on the edge of the village, or to the level crossing. "Can you see something?" he would ask her when she refused to go, and he'd give her a hug. "Is that where I shall die?" he asked. But Elza opened her eyes wide and shook her head.

"Mother, listen, if you can foretell so much, why didn't you prevent father from coming back from London? How come you didn't sense that he'd go to prison again?" Pali once asked his mother in an aggrieved tone.

"I did, I foresaw it all," said Elza sadly.

"Then why didn't you do something? Why didn't you speak? Why didn't you stop him?"

"I can only see what will be, but I can't change it."

"You don't mean to say that Destiny rules our lives, do you?" Pali asked heatedly.

"No, my boy. We ourselves and our surroundings are our destiny. We alone can shape ourselves and our surroundings, no one else can help us. I did warn your father not to leave London because I could see what would happen, but for the sake of his honour your father wanted to come home. And his conscience demanded that he side with the strikers. How could I have spoken against his honour and his conscience? If he hadn't acted in that way he'd have let himself down. I would have made the same decision in his place. Just as I chose to be deported along with my mother, although I could foresee the terrible things that happened. Because it was the honourable thing to do. Do you see what I'm getting at?"

243

It was the first time that Pali had discussed such things with his mother, and her gentle, soft words enthralled him. For the first time he felt that she regarded him not as a child but as an adult who was seriously interested in her opinion.

"But what do you feel when you're foreseeing something? How do you do it?" he asked.

"Just as we see the past. I compile it from indistinct images, as if they were from the past. Sometimes I have a feeling about moods or situations. But I don't like to talk about it, because these things are beyond explanation. I've only spoken to your father about it before and now I've spoken to you."

"Isn't it frightening?"

"I'm used to it. Just as everyone finds it natural to have images from the past."

"But I still don't understand, if you can foresee things, why can't you change them?"

"Can you change the past? You can't, can you? Though a lot of people try, especially these days. Nor can the future be changed, unless we change. Generally speaking, people can't see the present, only think they can. It's like when you look up to the starry sky and you accept that the stars are there, whereas you know that the visible heaven is the imprint of the situation millions of years ago. Many of the distant stars are now dead, exploded, but because of the enormous distance, the information hasn't reached us yet. Only later do people find out that everything around them, the present in which they live, has been falling to pieces before their very eyes, it's just that they haven't realised yet."

Elza paused for thought, and went on.

"I find it hard to explain. Perhaps your grandfather Samu was the only one who understood me, but I never spoke to him about this. I'm very sorry that you never had the chance to know him. You'd have got on well together."

The Jampot

Dávid and Isti were eleven when they set out on the great journey. Bit by bit they gathered the things they would need – a few sausage left-overs from the Vereses' pantry, two pots of apricot jam from the Goldsteins' store, some biscuits, half a loaf – and packed them into a bag along with a well-worn copy of Károly May's book on Indians. They'd worked everything out in minute detail, leaving nothing to chance. They had a precise itinerary, which had been checked on numerous occasions against the map in the Goldsteins' lexicon; they would sail down the stream to the Danube, down the river to the sea, then all they needed was to go in an arrow-straight line across the ocean to reach America. From New York they'd continue on horseback to the Wild West, where they'd make their fortunes panning for gold, and send lots of money back to the family. "This awful poverty will come to an end," said Dávid proudly to Isti, and they dreamed for a long time of how astonished the family would be and how happily they'd extol their achievement. On the evening of their departure they waited for everyone to be asleep and by the silvery light of the full moon stole out of their houses. They carried the Vereses' washtub down to the stream and, beating off the gnats, slipped it into the water between the reeds. In the dry conditions of late summer the stream was so shallow that three villages farther on, the tub grounded on the muddy, slimy bottom. In annoyance the boys dragged it onto the bank, ate the sausage and the bread, and went to sleep under a weeping willow, where they were found the next morning. István Veres and Samu Goldstein expressed their disapproval in differing ways. Isti received two stinging slaps, while Dávid had to listen to his father's reprimands for days; indeed, he was given lessons in both mathematics and geography. He had to calculate the precise length in kilometres of the planned journey and how many months it would have taken them at a speed of two kilometres per hour. What marine currents would they have had to contend with? Furthermore, Dávid had to answer a question which had no connection to mathematics or geography: was it his view that a Jewish boy was allowed to eat pig meat?

This escapade returned to Dávid's mind in December 1956 when, tired after the long flight but all a-quiver with excitement, they inched forward in the long queue towards the immigration officer at New York airport; and again, twenty years later, as he revisited Hungary for the first time. After Kennedy Airport in New York, Budapest's Ferihegy was more like a provincial bus station and the people seemed colourless and bad-tempered. Behind the glass window the youthful-looking policeman spent a long time examining Dávid's American passport, looking in turn at the document, then at Dávid. The passport was new, but the knotting in Dávid's stomach was the old one; it was the invisible hand that had gripped, crushed and twisted his stomach every time that he'd been checked in Hungary in former days. He greeted the sensation as an old friend: 'it's part and parcel of my native land, like *gulyás*, *pálinka* and *Matyó* needlework,' he thought. Since news had reached him, following the revolution, that Laci Bartos had been executed and Pál imprisoned, for years it hadn't so much as crossed his mind that he might go home. More recently, though, Isti had written several times that Hungary welcomed its citizens who'd gone abroad and wished to revisit with open arms; there was nothing to fear. Nonetheless his New York friends alarmed him, saying that the moment he set foot in Hungary he would be arrested. The frontier guard checked the passport against the details in a big book while Dávid shifted from foot to foot, growing increasingly nervous. Then the passport was given back and, wobbling at the knees, Dávid pushed his suitcase through Customs and into the entrance hall.

Outside the swing door he spent a while looking for his friend in the ring of people waiting and craning their necks. A paunchy, balding man pushed forward from the rest to embrace him. He and Isti laughed and looked each other over, admiringly comparing waist-measurements, then Isti roared with laughter and ruffled Dávid's black-tinted hair.

"You've gone mad! Do you tint your hair, like a woman?"

"In America you've got to stay young, otherwise nobody trusts you in the commercial world," said Dávid, embarrassed, as he carefully smoothed his hair down and looked furtively around to check who might have witnessed the distressing scene.

"You've obviously become an American," Isti slapped him on the back. "A real Yankee." And he fingered Dávid's check jacket, assessing the quality of the material. "Very nice!" he said approvingly.

Later, at home, he made Dávid strip to his underwear so that he could try on his shirt, trousers and jacket. Dressed in Isti's striped towelling bathrobe Dávid sprawled in an armchair laughing as his friend put his things on and admired himself in the mirror. Klári shook her head in the background, while from the other armchair their daughter Babi grinned with the full scorn of her teenage years.

"You're out of luck, because we even take the same shoe size," said Isti, after trying on Dávid's smart shoes. "Now I've become a real American as well," he laughed.

"You see," said Dávid, "there's nothing to it! That's all it takes!"

"Let's say you've brought these things for me," said Isti later.

"Right, let's say that," Dávid laughed, seeing the pleasure he'd given his friend. "Do you remember forty years ago, when my father bought the first kit for the Tövispuszta football team?" he asked, "That was the last time I saw you so happy about something to wear!"

That evening they went out to dinner at the Öreghárs. Dávid had to extract another outfit from his case because Isti couldn't be separated from the checked jacket, and insisted on being allowed to wear it out.

"Well, I'm interested in seeing whether there's anybody else you recognise," said Isti as they walked into the restaurant.

Dávid looked round, but didn't know who he was supposed to look at.

"Look at the band!" said Isti impatiently. "Don't you know the *prímás*?"

Csoki was facing fully towards them as he played, grinning broadly, his white teeth gleaming in his swarthy face.

"This beats everything, it's Csoki!" exclaimed Dávid, as he went up to the *prímás* and embraced him. "It's like going back thirty years!"

Isti took Dávid round the restaurant, introduced him to Auntie Bözsi and a number of other diners, and as he did so showed off his new acquisition, the check jacket. The habitués of the Öreghárs, small businessmen and civil servants, questioned Dávid about how long ago he'd left Hungary, what he was doing, how long he was staying. Once it became known that he was in the rag trade in New York there were some knowing smiles.

"He's a millionaire!" Isti boasted on his account.

"No way!" protested Dávid.

"He's a millionaire!" Isti repeated, nodding his head convincingly.

"We'd like to hear what happened to you, Mr. Pusztai," said a head of department from the Ministry, and indicated to the waiter to bring up another table for the new arrivals.

"These American success-stories always begin 'I arrived in New York forty years ago with ten dollars in my pocket, and now I own a factory and an apartment house'," said a small businessman at the end of the table. "Our stories start 'Forty years ago my father had a factory and an apartment house, and now we're happy if we've got ten dollars in our pockets'."

"I've never heard anyone say that, Patyi," said the department head, but the rest laughed heartily at the witty comment.

Dávid had never before spoken of his business successes, perhaps because he felt that his story was very modest by American standards, and no one had been very interested. Now he realised that in the land of his birth he was the American Dream incarnate. He thought it singularly amusing that when he, Anka and Peti had arrived in New York, Vince Goldstein had said word for word what Patyi had just quoted. Vince had been waiting for them at the airport; he'd sent their tickets to the refugee camp and had vouched for them to the American authorities so that they could obtain entry permits. They looked in awe at the grand entrance, with palm trees and a liveried door-porter who stood up from behind his desk and said "Good evening, Mr. Goldstein," to Vince, to which Vince courteously returned "Good evening, Ramon." The lift rose soundlessly to the sixth floor and stopped inside the flat. This consisted of a drawing room overlooking Central Park, a living-room decorated with paintings and statuary, and a variety of bedrooms opening off corridors, each with its own wardrobe and marble bathroom. When Vince took them to the guest room they simply stood for whole minutes, unable to believe their eyes. "Look, real nylon curtains," Anka was overcome by the lace curtains on the window, and crushed the material in her hand so she could enjoy seeing it spring back into shape. The lights in the park were already burning down below and a bluish mist enveloped the trees. "Nylon stockings, nylon coats, a nylon stork brings the nylon baby" sang Dávid happily. Vince was obviously not interested in what had happened to Dávid and his family. He hardly asked any questions, and if Dávid began talking about Uncle Henrik's family or the refugee camp he merely nodded, yes, you said that in your letter. They were served a light supper by the black housekeeper, 'a real negro' whispered Dávid to Anka, because it was there in New York that they saw dark-skinned people close up for the first time in their lives. Then Vince left them to themselves. "See you in the morning."

They were tired, but they couldn't sleep. Peti was the only one to doze straight off in the huge king-size bed, while Dávid and Anka talked until the small hours. Then, in the morning, Vince pressed two hundred dollars into Dávid's hand, together with a street-map of New York and an address in Brooklyn. "When I arrived in New York thirty years ago I had only ten dollars in my pocket," he said, "and look at me now. Having regard to the child and inflation, you're getting twenty times that much from me, but next thing I want to hear from you is that you're on your feet. First lesson," added Vince, raising an index finger, "the only thing that matters is what a man can do by his own strength." With that he ushered them out, or as one might say, ejected them from the flat.

Dávid and Anka worked out how to get to Brooklyn from the subway map. Carrying their few possessions and after much searching, they found their way to the Brooklyn address. The two-storey red brick building in Hewes street, Williamsburg, was rather like a warehouse, and when they rang the doorbell a bearded man with sidelocks, wearing a hat, came to the door. "Mr. Goldstein mentioned that his nephew would be looking for somewhere to live," said Jákob Feuerstein in a sing-song voice with a strong east Hungarian accent. He invited them into the drawing-room and called his family: his kerchiefed wife, three bearded, hatted sons and two bewigged women. The young people spoke Hungarian in broken fashion. Anka and Dávid blinked in confusion.

"Don't you wear a yarmulka?" Mrs. Feuerstein asked Dávid pleasantly enough, but her disapproval was evident. "At home we children only wore one in the house on religious occasions, and in synagogue," he answered. "We observe the law. If you're going to live with us, we'll expect the same of you," said Feuerstein. Dávid immediately received a skull-cap from him, while Anka was given a kerchief by his wife so that she could cover her hair as tradition demanded. The Feuersteins had set up a well equipped kosher kitchen for them, with separate cooking utensils and cutlery for meat and milk, in a little section of the house that overlooked the rear garden.

At first Dávid and his family found everything exciting, even in the monotonous district where they found themselves and especially after the conditions in Hungary and the refugee camp. "Can you smell the atmosphere of freedom?"

asked Anka in the street with a laugh, taking a deep breath of the heavy summer air. Dávid was fascinated by being able to buy chewing-gum in the corner shop, and looked at the range of different American cigarettes; in Hungary they all cost a fortune. "Chesterfield, like in films!" They looked in disbelief at the wide choice in the shops, dozens of different kinds of soap, butter, creams and washing-powder. They looked in amazement at the cars and the clothes that people wore. And they drank Coca-Cola. "What wealth, it's true what they say about America," they told one another.

Jákob and one of his sons kept an ironmonger's on the street side of the house where they lived, but Ishak, the eldest, worked in Vince Goldstein's diamond business in 47th Street. There Dávid too found employment, as a trainee salesman. The diamond-shop consisted in fact of a dozen little counters inside the shop, at each of which a black-suited salesman in a hat displayed goods. "This is Mr. Goldstein's shop," said Ishak the first time that he took Dávid to his workplace, pointing to one counter. "This counter is a shop?" asked Dávid in surprise. "Who could fill a whole big shop with diamonds?" replied Ishak. "A little one full of fire, as they say, like this one on the table is worth enough to keep our grandchildren as well as us." Dávid stared appreciatively at the little black velvet pouch of tiny, gleaming, blue-white stones. "It's harder to get into here than into Congress!" joked Ishak. He'd been learning the trade for years, and considered being employed by Vince Goldstein the best thing that had ever happened to him. "I didn't know that my uncle was an expert on diamonds as well," said Dávid, suitably impressed. "Mr. Goldstein understands business," replied Ishak. "This shop is just one of his investments, to him this is peanuts, as the saying goes." Dávid burst out laughing, and Ishak couldn't make out what had amused him so much. "It's nothing,"

Dávid laughed, "I was just remembering one of Uncle Henrik's stories."

Dávid went into Manhattan with Ishak every morning and it would be getting dark by the time they came home. Meanwhile Anka helped the women around the house, then went for walks in the park with them and Peti. On Fridays they observed the Sabbath-eve solemnities at sunset, as did everyone in the district, and Dávid went to pray in the synagogue with the men. The Feuersteins were good, hard-working people, but Dávid and Anka found it hard to talk to them. "If I've got to live my life like this among iron screws and bigoted women, I'd sooner jump in the river," said Anka one day. "I tell you straight, Stalinism was more entertaining than this!" "You think it's easy for me?" Dávid returned the question peevishly, scratching the top of his head under the yarmulka. "I've tried to get away from my Jewish background my whole life, to be like other people, and see what happens, first the anti-Semites persecute me, now the Jews are pulling me back into the net. If I weren't Jewish I wouldn't have got a job in the diamond business."

Dávid gradually learnt how to differentiate between diamonds on the basis of measurements, fire, colour and polish, and about emeralds, rubies, opals, tiger's eyes, aquamarines and other coloured stones. He learnt where they came from, how they came into being, which could be mounted in rings, ear-rings and pendants, and how. Gradually he fell in love with the stones. In the course of their walks Anka discovered a hippy jewellery boutique in Greenwich Village, and studied Native American, Indian and African jewels there. She was good at drawing, and in the evenings they started to dream of opening a tiny shop in the East Village where she would design jewellery, mainly using semi-precious stones, but they would try with diamonds too. They found premises that could be rented cheaply and at Anka's insistence Dávid mustered all his courage and called on Vince. He suggested diffidently that he might lend him some money to start up, to be repaid with interest naturally. Vince looked at him as if he were feeble-minded, and asked twice if he'd understood him correctly. Then he raised an index finger and said only this: "Lesson number two: Never lend to anyone, because when the time comes to repay they'll hate you!"

One day a tall, muscular man dressed in black came into the shop. "Are you Mr. Goldstein's nephew?" he asked Dávid. Receiving a positive answer, he asked for his address and informed him that at ten on Sunday morning a car would be waiting outside the door for them as they were invited to visit. "Visit who?" asked Dávid, not knowing what to make of it. "That's all there is to the message," said the man severely, then smiled.

On Sunday morning Dávid, Anka and Peti were waiting excitedly outside the Williamsburg house. At ten o'clock precisely a huge black Cadillac stopped in front of them, and the man who'd called on Dávid in the shop got out. He ceremoniously opened the back door of the limousine and waited while they took their seats. They'd only ever seen cars like this from the outside, and now at last they were able to touch the soft leather upholstery, the carpet on the floor, the bar-cupboard with its mahogany fittings and the gleaming chromium-plated handles. Almost without a sound the car sailed over the bridge into Manhattan, then through the city in a north-westerly direction, towards Connecticut. Peti lay back comfortably on the seat but Dávid and Anka stared through the window, not saying a word at first. "Doesn't New York look different from a car like this," said Dávid. "Wonder who feels we're so important?" they speculated. "Perhaps we're being kidnapped, but it can only be to a better place," said

Anka with a laugh. "Maybe they intend to use us to blackmail Vince, but they'll never squeeze a cent out of him." They turned off the freeway, and the road meandered between gentle hills, meadows and shady trees. The Cadillac went up an avenue of planes, patches of sunlight filtering through the foliage and playing on the windscreen. On both sides of the road two-storey, brick-built villas, colonial or English style, lay hidden in the depths of parks, scarcely visible for the vegetation that fringed the enormous grounds. They stopped at an elaborate wrought-iron gate which opened majestically. The car rolled on along the drive which curved between ornamental plants and slender cypresses and stopped in a parking-space beside the house. A number of similar limousines, Bentleys and Rolls Royces were already there. "Here we are," said the chauffeur, as he decorously opened the door. At the far end of the garden stood white baldaquin-like tents and beneath them large circular tables and chairs with beribboned backs. Ladies in summer dresses and picture hats were chatting to elegant gentlemen in blazers, who were smoking cigars. Under one of the baldaquins a cool jazz-band was playing Miles Davis. Farther on, beside the blue water of a pool, was a long table covered with plates, drinks and bottles; waiters in white tuxedos moved among the guests bearing silver trays.

"I'll introduce you to your hostess," said the chauffeur, leading them towards a middle-aged lady at the main table. She'd already noticed them at a distance, and as they came nearer said something to the others at her table, who all turned to look at them with interest. When they reached the table the lady smiled and held out her hand. "Well, let's look at you!" she said, retaining Dávid's hand in both of hers and studying his face. "You're a fine-looking young man," said she, "but you don't take after your father. I hope I haven't upset you by saying so, but your father was the love of my life!" 'My father was the love of her life?' Dávid pondered uncomprehendingly. 'But Samu never set foot outside Tövispuszta except when he was taken into forced labour.' "Oh yes, Henry was my beloved," said the lady, "I won't dare to say how many years ago." Anka looked at Dávid, not knowing what to say. For Dávid it all became clear. The lady was obviously Peggy, the blonde, blue-eyed girl from the family mythology, the love of Uncle Henrik's youth, the lady that Vince had separated him from when he got him to come home with news of grandfather's death. Dávid dared not tell her that he wasn't actually Henrik's son. The explanation would have been complicated and might have ruined Peggy's pleasure, and in any case Uncle Henrik had adopted him as his son, so he muttered a platitude and looked on, feeling rather foolish. He imagined Uncle Henrik at the lady's side in the company of the others at the table, then Peggy in Kresz Géza utca, but the visions didn't match up. He couldn't imagine that the awful Uncle Henrik, with his big nose, could have left such an impression in the heart of this elegant lady. As they talked it gradually emerged that after breaking up with Henrik Peggy had married a man from California, and had learnt of Vince's deceit only years later. Peggy's husband had become rich in land speculation, then obligingly died, leaving a vast fortune to his wife. She'd then moved to the east coast, and both before and since then had dreamed only of Henrik Goldstein. "Henry was like a Hollywood actor!" said Peggy to the others at the table. "Like Rudolf Valentino, or rather, Clark Gable." The others nodded understandingly and scrutinised Dávid's features to discover any similarity. 'Now they presumably think I take after my mother,' thought Dávid.

Even thirty years later Peggy had painful and hostile memories of Vince. "He's a nasty man, a really nasty man," she repeated. Nor did she want Dávid to work for him. When it turned out that Dávid had a degree in Economics, spoke German and even a little Russian, she introduced him to a friend, 'the boss of a fashion-house'. This turned out to be something of an exaggeration; the business involved having garments made up in Thailand to time-expired designer patterns for sale in South America and the Middle East.

Dávid thanked Vince for his help and resigned from the diamond shop. He and Anka carefully packed away yarmulka and kerchief and moved to a white, middle-class, Christian townhouse in New Jersey. "Now then, we've really arrived in America!" he then said with satisfaction. "I'd imagined something like this." And with that he fastened up a solid crucifix in the drawing-room, so that if the new neighbours came round they should see that they were to be trusted.

By the time their daughter was born Dávid was assistant economic director of the fashion house with a good salary. Peggy was delighted to stand as godmother to little Kati, and in the service, which was held in a chapel near her villa, Peti was christened at the same time. Anka found it harder and harder to cope with a life consisting of nothing but children, housework and shopping, and she vented her spleen on her husband as was only to be expected, since he was closest to her. When the little girl was a year old Dávid could see that the time was ripe for Anka to find some occupation of her own in which to exercise her talents. She had always dreamt of a little jewellery shop, and armed with a ten thousand dollars christening gift from Peggy, Dávid went to see Vince about buying diamonds from him at a good price. 'It'll be a good investment, and after all uncle can afford it, because as Ishak said, this is peanuts to Mr. Goldstein,' he thought, and grinned.

In the study of his Fifth Avenue flat Vince covered the lock of his wall-safe with his body, so that Dávid couldn't catch sight of the code, and took out a velvet bag of precious stones.

"You can have these at trade price," he said, with a magnifying lens in one eye. He passed another to Dávid, who picked over the diamonds, examined a number of coloured South African stones, but preferred a few half- and one-carat blue-white Indian brilliants. He pondered, then added a red diamond and a yellow one. "I can go up to ten thousand dollars," said Dávid. "Tell me what you can let me have for that." "Those and more," Vince nodded. "I suppose you know, my boy, why the Jews became diamond dealers?" Dávid didn't know. "Because they were for ever being persecuted and if they had to make their escape, diamonds were the easiest thing to put in their pockets. It's the same reason why they play the violin rather than the piano. Try running away with a piano!" Vince gave a little laugh at his brief but informative lecture, then placed the selected stones into a neat black velvet pouch; he carefully counted the ten thousand dollars that he received in exchange, put them all the same way round and placed them in his wallet.

Dávid could hardly wait to call on Ishak in 47th Street the next day and ask him to value his acquisitions. Ishak took his time examining the stones with a lens, humming as he did so. "What do you reckon they're worth?" asked Dávid suspiciously. "You might get eight thousand for them, if you can find somebody who doesn't know much about diamonds," said Ishak. "What?" Dávid burst out. "Impossible! I got them off Vince for ten thousand, trade price." Ishak shook his head and gave Dávid his lens. "See the polishing error on this stone? And the tiny inclusion in this one, there, on the right hand edge? And this one isn't pure either." Dávid fought back his tears. He felt the same wave of disappointment as when Henrik had given the bearing away to the boy next door.

At that very moment, in walked Vince. Dávid's face was contorted with rage. "You swindled me!" he shouted at his

258

uncle, almost in tears. "Hush!" Vince raised a finger to his lips. "Keep it down, you're not the only one here that speaks Hungarian." "I don't care," Dávid shouted, "Let 'em all find out what sort of man you are, who'll cheat his own family!" "It's not for my sake I say keep it down," said Vince, "but for yours. If you get the reputation for being gullible, from tomorrow everybody'll be swindling you!" Dávid stared at his uncle, astounded. "Lesson number four," and Vince, taking advantage of Dávid's confusion, raised the admonitory finger: "In business, never trust anybody, not even your own family!" "That was only lesson number three!" said Dávid, making a wry face. "But there won't be a number four."

"That was a good story. You see what capitalism does to people?" said the ministry department head in the Öreghárswhen Dávid had finished. And he added to himself: 'It's typical of you Jews to even swindle each other.' Then he looked round anxiously in case anyone had heard what he'd thought.

"Don't I say, you can't just expect things to come to you," added the small businessman.

The department head nodded in agreement.

"And are you still with the same company?" asked a boutique owner from Váci utca.

"I was made a partner, and some years later the business became ours," answered Dávid. "Now my wife runs the business, which is why she hasn't been able to come with me."

The next day Isti took Dávid to Tövispuszta. As the Zhiguli went though the city he looked at the concrete blocks of flats.

"In America the blacks and immigrants from Puerto Rico live in places like that. Who lives in them here?"

"Here it's the lucky ones," said Isti, a little offended. "They're glad to have somewhere to live."

The Zhiguli wound its way along the dusty country road, and Dávid looked at the yellowed, untidy verges, and the uniform, tent-roofed blocks that lined the main streets of villages.

"Is it compulsory for everyone to build the same kind of buildings?" he asked, this time more judiciously.

"Not compulsory at all, there are three patterns to choose from, but this is the cheapest and the windows and doors for this can be bought at Tüzép.[81] There are living-rooms and bathrooms in these, and if you look at the roof you can see there's television as well," boasted Isti.

"And what's become of the nice old peasant houses, with their porches?" Dávid enquired.

"They've been demolished. You can still find one or two in Tövispuszta, but who wants to live in a mud-brick house these days, when they can live in a brick-built one? Mostly the Gypsies at the end of the village, or daft artists from Budapest. People from Budapest have bought the oldest houses in the village and come out for summer holidays. Fatheads and city Jews come and play at being peasants, but I bet they'd hate them if they'd grown up in them like we did. Hungary's advanced a lot!"

'After a quarter of a century in America I feel like a foreigner, here in Hungary I'm a stranger now,' Dávid thought to himself. 'It's as if I'd got stuck in no-man's-land when I was crossing the frontier in '56.'

Elza and her family lived in an old peasant house in Tövispuszta. Even at a distance it could be seen that in the window and on the parapet of the porch there were nicely shaped earthenware jars for holding water and churning butter, glazed milk jugs and jam pots. In the corner of the porch was an old spinning wheel. "Been missing this, haven't you?" asked Isti as they reached the porch. "Young Pali's collected them in local villages and in Transylvania. Don't know what he sees in this old rubbish!"

Elza was so pleased that she didn't know what to offer her brother, and walked round him twice to get a good look at him. Pál gave Dávid a hug, then backed off and looked at him from a distance with his weary, gentle smile. Pál had aged, his hair was white, but Elza was as pretty as ever. Her green eyes gleamed, and her simple printed dress let it be clearly seen that her figure was still neat and trim. Dávid looked at her in delight.

"I've made chicken soup for you, but we've got some sausage as well, if you still like that," said Elza, poking fun at Dávid. "What can I spoil you with?"

"Heavens, how many years has it been since the last time we were all together?" Dávid brooded.

"Well," said Isti, slapping his thigh and standing up, "enjoy yourselves! I'll be back for you this evening to take you over to see János at Bátakér. We're throwing a bit of a party in your honour."

Sprawling in basket chairs on the porch, Dávid and Pál chatted. Elza was in and out with plates, glasses and a jug of wine as she laid the table, but joined in the conversation every time she appeared.

"We can't complain," said Pál. "We live a quiet life, out of the public eye, we read, write, listen to music."

"As Pál doesn't read the news and we have no TV, he doesn't know what's going on in the world," Elza added.

"I know precisely what's going on," replied Pál. "You don't need to read the papers or watch TV for that."

"But you're not being disturbed any more, are you?" asked Dávid anxiously.

"Nobody here's disturbed any more," said Pál, with perceptible scorn in his voice. "People are content. Same as the sow that quietly grunts and wallows happily in the mud, hoping that it might miss out on the pig-killing."

✻

Isti had just pulled up in front of Dr. János Szentágostony's house in Bátakér when a motorcyclist stopped beside them with a screech of brakes. A well-built man dismounted and removed his crash-helmet, shook out his curly hair, laughed at them with a gleam of blue eyes and waved to Isti. Then in a single movement he unzipped his jacket and revealed beneath it a clerical collar.

"This is our priest, Vili," Isti introduced him. "He's a great man, it's a pity he's being moved."

"Why's he being moved?" asked Dávid as they walked towards the house.

"Will you tell him, or shall I?" Isti turned to Vili.

"Leave it till later," said the priest.

The village celebrities, as they styled themselves, were all gathered at János': the priest, the chairman of the collective farm, the chief agronomist, the vet and the community Party secretary.

"Sometimes the schoolmaster comes as well, but he's such a stupid man, he can't even play *ulti*," [82] laughed the agronomist, a big man with a moustache.

"He prefers drinking," said the thin, dyspeptic-looking Party secretary.

"You're jealous, eh?" retorted the stocky, bald collective farm chairman.

"I could drink too, until I got this stomach trouble!"

"Comrade Veszelka suffers from irritable bowel

syndrome," said János emphatically, and winked at Dávid. "It used to be called having your nerves fuck you up," and he grinned. "That's right, my nerves fuck me up," the secretary confirmed. "If you were for ever being fucked about by the county, you wouldn't laugh so loud," he said, as the others laughed ever louder, a sure sign that this was a conversation that had taken place many a time.

"People who've got a street named after them in the village can't complain," said the vet.

"It's not named after me, it's my grandfather," replied the secretary in an offended tone.

"There are two streets that run into the square, towards the Soviet memorial, Veszelka utca and Kodelka utca. You remember, the death-squads hanged them in 1919," Isti explained to Dávid.

Dávid remembered the ghastly tale that old people had told when he was a boy, but he couldn't remember whether Iván Héjjas had cut off Veszelka's genitals before they were hanged and stuffed them into Kodelka's mouth, or *vice versa*.

"Well, let's have a drink so's we can go for a pee," said Isti, and went up to the table and plunged the corkscrew into the neck of a bottle of wine.

"Well, it's not so good if we don't drink," said the collective farm chairmen.

After the pheasant soup and the venison *pörkölt* with red wine, while the others were digesting and playing *ulti* inside, Dávid, János and Vili went and sat on the terrace and talked. 'Isti's always had a tendency to be frivolous, but a doctor, a former baron and a priest – how can they feel at ease in the company of a stupid Party secretary and a gormless collective farm chairman?' Dávid pondered silently. János seemed to read his thoughts, and as he filled his pipe he said:

"There's a saying here that there are three ways open to the Hungarian intelligentsia: the first is alcohol, the second suicide, and the third is impassable. But there is also a fourth: acknowledge that things are so and try to feel good. A slightly cynical viewpoint, but it works."

"What about Pál and Elza?" asked Dávid.

"Pál never had his feet on the ground, surely you know. He did more than ten years for his principles. Well, principles aren't worth that much! He's incredibly lucky to have a wife like her."

"I know how much you helped her while he was inside," said Dávid quietly. "Thank you."

János didn't answer, but his face clouded. Vili looked at him closely for a long moment.

"And why haven't you ever married?" asked Dávid.

János remained absorbed in filling his pipe.

"Vili and I have accepted celibacy, haven't we?" he said after a pause, looking at the priest with a forced laugh.

"Only you!" said the priest, but he didn't laugh.

"Well, say what you like, Vili has reinvigorated the faith in the village. When the old priest whom you remember was still here we were worried that the communists had stamped out religion. But since Vili has been here you couldn't drive the young women out of the church with pitchforks. Every woman constantly wants to go to confession. It's just as well that there's the grating between them, otherwise they'd be forcing themselves on this handsome man!"

"János, the things you say!" exclaimed Vili.

"All I do is go to confession. Anyway, I come to see you."

"And do people really confess things, Vili?" asked Dávid.

"Actually, weeks go by before anybody at last confesses a really juicy sin. Otherwise it's just the usual platitudes."

"Then why do people go?"

"So that the neighours can see them. And women come to complain about their husbands."

"The men hate Vili!" said János. "They spread a rumour about him that he was a paedophile, because he played football with the lads on Sunday morning on the field behind the church. It didn't bother anybody that the old priest used to grope the boys – that's how priests are, they said. But the fact that the women like Vili was more than they could take. And now he's being transferred. So, and how's your marriage? You and Anka getting along well?"

"As well as you can with your wife a quarter of a century on. When she's *not* there you miss her, when she *is* there she gets on your nerves."

"Tell you what, Dávid, let's take you hunting tonight," said Isti as he came out onto the terrace. The Party secretary and the agronomist grinned at his side.

"You go hunting?" asked Dávid.

"What did you think, that the pheasant and the stag fell into the pot this evening out of old age?" asked the agronomist.

"You go on," said János, "Vili and I will give it a miss."

They squeezed into the agronomist's Russian military commander's UAZ all-terrain car. Dávid was in front beside the agronomist, while Isti and the secretary were in the back with a bottle of plum *pálinka*. The agronomist took a double-barrelled shotgun and a box of ammunition from the boot and placed them in Dávid's hands. The feel of the weapon gave him a jolt of pride, and he felt the adrenalin begin to rise in his head.

"Ever been hunting?" asked the agronomist.

"Never."

"Well, you're going to be a bit lucky. We're going after hares."

The agronomist switched off the headlights and cut across the fields. The UAZ lurched over the furrows of the plough-land, then stopped in the middle. The agronomist took the gun from Dávid and loaded it with two cartridges.

"Wind the window down and keep your eyes open!" he said.

In the back Isti and Veszelka were chuckling loudly, passing the bottle of *pálinka* between them.

"Have a drop of shooter's water!" Isti offered the bottle to Dávid. "Then pass it on to Sanyi" – indicating the agronomist – "he might want to take a shot as well!"

"You should have seen when Isti came out hunting with the sub-machine gun and its drum magazine after the counter-revolution," said the secretary with a laugh. "He shot the wild boar to bits, there was more lead in them than meat."

"Are there no laws here about hunting?" asked Dávid in surprise. "In America I know there are."

"There are here too!" said the Party secretary. "We're the law."

"I'd like to see the game warden who'd dare say anything when Comrades Veres and Veszelka go hunting," Isti laughed. "Comrade Kádár's been hunting here as well. I went with him."

"There's a hare!" said the agronomist quietly, pointing towards the ploughed field. Dávid strained his eyes but could see nothing. He felt the blood pulsing in his veins with excitement. The agronomist switched the headlights on and there, between the two columns of light, sat a huge hare, its eyes shining as it looked at them, immobile.

"Wow, bloody hell, what a whopper!"

"Isn't that a dog?" asked Dávid uncertainly.

"So, you've only seen Easter bunnies before, eh? Well, take a shot at it, Dávid!"

The Jampot

Dávid leant out of the window and levelled the barrel at the animal. His hand shaking with excitement, he took aim and pulled the trigger. The gun recoiled with a loud bang and the hare leaped into the air, then fell back twitching convulsively.

"Why didn't the silly thing run away?" asked Dávid.

"A hare will never run into the lights. In Hungary even hares know where to draw the line! They'd rather die than cross it," said Isti with a laugh.

The Party secretary jumped out of the car and stumbled over the ploughed ground towards the wriggling animal. He kicked it hard in the head, and the dull sound was audible from the car. The hare flew half a yard then lay still. Veszelka picked it up by the ears and with a grin and a gesture of triumph brought it to Dávid, who felt pride, disgust and pity all at once.

A Trabant User's Manual

With her dark complexion, curly hair, big dark eyes and slim figure Kati Pusztai took after her mother Anka, whereas Peti was like his father, a flat-bottomed type of man with a rolling gait and an early tendency to put on weight. "It's just as well it's not the other way round," Dávid said with a chuckle when he was boasting about his daughter. "Just imagine, if a girl looked like me!" On the other hand, it seemed that the parents' personalities had crossed: Kati was like her father, easygoing and a little naive; Peti was moody and argumentative like his mother.

Pali Szentágostony thought the most beautiful avenue in Budapest would be the perfect setting for the socialist regime to display what it had to show. By the time that he'd strolled with his American cousins from Hősök tere to Bajcsy-Zsilinszky út it would be perfectly clear where they were. Pali started the social history walk, as he called it, from the Millennium monument, the plinth of the statues of the glorious leader Árpád and the tribal chiefs of the Honfoglalás.[83] The latter – seven in number, Álmos, Előd, Ond, Kond and the rest – looked unsuspectingly into the historic distance towards November 7 tér and Marx tér. A little farther on – Pali pointed in the direction of Dózsa György út – stands the

268

statue of a less glorious leader, Lenin. The statue of Stalin had formerly stood there, but in 1956 was pulled down and cut up with oxy-acetylene torches. Also on the left was the Yugoslav embassy, where Imre Nagy and his colleagues had sought political asylum after the revolution, but Kádár and Tito broke their word and the KGB enticed them out of the building. Farther along on the right was the Young Artists' Club, the centrally (i.e. Party-centrally) regulated artistic avant-garde. To the left was the journalists' headquarters, the centrally regulated freedom of the press. Again on the right, the featureless building of the Soviet embassy wedged in between the mansions. "Ideology gives it its beauty in contrast to the mansions," said Pali, keeping a straight face. Then on the corner came the building of the Chemokomplex Foreign Trade Enterprise. "At one time it was the headquarters of the Arrow-Cross, later of the ÁVH, so it's no wonder that it had a flavour akin to terror, like that of the mob," observed Pali. Meanwhile there came a brief account of the names of the road: Sugár út, Andrássy út, Sztálin út, Magyar Ifjúság útja, Népköztársaság útja[84] – all with colourful observations attached, together with the heart-warming prospect that, according to rumour, the magnificent radial road would one day become Kádár János út. The eight-sided Oktogon, now November 7 tér in honour of the Soviet October Revolution. To the right, the Opera House – a slight enthusiasm: it's like the one in Vienna, but perhaps more beautiful! Under the surface of the road runs Europe's first underground railway – more enthusiasm: built in the nineteenth century, because in those days Hungary… oh dear! By the time that they reached Bajcsy-Zsilinszky út – a brief account of the eponymous politician from the murder of Áchim to the opposition[85] – and Peti and Kati Pusztai really understood that they'd come to a foreign country.

"The names of streets are changed?" Kati expressed surprise in a strong American accent. "How can that be done? As if in New York Third Avenue or 42nd Street were changed?" She shook her head in disbelief. "I can't get my head around that."

Peti couldn't get his head around the Trabant. "Is it really made out of papier mâché?" he asked doubtfully, as if trying to second-guess a magic trick. But he really liked the Wartburg. "If I lived here, I'd certainly drive a car like that! Back home all the cars are similar, but these are so interesting!" said he appreciatively.

Peti had been a babe in arms when he had arrived in America with his parents, and his sister Kati had never been to the old country. Dávid had told them a lot about Hungary, about the war and the Fifties, but while the children were young these stories didn't interest them much. They wanted to be like other American children, and although they understood everything in their mother tongue they weren't inclined to speak it. After his visit to Hungary, however, their father was so overflowing with enthusiasm about his few days there that they decided to go the following summer and see the exotic communist country from which their parents had had to escape.

Pali was waiting for them at Ferihegy airport; Dávid had asked him to make the children love the old country. Peti and Kati had been worriedly searching out communist agents at the airport, and were sadly disappointed on the way into town by taxi not to see a single secret policeman anywhere, and not even one Russian soldier.

"Are the Russian soldiers very bloodthirsty?" asked Kati, prepared to hear the worst.

"After the war a lot of stories were told about them, how they raped women, plundered, took people away for 'little

270

jobs' from which they only came back years later. Most of it is probably true," said Pali. "It isn't excusing them, but when all's said and done they'd been fighting in an enemy country, one which had attacked them. Russian peasants or the Serbs of Novi Sad[86] would have tales to tell about Hungarian forces, because war-hardened soldiers are much the same the world over. Some things, however, are less talked about – for instance, that during the 1956 revolution a large proportion of the Soviet soldiers stationed here had to be replaced for fear that they wouldn't fire on Hungarians. The new arrivals were told by their officers that they'd be opposing German fascists, and when they found out the truth a lot of Soviet private soldiers went over to the revolutionaries. It's not hard to guess what became of them afterwards. Recently, though, I heard that a private defected from a Russian barracks somewhere in Hungary. He took refuge in Czechoslovakia, because he'd heard so much that was bad about the capitalist countries that he was afraid to go to Austria. The Czechs handed him back, he was court-martialled and shot."

The American cousins made an excellent audience. Pali took pleasure in telling them the legends of Budapest, about the missing tongues of the lions on the Lánchíd; the tunnel, into which the bridge is pushed when it rains, and the symbol of the volte-face, the Liberation monument on Gellert-hegy with the Russian soldier, which was originally to have been the memorial to Horthy's son who was killed on the Russian front.

After his first visit home Dávid came to Hungary regularly. Through the good offices of Isti and the civil servants that he met in the Öreghárs, he worked his way into several clothing factories. The managers were always only too pleased to see the American businessman who had such a keen sense of what to offer to whom: French perfume, jewellery, some cognac, a case of whisky, a designer watch or an exclusive fountain pen, or perhaps some foreign currency slipped into a bank account to enable the family to travel to the West in summer. Dávid had things made in Hungarian factories, and in the process topped up the goods in Isti and Klári's boutique. Once more the knowledge of Russian that he'd acquired with Henrik during the war proved useful; he joined forces with Hungarian factories in delivering goods to Russian and East European markets.

"Isti's like a brother to me," he told the children, and so later, when Pali took them to Tövispuszta they found it only natural to call on Isti's son.

Isti had scarcely seen Eni and his son for years. The Sárády family had brought Pityu up to a strict standard of Christian moral values: every Sunday they took him to church, he became an altar-boy, at Easter he sang at the head of the procession, and on such occasions didn't attend to his Pioneer duties, or later go to League of Communist Youth gatherings. "His lousy ÁVH father can go to Hell," said Dr. Sárády, his dignity reduced as the years went by, but with steadfast conviction in his voice. Even so, when Pityu reached the age of military conscription Eni called on Isti, at her father's instigation, to help arrange that the boy shouldn't be conscripted. Isti obliged, and since then had maintained contact. If he went to Tövispuszta he made sure that he saw his son. Encouraged by his grandfather, Pityu asked his father for the citation for his 'Worker and Peasant Power' medal. This showed that in 1956 Isti Veres had fought in the armed struggle against the counter-revolutionaries and gave his son an advantage in his application to enter technical university.

"We fought them with their own weapons!" Dr. Sárády triumphantly told his grandson. "Lie for lie!"

Pityu lived on a farmstead between Tövispuszta and Bátakér with his wife and two children.

"The farmstead used to belong to a Swabian, one Franci Mayer," said Pityu, "who was taken off by the Germans to Mathausen because he'd concealed people. He'd scarcely got back from the concentration camp when the communists relocated him to Germany along with a lot of other Swabians. He doesn't seem to have done too badly. The Mercedes that he came visiting in was so big that it couldn't turn the corners in the narrow streets in town. Through some administrative error the farmstead was left in Franci's name, he didn't know what to do with it, so he sold it to me cheap, and my father in the Interior Ministry sorted out the paperwork. Since then Mari and I have been living here."

"Pityu asked me to marry him ten years ago," said Mari with a laugh, "by saying 'Marry me if you want at least five children'."

"That's almost right," Pityu interrupted, "only I didn't say five, I said ten."

"And I agreed, but I never thought he'd hold me to it. Since then there's been a child every year to eighteen months."

"Is that because you're religious?" asked Peti.

"No. It's because we love children," replied Pityu cheerfully.

"Yes, but so many?" Kati was surprised.

"The more the merrier!" said Mari, rocking the smallest in her arms, a dark-blue-eyed Veres infant.

Pityu worked in the machine factory in town, and as a member of the Tövispuszta collective farm maintained its machinery. He also cultivated a bit of land in the vicinity of the farmstead as a domestic plot. He got up at three in the

273

morning, fed the chickens, pigs and cattle, then went off to the factory, from there to the machine station, and thence back home. In this way he was able to repay the bank loan with which he'd bought the farmstead.

When talk turned to money, grandfather Sárády always mentioned that one day the painting, the carpet and the watch would solve all their problems. All the family had to do was wait for him to be so kind as to pass away. "It wouldn't be worth selling at the moment," he kept repeating," because these days in this proletarian world things that are worth money have no value!" The notable items that symbolised the family's erstwhile wealth and elegance had to be mentioned with emphasis on the article: *the* painting, *the* carpet, *the* watch. And Dr. Sárády was glad to explain to all and sundry the salient features of each of these. The painting, a Caravaggio which had darkened almost beyond recognition, depicted, as far as could be made out, a wrinkled old man with an angel behind him. The carpet was 'a rosette Holbein, sixteenth-century, very valuable!' and the watch was a gold Patek, which could be worn as a medallion. Pityu was particularly interested in the little lady's watch; the back opened so it could be wound up with a tiny key. This was all that the Sárádys had managed to salvage of the family heirlooms when they were relocated, together with a cardboard box containing the buttons, belt, hat-badge and sword-belt of Béla's court dress. The elderly lawyer naturally clung to these articles; they now lived in the prefabricated block in town to which they'd moved after relocation was relaxed. The old people lived in one of the three rooms in the flat, Csenge in another, and Eni and Pityu in the third. Later, when Pityu was in his teens, the twin sisters shared a room and Pityu had the third to himself. "He's a bourgeois," joked his grandfather, "he's the only one with a room of his own." Pityu made his escape from that flat into marriage and the farmstead as soon as he could.

"I live the life of Jimmy Fülig," [87] Pityu laughed, "stoker at night, steward by day."

"So when do you sleep?" asked Kati in amazement – she had no idea who Jimmy Fülig was.

"Sleep? What's that?" Pityu pretended to be surprised. "That must be an American invention! I sleep in the factory, at my desk, during the shift," he added with a loud laugh. "Nobody notices there!"

They were drinking spritzers under the vine-wreathed pergola. There was an occasional breath of warm, summer breeze, and the sound of children's laughter came from the garden. The late afternoon sunshine filtered through the foliage of the vines, well-fed wasps buzzed among the leaves and an old dog, looking like a strange cross between a sheep and a bat, lay panting in the shade. The visitors felt that this really was a happy home.

"I've got good wine, but it gives you a thirst," said Pityu and laughed, as he filled up the tumblers with dense, tangy rosé from a glass jug.

"Father's told us that at one time good wine was produced in these parts. What's become of it?" asked Peti.

"You mean you don't like my wine?" Pityu joked. "Well, the good vineyards have been nationalised, and State agriculture produces undrinkable cheap wine from them. So I stick to my own!"

Pali remembered a conversation with his drinking friends in his university days, when they'd insisted that they would never have children because they weren't prepared 'to give hostages to society'. They were still able to remain free of them, but a child had to be sent to kindergarten and to school, taken to the doctor, couldn't be allowed to go hungry; for its sake one had to accept compromises at work, and the system gradually sucked one in. A fortnight later Olga tearfully announced that she was pregnant. He'd been wanting to break up with her for weeks, had just been putting it off, and now, if you please, he would be allowed to push the pram and to accept a lifelong responsibility. At first, Pali didn't know what to say. "If you want, we'll keep it," he forced the statement out, unconvincingly. As she sobbed, however, Olga burst out that he must think her a monster, but she couldn't imagine having a child. She said as she wept that she had for the first time in her life been to a library and looked at medical books to see what a two-week-old embryo looked like. Among the pictures she'd found one of a curette, and since then she didn't know which to be more afraid of – having a child or having an abortion. In the end Pali comforted her – if she didn't want to, then they wouldn't keep the child. Then with János' help a female doctor in Budapest put an end to the matter and two months later, amid great twinges of conscience, Pali parted from Olga. 'But with Pityu and Mari it's as if children are nothing but a blessing, without having to bargain with the political system,' he thought. 'The house is full of hard work, love, and cheerfulness,' he thought ironically, but then seriously, 'they're not bothered by bills for electricity, or charges for water and sewage, because they have no electricity nor drainage nor piped water. Pityu sees to everything around the house that needs mending, and Mari does the housekeeping so easily, that you'd think she hadn't got seven children running round her skirts. What's more, they somehow find the time to teach the three oldest, who are being educated at home because the farmstead's a long way from the school. In the kitchen garden behind the house they grow vegetables, they kill their own chickens and pigs – in a word (or rather three words): they live well.'

Since his childhood Pali had at times behaved like

an anxious, obedient boy and at others been sullen and awkward. Since his teens he'd been put off by bland old slogans which quite plainly didn't even ring true to those that uttered them, he'd found official art immeasurably dull, and these factors had drawn him to the 'alternative' communities, but his corresponding restraint prevented him from actually joining them. He'd bought *samizdat* publications in Galamb utca, been to concerts in the cellar at the nervous disorders clinic in Kulich Gyula tér, readings by dissident poets in the Hordó and to happenings at the college in Bercsényi utca, where he'd watched with an understanding expression as Biki writhed on the floor in a trance and set fire to his pubic hair, but he'd never been sufficiently radical and he felt an outsider everywhere. "The Count is something of an aristocrat!" people said to him. "Only a baron, only a baron!" he replied, but said it, of course, aristocratically. Then after a while he was no longer described in that way. He was also uncertain about Pityu's lifestyle; he liked it, the simple life secretly attracted him, but he couldn't imagine moving to a farmstead – especially not with seven children! He took Peti and Kati to see his uncle in Bátakér.

"I don't understand how most people can live the way they do, tired of work, tired of their relationship, tired of the children. They just sit in front of the television in the evening, watching all those fatheads arguing on the screen, then doze off over a glass of beer," he said.

"If you were looking for somewhere to live and had to support your family, you'd soon be more sympathetic, my dear Pali," said János. "Life is made up of the work and struggle of the day, smaller and greater compromises, that's where you have to find your enjoyment."

Peti and Kati nodded in agreement. "That's what we say in America as well."

"Have you found your enjoyment yet?" Pali asked János. "What's the matter?" asked János, pretending to be offended. "Are you finding fault with a shitty little catch–phrase?"

He and Pali laughed. Peti and Kati looked at one another uncertainly; they'd lost the thread of the conversation towards the end.

The door-bell rang. János went out into the hall, where an elderly couple were standing in the doorway.

"I'll be back in five minutes, just something to see to," he called into the room, and went into the surgery with the couple. In fact he was back before five minutes had elapsed.

"That started out as a heart-attack, but turned out to be just a cold," said János with a laugh. "The daily routine of a country doctor."

"And what do you do in such a case?" asked Peti.

"I prescribe a handkerchief."

"It seems to me," said Kati, slightly offended, "that you don't care much for people."

János pondered.

"In general, I do. It's only certain individuals that I don't. I dislike sick people most of all."

Kati couldn't believe her ears.

"A doctor who doesn't like the sick?"

"That's why I cure them," said János with a smile.

Kati was somewhat mollified.

"The only thing I'd never be able to get used to if I were a doctor is death," she said. "You do all that you can, and still you don't win. Do you remember the first person that died in your care, János?"

János thought.

"It was along time ago, when I was still a junior doctor, working in the emergency department. I was called out to

278

a patient and I could see that he was gasping for breath, on the point of suffocating. What it said in the book flashed into my mind, in such a situation a strong heart stimulant should be administered. I had just enough time to get the ampoule out of my bag, fill the syringe and inject it into his heart. He died at once. I massaged his chest with both hands, and the regular pressure brought him back. I gave him another injection. He died again. The family were just behind me, watching and weeping. I realised straight away that I'd made a bad decision, I shouldn't have given him that injection. I went on massaging his heart, getting more and more upset, and tried mouth-to-mouth resuscitation. He came round, then finally died. I'd killed him. The family were in tears, but shook my hand, said I'd done all that I could have. They even put my name forward for a medal. To this day, the only one I've been awarded."

Pali laughed. Kati and Peti looked at him, puzzled.

"Was János joking?" asked Kati in the street after they'd said goodbye to him. Her expression showed that she was still baffled.

"I don't think so," said Pali. "He's always at his funniest when he's talking seriously."

It was at the dance-house [88] that Kati Pusztai decided to become a Hungarian. "It seems that being Hungarian and being Jewish are like malaria, they get into your blood and you're never cured!" said Dávid afterwards. "I brought my children up as Americans and Christians, and now look – my daughter's become a Hungarian and my son's Jewish!"

Pali took Kati and Peti to Molnár utca on their very first visit to Budapest. After Muzsikás, Kalamajka struck up on stage with Béla Halmos. The group's vocalist, the tiny Évi Fábián, sang in her velvety-husky voice, swaying happily as she sang. Peti stood awkwardly by the wall – the ambiance and dancing didn't appear to be his scene at all – but Kati liked it and Pali urged her to join the circle. Then Évi Fábián, seeing her hesitate, went over, took her by the hand, gently led her into the audience as they danced and demonstrated a few steps to her. Half an hour later Kati, now flushed with exertion, was dancing and from then, when she was in Budapest, not a week went by without her going to Molnár utca. She sang Hungarian folksongs with obvious enjoyment and learnt the steps. It was there too that she met Gyuri, a university student with smiling eyes and a moustache, who spent every summer in Transylvania. He filmed the elderly peasants dancing with a portable camera and recorded the music on a tape-recorder, so as to teach the steps to the rest in the dance-house. He felt proud that the American girl had returned to her roots thanks to their folk-music.

David and Anka were very happy for Kati to go folk-dancing with a Hungarian society in New Brunswick, to which young second-generation Hungarians went, but when, after several months of ever more frequent correspondence with Gyuri, she announced that she would be spending next summer in Transylvania, they began to worry about the possible outcome. As they'd guessed with their parental instinct, things turned out precisely as they'd feared, and after a two-month stay in Transylvania Kati informed them that she was going to remain in Hungary with Gyuri.

When she'd previously heard talk of Transylvania Kati had always imagined grim cliffs, gloomy pine-forests and haunted castles, lit by the lightning of a stormy sky, in which Count Dracula, his fangs dripping blood, awaited his victims. From time to time the grotesque features of Frankenstein appeared in these images as well, since she regularly confused the two. As, however, they approached the Eastern Carpathians by train, hitch-hiking or on farm carts, and she saw the houses with their wooden porches, the shingled roofs and the elaborately carved Székely gates, she had the feeling that she'd come back to the real Hungary. The Transylvanian countryside and villages resembled the Hungary of her dreams much more than Tövispuszta did. All that spoiled the mood was the sight of the pre-fabricated estates that fringed the towns with their featureless, poor-quality houses and untidy, litter-strewn open spaces.

"The Neo-brutal is taking over everything everywhere," said Gyuri as he leant on his elbows by the train window. He was looking in the direction in which the train was going, the wind ruffling his hair. "Physical and spiritual rubbish is gradually overwhelming everything. Our children won't be able to see anything of what we can still enjoy."

Gyuri knew the region well and greeted a great number of people. On the edge of one village he ushered Kati into the garden of an ornately carved peasant house as if he were going home, dropped his rucksack on the porch and told her to do the same. Then they set off up the hillside.

"At this time in summer the sheep are up the hill," said Gyuri, "and old Julis and András are with them from dawn to dusk. At this time of year a lot of people live up there in the shepherds' huts. The Gödris only come down because the young ones don't live with them now, and they have to come and see to the animals."

"Where are the young ones?" asked Kati.

"Their daughter went to university in Bucharest and married a Romanian boy, and she'll probably stay there in the city. But their son got married in Hungary, I helped him. One of my fellow students married him by proxy so that he could come over. Previously in Romania he was a second-class citizen as a Hungarian, and now he's the same in Hungary as a refugee from Transylvania."

They climbed the soft, mossy track beside the stream through the forest, ducking under the wet branches. Now and then a little brook crossed the path and they laughed as they wobbled over it on the big stones. Birds chirped on the branches of the mighty beeches, in the stream white-bellied fish darted between the stones, and in the fresh forest air were the scents of woodland flowers and moss. Kati never stopped smiling. As they went, Gyuri told her how the Csángó[89] people had strayed there into the Gyimes valley, and why people spoke Hungarian although they were deep inside Romania. They left the stream, climbed a grassy slope and the hut in the clearing came into sight. It was a little wooden house with a porch, and beside it stood the summer kitchen and the sheep-fold. Old Julis was making *túró*[90] in the summer kitchen while András was restraining the *puli*,[91] which was barking loudly at the arrivals. The old man wore a black cloth cap, a long beaded shirt held at the waist by a leather belt, and a shabby leather waistcoat embroidered with wool. Tight linen trousers were tucked into the *bocskor*[92] on his feet.

"It's like a fairy-tale," Kati was enraptured as she looked at the gingerbread house on the luscious green pasture beneath the perfect azure of the sky, the two elderly folk, and the mountains fading to blue in the distance.

"Up here in the Carpathians fairy-tales still come true," said Gyuri proudly. "The thousand-year-old frontier is only a few kilometres away. We'll go to Gyimesbükk[93] tomorrow."

To Kati everything seemed magical. She'd only read of *puliszka*[94] in Hungarian folk-tales, and when Gyuri realised that she'd been brought up on Mickey Mouse he gave her some. She fussed around old Julis like a little girl, to see how she made *rakott puliszka*. Her eyes sparkled as she tasted *orda*,[95] and she wrinkled her nose at the taste of sloe *pálinka*.

"If you don't want it András will pour it away, because he doesn't like strong drink," said Gyuri.

"Says who?" asked the old man pithily. It was the first thing that he'd said since greeting them two hours earlier.

"Beg your pardon, I must be mistaken," said Gyuri with a laugh, winking at Julis. "András is so sparing with his words that it takes a glass or two of *pálinka* to get the odd one out of him. But if he dances, his feet tell a tale like you've never seen before. I'll show you a film."

The old man muttered something inaudible, but his eyes were smiling.

"Would you sing something for us, András?" asked Gyuri.

"There isn't time just now," replied András.

"Well then, I'll sing something for you, Gyuri," said Julis, "something I've never sung before. It's a song I learnt from my father. Only don't let anybody hear it, or we'll all find ourselves in jail."

With which Julis placed one hand on her hip and raised the other as if dancing a *csárdás*, and started to sing:

> Bells are ringing, it is almost dawn,
> Miklós Horthy is about to leave.
> His banner is red, white and green,
> His homeland the dear Hungarian soil,
> Miklós Horthy's men will defend it.

Goodness, even the Romanian mountains (once Hungarian) were astonished, because they hadn't heard such a song in a very long time.

As the sun sank towards the mountains András and the

puli drove the sheep back into the fold, and Julis, assisted by Kati, tidied up the kitchen and set off down to the village. By the time they reached the house, the light was fading and there were stars in the sky. Kati discovered to her surprise that the elderly couple slept not in the nice house with a porch but in a tiny place with one room and a kitchen next to it. Julis gave Kati and Gyuri a bed in the big house, in the guest room, and waited while, by the light of the oil lamp, Kati admired the bed that was piled high to the beams in the ceiling with a heap of bedclothes – pillows, quilts, bedspreads, 'the sewing' as Julis called the needlework, and then the bedclothes were gradually put away in the other room so that it would eventually be possible to sleep in the bed.

"If Julis and András don't sleep in this bed, what's the point of having it?" Kati was puzzled.

"It shows that we've done our best," said Julis proudly. "If anybody sees it they can admire it. Anybody that hasn't got such a thing hasn't done that."

"In these parts a made bed is like a Rolex watch in New York," Kati said with a laugh when Julis had said good night and she and Gyuri snuggled up together in the bed. "Somehow, these people are nearer to me than your embittered intellectual friends in Budapest or János Szentágostony in Tövispuszta – I can never tell with them whether they're being serious, and they seem to look down on everybody."

'One day I shall write an account of this tenants' meeting,' thought Pali Szentágostony as he listened to the discussion about the renovation of the roof and the cellar. He didn't say a thing, merely watched the people. He'd been living in the house in Várfok utca for eight years, and the two children,

Marci and Bence, had been born there. They'd moved to the Goldsteins' flat in Kresz Géza utca in the Fifties, as co-tenants with another family. Then after Henrik died, Anci had officially named Pali as tenant so that the co-tenancy shouldn't revert to the State, and certainly not to the dreadful Szabós, with whom they'd shared kitchen, larder and bathroom. "We can hear two Szabó families at once," said Anci in the sixties, "one on the radio,[96] the other through the wall." After she died Pali lived on in Kresz Géza utca for some years before finally reaching an agreement with the Szabós, and exchanging the one big flat for two smaller ones. Thus it was that Pali and his wife Éva came to be in Várfok utca. It was a house of character, and it was evident that over the centuries the walls had been patched and mended like those of a cathedral. The cellar did in fact date from the Middle Ages, a ground floor had been built onto it in the eighteenth century, extended towards the romantic garden at the turn of the nineteenth, renovated during the peaceful 1930s, and then, after the war, bomb damage was made good by converting the roof void into a further flat. However, while the stylistic elements of various cathedrals had been blended together by faith, hope and charity the house in Várfok utca was essentially supported by little more than ivy.

The occupants were as varied as the house itself. On the ground floor lived the Bánátys; the old man had been an Appeal Court judge, and before the war the whole house had been his; he tended the garden, or to be more exact, the rose bush in front of their window exclusively. Next were the Temesis. Father Temesi was a factory worker, a 'worker-guard'[97], and, in his secondary role, concierge; he kept the stairs clean and put out the dustbins first thing in the morning. Above them lived the Pajors, whose flat had been allotted to them in the fifties by the Interior Ministry. Next door to them were the alcoholic plumber Skorka and his family. Above them was the Székely family. He'd done a crash course in education, as a member of a peasant cadre, then graduated at technical university, but because of his defective schooling had always felt looked down on professionally. His three small, bullied, and identically crop-headed sons bore most of the brunt of this, since it was on them that Székely poured forth his wrath over the indignities that came his way. Next to them, on the garden side, lived Pali and his family, and finally at the very top two elderly sisters. One of them had been a nun in the Congregation of Daughters of Divine Love until it was dissolved in 1950, while the other had been a widow as long as anyone could remember – perhaps she'd been born as such. They went about like twins, dressed in black, buttoned to the throat, and never let anyone into their flat. They weren't seen for weeks on end and kept themselves apart from the world which caused them such grief. A deeply religious Transylvanian woman did their housework, shopped for them and attended to their needs.

The roof leaked and the cellar was rotting. The leak mainly bothered the Székelys because it was above them, and could only be mended via the sisters' flat, into which, as we know, no one was allowed. Székely's curses were futile, as were his threats to involve the council, the police, even the Warsaw Pact. The condition of the cellar gave rise to mould in the Bánáthys' flat, because the Székelys would only vote for renovation if the leaking roof were also mended, which, as we know, the sisters… Skorka could in fact have dealt with it, but he was damp from neither above nor beneath and so wasn't interested – he also asked to be left out of it all, he had enough problems. Temesi proposed that the cellar be put right, but the Bánátys wouldn't hear of it from him because in the Fifties he'd informed on the judge to the ÁVH. The Pajor family, the Ministry people, on the other hand no longer had their contacts with the housing department, and in recent years people had dared to loathe them more and more openly, so they merely said nothing, sat there with their mouths tightly shut, severe and stubborn. And so the roof leaked on and the cellar rotted away. And so it seemed it would continue to the end of time, for ever and ever.

The Inflatable Buddha

To this day I remember the strange item that my parents and I saw on the TV when I was ten. The reporter was investigating what had become of the enormous statue of Lenin that used to be outside the entrance to the Csepel ironworks – on one occasion (during the Kádár period, actually) the workers had sneaked a slice of bread and dripping into its outstretched hand by way of protest. Most of the facilities in the factory had been dismantled or sold off and the new foreign owners had closed them so that they shouldn't compete with goods manufactured abroad by multinationals for export to Hungary. Political statements and slogans vied with one another on the brick wall, the cavernous workshops echoed emptily, and the camera might have been in a ghost town as it panned the heaps of refuse in the roads between them. Then, in another building, the ironworkers revealed, after much urging, where the statue had been hidden. A crane raised a huge steel lid, and in the depths of the concrete-lined pit there stood Vladimir Il'ich Lenin, pointing defiantly, with the outstretched bronze hand that had once held bread and dripping, into the dark recesses of a concrete-lined tunnel: that was where the Way of Lenin led.

How many symbols of broken promise and murderous

ideology are still there to be excavated and reburied? What do stone walls, both beneath the earth and in the hearts of men, still conceal? Shall we ever be capable of telling one another our common story in such a way that everything will find its place? Or shall we each continue to regurgitate our own, to point the finger at one another, and will our stories go on and on, round and round, like the mindless babbling of lunatics?

That was how it started: I began to collect accounts of what people had experienced and what had become of them, using a tape-recorder and a camera, and then Tövispuszta returned to being called Szentágoston, as it had been when my grandfather was young. It was a strange feeling, a village bearing my name. And vice versa. Everything that had been on its head was at last back on its feet, or that too vice versa: one half of the country remembers things one way, the rest of it the other. The statue of St Augustine has been restored to its original position in the village square where for forty years the Soviet war memorial had stood, and the Soviets likewise have gone gallantly home. Veszelka utca and Kodelka utca have been given back their nice old names; once again they're known as Máramaros utca and Szentháromság utca, as they were before.[98] There was a splendid celebration. The bishop came in person and blessed the statue, the church choir has never sung more beautifully or been more numerous, and a lot of people put on the proud Hungarian garment of the thirties, the *bocskai*.[99] The tailor in town was busy for weeks and could scarcely meet the orders for the black, braided garments in which even spare tyres look smaller or at least more worthy of respect. Everything conspired to make it look as if the past bitter fifty or sixty years had been expunged from history – the defeat in war, the domination of the Arrow-Cross and the communists, the compromises of the Kádár period – and as if we had flown back in a time-machine to the happy years of the Thirties.

New political parties were formed and old ones re-established. The position wasn't the same as it had been when there was only one party to choose from, like butter in Közért.[100] In the end forty-six parties and groups competed with one another for our souls on the television screen, each proclaiming with finer slogans and symbols than the last the glories of the future or the past. Maize-cobs dangled, crosses glittered, the double cross nodded majestically with the orb and the crown, the carnation and the tulip bloomed, birds flew in national colours, and oranges smiled. 'Shall we be Democrats?' people pondered. 'If so, what sort? Hungarian, Free, Christian, Young or Social? And bourgeois, peasants or small-holders? Independent or national? Maybe socialists or workers?'

Of course, even in these circumstances there were those who were resigned. "It gets on my nerves!" lisped ex-community Party Secretary Veszelka, an expression which was delivered between his ill-fitting false teeth as "I' ge'sh on me nervsh!" Isti Veres said: "All this time we've been going on about finally wiping out the past, and now it looks as if the past is going to be the future." My grandfather Pál was the only one to continue calling the village Tövispuszta. "It will take a long time and a lot of wisdom for this village to become Szentágoston again," he said quietly.

✳

My Szentágostony grandfather and father didn't need land, but Pityu Veres did. He'd realised at the outset, when he worked on his little domestic holding, that he took a delight in ploughing, in the way that the plough turned over the furrows behind the tractor; he crumbled the soil in his palm, smelled it, kept an eye on the weather and waited eagerly for the harvest, and thought that there was no greater pleasure than seeing life spring again. Then, as the children grew, so did his responsibility; he wanted the best for them, and after it became possible to buy land with compensation vouchers[101] he caught himself looking more and more often at the area and at what others had, and the thrill of acquisition got hold of him. He felt that he could never have enough land. He would have liked to obtain some of the vouchers which were issued as an attempt to compensate those who'd suffered harm in the past years, and he would even have bought our family's land if he'd had enough money.

In support of his applications he also rewrote the story of his life. Previously he'd been known as István Veres junior, scion of a poor peasant family; his mother had kept the house and his father had worked for the Interior Ministry, and had distinguished himself in the defence of the Party HQ in Köztársaság tér. Now he used his other Christian name and called himself Hunor Veres, of an impoverished bourgeois family; the communists had thrown his grandfather into prison and relocated his family. "When all's said and done, that's true too," said he.

Dr. Béla Sárády didn't live to see moral reparation made to himself and his friends. As he'd promised he passed away, but with his compensation vouchers Pityu was only able to acquire a small parcel of land. He now pinned his hopes on the carpet, the Caravaggio, the Patek watch and the silver court dress buttons – all the more so as the proletarian world, as grandfather Sárády called it, in which value meant nothing, had now come to an end. He smartened up the Lada Niva in which he made his local rounds, packed up the heirlooms that remained from the Sárády family's glorious past, and took them up to Budapest to sell.

The valuer at Sotheby's, a tall former countess, her black hair worn in a chignon, assessed the items with a knowing eye. She began with the carpet.

"A nice Bokhara," she said, stroking the pile with a palm, "and in quite good condition."

"Bokhara?" Pityu was surprised. "My grandfather always said it was a rosetta Holbein, worth a great deal."

The valuer laughed.

"If it were a Holbein, so it would be!"

"Aren't these rosettes?" asked Pityu in a disappointed tone, nodding at the square patterns.

The countess was an experienced valuer and had witnessed many such disappointments, but she still found the moment painful when she had to confront families with the merciless fact that for generations they'd been deluding themselves with the glories of the past.

"The rosettes in Holbeins do have elaborately patterned borders, quite similar to Bokhara ornamentation, but this is without question a Bokhara," she said patiently, and turned the carpet over to show the knots. "And it's at least three hundred years younger than a Holbein. This is an early nineteenth-century carpet."

"So it's not worth so much, then?" asked Pityu, almost imploringly.

"It will sell, but there are a lot of these on the market, so I'm afraid it won't interest Sotheby's. But the Consignment Stores would certainly be glad to accept it. Let's look at the picture."

The valuer took the picture to the window, put it on a chair and surveyed it.

"This is interesting! But there's so much dirt on it. It hasn't been cleaned for ages."

"It's a Caravaggio," said Pityu.

The Inflatable Buddha

The countess raised her eyebrows and swallowed hard. Pityu followed her gaze as she looked at the bald old man in the picture, his back bent and his face wrinkled; he held a goose-quill in his hand and a book in his lap, and an angel, standing behind him and bending over the book, was guiding his hand as if teaching him to write.

"I'm sorry to have to disillusion you again," said the valuer. "Caravaggio did indeed paint a similar picture of St Matthew at the end of the sixteenth century, which was for a long time in the Kaiser Wilhelm Museum in Berlin, but was then destroyed. This may be a copy of it. It seems contemporary, so perhaps a less talented pupil copied it in Caravaggio's studio."

The countess stole a glance at Pityu. She was used to clients at this point either withdrawing into themselves or bursting out in offended humiliation. She waited to see which reaction Pityu would have.

"Couldn't you be mistaken?" asked Pityu with some hostility. "This was our family's most prized possession. My grandfather was from an old upper-class family."

"Of course I can be mistaken," said the valuer. "If you'd like a second opinion take it to the Museum of Fine Art and ask them. But I'm quite confident. Believe you me, I too would prefer these to be valuable items, because then I too would earn some commission. But I'm afraid that's not the case. And if I may give you some good advice: from all this it seems that your grandfather must have been a marvellous man, and your family an excellent family. These are only objects. My family's got nothing left either."

"But you're a countess, aren't you? People would be bowled over to hear this."

"Nobody's worth anything because of the glory of their ancestors. It's better to come to terms with that, believe me."

293

Pityu didn't believe her. He reached into his pocket for the Patek.

"Anyway, will you look at this as well?"

"I'm not really an expert on watches," she excused herself, "but I'll gladly take a look. It's a lovely little watch! Does it work?"

"I've never dared wind it up, but here's the key."

The countess carefully inserted the little key in its place and started to turn it. The key turned round and round, meeting no resistance.

"It can't be wound. I'm afraid that either the mechanism is broken or, worse, there isn't one. This happened often – if people wanted to cash in on something when times were hard they'd sell the gold case of a watch and only keep the mechanism, because that was the valuable part. In your position I wouldn't sell it. Your wife or daughter might wear it as a medallion. It's very beautiful!" said the valuer. "A lovely family memento."

Back in the Niva the wiper slapped crossly at the rain on the windscreen. Pityu's expression as he drove showed his utter displeasure. He was no longer angry at having failed to translate the heirlooms into land, but felt that the valuer had besmirched the family's past, stained its honour. As he kept his narrowed eyes on the misty road, he decided not to say a word at home about what had happened. He would say that he couldn't bring himself to part with the things, had changed his mind and let them continue to proclaim the glories of the Sárádys' past.

In the end Isti solved the financial problem: he persuaded Dávid to come into the business as a sleeping partner, to buy land jointly with Pityu-Hunor, who would work it with his family. By that time Pityu had eleven children, the oldest were competent at driving the tractor, ploughing, sowing and using the combine harvester, and with Isti's intervention and the help of the former chairman, the broken-down machinery of the dissolved collective farm became Pityu's at a knock-down price. He adroitly repaired the very familiar machines – he'd previously maintained them in the depot. Everything was going well. "All it takes is a bit of brains, that's all!" said Hunor-Pityu.

For years now I've been living in the Várfok utca flat. In the meantime my parents have divorced, my father has moved in with a female colleague, a young editor, but at least each member of the family managed to buy a flat with the money obtained from compensation vouchers. Thus at the age of twenty-five I came by Várfok utca. The occupants bought the flats from the local authority at advantageous prices; following the death of the sisters the Transylvanian woman obtained the roof conversion in exchange for care services, the Bánáthys' flat was sold by the judge's heirs, and so every impediment to the restoration of the roof was removed; the leak could be stopped and the rot in the cellar dealt with. The only problem was that finding a competent craftsman had become increasingly difficult.

Now even Matyi the handyman had to be called at least ten times before he'd pick up his mobile, whereas previously he'd been a model of reliability. He would stand there, his trousers held up by braces, in front of every piece of work like an overgrown child, waiting patiently for it to be admired. "I don't work for money," he used to say, "that's only a side issue, I work for praise." And truly, the work of his hands was an artistic creation, never less than perfect. With him in charge the wall was immaculate, even in light cast at a low angle, the wires ran so neatly, were so well arranged, that an artist might have drawn them; every piece of woodwork was accurate to a thousandth of a millimetre; and if he said that he would be there on Monday morning at eight o'clock, one could set one's watch by him. Impossible wasn't a word in his vocabulary. When one of his new men had the temerity to say of a job "This can't be done," Matyi answered with the question "Can't it? Well, let's see!" and he picked up the tools and did it. His employee merely grinned sardonically. But only until pay-day came. Then he realised, to his surprise, that his money was short. "You remember," Matyi said, "I did that job for you. I earned the money for that one!" Next time that "This can't be done" slipped out, all Matyi needed to say was "Well, let's see," and the man gave a start: "Beg your pardon, I'll have a go!"

"Send for Matyi!" was the habitual cry in our family when there was trouble with the water-pipes or the wiring, or if there was need of painter, French polisher or joiner. More recently, however, Matyi preferred to work in Austria and wasn't taking on small jobs for old customers.

"What's come over you, Matyi?" I asked him, when the great man finally attended to the renovations in Várfok utca. "You always used to be so obliging!"

"Nobody's obliging these days," he replied regretfully as he looked at the wall. "Not even me. Because people aren't that way with me. A colleague of mine said the other day that we ought to make that shelf for the kindergarten which he'd promised the woman that runs it. And I told him, we'd better take on work that'll keep the firm in business. 'But my son goes there!' he said. I said I couldn't care less. When I said it

I knew it wasn't a nice thing to say, but the trouble is, that's the way I think. I'm stuck in a chain of debt like other people. I can't behave in what I consider an honourable way any longer. I'm gradually stopping being ashamed of myself. Nobody's ashamed of themselves any more. They all just want to make a living, to survive. The big investors are all talk, but they invest in Romania, Dubai and Ukraine, and that's where they keep their main business. The State fleeces the people who pay their taxes honestly, while anybody who works in his shed and evades tax can work more cheaply and steals the work from others. The banks won't advance credit, because they're afraid they won't get their money back, but without credit there's no economy. The system's becoming more and more corrupt, but that's the only way to get work. Now that corruption has become natural, all we can do is protest at the level of it. And then there's the tax office, the police, the State apparatus, the mafia. I no longer know where the one ends and the other begins. They can all go and rot in Hell! If only somebody would come along and protect the honest Hungarian!"

The Öreghárs isn't what it used to be either. Following the change of regime, a number of former notables of Party and State kept on their regular table for a year or two. Former department heads from Party HQ, Central Committee secretaries and ministers, who'd been bitter adversaries in the Party hierarchy, now found that they had a common enemy – the change – and they downed their spritzers and did business together in perfect harmony. Actually they had no cause for complaint, since for the most part they'd helped themselves to hefty cuts from privatisation, or internationals had employed them, reckoning on their economic expertise and Russian political connections, from which corn and oil could be brought forth as if by magic. At the time Isti and Dávid had enjoyed themselves in their company, but then the company drifted apart. Some emigrated to the south of Spain or France, or to Miami, others retired to their Buda villas and never ventured forth without their bodyguards. "That wasn't a change of regime," said my great-uncle János, "it was one regime rotting nicely into another."

Csoki and his band no longer played at the Öreghárs. There was no demand, they were told, musak replaced them, and once a week there was live jazz played by young Roma musicians. When they played my girlfriend and I went along with a few friends to have a beer and listen to them. Auntie Bözsi had long ago retired, and a mysterious new owner who'd bought the restaurant from the local authority had engaged as manager one Elemér, a tubby, middle-aged man with close-cropped hair. It was said of him that he had strong connections with the underworld. He took me to his heart straight away because with my loud laugh I proved to be an appreciative audience for his stories. I think he liked my girlfriend Vali as well. Every time he saw her he said: "That girl's a witch, they have that sort of deceitful eyes and thick eyebrows." Elemér was a cheerful, good-humoured man. According to him he was one of six children by seven fathers. He'd last seen his mother when he was being taken off by train to Szabolcs, to the children's home, because she couldn't manage to look after her children. She hadn't said anything, just kissed him and left him, without even a backward glance. He could only tell from the heaving of her shoulders that she was sobbing. He grew up in State homes, and when he reached the age of eighteen was put out on the

street with a bag of potatoes and twelve thousand forints: he
was now an adult, and must live as best he could. He and a few
friends from the State home, mostly Roma, formed a gang. They
robbed cars and smuggled. He was a big, strong boy and was
taken on as bouncer at a disco. He had to throw the Gypsies out.
"Are you going to throw us out, brother?" asked his friends.
"If you come here, Hungarians won't," he answered. "Either
I throw you out, or I'll get thrown out. Then somebody else'll
come who'll throw us all out." Things became easier once he
became a cloakroom attendant. He went round the coats with
a stick, hit the pockets, and when he heard clinking removed
the small-change. Later on he stole a book of tickets from the
cloakroom at the Mákvirág nightclub, and from that gave
cloakroom tickets to guests who arrived tiddly in their smart
coats; then when they left, now plastered, and presented the
slip of paper he held his arms wide apart, there must be some
mistake, the esteemed guest had no coat there, he must have
left it at the Mákvirág, that was where the ticket was from.
The drunken guests would insist for a while, and then when
their demands became too noisy, the security boys threw
them out. Elemér sold the coats in the flea-market and gave
a reward to the security boys. In the Seventies some German
guests asked Elemér for grass.[102] He didn't even know what
they meant, but when it was explained to him, his eyes lit up.
"I'll get you some!"
    "I looked in the kitchen to see what grass cigarettes could
be made of. I mixed up tobacco with bay-leaves, pepper
and marjoram and sold it to them. Essentially, it was dried
vegetable soup, but they liked it a lot and came back for
more. They gave me a thousand forints for a cigarette – in the
seventies that was big money!" he raised a finger. We roared
with laughter, we found it so amusing. Elemér's career at the
disco came to an end when one evening a guest left a briefcase

with him, pointing out repeatedly that it was valuable, take good care of it. Naturally, he was given a Mákvirág ticket for it. As the guest went into the disco Elemér opened the briefcase. It contained six million forints. He went to see the manager and informed him angrily that he was resigning on the spot, and stormed out taking the briefcase with him.

"Marci, my boy, the boss'll be here tonight," Elemér whispered in my ear one evening. "We're throwing a birthday party for him in the cellar. I've persuaded him to let you and your girlfriend come."

My face cannot have registered the right degree of enthusiasm, because he went on.

"The Boss is a big man. Bigger than the Prime Minister! If he says something, even the politicians take note! Compared to him the other great brains are nothing."

I'd already heard about the Boss. He was spoken of in the city as head of the most influential underworld family, a total scoundrel, a common murderer. He bribed the leaders of the local authority, bought business premises cheap – as he had the Öreghárs – and sold them dear or rented them at a high price. He was said to run a protection racket and to be into prostitution, but it was hard to pin anything on him because the mafia was organised on a family basis, and if anyone became an informant he destroyed his family. Furthermore, the 'family' and the Roma liked him, because he helped anyone that he could with money and connections. He was truly a Godfather.

It was the first time that I'd been in the Öreghárs cellar. A moderately capable hand had decorated the walls with Greek frescoes, and little white-clothed tables stood at the base of alabaster Doric columns. At one table sat the Boss himself. He was a short man with strong features and lively, intelligent eyes. He examined us with a penetrating gaze.

The Inflatable Buddha

"Elemér's told me about you. What are you drinking?"
"A glass of wine, perhaps."
"The same for me, please," said Vali.
"Right, two glasses of wine," repeated the Boss. Immediately a big, swarthy man jumped up from the table and returned with two glasses of red wine.
"Elemér said that you were an artist," said the Boss.
"That's a bit of an exaggeration! But I try very hard to give expression to the world as I see it: I make videos, I take photographs and I write."
"I suppose somebody must want it," said the Boss, "otherwise you wouldn't be doing it. Don't you agree? What are you two going to have to drink?"
"Thank you, nothing more. We haven't drunk this yet," I excused myself.
The Boss looked at me hard, in silence.
"Ask for something!" whispered Elemér emphatically.
"Well," I corrected myself, "perhaps another wine, please."
The big man was on his feet at once, and placed another two glasses beside the first two, which we hadn't yet touched.
"Happy birthday!" I raised my glass towards the Boss. "May I ask, how many this is?"
"I'll tell you if you promise not to be startled! Thirty-seven."
I thought he looked at least fifty.
"I did thirteen years in prison, and it shows! But I'm not afraid of anybody! Look into my eyes!"
I did my best to comply with his request, but the Boss was leaning quite close to my face, and as he had a squint I couldn't decide on the spur of the moment which eye to look into.
"You see? Nobody!" he repeated, but this time so loudly

that people at the other tables looked at us. I began to feel less than comfortable, and I could see that Vali was slowly sliding down the chair in her nervousness.

"If I say Á, then it's Á!" said the Boss harshly. "What are you drinking?"

"Well, wine, if that's what we've been drinking already," I answered amenably, looking at the two almost untouched glasses in front of me. The big man jumped up and set more wine before us.

"And what business are you in?" I enquired. I've noticed that I'm always at my most impudent when I'm nervous.

The Boss was shocked at the question. He took a long look at my face: was I trying to provoke him?

"You know who I am?"

"Yes. I've heard."

"Right then. I'm into everything that can make me money."

"But what's your legal business?"

The Boss swallowed hard.

"All my businesses are legal. When my children were born I decided that I wasn't going back to prison. They go to the best private schools. I'm always telling them, don't be ashamed of being Gypsies but don't let yourselves be humiliated either. If I saw my children being taken advantage of I'd have somebody killed straight away."

"I'd be interested in the story of your life. Would you tell me?"

"What for?"

"I collect histories. I like to get to know about careers that are different from my own. I get the feeling that we're locked into our private little worlds, with everybody churning out their own grievances."

"It'd be no good my telling you the story of my life, you'd learn nothing from that. You have to solve your own problems."

The Inflatable Buddha

"That's a shame, I'd have been interested," I said.

"Here you are then: I was born in a lousy shack, and I didn't want my children to grow up in one as well. My life story's as simple as that. What d'you make of that?"

"All the same, I can try to understand it, can't I?"

"You all think that this can be understood. But you've got to experience it. When I was a boy university students would come round to the settlement to feel sorry for the Gypsies. They'd be very sympathetic, take photographs, film us, ask questions, make notes. Then they'd go home to their daddies and mummies on the Rózsadomb and have a good wash in case they'd brought any lice home. They'd even be political dissidents. They'd get a couple of thumps from the police and feel like heroes. D'you know how many thumps I've had? Now they've become paupers, or professors, bankers, Members of Parliament who come running to me for me to send a couple of thousand people to their mass meetings. They want me to do that in exchange for money to be set aside for the support of the Gypsies. They just shoot off their mouths, and everything stays the same. The cards have been dealt again, but it's the same old pack. Bunch of wankers!"

He looked hard into my eyes then pointed towards the door.

"See that black electric switch?"

Turn my head though I might, as I looked for the black switch where the Boss was pointing I could only see a white one. "It's white, isn't it?"

"It's black if I say so! I'll smash your face in!" shrieked the Boss. He jumped up, grabbed my shirt, hoisted me off my chair and raised his fist towards my face. I was petrified, Vali screamed. The other people sitting at the table merely watched in silence.

"All right," I said feebly, "it's black."

The Boss let me go. I sank back onto my chair, gasping.

"Well, there you are!" he said with a satisfied smile and patted me on the shoulder. "You gave the answer I was expecting. Intellectual young gentlemen all behave like that. That's why, if an intellectual and a primitive man come face to face, my money's on the primitive, because he's going to win. If you and your girlfriend fall out you aren't going to punch her in the mouth, because your father never hit your mother, nor your grandfather your grandmother. Though perhaps they should have. Anybody that's too intellectual always loses. The winners are the ones who have a sound balance of intellect and primitiveness. Now, another glass?"

"Thanks, I was just going to ask for one," I said eagerly.

The band struck up and everybody looked in their direction. It was Csoki and his band.

"Come on, let's have some dancing!" said Elemér, by now slightly tiddly, to ease the tension, and looked at the Boss as if asking permission. "What's your favourite tune?" he asked me.

"Same as the Boss', of course!" I said, gathering together the remains of my impudence.

The Boss raised his eyebrows and nodded. Elemér pulled Vali off her chair with me and hugged the two of us to him. The three of us began to dance together. We tottered around with him, ill at ease and trying to smile.

"Go and marry this lovely girl!" said Elemér. "And have a son! I'll give you a million if you have a son! Or d'you know what? I'll give you five million if you have a son! And if anybody fucks your girlfriend, I swear I'll cut his throat. I love you two!" he said, with tears in his eyes. "And d'you know why I love you? It's because you're so naive!"

✳

The Inflatable Buddha

Family and friends stood around the grave of my grandfather Pál Szentágostony. In silence there stood my grandmother Elza, János, my father Pali and my brother Bence. Isti, Pityu and Dávid had come too. We were like the cast at the end of a show, only we weren't taking a bow, I thought, as the priest spoke. He did his best to summarise my grandfather's life in the eulogy, and was perspiring visibly with the effort. He mopped his glistening forehead with a handkerchief as he spoke of the life and times of the family, of denigration, of Pál's years of imprisonment in communist days, the Christian faith which had sustained him, and the importance of Hungarianness, of which there was now greater need than ever.

The cottages of the former Tövispuszta were clearly visible in the valley beyond the stone statue of Christ on the cemetery hill – the statue on the head of which, according to legend, a little boy had placed a crown of thorns which he'd made himself. The village had officially been called Szentágoston for quite some time, but the villagers continued to call the area around the former farm servants' quarters Tövispuszta, to distinguish them from the developing Szentágoston side of the hill; after the closure of the mine and the surrounding industries they'd been occupied by unemployed families who eked out an existence on the dole. Our former mansion stood on the hilltop opposite; Pityu and his family had been living there for ten years.

Pityu had become a successful farmer and owned land as far as the eye could see, some of it cultivated by his tenants. He'd made good use of his father's and Dávid's money. He'd even bought the mansion from the bankrupt collective farm and had towers and a new wing built on, together with a huge terrace, wide steps, and in front of it a fountain which he'd seen in Germany. He was planning to build a wellness centre, and the new wing would be able to accommodate twenty or thirty visitors. The rosetta Holbein and the Caravaggio had finally found worthy positions. They hung on the walls in the big hall, declaring that Pityu wasn't some nouveau riche upstart like the entrepreneurs who were building new villas in Szentágoston, but a scion of the ancient, Christian, lordly Sárády family. He built a high wall round the mansion so that the envious might not stare at it, nor the Tövispuszta people rob him. "The wall protects us from the people of Tövispuszta but not, unfortunately, from the taxman, and he's a greater thief than any Gypsy," he used to say. That, of course, even he didn't take seriously.

As I listened to the priest my thoughts wandered. I considered what a good panoramic shot it would make with the hanging head of the sorrowful looking statue closing the picture on the right; or if I were to write a novel it could start with the stone Christ crowned with thorns. I'd been making a film about Tövispuszta for months, about the clashes that had slowly become everyday occurrences, the seething hatred. Tövispuszta people went over to Szentágoston to steal chickens, fruit and firewood, and to shoplift in the store. They even robbed poor old ladies who'd only the slenderest of pensions on which to subsist. People who didn't like this threatened them. "They don't know what work is!" said the people of Szentágoston. Which was true. There'd been no work in the area for twenty years, and a generation had grown up that had never seen its parents go to work. When I asked one Tövispuszta boy what he wanted to be when he grew up, he mumbled 'assistance'.

The everyday thieving and rowdiness reached such a pitch that the mayor requested the help of the Gárda.[103] That helpful body, in dress superficially a folk-dance team, but underneath riot police,[104] simply moved through Tövispuszta a few times and order was restored at once. No wonder the

The Inflatable Buddha

people of Szentágoston were grateful to them. "It's typical that the liberal bolshies immediately appeared for a protest, because sponging Gypsies matter more to them than honest Hungarians!" said the Gárda members. The black-uniformed Gárda, their supporters and the liberal bolshies shouted at each other and quarrelled.

I looked for familiar faces in the crowd to photograph. Among the Gárda I spotted Matyi, the handyman, with a few of his well-meaning friends who weren't allowed to be honourable, and a female porn star who was using the protest as a means of regaining her respectability. There were the grandchildren of Hetési and Székely, who were trying to redeem their Arrow-Cross grandfathers and a number of villagers who insisted that they weren't Tövispuszta people and were demonstrating against them. Then in the view-finder there appeared a well-known journalist who'd tried for ages to find his place on the political palette before at last succeeding: earlier he'd been a keen member of the staff of the communist party paper, then became a liberal, and here he was now with the Gárda. I saw men with narrow foreheads and hard faces who'd put on the uniform because they'd once again been denied what they considered their historical entitlement, had finally discovered whose fault it all was, and were now pinning their hopes on the Gárda to protect the fruits of their labours.

On the other side there was Veszelka, the ex-Party secretary, shaking his fist, together with a few dozen neurotic Jews who suspected that there were Nazis everywhere and were increasingly finding them. There were the old and new defenders of human rights, among them Tamás Kárász, my father's old dissident friend, who was now chanting slogans with a few old policemen who, in the Kádár period, had beaten him with rubber truncheons at the demonstrations by

307

the Batthyány statue. Well-known as a dissident writer, he was shouting together with his sometime informer and an erstwhile Party worker, who thirty years before had seen to it that his books were banned, and with his liberal friends, many of whom had only come because they were afraid that if they stayed away they would be cast out of his social circle. There was also old Temesi from Várfok utca. "We've come with the lads, old worker-guards who are still alive," the octogenarian told me, "If somebody would give us weapons we'd show these filthy Nazi youngsters what 'God of the Hungarians' means!"[105] I recalled that at the time of the elections I'd asked someone why he'd voted for the particular party that he'd chosen. The reply came "Because these only make me sick, I'm actually afraid of the rest," but which side he was on I can't remember. The Tövispuszta people, forgotten in the meantime by the demonstrators, were awaiting developments, a little apprehensively but with interest. Then the police appeared, carefully waiting for the moment when it was certain that there wasn't going to be any kind of riot, and forced their way between the opposing parties to prevent trouble. Meanwhile the priest was reading from the Bible. He quoted St Paul's words to Timothy: *For the time will come when they will not endure sound doctrine; but after their own lusts shall they heap unto themselves teachers, having itching ears; and they shall turn away their ears from the truth, and shall be turned unto fables.*[106] That was when I decided to let documentary film-making go hang. These people needed fables!

My grandfather was struck by a train on the level crossing while out on his evening walk. It never became clear whether that had in fact been his destiny, or whether he'd merely meant to refute Elza's presentiment. After grandfather's death my father woke up to the fact that he'd never really known him. Elza then gave him the essays which grandfather had written nightly over the years, and for days we feverishly read writings on philosophy, the history of science and culture, eastern religions, the economic crises of the Thirties and our own times, the power of the mob, esoterica and human behaviour.

"Good Lord!" said my father from time to time, raising his eyes from the page and looking at me, now flushed, now pale. "We were living here with him, and we didn't know who my father was. Your grandfather."

I scarcely knew my grandparents either, but everybody has told me that with my honey-blonde hair and grey-green eyes I'm the image of my grandmother. Bence and I, however, were born in Budapest and there we grew up, and we only came down to Szentágoston on important occasions and for a few days in the summer. "My summer grandchildren," grandmother Elza used to say, when our parents 'put us out to grass' in the summer, so that we could go back home bronzed and fattened up. On grandfather's death I awoke to the possibility that I might lose my grandmother too before I'd got to know her, and in recent times we've got her to talk more and more.

"Grandmother, do you understand these people?" I asked her after the Gárda demonstration.

"I suppose they mean well, but their grievances and fears have them on a string like puppeteers have their puppets. And while the past governs their actions it will be their future too. And unfortunately it will also be yours, you young people's, who think that the past is nothing to do with you," she replied.

*

My father pestered his mother for ages to let him give grandfather's manuscripts to a publisher. "People won't understand them," said grandmother Elza drily. "They didn't while he was alive, and they won't now he's dead. There'll be no point in mentioning them."

Eventually, however, she did yield to my father's requests for the writings to be published. In a few months the hermit of Tövispuszta's book became a nation-wide sensation, and Szentágoston a place of pilgrimage. University students came. Intellectuals sickened by politics, girls and women troubled in their womanhood, and ascetic-looking esoterics. They were accommodated in the new wing of the mansion and quoted and expounded Pál Szentágostony to one another, meditated in the jacuzzi, and chanted mantras in small groups in the grounds, seated cross-legged with eyes closed and thumbs and index fingers pressed together. Pityu took pleasure in telling the assembled enthusiasts what a wonderful man the master had been, how the air had glowed around him filling everybody with energy, how his aura had been little short of blinding, and how anyone that shook hands with him had felt a strange, warm electric shock. He even sold little framed pictures of my grandfather, for which there was regular hand-to-hand fighting among the devotees treading the path of enlightenment and love. One bald, muscular man wearing OM round his neck actually butted another determined esoteric for the last picture. My father bought a sports car with the royalties from the books and raced between Budapest and Szentágoston with his girlfriend, wearing baseball caps and sunglasses. Even Péter Pusztai came over from New York; he had, in the meantime, become a practising Jew, resumed the name of Goldstein, and very much looked down on his father for having forsaken the ancestral religion. He said that after reading Pál's books he had a better understanding of the Kabbala, the Jewish mystic work. Kati Pusztai came too, with her husband Gyuri and their four children, all dressed in Indian gauze, and at Pityu's suggestion set up a bio-food stall next to the mansion.

Since I was a boy I'd always felt that my great-uncle János was hiding a secret, but I couldn't make out what it might be. Since deciding to try and collect the tangled histories of Tövispuszta I've talked with him a great deal. His cynical tales amuse me, but on one occasion, when I burst out in supercilious laughter at the past, he cautioned me: "Don't you go thinking that you're innocent! You're all only young. Not yet fallen from grace."

And he pointed to the collection of things presented to him by his patients.

"So, clever clogs, have you succeeded in deciphering what's in people's heads?" he asked. "You too are aware that objects sometimes speak louder than words."

There was a porcelain dog with toothache, an icon, a terribly poor painting which portrayed János in a white coat with his stethoscope round his neck, an embroidered sampler proclaiming culinary wisdom, a red, heart-shaped box, a stuffed hedgehog and an orange, inflatable Buddha.

"This is particularly practical," said János of this last, "it's faith, wisdom and forgiveness all in one. True, the inside is empty, like life, and it's easily portable."

It was from János' collection that I acquired a taste for gathering objects as well as stories – yellowed documents, old newspapers, coffee-stained letters. From my father I begged

311

my great-grandfather's diary and a silver spoon embossed with a crown, from the Vereses I got the tulip-decorated chest on the lid of which Lucky Gizi had inscribed the most significant events in the family, the picture of Christ found its way to me, and I bought a Hanukkah candlestick in the local market – I was told that it had belonged to the Goldsteins or the Steiners; perhaps it's the smell of old things that evokes the past.

In his ironic way János told me a lot of tales about the Szentágostony family, my great-grandparents, my grandfather, grandmother and father, about the Vereses and the Goldsteins, but he didn't believe that these anecdotes could together form a historical narrative.

"How could truth emerge from a mass of living lies?" He shook his head. "It's like pieces of a jig-saw puzzle picked out of several different boxes, and what's more there are some missing, because anything at all discreditable has been rejected by the healing power of memory. Most people are unwittingly whirled along by history, from which I've been saved by my cynicism. I'd always have liked to observe things from a lofty viewpoint, as did Pál, but I always seemed to become just a bystander. So if you mean to write you ought to do it somehow like your grandfather: to crouch at God's feet and look at the world from both within and without, and purge your mind of all the policemen that various regimes have set in it to control your thoughts. But perhaps even then you won't be able to write what really matters in life. You can come up with ingenious plots, refined narrative techniques and linguistic inventions, but you won't be able to talk about what really matters because as you speak it'll be misunderstood, or it'll turn into feeble platitudes of no substance. As your grandfather's favourite Zen aphorism puts it: he that knows does not speak, he that speaks does not know."

"What really matters to you, János?" I asked.

He thought for a long moment. I could see that he was considering whether or not to tell me. Then, without saying a word, he rose heavily to his feet and made to leave the house. At the door he turned and beckoned to me. We climbed into his old car, drove through the village, up the winding road onto the Szentágoston hill and turned into a garden. From the top the whole of Szentágoston could be seen, the vineyards, and in the distance even the lake at Keszo". In the garden the cherry trees were in blossom. János didn't say a single word all the way. He got out of the car, shut the door and didn't even look round. Only the sound of the other door shutting told him that I was following him. On hearing the noises a plump woman of about thirty stepped out of the house; she suffered from Down's syndrome. With a strange, lop-sided smile on her lips she blinked her slanting, bulbous eyes timidly in the light and wiped her nose with the back of her hand. She was about to waddle towards János when she caught sight of me, took fright and turned back towards the door.

"This is Dóri, my daughter," said János.

Eyes wide, I stared inanely, first at János, then at the woman.

"You asked what really mattered to me. Well, she does: Dóri does. She's a lovechild! People say that they turn out well," he added with a faint smile. He went up to his daughter, gave her a hug and a kiss on the cheek, and stroked her head.

"This is Marci, your cousin, in a manner of speaking."

Dóri cocked her head to one side and looked at me. I did my best to conceal my repugnance, but I could tell that she sensed it, try though I might.

"Hello, Dóri," I said uncertainly.

"Dóri can't talk, but she understands everything," said János. "And she can be affectionate."

Out of the house came Dóri's mother, a calm-faced woman

with her hair in a chignon, and tried to ask us in, but János declined the invitation graciously.

"We were just passing and looked in to say hello," he said. "Well, we'll be off, my girl," he turned to his daughter, gave her another hug, and we climbed back into the car. As I looked in the rear-view mirror I could see Dóri looking questioningly after us until we disappeared from sight.

"I had a brief affair with Dóri's mother and then it turned out that she was pregnant; what was more, the child was going to have Down's syndrome," said János as we wound our way back down the hill. "I begged her to have an abortion, but she said that it would be her last chance to have a child. I'm ashamed to say it, but I prayed that it might be born dead. It was born, though, and for months just looked vacantly into space. It lay in its bed, ate, slept, defecated, and I thought I was going to die of grief and shame. Dóri must have been eighteen months old, when one day she was lying on the carpet, staring in front of her. I tried to draw her attention to me, spoke to her, clapped my hands, called out, but she took no notice of me at all. It was preposterous that I couldn't communicate with my own child, I told myself. I lay down beside her on the carpet and tried to see what she was looking at. Then I realised that as the shaft of light came in low through the window it was sparkling on the pile of the rug. Dóri was watching how silkily, splendidly, the golden yellow sunlight gleamed on the reddish strands of wool. And so we lay there together watching the beam of sunlight. Then for the very first time Dóri looked at me and began to examine me. She was obviously looking to see who this idiot was, lying on the floor looking at the carpet. You know, it's possible to understand anybody, you just have to lie down by them on the carpet. Dóri's got a weak heart. She won't live very much longer. Now God's going to take her from me when I've finally realised how much she matters to me. That's my punishment. When I told you in the garden that Dóri understood everything, I meant, everything that matters in life. Everything that will be missing from your book, because we don't know how to express it. We always talk about something else."

THE END

TRANSLATOR's

1. *Tövis* means 'thorn'. *Puszta* in a place meant the cluster of buildings that hous of an estate, together with the stables, gra. smithies etc. as is the case here. This is a rath. fashioned term (though a number of such plac ,, and a Hungarian ear will catch the other meanin of puszta: 'desolate, uncultivated' or a flat, steppe-like region of grassland.

2. A reference to the Treaty of Trianon (1920), under which Hungary lost some 60% of its territory.

3. Post-Trianon Hungary was popularly known as 'mutilated'.

4. Leading figure in the Hungarian Soviet Republic (1919). A large proportion of the commissars were of Jewish extraction.

5. The Soviet regime headed by Béla Kun which ruled in Hungary from March to August 1919.

6. The Hungarian version of *ratatouille*.

7. Not so much a new law, as the stricter application of the so-called *numerus clausus* law XXV of 1920, enforced to conform with German Nazi practice.

8. Because of this use of the 'cross barbed' the National Socialist Party was commonly known as the Arrow-Cross Party. I am indebted to Somerset Herald at the College of Arms, England for the information that there is no standard heraldic term denoting a square thus oriented – this specially invented (and approved!) term 'equilateral lozenge' may be the only good thing to come out of the Arrow-Cross.

9. Starting in 1938, Hungary passed a series of anti-Jewish measures in emulation of Germany's Nürnberg Laws. The first (29 May 1938) restricted the number of Jews in each commercial enterprise, in the press, among physicians, engineers and lawyers to 20%. Access to higher education was already restricted. The second anti-Jewish law (5 May 1939), for the first time, defined Jews racially: people with 2, 3 or 4 Jewish-born grandparents were declared Jewish. Their employment in government at any level was forbidden, they might not be editors of newspapers, their numbers were restricted to 6% among theatre and film actors, doctors, lawyers and engineers. Private companies were forbidden to employ more than 12% Jews. 250,000 Hungarian Jews lost their livelihoods. Most of them also lost the right to vote. The Third Jewish Law (9 August 1941) prohibited intermarriage and penalized sexual intercourse between Jews and non-Jews.

10. Pussy, pussy!

11. In Hungarian the word *aladár* both is a man's name and means 'turkey'.

12. The Hungarian verse is the first stanza of Attila József's *Mondd, mit érlel annak a sorsa*.

13. Eminent Hungarian poets of the 19th and early 20th centuries.

14. The Hungarian verse is the first stanza of Attila József's *Mikor az uccán átment a kedves*.

15. The familiar form of address, akin to the French *tu*. Among men, the elder will decide when it is to be used.

16. These are the words of a children's game-song of the 1930s.

Translator's Notes

17. *Viharsarok* (Storm Corner, 1937) is a real place on the lower Tisza, and Féja's account of the backwardness of life there was seen as a political indictment of the Horthy regime. *Puszták népe* (People of the Pusztas, 1936) is a partly autobiographical account of life in a vanishing, semi-feudal world. Lenin's *State and Revolution* (1917) was a seminal work of the Bolshevik revolution.

18. A public holiday in Hungary, commemorating the start of the 1848 revolution.

19. A reference to Hitler's restoration to Hungary in early 1939 of the 12,000 Km² Sub-carpathian region, ceded to Czechoslovakia under the Treaty of Trianon in 1920. Hungarian troops entered the area between 15–18 March.

20. The *Honfoglalás* (Occupation of the Land) under the tribal leader Árpád is traditionally dated 895 AD.

21. The racial origin of the Hungarians has been the subject of much dispute. One theory (now firmly discredited) was that they were of Scythian stock.

22. Lieutenant General Jenő Rátz was Minister of Defence from May to November 1938.

23. Ferenc Szálasi, leader of the Hungarian National Socialist (aka Arrow-Cross) Party, became Prime Minister and Head of State in October 1944, and was hanged 12 March 1946

24. Count Kűnó Klebelsberg, Minister of Education 1922–31.

25. "A mutilated Hungary is not a country! A whole Hungary is heaven!" The play on words *nem ország/mennyország* (not a country/heaven) means that this post-Trianon slogan cannot be effectively conveyed in English.

26. The *Felvidék* (Upper Hungary) is now mostly Slovakia;

the *Székelyföld* is a region of SE Transylvania, peopled largely by the Székely.

27. Pál Prónay (1874–1946?) was a hussar officer, prominent in the White Terror of 1930s. Arrested and deported by the Red Army in late 1945 he died in the *Gulag*. Count Albert Apponyi (1846–1933) was a distinguished politician and led the Hungarian delegation to the Versailles Peace Conference in 1920.

28. The anti-German swing in Yugoslavia took place on 27 March 1941. German forces entered the country on 2 April, Teleki's suicide occurred on 3 April, and Hungarian troops entered Yugoslavia on 11 April. Croatia had declared independence on 10 April, so that formally Yugoslavia no longer existed.

29. Henrik Werth, Chief of Staff until September 1941.

30. László Bárdossy, successor to Teleki as Prime Minister.

31. A reference to the battle of Borodino, 1812.

32. Defence law 1939:II which came into force in March 1939 provided the basis for this. 'Unreliable elements', mainly Jews, might not bear arms but were made to do heavy work in support of the forces. By the summer of 1940 sixty such Jewish units existed. Poorly clothed and fed, and on the eastern front especially in great danger, their survival rate was very low.

33. The massacre at Kamenets-Podolski, in Western Ukraine, was the first large-scale event in the 'Final Solution'. Some 18,000 Jews from Hungary arrived there by the end of August, having been marched from Körösmező (Ukrainian, Yasinya). Some 23,600 were murdered by *Einsatzgruppen* on 27/28 August.

34. A reference to the destruction of the Hungarian Second Army on the Don in January 1943.

35. This practice is commemorated by a monument on the Pest riverside consisting of a row of bronze model shoes. As it was the Arrow-Cross way to spray groups of victims with sub-machine gun fire, a few survived by jumping or falling into the Danube, less than fatally injured or even not injured at all, and swimming away.

36. 'Starred houses' were houses from which non-Jewish occupants had been removed for them to be occupied exclusively by Jews. Both parties were usually given at the most 24 hours notice of this, which caused great dissatisfaction. The entrances were then marked with the Star of David, and non-Jews were not allowed in.

37. 'Protected houses' were established by the embassies of a number of neutral nations, notably the Spanish, Swedish and Swiss, to house Jewish persons having connections with those countries who were in possession of the protective passports that they issued. This enabled assistance to be given with food supply, medical care and other humanitarian aid.

38. The anti-Habsburg wars of 1704–11 and 1848–49.

39. Horthy's Chief of Staff, commander of the First Army, he had defected to the Russians. The later famous Imre Nagy was also in the cabinet, the sole communist appointee.

40. Head of Soviet Security Services in SE Europe.

41. Elza has been addressing Pál formally, and his suggestion here is that she use the informal pronoun. Between a man and a woman it is usually the woman who initiates this, but here Pál is pulling rank!

42. Minister for the Interior, later Foreign Minister, he fell victim to a show trial in 1949.

43. Mátyás Rákosi, General Secretary of the Hungarian Communist Party at the time.

44. *Államvédelmi Hatóság*, State Security Authority, aka the Secret Police.

45. A prairie-like area or *puszta* in eastern Hungary, near Debrecen.

46. A pre-metric weight, approximately 100 Kg.

47. A Russian word meaning 'fist', used to denote a well-to-do peasant

48. A pre-metric measure, equal to 0.57 ha. or 1.42 English acres. Fifteen *hold* is therefore about twenty-one acres.

49. The communist-period popular song continues: shake in your shoes, for the repressed proletariat is rising.

50. Not for the sick or convalescent, but holiday accommodation. Another Russianism.

51. The communist youth organisation.

52. *arany* = gold, *kő* = stone.

53. The addition of -i to a place-name is a frequent means of producing a surname indicating association with the place. In the case of the nobility the suffix becomes -y and indicates ownership.

54. The commemoration of István I, first Christian king of Hungary (reigned 1000–1038).

55. These are all diminutives of the name István.

56. A tradition of celebrating the day of the year associated with one's given name. The custom originated with the calendar of saints; believers named after a particular

saint would celebrate that saint's feast day. Little if any religious significance remains today.

57. *Veres* is a dialectal form of *vörös* 'dark red'. Red wine and the Soviet army are *vörös*.

58. The Hungarian word for 'fair' is *búcsú*, which also means 'leave-taking'.

59. 20 August is traditionally the festival of both St István and of the new bread, made from the new flour of the recent harvest.

60. 'Rose Hill', a fashionable area of Buda.

61. The Kunmadaras incident occurred in May 1946, that in Miskolc in August the same year.

62. The present Dunaújváros, on the middle Danube, known as Sztálinváros from 1951 to 1961, was founded in 1950 on a greenfield site near the village of Dunapentele.

63. 'Free People', the Party daily paper.

64. Rajk, Pálffy and other victims of show trials were rehabilitated and were reburied on 6 October 1956.

65. A well-known writer of socialist leanings.

66. The hole was where the hammer, sickle and wheat-sheaf device had been cut out.

67. Corvin köz (a little street off Üllői út) and the neighouring Killián barracks were a key strategic point in October 1956, one of the last to fall to the Soviet forces.

68. A town in Pest county, a little to the east of Budapest.

69. This custom arose in the 1930s and spread through the social democratic workers' movement. The origin of the melody is uncertain; some ascribe it to Tchaikovsky, others to a Russian folk melody. The Hungarian words are by István Raics.

70. A stew made with pig's trotters.

71. Berkesz is a village in Szabolcs-Szatmár-Bereg county, north-eastern Hungary.

72. A well-known restaurant of the time on Blaha Lujza tér.

73. These pre-war names have been restored in modern Budapest.

74. A 1968 socialist documentary.

75. Distinguished Hungarian stage and film actor (1919–98).

76. The traditional external corridor at each level in an interior courtyard.

77. There was at the time a great shortage of telephone lines in Budapest.

78. One of the four pillars of Hungarian cuisine, a form of stew.

79. A 1968 Czech hit by Karel Gott which attained wide popularity.

80. A town on the Danube just north of Budapest, well known for its artistic connections.

81. *Tüzép* is a chain of building materials merchants.

82. A trick-taking game for three, played with the traditional Hungarian pack of 32 cards. The name derives from the aim to take the ultimate trick. The game is virtually unknown outside Hungary, though it is a remote derivative of the French *Mariage*.

83. 'Occupation of the Homeland', the arrival in the Carpathian Basin of the nomadic Magyar tribes under Árpád, traditionally dated 895 AD. The Millennium here means the 1,000th anniversary of this.

84. *Sugár* 'Radius' because of its straightness and location; Count Gyula Andrássy was Prime Minister in the

mid-19th century; *Magyar Ifjúság* 'Hungarian Youth'; *Népköztársaság* 'People's Republic'. Kádár became Head of State after 1956.

85. András Áchim was one of the first peasant Members of Parliament (first elected 1905). He was shot and killed in a quarrel by Endre Bajcsy-Zsilinszky's brother Gábor in 1911. Endre became a leader of the National Uprising Liberation Council, opposed to the Arrow-Cross, but was betrayed, arrested and hanged on 24 December 1944.

86. A reference to the massacre of Serb and Jewish civilians by Hungarian forces in January 1942.

87. A seafaring character in the novels of Jenő Rejtlő.

88. A very popular cultural movement which started in 1972 and which furthers the study and practice of Hungarian folk-music and dance.

89. A Hungarian-speaking minority in Romania.

90. Not unlike 'cottage cheese'.

91. A sheepdog, one of the ten native Hungarian breeds.

92. A kind of ankle-high boot, made of a single piece of leather.

93. The most easterly settlement in historical Transylvania.

94. A kind of porridge made from maize.

95. A cheese-like commodity made by boiling sheep's whey.

96. The Szabós on the radio were a very long-running soap-opera, with weekly programmes over forty-nine years.

97. The *munkásőrök* were a kind of communist party uniformed militia, never actually called to active service but influential in maintaining order in the Kádár period.

98. Máramaros is a town in Transylvania, *Szentháromság* means 'Holy Trinity'.

99. Named after the prince of Transylvania István Bocskai (reigned 1605–06), this is a close-fitting waist-length, long sleeved garment with braid/frogging on the chest and sleeves.

100. *Közért*, short for *Községi Élelmiszerkereskedelmi Rt.* 'Municipal Provision-trading Co.' had a chain of food shops in Budapest in the communist period.

101. These were negotiable securities issued by government in 1991 in an attempt to compensate, under certain conditions, citizens who had suffered unjustly under the previous regime.

102. The customers ask for *fű*, which means (ordinary) grass or herbs (culinary or medicinal), and is a slang term for marijuana.

103. The *Magyar Gárda Mozgalom*, Hungarian Guard Movement, a uniformed element of the right-wing Jobbik party, described by many as neo-Fascist.

104. Traditional folk-dance dress for men consists of white shirt, black trousers and waistcoat, and black George-boots; this is also the *Gárda* uniform. A black Trilby-type hat is commonly worn by dancers, but not by the *Gárda*.

105. The Old Testament name of Jehovah 'God of Hosts' (in Hungarian *Hadúr*) found its way into 19th-century literature and by a popular misconception became 'the God of the Hungarians', almost an extra member of the Holy Trinity.

106. Translator's note: Timothy II: 4,3-4.

ABOUT THE AUTHOR:

photographer: Kriszta Falus

András Kepes needs no introduction in his home country where he first worked in radio, followed by a distinguished career in TV, subsequently producing and hosting cultural programmes and documentaries across the globe. These confirmed his profile as one of the most recognised faces and voices in Hungary on a wide range of topics including film, native and minority cultures in far-flung territories and South American literature. His interviews with a long list of interesting and illustrious guests together with many of his documentaries have become Hungarian media history classics. He has received a number of honours and awards, among them a Pulitzer Memorial Prize in 1994.

Since 2010 András Kepes has been Dean of the Communication and Art Faculty of BKF (Budapest College of Communication and Business) where he is also Professor of Film and Media Studies. He has had several very popular non-fiction books published in Hungary where his first novel The Inflatable Buddha (*Tövispuszta*) is a bestseller.

ABOUT THE TRANSLATOR:

Bernard Adams read Modern & Medieval Languages at Pembroke College, Cambridge. Following a career in teaching, he moved to Hungary in 2006. He has had over 20 translations published and has been awarded 2 second places in John Dryden (UK) competitions, 2 PEN America awards, and a Füst Milán award for his translation work.

ABOUT ARMADILLO CENTRAL:

Armadillo Central is an independent publisher of new fiction, poetry and non-fiction, showcasing the best writing alongside original and limited edition art and photography. All available worldwide.

www.armadillocentral.com

Made in the USA
Las Vegas, NV
21 October 2021

32754944R00192